The Re-education of Mr. Darcy

A PRIDE & PREJUDICE VARIATION

By

Alexa Douglas

ISBN 978-1-7354461-0-3

For Finch

"A mind that is stretched by new experiences can never return to its old dimensions."

– Oliver Wendell Holmes

PROLOGUE

Janssen House, New York City, February 26th, 1815

Dearest Charlotte,

I have such glorious news to share: this summer I journey to England! I cannot wait to see you again, my dearest friend! It has been an age since Fate – that terrible lady! – required you to cross the ocean to live with your Lucas cousins, but it seems that she did not mean for us to be parted forever.

Last week I told Nanna Bennet of my vexation with Papa. He is determined that either Jane or I should marry John Pringle because he is "a good company man," despite being some twenty years my senior. Luckily, Jane is old enough to marry without Papa's consent, and she shall never want for suitors. Papa may force my hand, however, as it is more than a year until I am twenty-one. Nanna assured me that it could be prevented, and her solution is delightfully unexpected!

Grandpa and Nanna mean to take me, Jane and Lydia on a sort of "Grand Tour." Napoleon's wars are over and news of the recent peace treaty between America and England has just reached us, so Grandpa judges it safe to travel overseas. We are to visit England and Italy (and will be away for at least a year – clever Nanna!).

Mamma and Papa are not going. Papa cannot leave Bennet-Janssen Shipping in the hands of anyone else for such a long time, particularly given that trade with England is once again possible. He must move swiftly, Grandpa says, to take advantage of the opportunity. (Papa invites potential clients to dinner and card parties even now.) Mamma does not wish to give up her "society responsibilities." She is too near her goal of becoming Manhattan's grande dame, I think, to forfeit her position by an extended absence.

I was surprised that Papa permitted Lydia to go. She is barely fifteen – far too young to be brought out into society – and no less impetuous than when you left for England a year ago. Mamma asked Jane and me to "teach our headstrong Lydia some decorum" on our journey in hopes that she may behave like a lady when she is away from her wild friends. You shall judge our success for yourself when we see you in Hertfordshire.

Our journey shall take us first to Bath for a month at least, then to several seaside towns – Brighton and Dover and more besides. We visit our Bennet relatives at Longbourn in the autumn, though we cannot know how warmly we shall be received. Grandpa reminded us that his father left England alone and in secret. Great-Grandpa was the third son; his oldest brother was to inherit Longbourn and his second brother joined the church. His lot was to be the Army, though he begged to choose another profession. When his father presented him with an Army commission, he stole away! None of the American Bennets have been to England since, and there has been little contact. We can only hope that the current Thomas Bennet holds no grudge against our family.

What luck that you should be settled only a mile away! I entreat you to tell me again about our cousins. What books does Cousin Thomas read? What does Mrs. Bennet like to talk of? Is Mary always sermonizing? Has Kitty any conversation or accomplishments? And poor Tommy – has his health improved?

I enclose our itinerary so that you may direct your reply to our lodgings in England, as we shall depart New York when you receive this in early April. I rely on you to speak sense, my friend; I have known too much of silliness, with you gone away!

With great affection,

Elizabeth

Janssen House, New York City, March 30th, 1815

Elizabeth kept a bland smile on her face, but inwardly she wanted to kick someone. She would begin with Mr. Pringle, who leered at her now from the seat to her right.

"A pity we old bachelors must sit down to cards partnered with each other and not with the ladies, eh, Turner?" he said.

She had hoped that their upcoming journey would convince her father to cease his exhortations about an engagement. Instead, the pressure had only increased: John Pringle was in their drawing-room at least twice weekly with his iron-gray hair, protruding belly, and dark eyes that followed her possessively. She was careful never to be alone, lest he trap her into a compromise.

"A great pity," said Samuel Turner, smiling appreciatively at Jane. "I should certainly prefer the view."

Mr. Turner and his brother Joseph were this week's prospective clients, so Jane was forced to smile politely. She had endured many such evenings in the month past, though Jane had long ago learned to gracefully suffer unwanted masculine attention. At twenty-two, Jane was one of the loveliest women Elizabeth had ever seen. She was of medium height and shapely, with honey-blond curls framing a classically oval face. Tonight she dressed modestly, in silk that matched the cornflower blue of her eyes.

"I should be an inferior partner, sir," Jane said. "My sister is a far more accomplished player at whist than I. Were we to contend against Mr. Pringle and Elizabeth, I fear we should have no success at all."

"Nay, we cannot have that," said Mr. Pringle. "Not sporting to leave the client without a chance of winning. Speaking of which, Turner," he said as he laid down the last trump card, "I believe this brings us to five points, to the ladies' three."

"Congratulations on your win, gentlemen," said Jane.

Elizabeth excused herself and made her way to where her parents stood with Joseph Turner and his wife. She was grateful that the card-playing was done for the evening; it required a great deal of concentration to play well enough that the client won and Mr. Pringle did not suspect her of deliberately losing.

"My grandfather came to this country with nothing," Papa was saying. "He started as a clerk at Janssen Shipping, and he was so sharp that the old man took notice. Mr. Janssen had no family, you see, nor did my grandfather. They became very close. Like father and son, they were. Old Mr. Janssen made my grandfather a partner, and when the time came, Grandpa Bennet inherited the company. Bennet-Janssen has been a reliable, family-owned company ever since."

Elizabeth allowed her mind to wander. Papa told this story to every client; it would be some time before she was called upon to participate in the conversation. She immediately regretted her inattention, however. The scent of whisky, tobacco and sour sweat assailed her a moment before Mr. Pringle's bulk pressed against her back, his voice low in her ear.

"The company may yet remain in the family. There's no call for you to go gallivanting off through Europe, Miss Lizzy. If you throw in your lot with mine, I'll see that Bennet-Janssen-*Pringle* is more successful than ever. And we'll have a boy with my brilliant mind and your golden eyes to see it on from there."

He makes me an offer in a room full of people, Elizabeth thought. *Has Papa already settled it with him? How can I refuse without causing a scene?* Panic set in. Her heart pounded and her breath came shallow. She needed to escape but feared to move, lest he grab at her.

"Oh, Lizzy, you look terribly pale," said Jane. "Forgive us, Mr. Pringle, but my sister is unwell. I believe we must bid you good-night."

Jane wrapped an arm around Elizabeth's shoulder and guided her out of the room. Upstairs, behind a firmly closed door, Elizabeth's heart finally began to slow.

"What happened, Lizzy? You look as though you saw a ghost."

Elizabeth could not bring herself to repeat Mr. Pringle's words just yet. She tried for a smile. "How is it, Jane, that I attract only boorish men? Are they drawn to my sharp chin, do you suppose, or is it the set of my shoulders? Perhaps it is merely my diminutive stature, for they all speak to me as though I were a child."

"Oh, Lizzy! You know perfectly well that you are very pretty, and with those eyes you could ensnare any man you please. The sensible ones are merely frightened of your wit."

Elizabeth stared into the looking-glass. The woman reflected there had a willowy figure wrapped in russet silk; the color set off thick chestnut hair that fell past her shoulders in wide ringlets. Her skin was pale but tanned easily, with a barely-visible smattering of freckles across her nose, and her full lips were slightly too wide for her heart-shaped face. Her eyes were her distinguishing feature: large and amber, framed by thick, dark lashes.

"Well, I have no desire to ensnare Mr. Pringle, but he does not share my reticence." Shuddering, Elizabeth related his offer. "What am I to do, Jane? Papa is clearly determined to have him for a son-in-law."

"That is not entirely true, Elizabeth," said Mamma, entering the room. "I know that you have no wish to be further importuned about Mr. Pringle. The fact remains, however, that your father must have a successor, and your cousins have no interest in shipping. Your father relies on one of you to marry a man who can be a son to him, as your great-grandfather was to Mr. Janssen, so that the business may remain in family hands."

The panic began to return. *Which grasping socialite's son does Mamma intend for me? We know many who are fond of their own voices, but none with a head for business or any respect for a woman's mind.* Her mother surprised her, however.

"You must find such a man on your travels and bring him to New York. A younger son of a gentleman, perhaps, as your great-grandfather was. He must be sensible and intelligent, of excellent character, and not ashamed of making his fortune by hard work."

"But Mamma," Elizabeth said, "we shall remain in one place for no more than a few months at a time. How are we to know any gentleman well enough to ascertain his character, much less to secure him?"

"You are daughters of one of New York's first families. Jane is blessed with more beauty than most young men will meet with, and her gentle nature and skill with languages will also distinguish her. Elizabeth, your wit and musical talent are equally remarkable. You will doubtless attract the notice of many eligible young men, and you must endeavor to discover their character."

"And if we do not? If neither of us meets with such a young man, and we return to New York unwed?"

"Then one of you must marry Mr. Pringle."

PART I

AMICI E NEMICI

(FRIENDS AND ENEMIES)

CHAPTER ONE

IN WHICH ACQUAINTANCES ARE MADE

Ramsgate, Kent, August 1ˢᵗ, 1815

My Dear Charlotte,

We have been at Ramsgate only a week, and already I am delighted with it! I have enclosed a sketch which shows the brightly painted homes standing shoulder-to-shoulder along the wide stretch of beach that the locals call the Sands, and the long promenade just behind and well above the seashore. One meets with nearly everybody in the town on that promenade. Across the road is a row of quaint little shops; my favorite is the tiny bookshop – it is nearly invisible, with its recessed blue door hidden behind a great profusion of creeping vines. Judging by the books, its proprietor favors an educated female clientele.

I met our newest acquaintance there. We were forced by the narrow confines of the aisles to stand atop one another to reach the novels, so there was nothing for it but to introduce ourselves. Miss Georgiana Darcy is the younger sister of a Mr. Fitzwilliam Darcy, who I understand is the master of a great estate in Derbyshire. Miss Darcy is nearly sixteen, though she appears younger – such a delicate thing, with her translucent skin and huge blue eyes and pale golden hair! – and she has been very sheltered. She is at Ramsgate with her companion, a Mrs. Younge, and visited the bookshop to purchase her first novel. She was considering Frances Burney's works; I recommended Camilla. *For myself I selected* The Wanderer *– it is recently published, and from what I have heard it is far too radical for such an innocent as Miss Darcy but will do very well for me!*

My heart goes out to the girl, I confess. Miss Darcy's parents have both passed and her brother is much older; such a lonely way to grow up! She is very shy but wants only a bit of encouragement to become bright and bubbly, and it appears that the surest means to draw her out is music. She plays the pianoforte very well, though she lives in terror of display, so a duet proved to be just the thing. I am torn between wishing to carry her around safely in my pocket and pulling her along by the arm to acquaint her with the world. Jane feels much the same, though Lydia has no patience for her timidity and refers to her as "the little mouse."

Lydia's fancy is taken with another new acquaintance, a handsome young man that even dear Jane cannot think quite gentlemanly. (This fact alone should convey to you my opinion!) Mrs. Younge introduced Mr. George Wickham as a friend of her late husband. His manners were very pretty, but only moments later he winked at Lydia and lamented that men's "costumes" for sea-bathing are not half so elegant as the ones for ladies! Jane blushed for him, but he seemed unconcerned about the impropriety of speaking about male nudity with three unmarried ladies – one scarce more than a girl! It is surely too much to hope that Mrs. Younge does not introduce him to Miss Darcy.

Tomorrow we make our first attempt at sea-bathing, as it happens. I am exceedingly curious and shall write soon to tell you all about it. Until then I remain

Your affectionate friend,

Elizabeth

Ramsgate, Kent, August 1815

It was a glorious day. The sun was hot in a cloudless sky and a breeze blew steadily in from the ocean, bringing with it the scents of salt water, seaweed, and fish. Elizabeth was the first to venture into the sea – it looked inviting, but it was cold! She quite enjoyed the sensation of water pulling sand over her toes, however, so she carefully waded out until she stood knee-deep.

"Lizzy, wait for us!" Lydia called.

Elizabeth turned around. Moments later she was thrown to her knees by the crash of water against her back, only to be entirely drenched by the next wave. Staggering to her feet and wiping stinging water from her eyes, hair hanging in sodden ropes about her face, Elizabeth decided that sea-bathing for ladies was vastly overrated.

Jane squealed, fell, and disappeared under a wave. Elizabeth rushed forward and helped her to her feet.

"Thank you, Lizzy! Oh dear, I am sure I appear a drowned rat!"

"No more than I! If this is the typical experience of sea-bathing, I believe I must stay ashore or learn to swim. This is intolerable!"

"The water appears calmer ahead," said Lydia. "Do you suppose we can make it that far?" Without waiting for an answer, she charged through the breaking waves until the water was nearly to her chest. "It is much better here!" she shouted.

Elizabeth was already soaked to the skin. Shrugging, she struggled out another dozen feet until she stood next to Lydia, Jane following close behind. At this depth, they only swayed gently with the rise and fall of the waves.

After perhaps a quarter of an hour, Elizabeth noticed Jane's teeth chattering. Even Lydia had her fill, so they trudged back to their bathing-carts to change. Elizabeth peeled off the heavy woolen bathing costume and despairingly regarded her mangled curls in the tiny mirror. She dressed quickly in her own simple gown and wove her hair into a long plait, twisting the whole into a prim knot at the nape of her neck. Replacing her bonnet, she was pleased to see that the worst of the damage was hidden.

She emerged onto the Sands only a moment before Jane. Glancing around for Lydia, she was astonished to find her sister standing alone in conversation with Mr. Wickham! He kissed Lydia's hand, delivering a well-rehearsed compliment with an oily smile – some nonsense about summer roses and the bloom in her cheeks.

Lydia was taller than both of her sisters, with a womanly figure and golden caramel curls that softened the squareness of her jaw. The liveliness in her blue-gray eyes lent her features an attractiveness that was beginning to draw notice. *Far too much notice*, Elizabeth thought, watching Lydia preen under the empty flattery.

Jane's mouth tightened into a hard line. Elizabeth was astonished; her sister's feelings were rarely displayed. Jane led a simpering Lydia away, quietly remonstrating with her, while Elizabeth placed herself squarely in Mr. Wickham's path.

"Why Miss Elizabeth, do you not appreciate my compliments to your sister? Be assured that I think no less of you than of her."

"I beg you do not raise her expectations," she said. "She is young, and her fancy may be easily carried away by excessive praise."

"What, is seventeen considered young in America? I say, you are very strict about such things. But fear not, I have no designs on your sister."

"Lydia is *fifteen*, Mr. Wickham."

"I see. Yes, well, perhaps you are right. I shall endeavor to be more circumspect in future."

~ * ~

They chanced to meet with Mr. Wickham often in subsequent weeks. He came upon them at galleries and gardens, at the theater and at the Sands, but never when their grandparents or Georgiana accompanied them. Elizabeth could not believe this a coincidence, but Georgiana never mentioned him. Perhaps Mrs. Younge had kept him away from her charge after all?

Mr. Wickham favored them with exorbitant flattery and charming smiles. He told stories of shocking mistreatment at the hands of Mr. Darcy – opportunity obstructed, reputation tarnished, inheritance denied – but Lydia's was the only sympathetic ear. Try as she might, Elizabeth could not convince her sister that Mr. Wickham's tales might be exaggerated, if not entirely fabricated.

Georgiana's stories about her brother did not help matters. They often portrayed a man who was distant and taciturn, even resentful. Elizabeth was amazed that Georgiana could speak of him so affectionately.

One morning as they strolled in the gardens Elizabeth said, "Tell us more of your brother, Georgiana. I cannot make him out at all."

"He could not have been a playmate for you, being so much older," said Lydia. "From all you have said, he must have been a very dull brother indeed!"

"Oh, I would not have you think him harsh or unfeeling. He has always been very affectionate and generous with me. But he was twelve and already away at school when I was born, so he was grown before I began to know him at all." Georgiana looked wistful. "Father died unexpectedly these four years past. Fitzwilliam was only twenty-three, and since then he is forever attending to some matter of business or other. I do not believe that I have seen him truly laugh even once in all that time."

"It must have been very difficult for him, inheriting the responsibility of a great estate and the care of a sister at such a young age," Jane said.

Elizabeth suspected that the estate commandeered nearly all of Mr. Darcy's attention. *How else can he allow his sister to live alone, with none but a companion? Does he not see how much she desires his affection and care?*

Aloud, she said, "What sort of man is he? Is he *always* serious and responsible?"

"Fitzwilliam is generally reserved, particularly in unfamiliar company. My cousin Richard can tease him into a lighter mood, but we have scarcely seen Richard since he purchased a commission in the Army. Richard is 'Colonel Fitzwilliam' now, of course, so he has been mostly overseas with his regiment. It is only recently, with the years of war with both France and America finally over, that he is home for more than two weeks together. I believe Fitzwilliam missed him even more than I, though he did not say it."

"I cannot make out all these Fitzwilliams!" Lydia said. "How do they keep it straight?"

They stopped in a small glade perfumed with blooming roses. "It is very simple," Georgiana said. "My mother was Lady Anne Fitzwilliam, youngest daughter of the Earl of Matlock. She named my brother for her family and for my father: Fitzwilliam George Darcy."

"Why do you call him Fitzwilliam? It is such a ponderous name! Why not William, or Will?"

"It would not suit him. Mrs. Reynolds says he was always serious, even as a child; she has been our housekeeper since Fitzwilliam was small."

"What of your brother's interests? Does he dance?" asked Lydia.

"He does but rarely. Only when he is particularly acquainted with the lady, I believe."

"What of concerts, or the theater?" asked Jane.

"He enjoys plays and concerts, though he avoids London and the *ton* whenever he can. He says that to hear me play for him in the drawing-room at Pemberley is far preferable to the best concert in town."

"I suppose he prefers the company of books to that of people," Elizabeth said.

"Oh yes! Pemberley has a great library, and he is always buying more books. His choices for me run to history and Shakespeare, but Fitzwilliam reads extensively on many topics."

"That, at least, I understand. My grandfather has been buying books for me since I was small, on every subject you can imagine. My mother frets over it, but whenever she admonishes him Grandpa just smiles and buys another book!"

~ * ~

A few days later Elizabeth stood on the promenade above the Sands, waiting for her sisters to join her after their visit to the milliner's shop. Lydia had been wild for a new bonnet and Jane was content to accompany her, but Grandpa knew what thrilled Elizabeth's heart.

"We must take full advantage of a bookshop for bluestockings," he had said that morning, placing several bills in her hands. "Your sisters may amuse themselves with frippery, but I trust you shall put this to better use."

She had been delighted to discover a bound collection of Boulton and Watt's steam-engine patents, and the bookshop's proprietor had beamed, handing her the carefully wrapped tome. Now, feeling the weight of the book in her hands and hearing the inanities of feminine conversations taking place around her, Elizabeth was struck by her good fortune. *What might I have become, if I had no Grandpa Bennet to feed my appetite for knowledge?* Her sisters did not share her interests; indeed, many of her passions were considered subjects unfit for ladies.

Her musings were arrested by an unexpected sight: Georgiana ascended the stairs from the Sands on a man's arm, not twenty feet away. Their heads were bent together in an intimate *tête-à-tête*, and as they gained the promenade Elizabeth was astonished to recognize Mr. Wickham!

How dare he! She is a child! But why has she said nothing of him?

"Why, Georgiana! What a charming surprise this is. We had not thought to see you today!"

Georgiana started and removed her arm from Mr. Wickham's, blushing furiously.

"Elizabeth! It is indeed a surprise to see you! May... may I introduce my friend, Mr. George Wickham? He grew up at Pemberley, you know, his father was our steward. We came upon each other quite by accident some weeks ago and he has been most kind, walking with me whenever Mrs. Younge is ill with a headache."

Mr. Wickham bowed and flashed an easy smile, speaking all the proper words of introduction.

"You must join us," Elizabeth said. "My sisters will be finished at the milliner's soon. They shall be delighted to see you, Georgiana, and to meet Mr. Wickham."

"I fear I must reserve that pleasure for another day," said Mr. Wickham immediately. "I have just recalled a most pressing matter of business. I would be

14

grateful, Miss Bennet, if you would see Miss Darcy home safely." He bowed and departed, disappearing before either lady could utter a word.

Georgiana stood open-mouthed; Elizabeth took the younger girl's arm. "My dear, you have been very sly! You never dropped a word about your handsome beau."

"Oh, Lizzy, I am so glad you came upon us! I have been dying to tell you, but George insists we must keep it secret because I am not yet out."

"Has he proposed, then?"

"Not in so many words, but he speaks often of our life together."

"Where do you meet? I have never known you to be seen in company with any young man."

"He visits me at home. Mrs. Younge assures me that it is not improper because he was my father's godson and a close friend of my brother when they were boys, so he is very nearly family already."

"And what says your brother?"

Georgiana lowered her eyes. "I have not mentioned it to him. George says that Fitzwilliam nurses an irrational dislike for him because he is not wealthy. I hope that my brother will approve once he understands that I am truly in love, but... he *is* very proud. I fear that if he knows, he will separate us."

Elizabeth's heart pounded with fury. Mr. Darcy had much to answer for. *He entrusted his innocent sister to the care of an unfit companion. Surely it is no accident that Mrs. Younge allows her charge to walk out alone with a charming fortune-hunter!* After all Mr. Wickham's tales of woe, his attentions to Lydia and Georgiana could have no other motive.

Lydia, at least, has family to protect her. Georgiana is alone.

"Lizzy, are you quite well?"

"I am well, Georgiana. I was merely thinking on your dilemma. I am persuaded that your brother will not look kindly on Mr. Wickham's visits to your home, but perhaps we may reveal your renewed acquaintance in a manner that he must approve."

"Do you truly think so? Oh, I knew I should have asked your advice!"

"Here is my proposal: as Mrs. Younge often finds herself ill, you could stay with us for a time. Mr. Wickham may call upon you at our house, with my grandmother as chaperone. Your brother can hardly be displeased by such an arrangement."

"You are perfectly right, Lizzy! I shall discuss it with Mrs. Younge directly."

That evening, Elizabeth shared her concerns with Jane and her grandparents, describing in detail her conversation with Georgiana and her observations of Mr. Wickham. "Georgiana is entirely defenseless," she said. "She must come to us!"

"I agree, Elizabeth," said Nanna, "and she is welcome. But she may choose to remain where she is."

Elizabeth took Grandpa's hand. "Will you not write to Mr. Darcy?"

"It would be most improper, my dear. We have not been introduced, and I have no authority whatsoever as regards Miss Darcy. Besides, if she does come to us, there shall be no call for it in any case."

Elizabeth could not be satisfied; she was relieved when Jane stole into her room after all were abed. They talked late into the night, considering every alternative but reaching no conclusion.

The following morning, Elizabeth received a letter from Georgiana.

"My dearest Lizzy, I am delighted to tell you that Mrs. Younge is quite recovered and assures me that her health shall not prevent her from being a most diligent companion. She also promised to write to my brother herself and acquaint him with the fact that Mr. Wickham is in the neighbourhood. Therefore there is no need for us to impose upon your hospitality, though I am eternally grateful to you for extending the invitation and hope to call upon you in the course of the morning. Yours, etc."

"Well, my dear, we shall simply invite Miss Darcy to join our family party as often as possible," said Nanna.

"You shall see, Lizzy," Jane said. "We shall make such a nuisance of ourselves that Mr. Wickham shall give up in frustration and depart."

"You, a nuisance, Jane? I cannot envision it. Perhaps you should take lessons from Lydia."

Elizabeth's forced levity faltered when she met her grandfather's somber gaze. *No*, she thought, *Mr. Wickham will never willingly abandon his prize. We can only hope to take it from him.*

CHAPTER TWO

IN WHICH LOVE SAVES THE DAY

Ramsgate, Kent, August 18th, 1815

Dearest Charlotte,

 Ah, the folly of youth! Today I learned a valuable lesson: the dangers of indulging one's daughter too much or too little are equally great, and both leave the young lady vulnerable to the charms of a clever man. Lydia and Georgiana, as you may have guessed, are both in Mr. Wickham's thrall.

 Lydia is too much accustomed to her own way. I feared her presence on this journey, but she has certainly met her match in Nanna. After I revealed all to Jane and my grandparents, we spoke at length of Georgiana. Of Lydia Nanna said only, "She should see rather less of Mr. Wickham," and that was that. Lydia is now to accompany our grandparents until we depart for Hertfordshire, so that Jane and I may call very frequently upon Georgiana. Lydia disapproves of this plan, naturally. It is well that Nanna's capacity for firmness exceeds even her capacity for understatement. Grandpa calls it obstinacy, but with such fondness that he cannot possibly fault her for it.

 Georgiana, on the other hand, has been sheltered and directed all her life. She is incapable of imagining that, far from protecting her, Mrs. Younge seeks to further Mr. Wickham's schemes. I long to acquaint Georgiana with the whole of Mr. Wickham's behavior, but she has not a suspicious bone in her body. What if she refuses to believe me? I have no proof. She shall cling more tightly than ever to Mr. Wickham and he shall separate her from all who genuinely care for her.

 The pleasures of Ramsgate have faded before the difficulties of protecting two young women from Mr. Wickham's schemes, though in fairness I cannot say that at fifteen years old I would have seen through him any better than they. You are surely thinking that my passions for such unladylike topics as steam engines, abolition and the rights of women were their own protection, and you are right. My sister and friend have no such shields, however. I can only pray that Fortune smiles on us, and that when we depart for Hertfordshire the innocence and fortune of both young ladies remain intact.

Yours ever,

Elizabeth

Ramsgate, Kent, August 1815

Their plan worked tolerably well. In the week following Georgiana's stunning revelation, Elizabeth and Jane successfully arranged for Georgiana to spend most of every day with the Bennets. When she thanked her friends for their attentiveness – lamenting privately to Elizabeth that she had been unable to see her beau, so busy had they kept her – Elizabeth was forced to hide a triumphant smile.

"He is welcome to call here, Georgiana. You may introduce us, and I am sure that Nanna would be happy to chaperone his visits."

"Nay, Elizabeth. I could not bear to deceive your grandmother in such a way."

In truth, it was impossible to monopolize Georgiana's every moment. The day came when Georgiana was engaged to dine with another family; she parted from the Bennets after luncheon with promises to call again on the morrow.

"Lizzy, you shall wear a hole in the carpet if you continue this endless pacing," Nanna said.

"I know, Lizzy," said Lydia, "let us walk on the Sands. I daresay we could use the exercise."

"An excellent notion, my dear. By the time you return, Elizabeth may once again resemble a young woman and not a caged lioness."

They set off at once. Lydia kept up a stream of commentary that seldom required a response. At first Elizabeth gave her only half an ear, but Lydia's frequent mentions of Mr. Wickham soon captured Elizabeth's full attention.

"I say, is that not Wickham? There, up ahead," cried Lydia. Her expression rapidly soured. "Who is that girl with him?"

Elizabeth saw with horror that it was Georgiana; the girl held tightly to Mr. Wickham's arm, and his hand covered hers. Mrs. Younge stood some distance behind them, looking out to sea.

Lydia shouted as she strode rapidly toward them, heedless of the other beachgoers. "Wickham! What do you do here? I did not expect you for another half-hour! And who is this chit on your arm?"

Elizabeth halted in astonishment. Soon Lydia was several steps ahead of her, drawing every eye.

"Miss Lydia—" Mr. Wickham began.

Lydia halted in front of the pair, hands on hips. "Georgiana! Why are you with Wickham?"

"Why should I not be? Mr. Wickham is a very attentive and affectionate friend!"

Lydia scoffed. "What does he care about a timid little mouse like you? Wickham, why do you permit her to cling so? You came here to meet me!" She reached for Georgiana, attempting to pull the girl from Mr. Wickham's arm.

Georgiana slapped at Lydia's hands. "How dare you lay hands on me! Let go!" She held Mr. Wickham's arm in a vise-like grip, glaring at Lydia. "Why should my George come here to meet a girl he hardly knows?"

There was laughter from the nearby spectators. Mrs. Younge, noticing the commotion, hurried toward them as Elizabeth caught hold of Lydia.

"Now, ladies," said Mr. Wickham, "do please be reasonable. We can discuss this."

Neither paid him any attention. Lydia writhed in Elizabeth's grasp. "Wickham loves me! As soon as he has the money that your horrid brother owes him, we shall be married!"

"You shall not! *We* are to leave for Gretna Green at almost this moment! We shall be married in less than a week!"

"*ENOUGH!*" a new voice boomed.

Silence fell. Elizabeth looked up in surprise; she had been so focused on Lydia and Georgiana that she had not noticed anyone approach. Mr. Wickham's face drained of all color, while Georgiana's flushed crimson. Mrs. Younge began to back away.

The man upon whom every eye rested was tall, nearing thirty, with broad shoulders and long, powerful legs. His hands were balled into fists, the sleeves of his jacket bulging with the tension of muscle beneath. The breeze swept dark hair off his brow, and his pale eyes bore into Mr. Wickham.

He might be handsome if his countenance were not so forbidding, Elizabeth thought. Even before Georgiana said his name, she knew this must be Fitzwilliam Darcy.

He was closely followed by another man, shorter and dressed in a uniform that announced him to be an officer in His Majesty's Army. This could only be Georgiana's cousin, Colonel Richard Fitzwilliam. He moved like a cat; before Elizabeth knew where he had gone, he had Mr. Wickham's arms behind him in what appeared to be a painful grip.

"Please, do attempt to flee, you blackguard," he growled. "Not even Darcy would stop me from tearing you limb from limb, and I would very much appreciate the opportunity."

Mr. Wickham said nothing. He slumped in the colonel's grasp.

Lydia surged forward. "Wickham!"

Elizabeth planted herself in front of her sister. "Be silent, Lydia!" she hissed. "Can you not see that he lied to you? You have shamed us quite enough for one day! It is time we returned to the house."

Lydia continued to struggle, subsiding only when Mr. Wickham would not meet her eyes.

"I am very sorry for this display, Mr. Darcy," Elizabeth said. "I hope that you and Miss Darcy can forgive my sister's foolishness."

Mr. Darcy regarded her coldly. "It appears I must thank you for your timely intervention, Miss…"

"Bennet. Elizabeth Bennet."

Awareness entered his eyes and his countenance softened a fraction, though his tone remained frosty. "It is a pleasure to meet you, Miss Bennet, though I regret the circumstance. I hope we shall speak again before we leave Ramsgate."

"It would be my pleasure, Mr. Darcy. Good day to you, sir, and to you, Georgiana." She curtseyed briefly and turned for the stair, linking her arm tightly through her sister's.

Every eye followed them. Elizabeth lifted her chin and squared her shoulders; despite her sister's appalling behavior, she would not be cowed by strangers.

~ * ~

The following morning, Elizabeth picked at her breakfast. Lydia had remained in her room, speaking to nobody, since returning to the house. She did not disclose what cause she had to believe that Mr. Wickham loved her, nor how she had hoped to wed him with her sixteenth birthday yet half a year distant.

My attention was all on Georgiana, Elizabeth thought. *I assumed Lydia was safe with her family around her, but we nearly lost her, too.*

The butler entered and handed a card to Grandpa. They had not planned to receive visitors, but when he confirmed that Miss Darcy and two gentlemen were at the door, Grandpa instructed that they be shown in.

"I shall go to Lydia," said Jane. "Perhaps she will speak to me this morning."

Elizabeth took a deep breath to steady herself. She did not know precisely what to expect from this interview, but it was certain to be difficult.

The butler bowed their visitors into the room. "Mr. Darcy, Miss Darcy, and Colonel Fitzwilliam."

"Gentlemen, it is a pleasure to meet you. I am Andrew Bennet. This is my wife Esme and my granddaughter Elizabeth. Please make yourselves comfortable."

"I am very happy to see you all," Nanna said. "Particularly you, Georgiana."

Georgiana did not reply. She sat next to her cousin, eyes fixed on her lap.

Mr. Darcy remained standing. He took a position behind his sister, hands clasped behind his back. "Mr. Bennet, I must thank you for your letter. Were it not for your timely communication, I fear that my sister would have been compromised beyond any hope of concealment or restoration, and I would be forced to consign Mr. Wickham her dowry of thirty thousand pounds. I am sure I need not tell you that he is no longer at Ramsgate. Mrs. Younge has been dismissed without reference."

"No thanks are necessary, Mr. Darcy. We could not countenance the idea of a young lady as innocent as your sister being imposed upon. Once Elizabeth told me of it, I had no choice but to hope that a letter would reach you in time."

"It seems your friendship has been of invaluable benefit to my cousin, Miss Bennet," said Colonel Fitzwilliam. "Georgiana, I fear, has not yet learned to thank you for breaking her confidence, but I certainly do."

Georgiana finally raised her head. "How could you, Elizabeth?"

"I am so sorry, Georgiana. You seemed beyond the reach of reason, and I feared to warn you, lest I drive you further from safety."

"You really thought George would hurt me?"

"I did. Recall, dearest, that I also saw his indecent behavior toward my sister. Even then I did not know all! But no man who courts two girls of only fifteen years can be honorable. Mrs. Younge introduced him to us weeks ago, so it was evident that she was part of the scheme."

"You might have told me."

"I advised against it, my dear," said Nanna. "I am one of four sisters and have raised two daughters myself. There is no telling truth to a young woman whose heart is lost. The best one can do is try to protect her from herself."

"A friend would make the attempt, at least, rather than break faith."

Nanna smiled sadly. "You do not believe me now, but with time you will understand that only a true friend would have the courage to break your confidence."

Georgiana's gaze returned to her lap. The silence stretched.

"Miss Bennet," Mr. Darcy said, "Georgiana has spoken in her letters of your... American... views on society. I should hope that this incident will demonstrate to her the perils of associating with those who are beneath her. One cannot trust the motives of those of inferior birth."

Inferior birth? "American views?" What arrogance! Elizabeth controlled her temper for Georgiana's sake, but several moments passed before she could speak with tolerable civility. She forced her tone to be light. "Indeed, sir? This is quite shocking! How does one acquire nobly born servants, if one cannot trust those whose families have been in service for generations?"

Mr. Darcy glowered. "You misunderstand me, Miss Bennet. I speak not of servants, but of one's closest connections."

"I see. You desire your sister to understand that she cannot rely on those whose position in society is below her own to have her best interests at heart, if they seek to recommend themselves to her as a friend or suitor."

"Precisely."

"So a governess or paid companion would not make a suitable friend."

"She would not."

"And the son of a steward could never merit consideration as a husband."

"No indeed."

"What of the son or daughter of a family whose fortune was made in trade?"

"That would depend on whether the family was still involved in trade."

"And if they were?"

"Then they must be unsuitable as companions to the daughter of a gentleman."

Elizabeth registered Georgiana's panicked expression, though her gaze never wavered from Mr. Darcy. "Oh dear. I must apologize, Mr. Darcy, for

imposing myself and my unsuitable family on your sister. Truly, I had no understanding until this moment of how nefarious my motives must have been. I shall
be exceedingly sorry to lose Georgiana's friendship, but as you have made it clear
that I cannot be trusted, I see no other course."

Mr. Darcy's head snapped back as though she had struck him. Georgiana
and Colonel Fitzwilliam spoke at once.

"Oh, no, Elizabeth! You—"

"I believe what my cousin is trying to say—"

Georgiana rushed forward, taking Elizabeth's hands. "Oh Lizzy, do not say
such things! You are the dearest friend I have ever had. I know I am just a foolish,
ignorant girl, but I could not stand to lose you! Please say you are my friend!"
She began to weep.

Elizabeth wrapped an arm around the girl's shoulders. "Dearest Georgiana,
of course I am your friend. I am sorry that I frightened you. Please understand
that you are not to blame for any of this. And whatever your brother may think
of my family, you have my word that I shall always remain your friend and fierc-
est ally."

Georgiana sniffled and dabbed her face with a handkerchief. Clasping Elizabeth's hand, she looked fearfully at her brother. The colonel was speaking to
Mr. Darcy in low, urgent tones. Both men looked at Elizabeth.

"My dear Miss Bennet," said the colonel, "please do not think for a moment
that my cousin intended any slight against you or your family. Our dear Georgiana does not give her heart freely, and her devotion to you is the surest sign
that your friendship is of immeasurable value. We remove to London today, and
my cousins will soon return to Pemberley. It is our sincere wish that you will
correspond with Georgiana during your travels. I shall provide the direction."

"Thank you, Colonel. I am most grateful."

The colonel bowed low over her hand and Georgiana embraced her tightly.
Mr. Darcy shook Grandpa's hand and bowed very correctly to Nanna before
staring at Elizabeth, unspeaking, for several seconds.

"Good day, Mr. Darcy. Safe travels."

He nodded, stone-faced, and the door closed behind the three of them.

CHAPTER THREE

IN WHICH DARCY IS PUMMELED

Matlock House, London, 30th August 1815

My Dear Mother,

I promised to send you the earliest intelligence of my cousin Georgiana, and I shall not keep you in suspense: she is safe.

We must all be grateful that Mr. Bennet disregarded the conventions of propriety. Had he waited but a day longer to send his missive, Georgiana would have been lost. As it was, we arrived at Ramsgate to find her openly declaring Wickham's intent to carry her off to Gretna as soon as may be. Fortunately she is not yet out in society, so we may succeed in keeping this escapade from the notice of the ton.

You shall be surprised to hear that I am impressed by these Americans. I have not altered my opinion of their President; his declaration of war in 1812 distracted from our efforts to subdue Napoleon. One cannot hold the entire populace responsible for the idiocy of its leaders, however (how well do we know it! – one has only to consider our mad king), and the Bennets appear to be excellent people.

To be sure, Georgiana was at first angry with her friend Miss Elizabeth. Darcy quite cleverly turned that around, however, by openly questioning Miss Bennet's fitness to associate with her. I am not certain he knew himself to be doing so at the time, Miss Bennet manoeuvered him so deftly. The result was that Georgiana's devotion soon bestirred itself on Miss Bennet's behalf and dislodged her fury from that lady.

She has not yet learnt to aim her anger at its proper target, though you will doubtless aid her to view this misstep as merely a passing folly. I believe Miss Bennet will prove an able ally. You would heartily approve of her.

Your devoted son,

Richard

Darcy House, London, 4th September 1815

It was barely past noon when Darcy was forced to admit to himself that he was of no use to anybody. He could concentrate on nothing. He read and re-read his business correspondence without taking in a word, and even reading for leisure was impossible.

Since their return to London, he found himself awake each night until the small hours of the morning, eventually falling into exhausted slumber only to be hurtled into wakefulness by nightmares: Georgiana, hand outstretched as she disappeared into a wall of fog just out of his reach; Wickham forcing Georgiana into a trunk and locking her inside while Darcy watched helplessly; Mrs. Younge painting Georgiana's face to resemble a porcelain doll and placing her upon the auction block; Miss Bennet leveling a pistol at Darcy's chest as a weeping Georgiana quailed in terror of him.

He had believed, on waking yesterday from the last with his heart thundering, that no dream could be more disturbing. This morning's nightmare, however, proved the folly of such thoughts: his dream-self placed a sign marked *"Gratis"* around Georgiana's neck and walked unconcernedly away, the closing of his heavy study door silencing her cries. He awoke drenched in sweat and tangled in the bedclothes.

He kept to his rooms rather than suffer the pitying looks of the staff. In the harsh light of midday, Darcy scarcely recognized himself. His skin was lined and nearly the gray of his eyes, which were bloodshot and weighted down with great bruises. His hair was unkempt, his jaw unshaven, and he had bothered with neither cravat nor jacket.

I need a drink.

In his study, he poured himself a brandy and sat heavily in the deep leather chair, staring at the cold fireplace. Moments later, his cousin Richard Fitzwilliam sauntered in without knocking. Darcy groaned.

"Is that your first drink of the day, Darcy, or your last of the night? By your looks I would wager on the latter."

"What do you want, Fitzwilliam?"

"I came to inform you that you have just hired Mrs. Annesley to be Georgiana's new companion. Ordinarily I would take this opportunity to point out that I recommended her in preference to Mrs. Younge these three months past, but at present it appears that you need none of my help in feeling properly chastened. Have you a hair shirt already, then?"

Darcy gave him a baleful look.

"I say, this is a serious case." Fitzwilliam poured himself a drink. "Come now, old man, be reasonable. Mrs. Younge came with excellent references and Georgiana has never put a toe out of bounds. Besides, we all thought Wickham to be in Newcastle pursuing that brewery scheme. You could not have prevented this."

"I could have been with her. *Should* have been with her. What idiocy was it that persuaded me to send her with a woman she hardly knew to a place where she knew nobody?"

"Has she spoken to you about it?"

"No. She eats in silence, plays in silence, and otherwise keeps to her room. She will not even meet my eye!"

"Of course not. She blames herself, you know."

"What! How can that be possible? And how do you know this?"

"I spoke with her this morning before Mrs. Annesley's interview. She insisted that she should have discerned Wickham's falsity and Mrs. Younge's machinations. She berated her own stupidity in the most eloquent language."

"What could have given her the notion that she, who has no experience of the world, should have seen in Wickham and Mrs. Younge what many others, myself included, did not?"

"I believe the words 'How could you have been so taken in?' emerged from your mouth that first evening at Ramsgate."

Darcy passed a hand over his face. "I do not recollect it. I was not master of myself, I fear."

"And Georgiana's distress was even more acute than yours. Make no mistake, Darcy, *she* remembers those words. She feels your disappointment exceedingly, but has no notion of its true direction."

"I must speak to her."

"Indeed you must, but I suggest you attempt it only after you have slept and shaved. You appear now to have been attacked in the street; you would only terrify her further."

"I have not had a restful night in some days, I confess."

"Well, perhaps my other news shall ease your mind: Wickham is to be a militiaman! I called in a few favours, and he will soon be joining the Yorkshire militia, under the command of Colonel Forster."

"I fail to understand how this is helpful."

"If you knew Forster, no further explanation would be required. He is among the better commanders the militia has to offer. He tolerates none of the vices that are common amongst young men and is more than usually perceptive; rarely do men such as Wickham get past him. For surety I have provided some particulars about his newest lieutenant."

"Think you that Wickham shall remain at his post? I should take him for a deserter, if ever the situation became uncomfortable for him."

Fitzwilliam snorted. "Naturally he shall run; he is no more fit for the militia than he was for the clergy. You were wise to pay him off when he offered to resign all claim to the living at Kympton."

"Well, if he deserts his regiment then he may face the consequences without dragging my family name through the mud."

Fitzwilliam frowned at him. "Oh, he shall drag you into it. He always does. You should have let me kill him and be done, Darcy. And do not tell me what your father would have wished. Even George Darcy would have sanctioned an affair of honour, when it was his daughter's honour at stake."

Darcy closed his eyes and leaned back against the chair with a sigh. "Perhaps." He must have slept then, for when he next opened his eyes, Fitzwilliam had a book in one hand and a sandwich in the other. *At least I did not dream.*

Fitzwilliam eyed him speculatively. "You look less like a reanimated corpse, at least. That must be an improvement. Sandwich?"

Darcy found, to his surprise, that he was ravenous. He made short work of two sandwiches; he was contemplating a third when his cousin grinned at him. Darcy was instantly alert.

"While you slept just now, I dined with Georgiana. She had a letter from Miss Bennet today, who wonders if you accept knights in service in your household, or if nothing less than a baronet will do. I advised her to reply that a knight might do for the stables, but for household servants it must be a baron at the very least."

"You encourage Georgiana to laugh at me?"

"She must stop thinking of you as so near to divinity, old man! It will do her good. Besides, you might just as well have handed Miss Bennet a loaded pistol when you made that little speech, and then dared her to shoot you."

Darcy started, memory and nightmare twining together. He envisioned her ferocious expression and the deadly golden gaze that had lingered in his mind since that day at Ramsgate.

Just then Charles Bingley's jovial tones filtered in from the front hall. A moment later his friend stopped dead on the threshold. "Good God! Darcy, what has happened?"

"What brings you here, Bingley?" asked Fitzwilliam.

"Darcy was supposed to meet me at White's today, and when he did not arrive, I became concerned. Jones let me in."

"Jones must be quite uneasy, then. He let me in this morning without argument, and very nearly had a crease between his brows!"

Bingley's answering laugh died when he caught sight of Darcy's expression. "You must forgive me, Darcy, for my rudeness just now. But truly, you look very ill."

"Indeed, Bingley, he deserves your compassion," said Fitzwilliam. "He has met with a creature out of legend and did not come away unscathed."

"What are you going on about?" asked Bingley.

"A veritable Siren, she was. Lovely and gracious, with the most unearthly eyes. Golden eyes, large enough to swallow a man! And just when she seemed to have formed a perfect understanding with our hero, she tore him to shreds."

"Indeed! I was not aware that there was a woman in England who did not eagerly affirm every opinion Darcy uttered. How singular!"

"It is a great pity that you were not there to see her hoist Darcy with his own petard. It is an exceedingly unusual feat, and I have never seen a woman manage it."

"Are you quite finished?" Darcy growled.

Fitzwilliam only laughed.

"If you would prefer a more agreeable lady, Caroline remains quite at your disposal," said Bingley.

"You require her assistance far more than I," Darcy said testily. "Without a hostess, how are you ever to fill the ballroom of that country manor you were rattling on about? Nay, until you settle your affections on the same 'angel' for more than three weeks together, you must not attempt to foist your sister on me."

"As it happens, that is what I wished to talk to you about, Darcy. I remove to Hertfordshire next week, with Caroline, Louisa and Hurst. I should like you to join us. I let the house without spending above a half-hour in it, but it has been vacant these two years. I should very much appreciate whatever advice you might give me on improvements and management of the estate."

Darcy rolled his eyes, but he smiled. Bingley was ever the same: eager and impetuous, but too well-meaning to draw real censure. "It is fortunate that you only leased it. Should it prove unprofitable to return the house and property to a respectable state, you shall not be saddled with it above a twelvemonth, I daresay."

"You are quite right, Darcy. I should not like to purchase an estate until I know what I am about. Well? What say you?"

Darcy considered. "At the moment I have no concerns at Pemberley that cannot be managed by my steward, and I would appreciate the novelty of a challenge. I shall be happy to join you, Bingley. Where is this house again? And what is it called?"

"The estate is in Hertfordshire, only half a day's ride from here. It is called Netherfield."

CHAPTER FOUR

IN WHICH THE BENNETS MEET THE BENNETS

Ramsgate, Kent, September 5th, 1815

My dear Charlotte,

Just think! We shall arrive in Hertfordshire on the heels of this note! I do not call it a letter, for I am so eager to see you that I have no patience for writing.

Ramsgate has been far more sedate with Georgiana and Wickham both gone out of the country. We have had ample time to speculate about our Bennet relatives at Longbourn, and of course your information about them has been of incalculable value. I am most curious about Mary and Kitty. What shall we find to talk of? From what you have said – that Mary reads sermons instead of novels and Kitty reads not at all – I fear our conversations may be very dull indeed. I suppose we may pass the time rambling about the country as you have described – walking into Meryton or riding to Oakham Mount, perhaps.

I intend to be delighted with poor Tommy. It touches my heart that so young a child walks through life knowing he shall likely die before he reaches his majority. Thank you for telling me how greatly he enjoys card games; I have brought a cribbage board as a gift for his eighth birthday.

In your last letter, you said that the neighborhood was all a-twitter about a new tenant at Netherfield. Have you seen Mr. Bingley? Is he as handsome and charming as any young man of five thousand a year must naturally be, or is he merely an ordinary fellow in fine clothes after all?

With great anticipation,

Elizabeth

Meryton, Hertfordshire, September 1815

"Charlotte! Oh, my dear, you look remarkably well!" Elizabeth threw her arms about her friend as she stepped into the common room of the inn at Meryton.

Charlotte Lucas was intelligent and good-natured, one of the few at Mrs. Okill's School for Young Ladies to share Elizabeth's passion for reading. They soon became such intimate friends that Charlotte was nearly a fourth Bennet sister. Charlotte's parents had perished in the yellow fever epidemic of 1805, and her grandmother followed them these two years past. Having no other family in America, she went to live with her distant cousins in England.

Elizabeth had marveled at Charlotte's composure at this upending of her life, but her friend was an exceedingly pragmatic young woman. Charlotte had assured Elizabeth for many years that she was perfectly resigned to life as a governess, as it was unlikely that she would marry well. "I am quite the best mouse in the house," she would say. "I have perfectly ordinary brown hair and brown eyes and a pointed, twitchy nose, and I can make myself a tidy little nest anywhere." And indeed it was true, for she did not seem to regret leaving New York City for a rural English county.

"The country air agrees with me, Lizzy," she said now. "May I have the honor of introducing my cousin, Sir William Lucas."

Sir William was a genial man with open manners and a general eagerness to please. He issued them an invitation to the assembly in one week's time, to the delight of Elizabeth and Jane and the disappointment of Lydia, who was not permitted to attend.

Charlotte joined them for a light luncheon and described the other nearby families they would meet during their stay in Hertfordshire.

"What of this Mr. Bingley that everyone is talking of?" Jane asked.

"We have not yet seen him," Charlotte said. "He came down in a chaise and four to see the place last week and went away again immediately, but we expect him to return soon with a large party of friends. We do not know the particulars, though it would be well if the gentlemen outnumbered the ladies! Sir William shall call on him directly, so I shall have more intelligence to share with you soon."

After passing a pleasant hour with Charlotte, Elizabeth and her family set out for Longbourn. The curiosity of each family of Bennets regarding the other cannot be overstated, though Charlotte Lucas proved to be as valuable to her neighbors as she was to Elizabeth's family in describing the virtues and follies of each to the other.

Returning to the inn after supper, Elizabeth found that her family's opinions of their Bennet relations were similar, though Jane made more allowances for them and Lydia fewer.

Cousin Thomas was a bookish and somewhat contrary man who enjoyed laughing at his family and his neighbors but seemed pleased to be engaged by Grandpa on serious topics. Fanny Bennet was a gracious hostess and set an excellent table, but her manner was often unthinking and self-absorbed, and she seemed to require the utmost self-possession to speak civilly to Jane when the subject of Mr. Bingley arose.

"She cannot suppose that I shall carry him off with me to Italy," said Jane, "even if he does pay me any attention."

Mary was, at nineteen, filled with an air of self-righteousness and moral rectitude that astonished Elizabeth and offended even Jane. She had spent much of the evening delivering well-worn platitudes at inopportune times, seemingly oblivious to the awkwardness and insult she caused.

"She is too plain to attract a husband," said Lydia, "so she must tell herself and everybody else that she is too good for a man!"

Kitty was an unremarkable girl of seventeen, with no accomplishments or education to speak of. Only Lydia had been able to engage her in conversation; once they hit upon the subject of balls and handsome gentlemen, the two girls chatted happily for some time.

Young Tommy was a universal figure of sympathy. Thin and pale, he looked younger than his seven years.

"The poor dear, his lips were blue from nothing more than climbing the stairs! And he ate hardly anything at supper," Nanna said. "It is quite natural that his mother is so fretful about him."

"His body may be weak, but his mind is active," said Elizabeth. "He seems very like his father, now that I think on it. He reads extensively and observes everything around him. And he was exceedingly curious about America!"

"He seems lonely. His sisters have little enough to do with him. Perhaps we may bring him some cheer," said Lydia. "I wonder what we shall think of this other cousin who is expected Monday next. What was his name?"

"Collins. William Collins," said Grandpa. "He is to inherit Longbourn if Tommy dies without issue, which unfortunately seems likely."

"What could Mr. Collins mean in his letter, about making his cousins 'every possible amends'?"

"It was very presumptuous of him to speak so," said Nanna with some asperity. "I believe he means to marry one of the girls, expecting that he shall eventually take possession of their home."

It was soon clear that Mr. Collins did intend to choose a wife from among his cousins, though after making Jane's acquaintance he abandoned any pretense of interest in Mary or Kitty. He was an average-looking man of twenty-five, neither well-read nor clever. He was distinguished only by his manner. Elizabeth rejoiced that there were too many in their party to stay at Longbourn, for her patience was sorely tested by Mr. Collins's strange combination of pomposity and exaggerated deference. Jane frequently found it necessary to divert his attention to Mary, who of all of them was the only person to seek his company and conversation. Lydia abused him as the most stupid man of her acquaintance on either side of the Atlantic Ocean!

With others of their acquaintance they enjoyed conversation of a much more genial and productive nature. In particular, Sir William Lucas was soon able to provide a favorable description of Mr. Bingley: amiable, lively and well-looking, with a great deal of conversation and a fondness for dancing. He was, in short, everything a young man ought to be. The upcoming assembly was much talked of, as Mr. Bingley had declared his intention to attend with his sisters, his brother-in-law, and his oldest friend.

The following day all the Bennet girls and Mr. Collins walked from Longbourn to Meryton. Mr. Collins carried the conversation almost single-handedly, waxing eloquent about his noble patroness Lady Catherine de Bourgh, her estate at Rosings Park, and the extraordinary notice and condescension she showed him.

She sounds like an insufferable busybody, Elizabeth thought.

"I intend most assiduously to follow her advice to find a sensible young woman to marry, not brought up too high, as soon as may be," Mr. Collins was saying with a lingering glance at Jane.

"You needn't look at Jane like that, Mr. Collins," Lydia said. "Our family is exceedingly wealthy, you know. We move in the first circles in Manhattan."

"My dear young cousin, I am sure you believe yourselves to be important, but it cannot be so. Your country has hardly any true gentlemen and you have abandoned the nobility entirely. Even your wealthiest families are in trade. Your connections must be rated as lower than your cousins', as their father is a gentleman."

Lydia and Elizabeth both bristled, but it was Jane who spoke. "Perhaps you can tell us what it means to be a gentleman. After all, is Mr. Bingley's fortune not from trade? And yet the neighborhood speaks of him as though he were a gentleman."

"I cannot be surprised at your ignorance; I pray you do not think that it lessens my opinion of you. A gentleman possesses an independent income, most often from the proceeds of an estate. I am profoundly humbled by the knowledge that if God should call poor Tommy home while he is still a child, as must surely happen, then I shall become a gentleman myself. Though of course that day may be many years from now."

An awkward silence fell; even Mary frowned at this speech. Nobody said another word until they reached Meryton, where they found Charlotte and Sir William in conversation with a distinguished-looking man of about forty. He was introduced as Colonel Forster, of the Yorkshire militia, which was to be quartered at Meryton the whole winter.

They were soon joined by two other officers and a young woman of about Kitty's age, who proved to be the colonel's wife of only a few weeks. Lydia entered readily into conversation with the newcomers, complaining loudly about being prevented from attending the assembly. Elizabeth immediately took her sister aside, but her attempts to urge Lydia to some decorum fell on deaf ears. Jane was left to make their excuses and the three of them returned to the inn.

~ * ~

The following afternoon, Elizabeth and Jane dressed with more than their usual care. Mindful that the finery to which they were accustomed was far beyond the best dresses likely to be owned by the ladies of the neighborhood, they wore understated jewelry and the simplest of their evening gowns. Jane's was pale yellow silk trimmed with delicate lace and tiny beads; Elizabeth favored an ivory satin with elaborate floral embroidery at the sleeves and hem.

Kitty exclaimed over their hair, which they had arranged in the very elaborate styles favored by the Manhattan elite. She was particularly envious of the diamond-studded butterfly pins securing Jane's honey-blond braids and Elizabeth's ivory and mother-of-pearl combs.

Mr. Collins was uncharacteristically silent in the face of Kitty's enthusiasm. Jane smiled at the brief reprieve; she had been unable to refuse his request to dance the first set with her.

Mary sighed. "I take little pleasure in a ball. One must observe the social conventions, of course. It is a woman's duty to find a suitable husband, that she might not be a burden to her family. But were I to consult only my own feelings, I should infinitely prefer to study Fordyce's sermons. I consider the improvement of the female mind to be a far more beneficial pursuit."

Mr. Collins agreed, pronouncing the novel to be the most seditious form of the written word ever published. Elizabeth rolled her eyes, but he was too enraptured by his own voice to notice. He was interrupted only by the signal that the dancing was shortly to begin.

Elizabeth observed the first set from the side of the room, mortified on her sister's behalf. It was agony to watch lovely, graceful Jane attempt to gently direct Mr. Collins to move the correct way and keep her skirts free from his clumsy toes. Elizabeth had not even Charlotte's company to soothe her, for Charlotte had taken her place at the head of the dance with her cousin John Lucas.

There was a stir by the doors. A small and very elegantly dressed party entered and were introduced as Mr. Charles Bingley, Miss Caroline Bingley, Mr. and Mrs. Arthur Hurst, and Mr. Fitzwilliam Darcy. Sir William hurried across the room to welcome the newcomers.

Elizabeth stood, stunned. She was entirely insensible of Jane's solicitous exclamations over her suddenly pale appearance and Mr. Collins's attempt to claim her hand for the next set. Her mind was awhirl. *Mr. Darcy* was Mr. Bingley's oldest friend?

This does not speak well of Mr. Bingley, she thought. Her confusion only increased as she observed Mr. Bingley enter into easy conversation with Sir William. He begged introduction to every local family, his manners open and pleasing.

Elizabeth mechanically allowed Mr. Collins to lead her to the floor; fortunately, her feet knew the steps of the quadrille. She was roused to consciousness when Mr. Collins trod on her skirt, to find that he was speaking to her.

"Indeed, who could have predicted that I should meet with one of Lady Catherine's nephews here? His estate is quite the equal of Rosings, though I have never seen it. I must beg your pardon, Miss Elizabeth, for I should be remiss if I did not instantly introduce myself to Mr. Darcy when this set is complete. I am happily able to inform him that Lady Catherine is in excellent health!"

Elizabeth, mortified now far more than she had believed possible, attempted in vain to persuade him of the impropriety of such an imposition. Mr.

Collins condescendingly reminded her that she was a female and an American, and thus could not understand that he, as a clergyman – particularly one so fortunate as to be distinguished by the patronage of Lady Catherine de Bourgh – was quite equal in importance to a gentleman such as Mr. Darcy.

He released her when the music ended, colliding with other couples in his haste to make his way to where Mr. Darcy stood. Elizabeth found Jane standing with Charlotte and Mr. Bingley, who exclaimed at the astonishing coincidence that Elizabeth's friend should have settled nearly next door to her relations. He expressed himself in such a genial and gentlemanly manner that Elizabeth found she could not object when he solicited Jane's hand for the next set, despite what she knew of his friend.

Finally able to speak to Charlotte at leisure, Elizabeth learned that Mr. Bingley was as amiable and attentive a partner as his manners promised.

"His sisters do not seem nearly so pleased with their company," Elizabeth said.

"Quite so, though they behaved very properly toward me. Mr. Darcy has looked at you several times, Lizzy. I thought you met him only once. It appears you made quite an impression!"

"If that is so, it is only because he found me as disagreeable as I found him." Elizabeth searched the room, finally spotting Mr. Darcy. He instantly turned his face to the side, and she laughed. "He was so arrogant! It was all I could do to keep a civil tongue in my head. I confess it gave me great pleasure to bait him. Truly, Charlotte, I believe he acknowledged me when they left the house only because propriety demanded it. Nanna tried to chastise me, but Grandpa declared that it was an excellent set-down, and well deserved."

Charlotte's grin disappeared as she rearranged her features into a mask of pleasant modesty. "He is coming this way, Lizzy! Let us see if he gives you the cut direct!"

Nearly every lady on the periphery of the room followed his progress with their eyes, Elizabeth saw. He gave her a very perfunctory bow and walked on, seeming not to hear Charlotte's quiet laughter.

Elizabeth danced the next with Mr. Bingley. She took the opportunity to inquire about his friendship with Mr. Darcy.

"I say, Miss Elizabeth! I had no idea you were acquainted with Darcy!"

"We met once at Ramsgate. His sister Georgiana and I became great friends there, and they called in the morning before removing to London. It was such a small thing, I cannot be surprised that he did not think to mention it."

"Miss Darcy is so shy that I have scarcely spoken to her, for all the years that Darcy and I have been friends. If you befriended her then you must be a singular person indeed!"

"That is kind of you to say, but it is not so astonishing. We share a love of music. How did you and Mr. Darcy become friends?"

"We met at Cambridge. I struggled with mathematics, he with social intercourse. We began with an agreement, each to serve as tutor to the other. Before long we began to enjoy each other's company for its own sake."

"How singular! Your temperaments appear so dissimilar."

"Oh, certainly! Darcy is quite the most intelligent person I know. He would be intimidating indeed if I could not laugh at him for his awkwardness around any new person he meets. I believe that I have benefited far more from our friendship than he!"

After supper, Elizabeth was again forced to sit out for want of a partner. She was not alone, however, in observing that Mr. Bingley danced with Jane a second time.

"Mr. Bingley seems quite delighted with your sister," Charlotte said.

"He seems delighted with everyone he meets! I am amazed that he and Mr. Darcy can be friends."

"Perhaps Mr. Darcy is more amiable in familiar company."

"How can you think so? See how he strides around the room, looking disdainfully at everybody and never entering into conversation unless it cannot be avoided! How could such a man ever be amiable?"

"He knows scarcely anybody here, Lizzy."

"Very true, and of course nobody can ever be introduced in a ballroom."

Mr. Darcy stopped his pacing near them as the music ended and the dancers left the floor. Mr. Bingley brought him a drink, abusing him genially for standing about in so stupid a manner. Mr. Bingley could not convince his friend to dance, however, for all his good-natured mockery. Mr. Darcy emphatically refused, on the grounds of its being a degradation to be partnered with any but Bingley's sisters.

"How can you say so? The Miss Bennets are delightful and lovely young ladies – the American ones, at any rate. I hear that over there, the Bennets are quite as distinguished as the Darcys. Are you blind, man?"

"The eldest Miss Bennet is certainly very handsome."

"A fine concession! What of Miss Elizabeth? I find you know each other, and yet I have not seen you speak two words to her all evening. Surely it cannot be a degradation to dance with her! It will be but the work of a moment to solicit her hand; she sits just over there."

Mr. Darcy glanced around; Elizabeth pretended interest in something across the room. "I am acquainted with Miss Elizabeth. She might be tolerable to some men, but she is certainly not handsome enough to tempt me. Her features must be remarkably fine to counteract the forwardness and impertinence of her manner. Were her sister not so modest, I should mark it down to her American upbringing. But no; it must be her own temper that is so brash, and there is not sufficient beauty in her form or face to induce me to entrap myself into half an hour's conversation with her, much less dancing, which you know I detest."

Charlotte's expression mirrored Elizabeth's own slack-jawed disbelief. Neither said a word, however, so intent were they on hearing Mr. Bingley's reply.

"Darcy, those may be the most ungentlemanly words I have ever heard you utter. I sincerely hope that I am the only person to have heard them."

Mr. Darcy stiffened. "Perhaps you should not have importuned me on this subject."

"This is not the first circumstance in which I have attempted to encourage you to sociability, but it shall certainly be the last!" Bingley said. "I have not the smallest idea what led you to form such an opinion. I find Miss Elizabeth to be witty and vivacious, and her sister is quite the most angelic creature I ever beheld."

Elizabeth winked at Charlotte. *Naturally he likes her! At least he isn't as hateful as his friend.*

Mr. Bingley paused, his tone softening. "I am sorry that I persuaded you to accompany us, for you are clearly not fit for company tonight. Please call for the carriage and return to Netherfield whenever you choose. Only send it back for us."

"Thank you, Bingley. I regret that I am a poor companion this evening." He promptly made for the door, walking past a simpering Miss Bingley without a glance.

"It seems Miss Bingley is not handsome enough to tempt him either," said Charlotte.

Elizabeth pulled Charlotte across the room, biting her lip hard to suppress the laughter that erupted as they burst onto a balcony overlooking the street. It was some time before either could speak.

"Well, Lizzy, you certainly did make *quite* an impression!"

Elizabeth could only nod, gasping for breath as she wiped tears of laughter from her cheeks. Glancing in the direction of the street, she saw Mr. Darcy poised to enter a carriage. He was looking directly at her.

Their eyes met. Elizabeth was almost certain that she saw the flush on Mr. Darcy's cheeks climb to his hairline before he stepped into the carriage and closed the door firmly behind him.

CHAPTER FIVE

IN WHICH CHICKENS COME HOME TO ROOST

Netherfield, Hertfordshire, 4ᵗʰ October 1815

Fitzwilliam,

Am I never to be allowed to put Ramsgate out of my mind? Three weeks past, Bingley implored me to attend the local assembly. I agreed, against my better judgment, and what should I find but that the American minx is in the neighbourhood! The most prominent family hereabouts is also named Bennet, and these relations are more vulgar even than the Americans. The father is indolent, the mother rapacious, and the eldest daughter sanctimonious.

Worst of all is the cousin, Mr. Collins. Lady Catherine has gifted him the living at Hunsford, it seems. Never have I seen a more pompous imbecile! He introduced himself to me directly and thrice referred to Anne as my fiancée. Little wonder that Lady Catherine likes him; he speaks as though she were second only to Christ. I said as little as I could, but he appeared insensible of the insult in his behaviour to me, or mine to him.

If that were not sufficient misery, your scheme to engage Wickham with the Yorkshire militia has delivered him to my doorstep! The regiment is quartered at Meryton, and we encountered each other in the street last week when Bingley stopped to speak to the Bennet ladies and their odious cousin.

Bingley is quite taken with Miss Elizabeth's elder sister Jane. She is nothing objectionable in herself, but Bingley seems unable to comprehend that her family and connections must make her a wholly inappropriate object for his affections. The youngest sister, Miss Lydia, was again making a spectacle of herself. She flirted extravagantly with two of the officers and paid no heed to her grandmother's attempts to silence her.

Wickham, meanwhile, attempted to ingratiate himself with Miss Elizabeth, who at least had the sense to repudiate him. His countenance when he saw me was, perhaps, the only satisfying aspect of that scene. It took him a moment to summon his usual insolent smile, and in that moment he went quite white. He appears to have avoided me since then, though the inferior society of the neighbourhood makes that a relatively easy task. I go into society but rarely here, even by my standards.

My only consolation in all this is that Georgiana is at home with Mrs. Annesley, Mrs. Reynolds, and your mother. She begins to sound more like herself in her letters, which relieves my mind somewhat.

Pray write soon with the particulars you gave Colonel Forster about Wickham. I may require them.

– Darcy

Hertfordshire, October 1815

Darcy escaped the house before the others were awake. It was his only certainty of avoiding Miss Bingley, who was sure to find him whenever he was in the house. His morning rides also provided an opportunity for silence and reflection, both of which he required to restore his equilibrium. Unfortunately his reflections did not soothe him, for he was increasingly preoccupied with Elizabeth Bennet.

Every encounter with her was painful. Despite the frequency with which he begged off invitations, he was sure to see her and Miss Lucas at any party he attended. He found himself unable to speak to either lady, paralyzed as he was by mortification.

He had been in a particularly black humour that night, having just discovered that Wickham was to arrive within the week. It left him entirely unequal to encountering the young American woman who had so skillfully gutted him with his own words.

He saw her within seconds of entering the ballroom, her countenance frozen in astonishment not dissimilar to his own. She drew his gaze throughout the evening with her liveliness and grace, even when forced to endure the unpardonable Mr. Collins. He caught her looking his way once, a wicked gleam in her remarkable eyes. He looked away before she could see how greatly she discomfited him.

He had spoken of her to Bingley with vehement derision, intending only that he should never again be subjected to her mockery. Bingley had rightly pronounced his behaviour to be ungentlemanly, though Darcy was not sorry for it.

Until he discovered that he had been overheard.

Had she raged in fury, he believed he could have borne it. He might even have been able to apologize, for he certainly deserved her fury. It was her mirth that silenced him.

He had little experience of being laughed at. This woman, however – she had so little consideration for his good opinion that she was able to treat his disdain as an excellent joke! He had delivered her a grievous insult within her hearing, and she laughed until tears streamed down her face.

From this, he knew not how to recover. In company he was stiff, tongue-tied and barely civil. Miss Elizabeth appeared entirely unaffected, though the only man she avoided more assiduously than himself was Mr. Collins.

Now Darcy was encountering her on his morning rides. He had come upon her walking alone across the fields the week previous; face hot and unable to say a word, he stared until she dropped a shallow curtsey and turned away. Three days ago, a horse and rider flew past him on the road to Oakham Mount. He had time only to catch a glimpse of dark hair and a deep green riding habit before she was gone.

Perhaps I shall see her again this morning. He was appalled at the thought.

He entered the small copse of trees that bordered the Longbourn property and pulled up short. Miss Elizabeth appeared to be hiding there; she held her finger in front of her lips with such a forceful expression that he instantly obeyed.

Mr. Collins's voice could be heard through the trees. "Miss Elizabeth? Did I truly see you walking the grove in hopes of meeting me, or was that merely my fancy playing tricks on my eyes?"

Her eyes rolled and her mouth set in a firm line.

Naturally the fool is unable to conceive that she might walk out alone merely for the enjoyment of it. Collins's attentions toward her had become marked in the face of Bingley's obvious preference for her elder sister. Darcy spurred his mount forward, nearly colliding with Mr. Collins as he emerged from the trees. With a quick backward glance, he was relieved to see that Miss Elizabeth remained hidden from sight.

Collins greeted him in an exaggeratedly solicitous manner. Darcy cut him off in his most imperious tone, the one Fitzwilliam called his "Lady Catherine voice."

"Mr. Collins. Did I hear you calling out to a young lady just now? Are you, a man of the cloth, attempting to compromise a respectable maiden?"

The man reddened and spluttered. "Of course I was not— I would never— I have far too much respect for my noble patroness to even contemplate such a thing!"

"Then it is fortunate that no young lady is about. You heard my horse walking through the trees."

"Oh. Yes. Of course, Mr. Darcy. You are quite right. I was mistaken."

"I expect never to hear of such behaviour on your part again. My aunt would take an exceedingly dim view of having a rake residing in the parsonage."

"Of course. You may rest assured that I have no intent to... ah... materially damage the reputation of any young lady. I bid you good day, sir." Mr. Collins bowed deeply and scuttled away.

Darcy watched until Collins had entered the house before returning to Miss Bennet. She stood, hand pressed firmly over her mouth, eyes wide with surprise and laughter. When she met his eye, another emotion briefly overwhelmed her – relief – and she sat down hard on the trunk of an overturned tree. Her whole body shook with laughter or fear or pain, or perhaps a combination of all three.

Concerned, he dismounted and took a step toward her, keeping his voice low. "Are you well, Miss Bennet?"

She nodded, arms clasped tight across her body. "Yes, thank you, Mr. Darcy. I am excessively grateful for the service you rendered me just now. I had no idea that he had taken note of my favorite solitary path, which of course shall no longer be my favorite path. I—"

She stopped herself with a glance at him, followed by a wry half-smile and a shake of the head that seemed to be for herself alone.

It struck him that they were in a secluded copse, quite alone. He fought down the flush warming his cheeks. *What is it about this woman that has me blushing like a schoolboy?* He was unable to meet her eyes.

"It is nothing, Miss Bennet," he managed. "No woman deserves to be saddled with Mr. Collins except by her own choosing."

"Not even me? Your opinion of Mr. Collins must be low indeed."

Darcy grimaced.

"I am sorry," she said quickly, "that was ungenerous of me. I *am* very grateful to you, sir. I shall interfere no longer with your enjoyment of your ride. Good day, Mr. Darcy." She curtseyed, eyes on the ground, and walked rapidly away without waiting for his reply.

~ * ~

Not long afterward, a new circumstance excited the attention of the whole neighbourhood. Darcy followed Bingley into Netherfield's drawing-room one morning to find Jane and Elizabeth Bennet, along with their grandmother, calling on Miss Bingley and Mrs. Hurst.

"A thief, Mrs. Bennet?" Mrs. Hurst was saying. "How dreadful!"

"Indeed! Mrs. Long was the first to notice jewelry missing, two weeks past. Last week Mr. Purvis discovered all of his late wife's jewels gone from the safe."

"Has the magistrate any idea who might be responsible?" asked Darcy.

"I believe he will soon. Our cousins Thomas and Fanny Bennet hosted a dinner two days past; Fanny noticed several items missing when she put her jewels away afterward. She told Sir William immediately."

"Sir William is the local magistrate?" Darcy asked, keeping his tone neutral.

"He is. He takes his duty very seriously."

Perhaps, Darcy thought, *but he lacks the necessary power of mind to suspect his neighbours in such a scheme.*

"Does he believe there to be a connection between the thefts?" Bingley asked.

Jane Bennet answered. "Yes. Mr. Purvis had a large party of gentlemen to shoot some weeks back, and the Longs had recently hosted a card party."

Darcy frowned, a suspicion already fully bloomed in his mind. "Mrs. Bennet," he said, "were any of the officers of the regiment invited to these events?"

Mrs. Bennet and Miss Elizabeth regarded him with identical shrewd expressions.

"I can answer in the affirmative for Mrs. Long and my cousin. I do not know about the shooting party. Do you suspect an officer, then?"

The eyes of every person in the room were on him now.

"One cannot be too eager to eliminate any person as a possibility. Indeed, we cannot even be certain that only one person is responsible."

Mrs. Bennet lifted a brow at him, as though they shared a secret. "Then we must also consider the possible involvement of a lady."

This possibility had not occurred to him. His first impulse was to reject the very idea, as others were doing. Noting the look that passed between Mrs. Bennet and Miss Elizabeth, he realized how easy it would be to persuade a naïve young woman to aid in such a scheme, all unaware of the role she played.

Darcy excused himself, forming his resolution even as the thought occurred, strangely gratified by Mrs. Bennet's approving nod as he departed. A half-hour later he was shown into the vestibule of Colonel Forster's command tent, where he found Andrew Bennet waiting for an interview.

"Good day, Mr. Bennet. I just saw your wife at Netherfield. She told us of the recent thefts in the neighbourhood."

"Then I imagine we are here on the same business. I came to speak to Colonel Forster about one of his lieutenants."

Darcy nodded agreement. He found the man's directness unnerving.

"Let us proceed together. I suspect you have rather more pertinent information, but I feel it necessary to call attention to his behavior toward... Lydia." Mr. Bennet looked at him meaningfully.

Darcy understood. "I am most grateful to you, sir. I can provide particulars about financial concerns."

Mr. Bennet smiled with a degree of grim satisfaction that made Darcy glad they were allied in this cause. He felt a momentary pang of sympathy for Wickham's accomplices. They had no idea how formidable an adversary they had gained.

~ * ~

The following Friday saw the assembly rooms in Meryton filled to capacity for the monthly ball. Darcy, to Bingley's evident surprise, insisted on attending. His ostensible reason was to ensure, at the request of Colonel Forster, that the story passed around the neighbourhood bore at least passing resemblance to the facts. He was not prepared to admit, even to himself, the true reason for his interest.

The name on everybody's lips was Wickham's. Such a handsome young man! So charming, and yet all this time a villain! To think that he had stolen precious family jewels, all to cover hundreds of pounds in gaming debts! Fortunately, the part played by the sixteen-year-old niece of Mrs. Long was generally unknown.

Colonel Forster was the hero of the day, having been given the entirety of the credit for discovering Wickham's treachery. The Colonel had argued strenuously against this, but Darcy and Mr. Bennet were firm. Because the charges were brought in the military courts, the proceedings were not open to the public, and thus no whisper of the events at Ramsgate emerged.

Darcy had seen Wickham only once. With a smug smile, Wickham promised to say nothing about Georgiana's licentious behavior if Darcy would see him freed and purchase him a commission in a different corps. Wickham had every reason to expect him to agree; Darcy had made many such bargains to protect his father's name.

This time was different. Wickham's smile fell away at Darcy's counterproposal. Wickham would remain silent about *both* young ladies and Darcy would not bring charges for the mountain of unpaid debt that he had purchased, most recently at Meryton. Wickham must take his choice: transportation to Australia, or debtors' prison. He was set to take ship the following Tuesday.

Military justice moves swiftly, at least.

Darcy's musings were interrupted by the arrival of the Americans. Bingley hurried over to greet Jane Bennet, who graced Bingley with one of her tranquil smiles. Darcy could not make out her feelings for Bingley. Her countenance was invariably serene; were Bingley ever to see any burst of feeling which bespoke true attachment, his friend might be in real danger.

He saw movement in the corner of his eye. Mr. Collins had also noted Miss Elizabeth's arrival, and Darcy moved swiftly to head the man off. He paid his respects first to Mr. and Mrs. Bennet; their greeting was coolly polite, for which he could hardly blame them. Even if Miss Elizabeth had not told them of his behaviour at the assembly in September, they had witnessed his ungracious speech at Ramsgate and had seen little since then to soften their opinion of him.

It is time to begin making amends.

He bowed low over Miss Elizabeth's hand. She schooled her expression, surprise evident only in the slight lift of her brow. His voice failed him; heart beating in his throat like a drum, he coughed and began again.

"I fear I may be too late, madam, as I see your card is already quite full. I had hoped to have the pleasure of dancing with you this evening."

She assessed him for a very long moment. Glancing at Mr. Collins, she appeared to come to a decision. "You are fortunate, Mr. Darcy," she said with an arch smile. "I still have the first and the last."

"Then I shall be honoured to claim the first." *Under no circumstances shall I permit this buffoon to have that pleasure.*

Mr. Collins was left to beg the favour of the last set, to which she graciously consented. As Darcy escorted her to the floor, ignoring Bingley's frankly astonished expression, he was darkly curious to discover if Elizabeth Bennet would "turn her ankle" in the course of the evening.

CHAPTER SIX

IN WHICH ELIZABETH ATTEMPTS A CHARACTER SKETCH

Meryton, Hertfordshire, November 1ˢᵗ, 1815

My dearest Georgiana,

How much has happened in just two days! I trust your brother has told you of the hunt for the neighborhood thief, and of Mr. Wickham's arrest. He shall shortly be transported, and I cannot be sorry for him. My pity is all for the innocent young ladies of Australia! But you shall hear no more of Wickham from me.

I must instead tell you about the service your brother rendered me at last night's assembly. For the second time in as many weeks, his timely intervention saved me from the mortification of my cousin Mr. Collins's addresses. We had not been inside the room five minutes before I saw your brother approaching, moments ahead of Mr. Collins. I had taken pains before the assembly to evade my cousin and fill my dance card, but through an inexplicable twist of Fate, both the first set and the last were vacant!

How delighted I was to offer someone – anyone, truly, would have done for me in that moment – the first set! I must own that I abused your brother heartily for his usual refusal to dance, as he is quite an accomplished partner. He accepted his thrashing with admirable grace and even apologized for refusing to stand up with me at last month's assembly. (I did not tell you about that at the time, my dear, for he was quite rude, and I was terribly angry.)

I was overcome with headache by one o'clock and gave my regrets to Mr. Collins. He is persistent, however! This morning we called at Longbourn. The young people enjoyed a walk around the little wilderness at one side of the *lawn, for the day was very fine. Mr. Collins caught me alone and instantly made me a proposal of marriage! I cannot tell you how many times I ardently refused him, but he would not understand me. Eventually I gave over every attempt at civility and ran away to seek out my grandfather.*

Oh, Georgiana, to see Grandpa's face when I entreated him to intervene! Cousin Thomas allowed them the use of the library for a private conference. Shall you think me very wicked when I confess that I could not help listening at the door? If you do, then you must also think so of my cousin, for he stood next to me, looking quite delighted by Mr. Collins's attempts to defend himself against the invective Grandpa hurled at him.

I spent the rest of the day at Lucas Lodge with my dear friend Charlotte, so I did not see Mr. Collins again until supper. You may imagine my astonishment when my cousin Thomas announced Mary's engagement – to none other than Mr. Collins! Mary was apparently quite solicitous of Mr. Collins's feelings after his disappointment of the morning, and as his visit in Hertfordshire is nearly done, he wasted no time.

If I am to be charitable, I must say that he and Mary should do well together. She truly admires him and might even come to think nearly as well of Lady Catherine as he!

Your exhausted friend,

Elizabeth

Hertfordshire, November 1815

Returning to Longbourn after a lovely day, Elizabeth could not quite manage to ignore her discomposure.

Their outing, a picnic at Oakham Mount, had been Lydia's doing – a gift for Tommy's eighth birthday. The Lucases had joined them, and the entire party had taken great care of the boy. His small face shone with delight as the gentlemen took turns carrying him on their backs up the hill to enjoy the views.

There had even been a brief game in which Mr. Bingley and John Lucas ran across the field, each with a boy on his shoulders attempting to pelt the other with small seed-filled bags. This had rapidly proved to be too much exertion for Tommy, but the raucous shouts and laughter – even the servants cheered Tommy's every hit – were the highlight of the afternoon.

Elizabeth had presented Tommy with his new cribbage board after luncheon. He immediately begged to learn the game, and Mr. Darcy cheerfully appointed himself Tommy's advisor. Between Mr. Darcy's strategies and her abysmal cards, Elizabeth was thoroughly trounced.

"What a pity Jane did not advise you," she told Tommy with a wink. "She would not have encouraged you to be so cruel!" Her merriment faded to confusion, however, when she found Mr. Darcy smiling warmly at her.

Now, watching him tend to Tommy's comfort, she frowned in consternation. "Mr. Darcy baffles me, Charlotte."

Beside her, Charlotte laughed. "Is he so difficult to understand? To be sure, his behavior has been somewhat inconstant, but I believe there is a simple explanation."

"Somewhat inconstant? He publicly disdains me, avoids me for a month, then rescues me from the attentions of Mr. Collins – twice! – and then speaks not a word to me until today! And today he has been positively gentlemanly. Friendly, even! What *can* he be about?"

"You fascinate him, Lizzy. His eyes are often on you. But consider: he is the nephew of an earl and the master of one of the greatest estates in England, which by all accounts has increased in prosperity under his management."

"You mean to say, I suppose, that he naturally believes himself superior."

"Precisely."

Elizabeth sighed. "He needn't be so offensive about it."

"Very true, Lizzy, though you *are* quite impertinent. I suspect he has never met a lady with the temerity to argue with him."

"This explains why Mr. Darcy should seek to avoid me. How can you account for the rest?"

"The very same explanation. He is intrigued and repelled by you at once."

Elizabeth considered this. "Your theory is compelling, but I cannot credit myself with such powers of attraction. Mr. Darcy's antipathy to Mr. Collins requires no feelings of gallantry toward me, for example."

"I might allow that, but what of today? He smiled at you, Lizzy!"

"Dear Tommy has such a profound effect on us all, why should Mr. Darcy be excepted? Even Mary has been smiling and sociable!"

"You may deny it all you like, Lizzy, but I shall be proven right in the end."

~ * ~

Late that evening, Elizabeth and her sisters sat companionably on Jane's bed with cups of chocolate, prepared to giggle and gossip as they had done since childhood.

"Jane, it is your turn for telling truth, so you must tell us what we all want to know," Lydia said.

"What is that, dear?"

"When shall Mr. Bingley propose, and shall you accept him?"

Jane blushed to the roots of her hair.

"What! Has he proposed already? Why did you say nothing before?"

Jane resolutely shook her head. "No, Lydia. He has made no declaration."

"Then he certainly shall! Do not you agree, Lizzy?"

"I agree that he likes Jane very much, and I believe he wants only encouragement to declare himself. But shall you give it, Jane? What are your own feelings?"

"I hardly know," Jane sighed. "He is sensible, amiable and generous, to be sure. I enjoy his company very much. But I do not know if he is clever, or steady."

"Or if he should like to run our father's business."

At Lydia's confused exclamation, Elizabeth shared their mother's ultimatum.

"Mr. Pringle! How perfectly horrible! He is ancient and dull. Surely Papa would not be so cruel!"

"Papa has been quite persistent," Jane said. "Mr. Bingley would certainly make a far more agreeable husband."

"That is precisely the problem, is it not, Jane?" asked Elizabeth. "His temper is so easy that it is but the work of a moment to persuade him. That cannot be an advantage, to his wife or to any in his employ."

"Lizzy, I believe you judge him too harshly."

"Do I, Jane? When Kitty told Mr. Bingley today that he must give a ball, he settled on the date and the guest list in ten minutes. And his sister not even there!"

"Oh, Lizzy. What harm is there in ready agreement to something of no great import?"

"None, but did you not doubt his steadiness? I fear he has but little. He said himself that if he should decide to quit a place, he should be off in five minutes. And he does nothing with Netherfield unless Mr. Darcy recommends it."

"Mr. Bingley invited Mr. Darcy to Netherfield because he has no experience in managing an estate. He means to learn."

"My dear Jane, one does not learn by allowing another to dictate all!"

Lydia giggled. "Lizzy, you speak as though Mr. Bingley were a marionette and Mr. Darcy the puppeteer!"

"Precisely. How should a man so easily persuaded oversee a modest country estate, much less a company with hundreds of workers on three continents?"

"We must discover if Mr. Bingley can be steady, then. But how are we to know?"

"Perhaps this ball shall give us a hint. If the guest list becomes only fashionable London acquaintances or he gives it up entirely, we shall know he has been swayed."

~ * ~

The ball was held on the 21st of November. Elizabeth had never seen Netherfield looking so grand: the house was overflowing with fresh evergreen boughs, white ribbon and silver candlesticks. Every prominent local family was in attendance, but Mr. Bingley had eyes only for Jane.

Her sister was exceedingly elegant this evening. A layer of gauzy white lace softened the dark blue satin of the gown beneath, which matched the sapphires at her ears and throat. Her hair was held back by a delicate tiara, golden curls draped over one shoulder.

Elizabeth's gown was of white satin, worked on the bodice and hem with silver embroidery that gleamed in the candlelight. Caroline Bingley gushed over the exotic black pearl necklace and earrings that had been her grandparents' gift for her twentieth birthday. *That may be the first sincere compliment I have ever heard Miss Bingley utter,* she thought.

It was a very enjoyable evening. The musicians were excellent, and Elizabeth never wanted for a partner. The only sour note was that Mr. Darcy had very early solicited her hand for the supper set. She could hardly refuse, but she knew not how they were to fill an hour of conversation. When the time came, however, she found that Mr. Darcy did not share her anxiety, for he initially said nothing at all.

On reflection, she discovered that when they danced together at Meryton, all their conversation was begun on her side. She had just determined that a half-hour of silence would provide excellent opportunity to observe her neighbors when he finally spoke.

"Are you well, Miss Bennet?"

"I am, sir. Think you that I appear ill?"

"Nay, only that you are uncharacteristically silent."

"Whereas your silence is entirely expected." She flashed a mischievous grin. "How shall we proceed, Mr. Darcy? Is it to be charades, or shall we wrap ourselves in an air of mystery and continue as we were?"

He chuckled. "Have you no taste for conversation, then?"

"Do not mistake me, sir, for you must know that I consider conversation to be indispensable. At present, however, I think only of *your* distaste for it."

He looked at her curiously. "Pray tell, for what purpose do you find it so necessary?"

"Why, for the illumination of character, of course."

"Is that all! Is it not possible to discover a person's character without meaningless discourse?"

"One may observe how a person behaves, or inquire after them, but this may be unreliable. Meaningless discourse is little better."

"Unreliable?"

"Do you not think so? Have you not been acquainted with those whose public behavior portrays a vastly different character than their private acts reveal?"

Mr. Darcy's jaw clenched, and he nodded almost imperceptibly. "Such persons rarely speak their true thoughts aloud. Indeed, I should venture to say that one of the tenets of well-bred society is to conceal one's true opinions when in company."

"Only when one's true opinion is hurtful to others, I hope. One should freely reveal everything wise or charitable."

"Naturally. But I have always believed that one's true character is displayed by one's conduct, particularly such private acts as you describe."

"Ah, but how does a mere acquaintance discover such acts, to fairly judge one's character? Nay, sir, that shall never do. I say again, conversation is essential."

"Do enlighten me, Miss Bennet."

"I do not speak of meaningless discourse, sir. Only with the mutual exchange of ideas on topics of substance may one ascertain the *motive* for another's behavior." She was struck by a recollection and laughed. "This conversation, indeed, puts me in mind of my former headmistress, Mrs. Okill. She regularly recited maxims on the subject."

"Maxims? Does one dare inquire?"

"Oh, they are nothing a gentleman could not hear. One in particular she said very often." Elizabeth assumed a ponderous expression and a pinched, nasal voice. "No young lady should marry a man with whom she cannot converse with pleasure. When children are grown, spouses must entertain each other."

Mr. Darcy's lips quirked. The music ended and he offered his arm.

Elizabeth went on. "There was also, 'A lady skilled in conversation invites a gentleman to tell her not pretty lies, but deep truths.' My grandmother is the embodiment of that maxim, as you may have observed. My favorite, however, was always, 'A conversation is a journey. Together the voyagers may discover new delights… or abject horrors.'"

He laughed outright. "An apt metaphor. Sadly, my own attempts have tended toward the horrors. I fear I am ill-qualified to recommend myself to strangers."

"How can that be? Why should a man of sense and education, who has lived in the world, be ill-qualified to recommend himself to strangers?"

"I can answer that very readily," said Mr. Bingley, approaching with Jane as they made their way to the dining-room. "He will not give himself the trouble to pretend interest in their concerns."

Jane gasped. "As ungenerous a speech as I have ever heard from you, sir!"

"I say no more than Miss Elizabeth knows herself already. But perhaps she has not yet divined the reason." Mr. Bingley grinned.

"I cannot say that I have."

"Why, so that he need not suffer the attacks of the impertinent or the inferior! A single man of fortune is always assumed to be in want of a wife or a poor relation to support." Mr. Bingley clapped his friend on the shoulder. "When a man finds little enjoyment in idle conversation, it is best to go about looking as fierce as possible, eh, Darcy?"

Mr. Darcy said nothing, merely lifted a brow at his friend with a cold, steady look.

Bingley only laughed. "There, now! That is exactly the expression. Admirably displayed, Darcy!"

Elizabeth checked her laughter, perceiving that Mr. Darcy was truly offended. His silence persisted through the first two courses, though he seemed to attend closely to her other conversations. Eventually she determined that she could not publicly ignore him for the whole of the meal, despite his rudeness.

"How does Georgiana? Shall her aunt stay long with her at Pemberley?"

"No, Lady Matlock returns to Derwent Court within the week to prepare for her annual Christmas party. Georgiana shall remain at Pemberley with Mrs. Annesley."

Elizabeth kept her tone neutral. "Georgiana speaks very highly of Mrs. Annesley's elegance and decorum."

"She is a very genteel woman. She sets an excellent example for my sister." He lapsed again into silence.

Elizabeth tried again. "Shall you and Georgiana be in town this winter?"

"It is likely that I shall, but Georgiana prefers Pemberley to Darcy House."

"Does she indeed, even under such circumstances? How singular! I should not have thought so."

A frown creased his brow. "Pray, what circumstances do you mean?"

"A large house is cold comfort when it is filled only with servants and a paid companion."

"I assure you, madam, my sister is quite contented there."

Elizabeth only looked at him for a long moment, then turned back to her plate.

His voice was low and tense. "What claims have you to contradict my knowledge of my sister?"

"I am her intimate friend and correspondent, sir. She does not fear to disclose her feelings to me."

His countenance hardened. "Miss Bennet, if you have something of which to accuse me—." Elizabeth could not have said if it was the harshness of his tone or Mr. Bingley's sudden look of alarm that stopped him.

Mr. Darcy stood abruptly. "It is quite warm, is it not, Miss Elizabeth? Perhaps you might be more comfortable in the next room."

Elizabeth murmured indistinct thanks, nodding to Jane and Mr. Bingley with a serenity she did not feel. Mr. Darcy accosted her again the moment they could speak without being overheard.

"Do you accuse me, Miss Bennet, of frightening Georgiana?"

Elizabeth did not reply.

"I am not only her brother, but her guardian. It is my duty to shelter and protect her."

"You have succeeded admirably, then. She is entirely unacquainted with the ways of the world."

"She is safe."

Elizabeth scoffed. "Oh, aye, she is in no danger at all. No danger of making any friends, nor of learning to overcome her natural reticence, nor of exercising her own judgment, nor even of setting a foot out of doors without your knowledge! I am sure it is very convenient for you to keep such a timid bird in your gilded cage."

"You would have me allow her to continue in her own establishment, I suppose? I shall do no such thing! Her judgment is not equal to such independence."

"Of course not! She is but sixteen, raised in a great lonely house by servants, with no playmates to speak of. She has little in common with her schoolfellows, and she can purchase the attention of her faultless paragon of a brother only by such compliance and accomplishments as might earn his approval!"

Mr. Darcy's posture was rigid with fury. "You accuse me of neglect, I see."

Elizabeth was suddenly aware of how he loomed over her. She took several deep breaths, attempting to moderate her tone. "How is Georgiana to improve her powers of perception when all she sees is familiar to her? How may she learn to judge rightly, when she is given no opportunity to make even small mistakes?"

There was no alteration in his countenance. He glared, eyes gray and hard as steel. Elizabeth faced him squarely, looking up at him with all the seriousness she could muster.

"Mr. Darcy, can you not see that Georgiana requires assurance that her brother loves and trusts her? She relied on her own judgment for the first time in her life, with catastrophic results. Now she fears to trust herself at all." Her voice caught. When she continued, it was just above a whisper. "How is she to believe herself worthy of any man's good opinion, when the one she holds in the highest esteem appears to want nothing to do with her?"

For the second time, he reacted as though she had slapped him. His eyes widened and the color drained from his face, fury replaced by an emotion she could not name.

"You have said quite enough, madam. I perfectly comprehend your feelings. Pray, excuse me."

Elizabeth took a moment to compose herself after he had gone. What had possessed her to attack Mr. Darcy with such spirit, and in such a public place? She was grateful that they would remove to London very soon. With luck, they would see little of him there.

It was a great consolation that Charlotte had agreed to visit them after Christmas. She very much wanted to retain Charlotte's company and good sense, and she had seen quite enough of Hertfordshire.

CHAPTER SEVEN

IN WHICH DARCY'S MOTIVES ARE QUESTIONED

Netherfield, Hertfordshire, 25ᵗʰ November 1815

Fitzwilliam,

This shall be my last letter from Hertfordshire, as we are to remove to town on Monday next. The Americans departed today; they shall take a house for the winter and travel to Italy in the spring, it seems. Bingley is already fretting about the loss of Jane Bennet, though I wager that after a fortnight in the broader society of London, he shall meet his next "angel" and the allure of Miss Bennet shall fade.

I have lately been giving a great deal of thought to Georgiana's situation at Pemberley, particularly in light of the manner in which Mr. Bennet is handling the behaviour of his youngest granddaughter. Lydia Bennet, you recall, was the one vying for Wickham's affections; her lack of decorum with the militia officers in Meryton has been equally egregious. She is therefore being left in Hertfordshire as a companion to her young cousin Tommy.

Mr. Bennet revealed his motive for this decision over brandy last evening at a dinner party hosted by Colonel Forster, at which every officer was present. Miss Lydia's natural high spirits and dependence on her own judgment make her perfectly indifferent to the admonitions of her family, he said, but serve her very well in support of her cousin. Her genuine affection for him and her desire to be distinguished – particularly in comparison to her sisters – also make it likely that she will succeed in the task now set before her.

To aid her motivation, she shall be permitted to travel to Italy only if she demonstrates more steadiness and decorum than she has heretofore shown. He also made it known that if she marries without his consent her dowry is forfeit, and that any man that ruins her should expect swift and severe retribution. His role in Wickham's capture is not generally known but no man there doubted his capacity to deal out suffering, despite his age.

You may well wonder how this pertains to Georgiana, whose character could not be more opposed to Lydia Bennet's. What struck me about Mr. Bennet's plan is that, instead of attempting to subdue his granddaughter's temperament, he is relying on it. After much reflection I begin to believe that my actions as regards Georgiana, though intended to protect her, have done naught but repress her naturally affectionate temper and increase her fears. I hope you may call at Darcy House on Tuesday next; your advice on this point will be welcome.

Until then—

Darcy

Darcy House, London, December 1815

Darcy bounded down the steps to assist Georgiana out of the carriage. She eagerly embraced him, eyes bright and countenance glowing with happiness.

Her steps were light as she cheerfully recounted the pleasures of the journey, but when Darcy observed her more closely he saw that she was thin and pale, with dark circles beneath her eyes. He frowned, concerned. She stopped mid-sentence, eyes dropping to the floor.

"Georgiana, what is the matter? Please, look at me."

She glanced up and then down again. "You looked displeased, brother. I thought my chatter must be irksome to you."

"Not at all, my dear." He gently lifted her chin until she met his eyes. "I was merely concerned; it appears that you are not entirely well."

When she did not answer, he dropped her chin and focused on the tea tray. "After we have had some refreshment, there is something I should like to tell you. Then, perhaps, you may feel sufficiently comfortable to tell me how you have been." He took care to speak kindly, and she relaxed a fraction.

He had spent the week debating with himself about what to say. He could not bring himself to share Miss Bennet's exact words, nor the dream that had now recurred several times; the image of Miss Bennet aiming a pistol at his chest, arm protectively around Georgiana, was entirely too apt.

His sister nibbled at a pastry that she would have devoured only six months ago. Wincing internally, Darcy recalled that dreadful argument – *can you not see that Georgiana requires assurance that her brother loves her?*

"Georgiana," he said gently, "I owe you an apology. I must thank your friend Miss Elizabeth for calling it to my attention."

Her eyes were wide. "I had no idea of her saying anything about me at all!"

"I can easily believe it. She was not gentle in her remonstrance, and she had no reason to believe that it had any beneficial effect. I shall spare you – and myself – the details, but she gave me to understand how lonely you have been, and that to be left alone at Pemberley was more punishment than protection."

"Oh my! Fitzwilliam, you *must* believe that I never said anything of the sort to her!"

He took her hands in his. "Do not be alarmed, dearest. What I feel is not anger, but regret. You are my sister. It was my responsibility to ease your suffering, but I could not even see it. I was too engrossed in my own concerns."

She began to weep, leaning against his chest and crying into his shoulder as she had not done since she was a child. He found himself rocking her gently, chin tucked into her hair and blinking back tears of his own.

"I know not what to do, nor to think," she said, her voice muffled by his jacket. "I lay awake questioning everything. Mrs. Annesley is kind, but she cannot be a friend. Aunt Eleanor means well, but she gives advice that I have not courage enough to follow. I did not want to cause more trouble for you by asking to come to town, but I am so glad to be here."

He smiled wryly. "I do not know how much help I can be to you, Georgiana. I have been too blind to have faith in my own judgment on that score. But you shall have as much of my time as you can tolerate – we shall attend concerts and plays, and anything else you desire."

"That sounds lovely, Fitzwilliam. I cannot recall when last I had the prospect of such pleasures with you! There is only one thing more which I could ask."

"You have only to name it."

"Might I call on Elizabeth? Mr. Bennet has taken a house for them in Dover Street. I know you do not like her, but I feel quite easy with her. She is so clever, and Jane is so calm, I feel that I might ask them anything."

"Of course you may, and they may call upon you here. I do not dislike Miss Elizabeth, dearest. I cannot pretend to enjoy her rebukes, but her counsel has always been sound."

~ * ~

"Well, now you've done it, Darcy."

Darcy looked up in surprise as his grinning cousin dropped casually into the empty chair opposite.

"Done what, Fitzwilliam?"

"You've gone and made the paper. The society pages, no less!"

Bingley, next to him, laughed. "Indeed, it is the most pressing news among the ladies of the *ton*. You are on the hunt for a society wife at last, they say!"

"So, to what do society's most formidable matrons owe the honor? You cannot pin this on Georgiana, old man. Not even she, were she out in society, could induce you to be seen in company four or five nights every week."

Darcy's lips pressed into a firm line. Not for anything would he speak the truth aloud.

"Nay, Darcy, that shall not do," said Bingley. "This is White's! There are no gossiping matrons here to spread your tale, and there can be no common explanation for such extraordinary behaviour. Let us hear it!"

Darcy looked pointedly across the room to where several younger men – dandies all – could be clearly heard trading rumours and salacious remarks about the eligible young ladies of their acquaintance.

Bingley shrugged. "Keep your voice low, then, but by all means, do tell us why you have suddenly acquired a taste for society that you have hitherto disdained."

Darcy weighed his words carefully. "Let us say that I am unlikely ever to wed if I keep to my study, and I am disinclined to allow my relations to choose my bride."

"Ha! How grim you are about it, Darcy! What a pity that we are off to Scarborough for Christmas. I should very much enjoy the sight of Caroline duelling with the other ladies for the favour of your attention!"

Darcy seized the opportunity to redirect the topic, ignoring Fitzwilliam's thoughtful gaze. "Indeed, I have scarcely seen you since we returned to town. Where have you been hiding?"

"Caroline has engaged us for endless dinners and parties. I thought at first that her aim was to secure a husband, so I have been excessively happy to escort her, but recently I suspect that she has another view in mind."

"She is looking to find you a suitably elegant wife, one assumes," Fitzwilliam said.

"I believe so. She has recently befriended Miss Elliot, whom we seem to encounter everywhere."

"Is Miss Elliot the daughter of Sir Walter Elliot?" Darcy asked.

"Yes, the eldest. Her younger sister is lately married, I understand, to a gentleman of the Navy."

"Very true, and Mrs. Wentworth is a treasure," said Fitzwilliam. "I do not know her sister, but the daughter of a baronet is certainly an eligible match."

"Miss Elliot is quite possibly older than you are, Colonel. I believe I can do better than a woman already on the shelf. Besides, her conversation is comprised entirely of insipid anecdotes about her cousin the Viscontess Dalrymple and raptures about the drawing-rooms of her father's house in Bath."

Fitzwilliam laughed heartily. "The conversation alone must put a sensible man off the idea of such a wife. I begin to think you may yet choose a lady for something more substantial than blond curls, blue eyes and a sweet temper."

Bingley protested the unfairness of this characterization, but could not long withstand the jocular accusations of one friend and the gravely amused affirmation of the other. Unwilling to concede defeat, he wished them a happy Christmas and departed in very good humour.

"When do you travel to Matlock for your mother's Christmas party?" Darcy asked.

"Oh, did I not tell you? Many of her usual guests are away on the Continent, so she and Father have changed their plans. They arrive in town tomorrow. She means to host a New Year's Eve party at Matlock House instead."

"Is this to be one of her grand affairs, to which half the city is invited?"

"Quite likely, knowing Mother." He grinned at Darcy's expression. "You shall have to make an appearance, old man. It should not surprise me if the Americans are invited as well." Fitzwilliam's tone was casual, but he eyed Darcy carefully.

"I was not aware that your mother was acquainted with the Bennets."

"Georgiana apparently spoke so glowingly of her dear friend Miss Elizabeth that Mother determined to call as soon as she discovered that the family was in town."

Darcy kept his expression neutral. "Hmm."

"Bingley's sister is scheming to keep him away from them, I suppose."

"She is. The stratagem appears to be having at least half of the desired effect; she has not heard him mention Jane Bennet in over a week."

They returned to Darcy House, where feminine laughter could be heard from the direction of the drawing-room. Fitzwilliam's eyebrows raised in question.

"The Bennet ladies were to call on Georgiana today," said Darcy. "I did not expect they would still be here."

"Shall we join them, or leave them to it?"

Darcy hesitated.

Georgiana's voice carried down the hall: "How remarkable, Mrs. Bennet!"

He was halfway to the drawing-room before he was aware of having taken a step. Fitzwilliam smirked.

Mrs. Bennet could now be clearly heard. "On the contrary, my dear, it has been fifty years since my family moved to New York from London. The most remarkable thing is how many things are just as I recall them!"

They entered the drawing-room to the obligatory round of polite greetings.

"Mrs. Bennet was just telling us that she grew up in London as a girl," Georgiana said. "I cannot imagine what it must be like to cross the ocean for an entirely new life in another country!"

Fitzwilliam nodded. "It must be exciting. I have never seen New York; I imagine it is quite different from London."

"Oh, yes. I fancied myself very worldly at fifteen and was prepared to be unimpressed, but I was astonished by the energy of the place! There seems always to be someone hurrying about, of every station in life."

"What led your family to leave London?" Georgiana asked, eyes wide with eager curiosity.

"My father was brought over to replace the son of old Mr. Bennet as the manager of Bennet-Janssen's New York office. None of us expected that the charming young man who met us at the dock was the selfsame person! He looked no older than my eldest brother, who was not twenty!"

Fitzwilliam and Georgiana's faces mirrored his own surprise, but the Misses Bennet merely looked on with fond indulgence. *Clearly this is an oft-told family story.*

"To be in such a position at that age is quite singular," he said.

Miss Elizabeth smiled proudly. "Our grandfather is a singular man, Mr. Darcy. Great-Grandpa was fond of boasting of him."

"When Lizzy and I were small," Miss Bennet said, "he told us of the summer that Grandpa decided to sell cold water for a penny a glass. He was only eight years old, and every day he had a line of customers around the block!"

Mrs. Bennet took up the tale. "After that, Papa Bennet brought Andrew to the office nearly every day. He made him the manager at seventeen; my father was brought in a year later so that Andrew could devote himself to his studies at King's College."

"By Jove, that is extraordinary!" said Fitzwilliam. "When I consider my own employments at seventeen, I cannot boast of achieving anything of particular merit."

Not long afterward the Bennet ladies took their leave with great affection for Georgiana. Darcy and Fitzwilliam remained a short time to hear her effusions over the felicity of having such clever and charming friends.

"I have not seen Georgiana speak with such ease and animation since she was a child," said Fitzwilliam as they retired to the library. He fixed Darcy with a very direct look. "Tell me again, if you would, why the Bennet family is so wholly inappropriate."

Darcy sighed. "I must agree that their affectionate ease has been beneficial for Georgiana's spirits, but surely you must see the vulgarity in them. To speak so openly – with pride, even – of a fortune earned directly by trade must inevitably separate them from the first circles. Indeed, their very directness of speech – Miss Elizabeth and Mr. Bennet in particular, to say nothing of Miss Lydia – is inelegant at best."

"You say nothing that my parents would not echo. I must confess, however, that I have great respect for enterprising men. In my profession, it is the officers who refuse to endure effort or hardship because they fancy themselves gentlemen who lead men to their deaths with frightening regularity."

"There is a distinct difference between a gentleman's son who enters a respectable profession and a commoner who happens to prosper in business, Fitzwilliam."

"On that we agree, but I doubt that our concordance of mind extends to the exact nature of that difference."

"You argue that the commoner is superior, then?"

"I argue that there is nothing admirable in spending one's life entirely at leisure. You are not an example of the gentlemen of whom I speak; you were taught to manage your estate attentively, which requires effort. One might even call it 'work,' though you take pains to disguise it."

"There is nothing admirable in leaving one's estate entirely to the care of a steward."

"Indeed," Fitzwilliam said amiably. "As I said, I admire an enterprising man. But consider for a moment those dandies at White's today, who had nothing better to occupy their time than idle gossip and plotting the ruination of respectable young women."

"You know my opinion of such men."

Fitzwilliam's gaze turned steely. "I do, and yet you tell me that I must esteem them more highly than Mr. Bennet, because they are the firstborn sons of gentlemen. Somerton is the worst of them, and he is the son of a duke. Are we truly to look up to him with respect?"

Darcy could not think of a reply. As often happened in such debates, his cousin's pragmatism triumphed over his own principle.

To his credit, Fitzwilliam did not press his point. Instead, he smirked. "I wonder if, perhaps, there is another reason you are so determined to think ill of the Bennets."

"What nonsense are you spouting now, Richard?"

Darcy silently kicked himself for speaking before he had collected his thoughts. His cousin knew that Darcy only used his first name when he was truly rattled; Darcy would never hear the end of this.

He had underestimated Fitzwilliam, however. His cousin's eyes were sympathetic, not gleeful.

"You may tell as many lies as you like to Bingley, my friend, but I am not fooled. You are not so desperate as to bind yourself to one of those grasping society maidens whose company you have long shunned."

Again, Darcy said nothing in reply. He kept his face as neutral as possible; Fitzwilliam's ability to discern his true feelings was both uncanny and unnerving.

Fitzwilliam made to leave but paused as he passed Darcy's chair, placing a friendly hand on his shoulder.

"You should be grateful that I can see through you as I do, Darcy," he said quietly. "Were I less discerning, you should find me a determined rival. She is quite extraordinary." He left without another word.

Darcy remained where he was, staring unseeing at the fire and attempting to subdue the riot of thoughts and feelings crowding his mind and heart, until the room was lit by nothing more than embers.

CHAPTER EIGHT

IN WHICH ELIZABETH HOBNOBS WITH THE ELITE

Dover Street, London, December 30th, 1815

Dear Charlotte,

What a surprising visitor we had today! Georgiana called with her aunt, the Countess of Matlock. Her Ladyship was everything elegant and gracious, and I can now say with confidence that Colonel Fitzwilliam derives his sharp eyes and ready wit from his mother. It was apparently through my letters to Georgiana that she developed a curiosity to meet me, but she spent far more time taking Nanna's measure than mine.

It was quite something to see! I imagined myself to be observing a jousting match – each combatant would lower her lance but the other would expertly deflect its point, and neither ever showed signs of being unseated. By the end they appeared enormously pleased with one another. Before she left, Lady Matlock invited our family to her New Year's Eve gala. The housekeeper assures us that the Countess's parties are legendary, and that the cream of society shall be there. Dearest Jane quailed a bit at that, but I find my courage is equal to the idea of meeting with so many elevated persons.

Speaking of Jane, I cannot make her out. We have been a month in London, and in that time have seen Mr. Bingley only once. I am convinced that this must be deliberate. Even Jane believes it to be so, but she maintains that Mr. Bingley must never have been very attached to her at all. Miss Bingley writes occasionally, always mentioning a Miss Elizabeth Elliot, whose father is a baronet. We are naturally to believe that she has captured Mr. Bingley's heart, though we hear no such news. Jane's countenance is serene, but she changes the subject whenever the Bingleys are mentioned and will not speak of him even to me. I know not how to comfort her, Charlotte! If you have wisdom to offer, I am ready to hear it.

I pray you to give the Lucases my best wishes. I eagerly await your arrival in town, when I shall tell you all about Lady Matlock's gala! Until then, I remain

Your dear friend,

Elizabeth

Matlock House, London, December 31st, 1815

The mantel clock chimed eleven as Elizabeth made her way to the divan in the drawing-room where she had left her grandmother and Jane. Her progress was slow; there were guests milling about everywhere, with more arriving regularly. Finally she halted, unable to find a path that would not put her directly in someone's way. Catching Jane's eye through the crowd, she lifted the glasses of wine she carried and glanced around her with an amused shrug.

A susurration of skirts and feminine whispers from the doorway diverted her attention. Mr. Darcy's tall figure stepped into view, followed by Colonel Fitzwilliam. She was struck by how Mr. Darcy seemed to tower over the admirers now crowding around him, all of them decidedly young and female. Murmurs of "Mr. Darcy" reached her ears; it put her in mind of waves breaking on The Sands at Ramsgate.

The newspapers were breathless with speculation over Mr. Darcy's dramatic entrée into society this Season, though the only question they considered worthy of discussion was which young lady had prompted this astonishing change. Elizabeth had certainly observed no evidence of preference on his part; indeed, she would not have believed him capable of warmth at all had she not seen him interact with his cousin and sister. On more than one occasion she had entered a room to see him laughing with the colonel, only for his ease to vanish the moment he caught sight of their party.

Tonight his posture was stiff and formal, his countenance frozen into a mask of politeness that should have forbade any lady of discernment to approach him. Perhaps unsurprisingly, it had no such effect.

Elizabeth battled an urge to laugh aloud, watching him bow with excruciating precision to each successive wave in the sea of ladies. So captivated was she that she was helpless to hide her mirth even when he met her eyes. Something unreadable flashed in his expression and she promptly turned away, biting her lip in an effort to school her features.

"May I be of some assistance, madam?" came Colonel Fitzwilliam's voice from behind her.

She turned, surprised; she had not noticed him leave his cousin's side.

"You appear to be overburdened and stranded," he said, taking a glass from her.

She nodded, not yet trusting her voice.

"Follow me," he said. "Once more into the breach!"

Elizabeth stayed close behind him as he navigated through the clusters of people, greeting many with effusive good humor. In short order he bowed gallantly to her grandmother, presenting her with the wine glass he carried.

"Thank you for rescuing my sister," said Jane.

"Think nothing of it, Miss Bennet. I am always pleased to come to the aid of a damsel in distress. Miss Elizabeth, might I persuade you to favor me with a dance? I commend your relations for defending their seat against all comers – I wager that Lady Middleton will be offering to purchase that space on the cushions before the night is half gone – but as we are obliged for the moment to stand, shall we not take a turn together?"

Finally permitted by the absurdity of this speech to laugh aloud, she happily consented.

"I could not permit you to perish of apoplexy," he said when they had passed out of the room. "You looked to be in mortal peril when I found you."

"I have never observed a scene quite like it. Your cousin appeared an automaton!"

The colonel's full-throated laughter drew attention, but the curiosity and occasional censure faded into amusement when he lamented the dangers of escorting a witty young lady. The curious glances shifted to her, but he did not stop to make introductions.

"We should let them wonder what lady has rendered me uncouth with amusement," he said.

She smiled archly. "Tell me, Colonel, did you develop such a keen mind for strategy in the Army, or was it learned at your mother's knee?"

He laughed again as they joined the set and kept up a lively conversation during the dance. Afterward they made their way to the refreshment table, where the colonel was hailed by a tall man in a dark blue uniform whose hearty voice might easily have carried across the house.

"Wentworth! Delighted to see you," said Colonel Fitzwilliam, introducing her. "This intrepid gentleman is Captain Frederick Wentworth of the Navy. He has my everlasting gratitude for being the means of returning my regiment to English soil once Napoleon's ambitions finally got the better of him."

The captain's manners were easy and open. Glancing at Elizabeth, he declared that wartime topics had no place on a night of festivities. Elizabeth surmised that he'd seen action in the recent conflict between their countries and was grateful for his forbearance.

He earned her further esteem by introducing her to his wife. Anne Wentworth was a petite and pretty woman nearing thirty, and a very little conversation proved her to be well-educated and sensible. They delightedly compared observations on travel, with frequent additions and amusing anecdotes from the gentlemen, pausing only to join the assembled guests in counting down the seconds to the New Year.

They were toasting merrily to new adventures when the party was approached by another pair. These proved to be Mrs. Wentworth's father and sister, whose polite greeting turned positively rancid when they learned that Elizabeth was American.

Sir Walter Elliot opined that he had never seen a tolerable face among them, though he allowed that he knew very few Americans. Miss Elliot declared herself shocked that her brother could speak with such civility to any citizen of the country whose shores he was so recently blockading! Though of course she meant no offense, she assured Elizabeth with glib insincerity.

The Wentworths were mortified, but Elizabeth was able to reply with genuine unconcern that she was not in the least offended. *Miss Elliot has elevated rudeness to absurdity. That I am not laughing at her is a triumph!*

The captain steered the conversation back to the topic of traveling for pleasure. Miss Elliot interrupted to express her disdain for the expense and inconvenience when she suddenly looked past them, her sneer becoming a simper.

Following her gaze, Colonel Fitzwilliam grinned. "Darcy! We quite despaired of you."

"You must teach me the trick of melting through crowds as you do, Fitzwilliam." Mr. Darcy bowed to Elizabeth. "Good evening, Miss Bennet. Your grandmother was just sharing my cousin's conjecture about the value of her seat. She requested that I dispatch him back to serve as her auctioneer."

"I am ever at that gracious lady's service," said the colonel. He made the necessary introductions before clapping his cousin on the back. "Your error is that you stop moving, my friend." He departed the ballroom as he had entered it, greeting all he passed without once breaking stride.

Sir Walter began what could only be described as an interrogation, quizzing Mr. Darcy minutely about the Pemberley estate. Elizabeth was forced to bite her lip again to keep from laughing as Miss Elliot maneuvered herself closer, fluttering her lashes and resting her hand on Mr. Darcy's arm.

Caroline Bingley is surely deceiving either herself or Jane, Elizabeth thought. *If Mr. Bingley's regard for this woman is not fictitious, I must entirely discredit my own judgment.*

Elizabeth's amusement did not last long. Mr. Darcy steadily repressed every attempt to engage him in conversation. His coldness toward the Elliots required no explanation, but neither Captain Wentworth's geniality nor his wife's intelligent cordiality could elicit more than the minimum required for the sake of politeness. Elizabeth herself he ignored entirely, as Sir Walter and Miss Elliot were now studiously doing. He even turned so that his back was to her!

Nearby onlookers who had observed her with smiles and curiosity when Colonel Fitzwilliam was her companion now turned their faces from her with cool expressions. She was grateful when Mrs. Wentworth directed her toward the refreshment table, arms companionably linked.

Her relief was to be short-lived, however, for Captain Wentworth soon claimed his wife for the next set. Mrs. Wentworth went with a regretful press of Elizabeth's hand, but Elizabeth could not begrudge them the pleasure of dancing together; they were clearly very much in love. She had just resolved to return to her family when she found herself accosted by Mr. Darcy, with an invitation to join the set.

Elizabeth could hardly believe her ears. She stared at him blankly for a moment, then caught sight of Miss Elliot behind him and understood. She was an ideal partner: she would not pursue him, and they both knew what he thought of her. For half an hour he could ignore the scores of female eyes trained on his person, which must far outweigh the cost of uttering a handful of sentences to her.

She nearly refused him. She was not inclined to dance again this evening, nor was she so kindly disposed as to wish to save him from Miss Elliot. Quite the contrary! Despite her anger, she kept the pleasant façade that she had long ago perfected firmly in place; nobody need know how painfully his rudeness had stung her. Then she noticed the eager curiosity of those around her – the same people who turned away disdainfully when Mr. Darcy did so. Lifting her chin, she wrapped her pride around her like a cloak and nodded her acceptance.

They had last danced together at Netherfield, and once again they began the set in silence. Elizabeth was grateful. She could think of nothing polite to say, and the expressions of the women around her served only to crystallize her dislike.

Mr. Darcy gave her a curious look. "Shall we not have some conversation, Miss Bennet?"

"Certainly, if you desire it."

"What should be the topic of our discourse?"

"You must not ask me, Mr. Darcy," she said, taking care to keep her tone even. "I am not equal to the task of choosing a subject that would be of interest."

His brow lifted in surprise, but then he smiled. "Perhaps you might share the thought that so diverted you when I saw you in the drawing-room earlier this evening?"

She glanced sidelong at him. Recalling the ridiculous automaton he appeared, she allowed herself the tiniest of smiles. "Nay, sir, that would not do at all."

"So you *were* laughing at me!" he chuckled. "I thought it might be so. Come, Miss Bennet, you see I am not afraid of you. Please, enlighten me."

Elizabeth considered him for several long moments. "Nay, I see what you are about," she said finally. "You think to expose me here, surrounded by the most elevated society. You know how dearly I like to laugh at nonsense, and you shall all be free to despise me for my vulgarity."

It cost her some effort to keep her tone light, and his countenance told her that he was not certain how to receive this accusation. A smile was waiting to form there, but his eyes searched hers for confirmation that she was indeed joking.

She attempted a saucy expression, but it felt brittle. "I recall your admonition that one of the tenets of well-bred society is to conceal one's true opinions, and so I shall thwart your scheme and refuse to admit that I was at all diverted when you saw me earlier this evening." She tossed her head, chin high. "Now, despise me if you dare."

"Indeed, I do not dare." He was smiling now, but his eyes still held a question.

She avoided his gaze, fuming behind her façade, and he lapsed again into silence. *Insolent man! I understand well enough that my company is only desirable as an escape from the rapacious Miss Elliot; is that not sufficient insult? Must he add injury by inviting me to give him further cause for mockery?*

His occasional gallantry in Hertfordshire notwithstanding, Mr. Darcy's behavior had repeatedly confirmed her first impression: that he despised everyone he believed to be beneath him, herself included. Indeed, she had regular opportunity to observe that his behavior toward all but his closest family and friends was at best cool and at worst repugnant.

The music ended and Elizabeth sighed inwardly with relief. She wanted nothing more than to return to her family and depart this wretched house. Unfortunately, her distress was visible. Mrs. Wentworth took her hand and asked after her health with kind solicitude.

Pleading a headache, Elizabeth voiced her desire to return to her grandmother's side. Mr. Darcy, no doubt observing the encroachment of Miss Elliot and several other young ladies who were eager to be his next partner, offered to escort her.

"I thank you, Mr. Darcy," she said as evenly as she could manage, speaking to his waistcoat, "but I would not wish to inconvenience you."

He stiffened and assured her in frosty tones that it was no inconvenience. Elizabeth could not now refuse his escort, so she contented herself by arranging to call upon Mrs. Wentworth very soon.

Mr. Darcy employed the tactic so effectively demonstrated by his cousin, nodding his greetings without slowing his pace. The crowds parted for him as though he were Moses before the Red Sea, whispers following as they passed. No sooner had they stepped through the door to the drawing-room than their progress was halted by the Earl of Matlock.

"There you are, Darcy! I wondered where you had taken yourself off to. Richard told me you could be found on the dance floor, but of course that was patently absurd." Only then did he appear to notice Elizabeth. "Oh, I beg your pardon, madam. Shall you introduce me to this young lady, Darcy?"

Mr. Darcy obliged, and Lord Matlock bowed correctly. "I have recently been so unfortunate as to make your grandfather's acquaintance, Miss Bennet."

Elizabeth was unable to mask her surprise and discomposure at such a statement.

"Oh, have no fear, madam, the misfortune is entirely to my pocketbook. Your grandfather is an exceedingly shrewd card player. He is so affable that a man does not realize that he is being fleeced until the thing is done and he stands there, shivering!"

Elizabeth smiled politely, only somewhat mollified.

"My lord, for shame!" Lady Matlock appeared, favoring her husband with an exaggerated frown. "You would have this delightful young woman believing that we have no manners at all! Do forgive my husband, dear. It is not often that he is bested at the card tables."

"I meant no offense, Miss Bennet, truly," Lord Matlock said. "And I fear I have quite rudely interrupted your *tête-à-tête* with my nephew here. Please, do not let me keep you any longer."

"I thank you, my lord, but Mr. Darcy was merely assisting me to find my grandmother." She nodded toward the divan. "She is just there, and I feel quite certain that I can manage the remaining distance on my own."

Elizabeth looked up at Mr. Darcy. She read consternation and confusion in his eyes, but his face remained impassive. "Thank you, sir. I bid you good evening."

Lady Matlock took her arm. "Let me join you, Miss Bennet. I was just coming to speak to your grandmother."

Elizabeth's anger began to recede in the face of their hostess's pleasant conversation. The countess, they discovered, had traveled in America with her husband many years previously; they spoke genially of New York for several minutes.

Elizabeth's headache was, by now, a determined reality. Her grandmother, seeing that she was unwell and satisfied that they had fulfilled their obligation, summoned her husband and their carriage. As Elizabeth watched Matlock House disappear behind them, she leaned her head on Jane's shoulder. *I do not think that I have ever been so happy to leave a place in my life.*

CHAPTER NINE

IN WHICH DARCY ENGAGES IN A TACTICAL RETREAT

Matlock House, London, 26th January 1816

My dear Nephew,

I received your letter this morning and I regret that I cannot provide the reassurance you seek. I understand that it was not your intent to cause such havoc, but you could not have met with more success if it had indeed been your desire.

The snub to Miss Elliot was readily smoothed over, though Richard desires me to tell you that your debt to him for his efforts on that score will not be satisfied by the usual methods. I imagine that you suppose me not to know the means by which you bribe each other for such favours, but our cabinet would benefit by the addition of some fine French cognac; Richard is by no means alone in his efforts to redeem your faux pas.

I have thrice called on the Bennet ladies. Mrs. Bennet and Miss Bennet have been more gracious than I had any reason to expect, given the sudden change in their social fortunes. I have yet to see Miss Elizabeth; her family tells me that she is much engaged with her friend Miss Lucas. We have invited them to join us in our box at the theatre tonight; I only hope that Miss Elizabeth does not plead illness. I should like to know her better, after all that Richard has said in her favour, and I am determined to be of use to her. Surely she cannot be so obstinate as to refuse the assistance I wish to provide!

Can you truly have been unaware of the degree of offence you gave? Americans do not judge class distinctions with the same degree of precision that we observe, but there are few families with higher social standing than the Bennets. This was true even when your uncle and I visited New York more than a decade past. Why you should choose to publicly affront them I cannot imagine, but on this point I have said enough.

I shall advise you when it is safe to return to London and make your own apologies. At present any such venture on your part would be viewed as further mockery, but if our efforts succeed then you may yet have a month or more to deliver your "mea culpa" before the family departs for Italy. I shall strive to make it so. Until then, I remain

Your loving Aunt,

Eleanor

Pemberley, Derbyshire, 2nd February 1816

Darcy set down his aunt's letter with a sigh and stared through the window at the bleak midwinter landscape, a leaden feeling growing in the pit of his stomach. It was many years since he was unable to find comfort in his own home, but even here he could not escape the sense of judgment.

It is not as though I set out to affront Elizabeth Bennet, or even Miss Elliot. I hoped merely to avoid arousing Miss Bennet's expectations and allay Miss Elliot's suspicions. How was I to know that my actions would be observed so minutely, or misinterpreted so broadly?

He had employed this defence, often several times daily, over the past weeks. It had done nothing to exonerate him in the eyes of his family, and recently even he could not give credit to such foolish assertions. His explanation had certainly done nothing to soften Fitzwilliam's anger.

He had never seen his cousin in such a towering rage. Fitzwilliam had barged into his study at Darcy House a week following the New Year's Eve gala, slamming the door and barking at Darcy to justify himself. Had any other person intruded upon him in this manner he would have thrown them out, but he was so taken aback that he felt only astonished confusion.

It took some time before he understood the source of his cousin's anger, and he was filled with the same bewildered impotence every time he recalled the conversation. Though he had protested repeatedly that he was ignorant of what Fitzwilliam was accusing him, nothing he said could stop the torrent of vitriol.

"When first I learned of it, I could not credit it. Indeed, I know you better than any man alive, and I refused to believe that you would behave so."

Fitzwilliam was shouting by then. "I defended you to friends and strangers alike, Darcy! Do you know, Somerton took great delight in assuring me that even *he* would not treat a lady thus, American or no. *SOMERTON!*"

Fitzwilliam stood, jaw clenched and fists balled, visibly restraining himself from punching something.

Or someone, Darcy realized. He judged it unwise to speak. When his cousin no longer appeared poised to pummel him he said, "Truly, Fitzwilliam, I do not understand you. What am I supposed to have done?"

Fitzwilliam stared at him with undisguised astonishment. His anger resurfaced, tinged now with contempt. "Immediately after I left you in our aunt's ballroom you gave Miss Elizabeth Bennet the cut direct, and then proceeded to insult Miss Elliot and make a mockery of Miss Elizabeth. Indeed, Darcy, until I heard the tale directly from Wentworth this morning, I did not believe you capable of it. You are often offensive, but never cruel."

What followed, once Fitzwilliam became convinced that Darcy's incredulity was genuine, was an excruciating demolition of his defences. The rationale for his behaviour, which to him appeared self-evident, mystified his cousin.

Society's interpretation, which – he was given to understand in the strongest possible language – was also Miss Elizabeth's belief, was that he considered Miss Elizabeth Bennet to be so far beneath contempt that to single her out for a dance, and laugh while doing so, was evidence of his derision.

And so closely was his behaviour examined that the cream of society suddenly found that one of the wealthiest and most respected families in America was entirely beneath their notice.

"They are being treated as pariahs among all good society, Darcy," Fitzwilliam said. "Dammit, man, I stood aside for you because I thought you loved her! I hoped, certainly, that at last you might learn to love something better than your pride. God knows that you do not love your reputation better, for you might then make some effort to be gracious in society."

Darcy could think of nothing to say that would not sound false or weak.

Fitzwilliam's direct gaze, which saw through him far too often for his comfort, now felt like a sword in the chest. His parting words were deadly.

"Your defect, cousin, is that you value your own comfort above that of every other creature. A man cannot love a woman whose worth he views as inferior to his own."

Fitzwilliam strode out, turning in the doorway. Looking every inch the seasoned battle commander he said, "I shall do all in my power to restore her standing in society, Darcy, but for her sake alone. If you interfere or attempt to undermine my efforts, I shall cut you down where you stand."

Darcy had remained in his study late into the night. Disbelief and indignation eventually gave way to despair. His sleep was again interrupted by nightmares, leaving him looking gray and unwell. He instructed his staff that he was not at home to anyone, not even family, and retreated to his study. By the afternoon he began to be resigned; he considered what he might do to repair the damage he had apparently done.

When he called at Matlock House the following day, Fitzwilliam was out. Uncle Henry assured him with genial unconcern that the whole debacle would be forgotten in a fortnight, but Aunt Eleanor was less sanguine. She had been the one to advise him to depart immediately for Pemberley.

"You have never taken the trouble to be more than civil among the *ton*," she said. "Now everything you say and do will be examined for deeper meaning, none of which will present you in a more amiable light."

It was only then that Darcy had truly believed Fitzwilliam was not exaggerating. Even so, he could not countenance the idea of fleeing London; he did not wish to be seen as a coward or a disgrace.

His aunt was having none of it. "When one is standing in a hole, one would be well advised to cease digging!"

She described how every action he had thought to take would be perverted to support society's current narrative: an apology would be viewed as insincere, whereas a social invitation would give license for all of society to openly mock Miss Bennet.

Ultimately, he conceded that removing himself was the only acceptable choice. "How shall I explain this to Georgiana?" he asked his aunt.

"You must be the one to decide how much or how little she should know, though I would advise you to tell her more than you might wish to say at present. Recall that she thinks very highly of Miss Bennet and her family, and it is impossible that she is ignorant of the business by now."

When it came to it, however, he could not face the notion of spending four days in a carriage with an angry and disappointed sister. He said only that they must return to Pemberley, vowing to himself that he would reveal the rest once they were home. She asked him no questions, retreating to her room with a nod.

In retrospect he should have understood this as a warning, but he was simply grateful that he need not explain himself yet.

Georgiana was withdrawn and resolutely silent on the first day of the journey. Not even Mrs. Annesley's gentle admonitions could induce his sister to speak. Darcy realized that he was too late to avoid her anger and disappointment, so that evening he took her aside at the inn. Haltingly he confessed to his behaviour in the ballroom; it was difficult to explain his actions without speaking of his deeper feelings.

Georgiana was unimpressed. She said only, "I have not your experience of the world, brother, but even I know what is meant when a gentleman pointedly ignores a lady to whom he is known to be well acquainted." Turning on her heel, she left him standing open-mouthed in the inn's private parlour.

Mrs. Annesley explained afterward that they had called on the Bennet family a day or two after the gala to find the family not at home to visitors. Before the first week had passed they heard the gossip everywhere they went; young ladies tittered behind their fans when they recognized Georgiana, the boldest among them congratulating her for having a brother so ready to "put the insolent American chit in her place."

Georgiana had remained grave and nearly silent in his company since then. She asked formally for permission to continue corresponding with Miss Elizabeth and appeared relieved when he encouraged her to do so. When he added that he hoped, in time, to apologize to Miss Elizabeth and renew their acquaintance, Georgiana's disbelief was nearly as painful as Fitzwilliam's contempt.

Darcy had hoped that the familiarity and comfort of Pemberley would allow them to resume their usual routines, but Georgiana's cool formality continued and she spent as little time with him as possible. This was different than her avoidance of him after Ramsgate; then she had judged herself rather than him, he realized, and he had been so caught up in his own wretchedness that it had required Fitzwilliam's intervention for him to attend to Georgiana's.

He also experienced a new sense of loneliness. It was not uncommon for him to be at Pemberley without the company of friends or family, but the presence of his determinedly remote sister brought home to him how correct Miss Bennet's accusation had been last November: a large house was indeed cold comfort when filled with none but servants and a paid companion. He discovered only now, when its absence was so glaring, that he had taken his sister's adoring solicitude for granted.

He had neither seen nor heard from Fitzwilliam in weeks, though Darcy heard something of his efforts from his cousin's letters to Georgiana. Through the combined efforts of Fitzwilliam and Captain Wentworth both the Army and Navy had rallied around the Bennet family, doing much to restore their respectability. Darcy was grateful; Fitzwilliam's departing sword thrust returned to him often.

Can it be true that I think only of my own comfort? No; I am a doting brother and a generous landlord. How often has Mrs. Reynolds assured me of my superiority as a master?

Now, however, he viewed himself with the same bleak honesty that he had seen in Fitzwilliam's eyes that day. It was this morning's letter from Bingley, who knew little of what had transpired in London, that forced Darcy to consider himself with greater honesty. In his hurried scrawl Bingley had written that *Caroline is grown entirely too willful, and thinks to command me as though I were a child. I have finally determined to borrow some of your habitual incivility and instruct her, without regard to the offence that she or any other of the family might feel, in her proper role.*

In the face of such a casual remark, written – Darcy had no doubt – without a thought that it might cause offence to its reader, Darcy finally admitted the justice of what all those closest to him had long said: he made no real effort to ensure the comfort of others in society, particularly if it might come at the expense of his own. Even among those for whose comfort he was responsible, he did nothing for their benefit which might truly inconvenience himself without extraordinary cause.

He reviewed every instance in which he had privately applauded his own actions, or seen them publicly praised, and was disgusted when he could find none which might redeem him. When he considered his behaviour toward the Bennets – and Miss Elizabeth in particular – he could not remain still, so great was his discomfort.

He must reform his behaviour, he decided, beginning with his own family. He would be more considerate of Georgiana, and he would write to Fitzwilliam to admit his own fault and express his sincere gratitude for his cousin's honesty and forbearance.

He considered the possibility that Fitzwilliam might succeed where he had failed in earning Elizabeth Bennet's regard. The sudden constriction in his chest confirmed that he was not prepared to concede defeat on that score, but the obstacles ahead appeared insurmountable.

I must not only beg her forgiveness, he thought, *I must earn it. But how am I to do so when she will very likely refuse even to speak to me, should I ever see her again?*

CHAPTER TEN

IN WHICH ELIZABETH IS ASTONISHED

Dover Street, London, February 14th, 1816

Dear Lydia,

What a delight it was, to hear how well Tommy is doing! It is fortunate that you have such a passion for painting, else he might never have discovered his own! Pray tell him that I am eager to play cribbage with his first deck of cards, if he can bear to risk damage to the pictures, and that his idea to illustrate them with famous English royals is inspired.

Our small corner of London grows ever larger, thanks to the determined efforts of Colonel Fitzwilliam, Captain Wentworth, and Lady Matlock. Since our evening at the theater last month, most of our acquaintance among the elevated set have resumed calling in Dover Street and will deign to speak to us in public. We are often in company with the Wentworths, and dear Anne has been a treasure. We all adore her. She has Jane's goodness and Nanna's spine, and if she has any flaw I have yet to find it!

Grandpa's business contacts have also kept us from being entirely bereft of company. I believe I told you of Mr. Robert Lewis, who attended a dinner party at the house several weeks past; he will take ship with us as far as Lisbon, to assume the management of the office there. He is now a regular visitor and Charlotte is clearly the object of his interest, though he comes ostensibly to study Portuguese.

Charlotte is nearly as facile with languages as Jane, of course, so while Jane drills me in Italian – in which I make slow but steady progress, I am pleased to say – Charlotte and Mr. Lewis hammer away at Portuguese. I teased her for her eagerness to study with him, to which she replied that she merely enjoys learning a new language. Naturally I laughed at her.

She has always insisted that she is not romantic, but Mr. Lewis certainly is! She says that she does not know quite what to think of him, but I suspect she is merely made cautious by the thought of living in Portugal. Her cheerful pragmatism allows her always to land on her feet, however, and he seems an excellent man. When she finally discovers how dearly she loves him – which is obvious to all except for the two in question – I believe they shall be very happy together.

Give Tommy a kiss for me, and do please include some of your sketches, and his, in your next letter, that I might share them; we are all eager to see his progress!

Your loving sister,

Elizabeth

London, March 1816

Mr. and Mrs. Lewis were married on the morning of the equinox, with the early flowers showing their faces to the springtime sun.

Charlotte had chosen to be married from Dover Street, so Elizabeth found herself standing with Lydia in the garden as they waited for the Lucases to pay their respects to the happy couple.

"Can you believe it, Lydia? Our Charlotte, so certain that she was destined to be a governess, is the first of us to marry after all!"

"Oh! Lizzy, I thought I should die of laughter when you told me she was to be married for love! I would never have believed that Charlotte would swoon for fancy words from a handsome man!"

Elizabeth laughed. "I wager that had the words been spoken in English, you would be right. It was Portuguese that transformed her into the starry-eyed woman you see there!"

"What an adventure that shall be, living in Lisbon and knowing no one at all! What fun she shall have!"

"Only you would think so! Though if she is anxious, she says naught about it. I believe that we might drop those two anywhere in the world together and find that they shall thrive."

Lydia sighed dramatically. "I hope one day I shall fall in love with someone who shall take *me* on such an adventure!"

"For your sake, Lydia, I hope he is as practical as he is adventurous, like our Mr. Lewis!"

"La, you fret over me as badly as our cousin Mrs. Bennet, Lizzy. I am like Charlotte, you know. I land on my feet."

Elizabeth only smiled fondly and shook her head; it was useless to argue with Lydia about such assertions. They made their way to give their best wishes to the bride and groom, and Lydia shared her enthusiasm for their upcoming voyage.

"She is irrepressible, I see," said Charlotte.

"It will require far more than four months in the country to temper her spirits, Charlotte," Elizabeth said. "In fairness, though, our cousins give a very favorable report of her behavior in Hertfordshire after we departed, despite the militia's ongoing presence."

"Has your grandfather agreed to allow her to accompany you to Italy, then?"

"He has, and with our departure less than two weeks distant, she shall remain with us in London."

"Let us hope that her behavior continues to do credit to her family."

Charlotte turned to greet Colonel Fitzwilliam, who offered his hearty congratulations. He spoke with great pleasure of Lisbon, promising to write a letter of introduction to several of his friends there. At length the colonel invited Elizabeth to take a turn with him around the garden. She readily consented; judging by his countenance, his request was not an idle one.

They strolled pleasantly for a short while. "I confess I have no thrilling tales of Italy with which to regale you, Miss Bennet," he said. "I was far too young to have taken a Grand Tour before Napoleon came to power. You must be the one to advise me."

Elizabeth was happy to make such a promise. She wondered if the colonel would ask her to write to him, or even to remain in England by his side. It was difficult to be certain with a man whose manners were so uniformly genial, but she suspected that he felt some partiality toward her. She had given a great deal of thought to her answer, should he make her an offer.

She very much enjoyed his company. He was a good man, gentlemanly and well-informed, and his respect for her own intelligence was evident. His family and profession were concerns, though her fortune would make his continued service in the army unnecessary, and he might even be persuaded to live in New York.

Her primary cause for doubt was her own feelings. She liked him very much but did not believe she loved him, at least not as she imagined love must feel. She thought perhaps that love might grow in the soil of friendship and esteem, however; she would, she decided, accept him if he asked for her hand.

His question, when it came, was not at all what she had anticipated.

"Miss Bennet," he said, "my cousin Darcy is recently returned to town and very desirous of making his amends to you, if you will permit it. Will you speak to him?"

Elizabeth could only stare at him.

"I must say that I understand your surprise. Indeed, when I discovered what he had done I threatened him with bodily injury if he took any action that might cause further harm to you or your family."

Elizabeth's gaze was questioning; the colonel was justly known for his figures of speech. He nodded gravely.

"Why, then, are you here today pleading his case?" she asked.

"It was some weeks before I could bring myself to speak to him," the colonel admitted. "Several more before I could forgive him myself. I know," he said, forestalling her, "that it is far easier for me to forgive; we have been close since childhood and it was not my family he affronted. I do not ask that you forgive, only that you hear his apology."

"You believe him to be truly sorry?"

"I do."

Elizabeth was grateful that he did not attempt to make the apology on his cousin's behalf, nor tell her why she must forgive the man. Had he done so she would certainly have refused his request. Looking at him, she realized that he understood this. The decision was truly hers to make.

She sighed. "If that be the case, I shall hear him out."

He nodded, satisfied. "May I tell him that he may call on you?"

"No. I would not want those with wagging tongues to see his carriage at our door and spread the tale that three months' absence was all the penance required for him to be received in Dover Street."

The colonel smiled. "Either you have been speaking to my mother, or I am not the only one to have had an education in strategy. What shall I tell my cousin, then?"

Elizabeth thought for several moments. "Tell him that I shall be riding in Hyde Park on Friday. I shall be near the deer pond at one o'clock."

"That is quite a public arena in which to have such a conversation," he said, brow raised.

Elizabeth's chin went up in defiance. "If he can feel free to insult me before all of London society, he can apologize in the same manner."

"I shall tell him," said the colonel with a grim smile. "I wager we shall both get the measure of him."

~ * ~

Spring continued mild and sunny, enticing Londoners to be out of doors. Hyde Park was too crowded for Elizabeth and her grandfather to give the horses a proper run; Elizabeth's horse pranced to the side, responding to the pressure of her knee.

"Relax, Elizabeth," Grandpa said. "You have only to listen to him."

"Think you that he will show himself?"

Her grandfather responded by nodding toward two riders approaching from the north. Elizabeth recognized Colonel Fitzwilliam's uniform first, then made out Mr. Darcy's features. She fixed her pleasant façade in place and focused on breathing slowly and deeply.

Mr. Darcy's greeting was stiff and formal. He fell in beside her, the colonel taking up a position alongside her grandfather with an easy nod. They rode in silence until the two chaperones fell behind, out of earshot.

"I must thank you, Miss Bennet, for agreeing to speak with me," Mr. Darcy said. "You are more charitable than most ladies would be in such a circumstance."

"You chose your ambassador well."

"I am certain my cousin was…quite frank in his assessment."

"That is why I trusted it." She met his eyes. "I abhor disguise, and I prefer to hear the truth directly than be forced to guess at it."

Mr. Darcy grimaced. "The truth is…somewhat painful for me to admit, Miss Bennet."

She lifted an eyebrow, careful to keep her expression otherwise neutral.

He nodded, flushing. "Indeed, madam, you are correct. Under the circumstances, the pain of exposing myself to you is a mere trifle."

Elizabeth waited, regarding him steadily.

He sighed. "I am particularly prone to giving offense when I am discomfited, as I often am among those I do not know well. I find it difficult to catch the flow of others' conversation at the best of times. In a setting such as my aunt's gala, it is infinitely worse. I feel like a fox surrounded by slavering hounds, at the mercy of dozens of huntresses. Bingley and my cousin have each rescued me from being trapped into a compromise on more than one such occasion."

"I can well believe it," she said sourly. There were a few young women among her acquaintance who had used such a ploy to ensnare wealthy husbands; none were even tolerably contented afterward. *"Resentment and scorn make a poor foundation for a marriage,"* Elizabeth's mother had said.

Worst was Sophia Harding: already twenty-five and becoming desperate, she had gambled particularly poorly. The rake with whom she had long been besotted had no compunction allowing her reputation to suffer; indeed, if her former friends were to be believed, he openly embellished the tale of what she had permitted him to do in the privacy of her father's library. Utterly ruined and disowned by her furious family, Miss Harding had joined a troupe of actors headed west only a few months before the Bennets departed for England.

Mr. Darcy's voice drew Elizabeth's attention back to the present.

"You may well wonder what these difficulties have to do with you. After all, you and your sisters are among the only young women of my acquaintance who do not appear to pose any such risk. The truth...."

There was another lengthy pause. He took a took a deep breath, appearing to steel himself.

"The truth, Miss Bennet, is that you discomfit me exceedingly. Almost from the first moment of our acquaintance, I have struggled against my very great admiration and regard for you."

Elizabeth's grip on the reins slackened, and it was only long habit that kept her in the saddle. She blinked stupidly at Mr. Darcy in slack-jawed amazement. Even Charlotte, who had insisted in Hertfordshire that he fancied Elizabeth, had been forced to concede that it was not likely after all when Elizabeth and Jane described his behavior in London.

And now this? The man is incomprehensible!

Her horse, sensing his rider's inattention, wandered to a patch of clover and lowered his head to eat. Mr. Darcy followed; he faced her, his color high, appearing nearly as surprised as she felt.

"I believed that you must suspect my feelings, Miss Bennet," he said, "from the preference I had long shown you over any other woman."

Elizabeth closed her mouth with a snap. It took her a moment to find her voice. "Silence and avoidance do not indicate a preference, Mr. Darcy. Quite the opposite."

"I feared creating an expectation among society, but particularly in you, of my proposals," he said stiffly. "My better judgment warned me that displaying my preference was cruel, when I could not consider marriage to a woman whose condition in life was so decidedly below my own."

She clamped her jaw shut, nearly lightheaded with fury. *He is simply confirming what you already knew, Elizabeth.* She focused on her breathing until she could trust her voice to remain even. "Am I to understand that when you caught yourself speaking to me cordially at your aunt's gala, you believed I was in expectation of an imminent proposal of marriage?"

"The reactions of Sir Walter and his daughter certainly indicated that they suspected my partiality."

"And you judged that a direct cut was the most effective way to silence those suspicions." The words came out before she could temper them; her tone was icy.

Mr. Darcy's response was equally cold. "I did not cut you, Miss Bennet. You will recall that I shortly thereafter asked you to dance."

"Yes, when it was obvious to all that Miss Elliot was unwilling to seek elsewhere for masculine attention."

"I had no desire to dance with *Miss Elliot.*"

They glared at each other for several long moments.

"I was given to understand that your desire was to apologize, Mr. Darcy," Elizabeth said eventually. "I have yet to hear a word of remorse. Was I misinformed?"

It was Mr. Darcy's turn to wrestle for control of himself; she could see the muscles working in his jaw. Finally his shoulders relaxed somewhat, and when he spoke his voice was formal but not uncivil.

"I apologize, Miss Bennet, to you and your family, for the harm my behavior caused to your standing in society. It was never my intent to imply that you were in any way unworthy of my attention or esteem."

Elizabeth waited, but he said no more. "I confess that I cannot reconcile that statement with your earlier one, sir," she said. "You have long implied, and just now stated outright, that you consider my family to be decidedly beneath you. How, then, am I to believe that you find me worthy of your attention and esteem?"

"I have already explained the motive for my reserve toward you, madam. Had you not possessed so many admirable qualities, I should never have struggled at all. I do not mean to offend. The social inferiority of your family is not a matter for debate; it is simply a fact."

"Because I am an American."

"Only in part. Primarily because your family is in trade. Were your father a gentleman—"

"You would prefer the daughter of a slaveowner?"

His eyes widened. "I said no such thing, Miss Bennet."

"Did you not? As my cousin Mr. Collins reminded me, Mr. Darcy, there are few Americans who might merit the term 'gentleman,' as you understand it. The only American families who live entirely at leisure off the earnings of large estates are the plantation owners of the South, and their profits are earned on the backs of human beings who are ripped from their families, tortured, violated, and forced to work in conditions that no white man would tolerate."

She glared at him with undisguised contempt. "If you seek to convince me that my family's social position would materially benefit if my father was a 'gentleman,' you may depart at once. I have nothing further to say to you."

Mr. Darcy appeared entirely taken aback. He looked around, which brought Elizabeth's attention back to their surroundings; fortunately, the only people close enough to them to have overheard her outburst were her grandfather and Colonel Fitzwilliam. The colonel appeared ready to close the distance, but her grandfather held out a hand. He raised his eyebrows at her; was she well?

She took a deep breath to steady herself and nodded. Grandpa spoke briefly to the colonel and both men subsided.

Mr. Darcy was watching her closely. "I most sincerely apologize, Miss Bennet. I spoke from ignorance. I must bow to your superior understanding of your own country, and I can most fervently assure you that I have no intention of advocating in favor of human bondage."

"Thank you," she said. "The English have made far greater strides in this regard than we."

His brows lifted. "You accept my apology?"

"The latter one, yes."

"But not the former?"

"I cannot, Mr. Darcy." She spoke with greater equanimity than she had felt all afternoon. "I believe that it was not your intent to influence society to cut me or my family. Yet you apologized only for that which was entirely outside your control – how others interpreted your behavior. A sincere apology, like the one you just gave me, acknowledges the wrong that one has done to another and includes the means, or at least the promise, not to repeat the offense."

Mr. Darcy's brows knitted, his gaze downward. He opened his mouth as if to speak and then closed it again, frowning.

"If I may be frank, I do not believe it is presently within your power to deliver a sincere apology," she said.

His eyes leapt up to meet hers and he flushed, clearly offended.

She strove to keep her tone as neutral as possible. "To truly regret your behavior to me, not just on that evening but on nearly every occasion in which we have been in company, you must be convinced that it is the height of poor manners to treat your social inferiors with disdain, or even indifference. Or you must be convinced that I am not, in fact, your social inferior. As you believe neither of these things, how can you possibly make an honest apology?"

His expression clouded. "I take it that you are convinced of both of these things, Miss Bennet?"

"I am, sir. Do not mistake me; I am not insensible of class. I have been taught, however, that no one who seeks to use their talents to best advantage in the service of others is beneath me. There is nothing shameful in work. The profligate, however – the selfish, the faithless, the exploitative – those persons *are* beneath me, no matter their birth, education, or fortune."

Elizabeth could see by his expression that he immediately rejected her first assertions but could not entirely disagree with the last. When he spoke, his voice betrayed his tension.

"Should not one respect one's betters?"

"If they are indeed better, yes, of course. And if one is properly humble, there are many better. Those merely fortunate enough to have been born into wealth and privilege deserve respectful address and common civility, but if they are of low character then they do not merit genuine respect."

Mr. Darcy's consternation increased with every word she spoke, but he was visibly battling his inclination to argue. It occurred to Elizabeth that *he*, at least, was attempting to avoid giving further offense.

She sighed. "Mr. Darcy, we see so differently on this point that it is useless to canvass it further. We were simply taught to place a greater value on different things. It pains me to say that I cannot accept your apology, though I truly do believe that it was not your intent to bring injury to my family."

"I thank you for that concession, Miss Bennet," he said, formality returning. "I shall think on what you have said. Perhaps we shall have the opportunity to speak further before you depart."

"Perhaps," she replied noncommittally. "I hope that I may continue to correspond with Georgiana."

"Of course, madam," he said with a stiff bow. "A good day to you, and should we not meet again before you sail, please accept my best wishes for your health and happiness."

CHAPTER ELEVEN

IN WHICH DARCY EXPANDS HIS HORIZONS

Darcy House, London, 23rd March 1816

Dear Aunt Catherine,

I received your recent letter with the detailed accounting of items requiring my attention at Rosings. I regret to inform you that my annual visit shall be unavoidably delayed, and I therefore shall be unable to remain for the usual month. Given the large number of estate matters to be dealt with, Richard shall accompany me; as we are likely to be poor company, Georgiana will join us as well.

As to the other matter mentioned in your letter: this is the final time I shall address this subject. While I have great respect for my cousin Anne, I will not marry her. She and I are in complete accord that a union between us would suit neither our mutual preference nor our individual temperaments. I am exceedingly happy to instruct her in the management of Rosings, but I shall not be its master.

Understand, madam, that I will not be further importuned on this subject. Should you bring it to my attention again, directly or through another, you shall not see me again in Kent. You are fortunate to have an excellent steward; I shall provide my recommendations via post on the items you have enumerated and encourage you to empower him to take appropriate action.

Barring that, you should expect our arrival on May 1 and we shall remain for a fortnight. I shall contact your steward to make arrangements for several tasks which must be completed before our arrival, if we are to make the best use of our limited time. Until then—

Your devoted nephew,

F. Darcy

London, April 1816

Darcy could feel beads of sweat rolling down his face. It had been some time since he had last accepted Fitzwilliam's offer to fence, and this match required all his concentration.

The two had attracted a crowd, for though Darcy was an excellent swordsman and had the longer reach, his cousin moved with lithe, athletic grace and fought with greater strategy. Darcy was rarely able to best Fitzwilliam, though it was typically a near thing.

Today he was intensely grateful for the opportunity to silence his thoughts and allow his frustration and disappointment to fuel his sword arm. He should have been nearing exhaustion by now, but he merely felt coldly determined. Fitzwilliam, though, appeared to be flagging.

That might be a ruse.

Even as the thought occurred, his cousin suddenly advanced with a flurry of rapid attacks. Darcy parried furiously but was not swift enough to counter them all. He felt the tip of Fitzwilliam's steel press into his shoulder.

"Hit acknowledged," he said tightly.

Both men relaxed and Darcy mopped his brow. The crowd applauded.

"Well fought, cousin," Fitzwilliam said, offering his hand. He was breathing heavily. "You might have had me if we kept on much longer."

A half-hour later, Darcy relaxed into the well-sprung seat of his carriage. Beside him, Fitzwilliam fixed him with the direct look that Darcy had been dreading.

"It has been more than a week, Darcy," Fitzwilliam said into the silence. "I have permitted you to stew quite long enough. She sailed this morning, so you are no longer in any danger of encountering her in society. Now tell me; what said she to your apology?"

Darcy sighed and closed his eyes. No part of him wanted to discuss this, but his own thoughts had been traveling in circles for days. *Perhaps it is time to tell him the whole sorry tale.*

"She said that I could not offer a proper apology because I was not truly distressed by my own behaviour, only by its consequences," he said dully, speaking to the ceiling.

Fitzwilliam gave him a startled look. "That is a singular interpretation."

Darcy grimaced. "She was justified, Fitzwilliam. When we are seated before the fire in my study, brandy in hand, I shall tell you all."

"I believe I must send word to my mother that I shall be absent for dinner this evening," his cousin said, his gaze assessing.

Darcy only nodded.

~ * ~

It was difficult to begin. Darcy stared at the liquid swirling in his glass, considering.

"Start at Ramsgate," Fitzwilliam prompted. "If you are to tell all, then you must begin at the beginning."

Haltingly Darcy began to speak. When he came to the first assembly at Meryton, the words caught in his throat. He had apologized to Elizabeth but had never spoken of it to another soul, not even Bingley. His voice hoarse, he ground out the tale.

His cousin stared at him, mouth agape, before swallowing his brandy in a single gulp. "Good God, man! That she ever spoke another word to you is extraordinary! You have chosen your lady exceedingly well, though you really must overcome your eagerness to insert your own foot into your mouth." Fitzwilliam refilled his glass and looked at Darcy with great curiosity. "How ever did you manage a conversation with her after that?"

Darcy chuckled darkly. "I hardly know. I was terrified of her." He thought for several moments, then his mind's eye saw her hiding from Mr. Collins in a copse of trees. He smiled. "I recall it now; I came to her rescue."

It was as though a dam had broken. For two hours the words poured out, interrupted only by food and drink. Fitzwilliam was an excellent audience, laughing and congratulating him with spirit when he had justly earned it, groaning and smacking his own forehead whenever Darcy admitted to something particularly idiotic, which was far more frequent.

"I have spent the last week debating with myself," Darcy finished. "Is it possible to love a woman who despises you? Is it insanity to hope that her opinion might be altered? And does one such as I have the means with which to alter it?"

Fitzwilliam shook his head in apparent disbelief. "First let us clarify one or two points, shall we?"

Darcy returned a wary nod.

"Do you admire Miss Elizabeth Bennet?"

"Fitzwilliam, I thought that should be obvious by now."

"Answer the question, man."

Darcy sighed. "I do. Very much."

"And what is it, precisely, that you admire about her?"

He considered. "I admire her quickness of mind and her adventurous spirit. I admire her courage and her devotion." He gave his cousin a half-smile. "And, loath as I am to admit it, I admire that she will give me an honest tongue-lashing, but never an insincere compliment."

Fitzwilliam smirked. "Not a word about the attractiveness of her person? I am impressed."

Darcy flushed. "She is lovely, Fitzwilliam, as you well know. Her eyes are extraordinary."

"And her brash, forward, vulgar manner? What of that?"

Darcy paused; when had he ceased thinking of her in those terms? "On closer acquaintance, I find that I prefer her directness to the fashionable *ennui* of other young ladies."

"And yet she is unmarriageable, because she is beneath you."

Darcy squirmed in his seat. "Yes."

Fitzwilliam regarded him levelly. "You are a hypocrite, old man. You despise the *ton* for their falsity and their politicking. You admire a woman who plays none of their games. And yet you will not marry her *because* she plays none of their games and *because* they insist that she is inferior."

They sat in silence for several minutes while Darcy considered this. He had never questioned the social order that his parents had instilled in him as right and proper. Yet his cousin was correct; he despised most of his own class.

His thoughts must have shown on his face, for Fitzwilliam spoke again. "Why, if she is unworthy to be mistress of Pemberley, do you care that she despises you?"

Darcy blinked at him, flummoxed.

His cousin continued, ruthless. "Should you not make every attempt to root out whatever tender feelings you harbor for her? A task made easier, no doubt, by her contempt. You should be grateful for it!"

Darcy's heart rebelled at these words. He fought down an angry retort and sat, stewing.

"Your defect is that you value your own comfort over that of every other creature." His cousin's parting thrust, so many months ago, came unbidden to his mind. He saw himself as Elizabeth must: a man quite comfortable in the belief that he was superior, solely by virtue of his birth.

My very existence is comfortable; I have endured grief, but not privation. And what am I doing now, but seeking a way to gain what I desire with no discomfort to myself?

What if I should succeed?

The thought rooted him in place, brandy glass halfway to his mouth. He set it down carefully as his imagination took flight: Elizabeth begging his forgiveness, grateful for the extraordinary condescension of his notice. Elizabeth demure and deferential in her adoration, content with whatever crumbs of affection he offered.

Impossible! She would not permit herself to be so meek and downtrodden, so like the ladies she disdains.

I should disdain her too, were she like them, he realized. Nor could he countenance the thought of keeping her as a mistress. The very idea made him squirm again.

Suddenly a new realization struck. He might never see her again – she would likely avoid him when she returned to England, if they did not simply sail directly to America. *No,* he thought. *Intolerable! But what is the alternative? If I do discomfit myself, what can I hope to achieve?*

What would she have him do?

"You must be convinced that it is the height of poor manners to treat your social inferiors with disdain, or even indifference," she had said. *"Or you must be convinced that I am not, in fact, your social inferior."*

Was it even possible? *Of course it is. Fitzwilliam manages it.* He looked at his cousin appraisingly. Richard Fitzwilliam was the son of an earl, yet he readily befriended those far below him.

For the first time, it occurred to Darcy that his cousin's talent for making his way in any society was not merely because of his affable temper. Fitzwilliam had made it clear that he respected Andrew Bennet far more than that arse Somerton, entirely on personal merit. And he had cheered when Darcy related Miss Elizabeth's speech about those who were beneath her.

Fitzwilliam looked back at him now, a questioning brow lifted.

"I believe I must expand my acquaintance," Darcy said slowly. "How may I begin?"

Fitzwilliam grinned.

~ * ~

The month that followed was unlike any in Darcy's life.

Fitzwilliam introduced him to dozens of people with whom he would never previously have deigned to speak. His cousin particularly insisted that he become properly acquainted with the Wentworths, and he was mortified to discover how ill-judged had been his dismissal of them at his aunt's gala. The captain, though the son of a clergyman, comported himself with confident intelligence and very gentlemanly manners. His wife's mind, manners, and conversation were far superior to those of her sister and father; Darcy soon valued her so highly that he begged the favour of introducing her to his sister.

In Anne Wentworth he saw a steady character and excellent judgment, with manners mild and generous enough that his sister would likely feel quite as secure in seeking her counsel as she had the Miss Bennets'. His hopes were rewarded when, after only a few evenings spent in company, Georgiana asked if she might not look upon Mrs. Wentworth as a sort of mentor.

"You have the Wentworths to thank for Miss Elizabeth's restoration in society, nearly to the same degree as my mother," Fitzwilliam said when Darcy told him of Georgiana's delight with her new friend. "Frederick Wentworth is quite well-connected through his brother, Admiral Croft, and those Navy men brook no insult to any that they consider one of their own. Their wives are even more ferocious."

Darcy glanced at the clock; they were waiting for Georgiana to descend, as they had been invited to dine with an acquaintance of Fitzwilliam's and the invitation had been extended to include Georgiana.

Darcy had hesitated at first, but Fitzwilliam had reassured him. "There will be another young lady near to her age, Darcy, and we are their only guests. I think it excellent practice for you both."

Georgiana appeared, looking as though she were attempting to master her nerves. Her golden hair and pale yellow gown were both done in a more sophisticated style than she usually wore, and Darcy was suddenly struck by the fact that her seventeenth birthday was only a few months distant. His aunt would be planning her introduction into society by this time next year.

Fitzwilliam is right to demand that we both practice at making new acquaintances.

"Tell me again about the Gardiners," Georgiana asked. "I fear I shall forget everything you have said of them when we meet!"

Fitzwilliam squeezed her hand in reassurance. "I met them in January, when I was so often with the Bennet family. Edward Gardiner owns a very successful import company, and he does business with Mr. Bennet. The ladies were quite pleased to make his acquaintance, as he imports some of the best quality silk in London." He glanced sidelong at Darcy. "Mr. Gardiner is also the brother of Mrs. Fanny Bennet, of Longbourn in Hertfordshire, so they have a family connection."

Darcy's brows went up; Fitzwilliam had conveniently failed to mention this.

"Put away your scowl, Darcy! I should think you trusted me by now." He turned back to Georgiana. "Madeline Gardiner is a delightful woman who knows of your family; she lived in Lambton as a girl. There will be only one other guest. Their niece Kitty Bennet, who is eighteen, is visiting from Longbourn."

They arrived in Gracechurch Street, at a modest but handsome and well-kept home. The Gardiners proved to be exactly as Fitzwilliam had described: intelligent, cultured, sensible people of lively conversation and impeccable manners. Had he met Mr. Gardiner under other circumstances, Darcy realized with some surprise, he would have assumed him to be a gentleman. That he was the brother of Mrs. Bennet was astonishing.

Their hosts were, at first, careful in their interactions with him and Georgiana, but Darcy found that he desired the good opinion of these people and exerted himself to be agreeable. Georgiana was soon put at ease by Mrs. Gardiner's kind attentions, and Kitty Bennet – who had been so blandly inoffensive as to be invisible in Hertfordshire – chatted warmly with her.

Miss Kitty and her brother were engaged in a campaign to add a dog to the family home at Longbourn and begged for anecdotes to support their position. Georgiana spoke fondly of her horse, and Mr. Gardiner shared his pleasure at befriending the cat that took up residence in his first warehouse. Mrs. Gardiner spoke of a schoolfellow whose father had brought back a parrot from the East Indies that said some very shocking things, indeed; the girls both tittered, cheeks aflame, as the adults laughed heartily.

With a grin in Fitzwilliam's direction, Darcy told of the time when twelve-year-old Richard had convinced ten-year-old Darcy, who was visiting at Matlock for the Christmas holidays, to keep a fox as a pet. "A great snowstorm blew in, so we determined that we must bring him into the house," he said with a chuckle.

The adults were laughing even before he finished speaking, and Georgiana and Miss Kitty wore nearly identical expressions of confusion.

"What happened, brother?" said Georgiana.

"You know that foxes make dens, of course," said Fitzwilliam.

Georgiana's eyes grew wide.

Darcy grinned at his cousin again. "This fine fellow decided that Arthur's mattress was the ideal spot. He would disappear for hours, and we had no notion of where he had gone. We only discovered it when we were all awakened by shrieking from that part of the house at sunrise on the third day. It seems our small friend had emerged from his den and, seeing Arthur's foot moving under the coverlet, attempted to catch his breakfast."

As the entire party laughed loudly, Darcy caught Fitzwilliam's nod of approval and Georgiana's gaze, warm and affectionate for the first time in months. He felt absurdly happy.

~ * ~

The next morning, Darcy sat with Fitzwilliam and Georgiana in the breakfast-room.

"I heartily approve of both of your efforts to be sociable," Fitzwilliam said. "Darcy, you outdid yourself. I had nearly forgotten about that little adventure."

"Thank you ever so much for telling it," Georgiana said, eyes dancing. "I enjoy hearing stories of when you were young. I cannot recall when I last laughed so long!"

Darcy's reply was interrupted by a commotion in the front hall, followed by an imperious voice that carried clearly to where they sat.

"Where is my nephew? Take me to him at once!"

Georgiana's delighted expression vanished. Darcy exchanged a look with Fitzwilliam; he stood as his aunt entered on Jones's heels. She was dressed in a heavy brocade gown and furs, her cheeks excessively rouged. Her ever-present frown carved deep lines into her face.

"Lady Catherine," he said. "This is quite unexpected."

She glared at him, ignoring the other occupants of the room. "Surely you understand the reason for my journey."

"Indeed, madam, I am quite unable to account for it."

"I received your letter, with the preposterous threat that you would not be coming into Kent. Three days ago I received another communication, that you have been seen consorting with up-jumped commoners in uniform." She jabbed a finger in Georgiana's direction, outrage mounting. "Also, that you were engaged to dine with your young sister at a *tradesman's* house!"

"Another communication?" Mr. Collins, I suppose, through his wife. Kitty Bennet must have written to her sister of the dinner.

Lady Catherine lifted her nose in the air, her tone becoming ponderous. "I knew it must be a scandalous falsehood; you have long understood your duty. I came at once to make my sentiments known to you."

"I wonder that you took the trouble of coming so far," Darcy said. It was all he could do to keep his countenance; he wished to thunder at her for her insolence, but he also wanted to laugh. Her expression was nearly identical to Elizabeth's portrayal of her headmistress, while they danced together at Netherfield. For a moment laughter nearly won out, and the corners of his mouth turned up.

This only enraged his aunt further. "How dare you smirk at me! How dare you threaten to abandon your fiancée! You have been intended for each other since infancy! It was your mother's favorite wish, as well as mine!"

"I should think she might have mentioned such a thing," he said mildly.

"I will not be interrupted! You will come to Rosings and fulfill your obligation to Anne and to the estate at once!"

"I will not."

Darcy held up a hand as she opened her mouth to shout at him again. He was truly angry now. He could tolerate her intrusion for the sake of their family relationship, but it was insupportable for her to order him about in his own house, as though he were still in short pants.

She was accustomed to dictating to all those around her. *It is long past time,* he thought grimly, *that she understands that my decisions are not hers to make.*

"I informed you in the most direct language of the consequences," he said, "should you continue to advance this fiction that I am engaged to my cousin. I do not give my word lightly. I will not go into Kent while your behaviour continues thus. And if you say another word about it, I shall have you removed from this house."

"Impertinent boy! Anne is—"

"Jones!"

The door opened immediately; Jones stood there, four footmen behind him. "How may I be of service, sir?"

Darcy glared at his aunt. She was nearly purple with rage but remained silent, teeth grinding. He spoke without taking his eyes from her. "Jones, if you hear Lady Catherine speak of my imaginary engagement to her daughter Anne de Bourgh, please escort her from the premises. You have my leave to enter the room directly, should it be necessary."

"Very good, sir." Jones bowed and closed the door.

"As for the other accusation you spat in my face, Lady Catherine—"

"Do you deny it?"

"I have no wish to deny it. Richard has been so good as to introduce me to his fellow officers and to the estimable Captain Wentworth of the Navy, along with his wife."

"You are a Darcy! Why should you lower yourself to associate with those of obscure birth, merely because they did not drown out in the ocean somewhere?"

"My parents think very highly of Captain and Mrs. Wentworth, Aunt," Fitzwilliam said. "Indeed, Father spoke in his last letter of how fortunate we are to be acquainted with so many excellent officers of the Navy."

"My brother is a sentimental fool." Her glance fell on Georgiana. "And what of the tradesman? Surely you cannot give credit to such blatant lies! You have far too high a respect for your duty to Georgiana to sully her reputation by association with trade."

Darcy privately worried that maintaining an acquaintance with a tradesman's family would taint Georgiana's debut, but he would be damned if he would admit it. He smiled instead, knowing it would provoke his aunt. "Georgiana and I were just telling Fitzwilliam how grateful we are that he introduced us to the Gardiners. I cannot recall the last time I enjoyed a dinner party so greatly."

His aunt glowered at him, and then at Georgiana. "Do not lie to me, girl. Are you not ashamed to have your name spoken alongside theirs?"

Georgiana looked as though she wanted to disappear. Eyes lowered, she spoke softly. "The Gardiners seem to be excellent people."

Lady Catherine threw up her hands. "Darcy, have you taken leave of your senses? It was allowable – just — when you befriended that boy, the son of the tradesman. He, at least, might purchase an estate and attempt to be respectable! But you were seen in company with that dreadfully vulgar American girl, whose family has been in trade for generations! When you cut her at my sister's ball, I believed you might finally have learned to properly value your family's legacy, but—"

"Enough! I will hear no more, Lady Catherine!" He was furious and ashamed. Whatever his own struggles might be, his aunt knew nothing of Bingley or Elizabeth. He fought to master himself, and his voice was deceptively calm when he spoke again.

"You have long instructed me as to what is due to those persons who occupy the most elevated positions in society. I have also been advised that if those persons are of low character, then one owes them civility but not respect." His tone became icy. "Your behaviour, madam, is so offensive that you should fear to pass judgment on any other person. It certainly does not merit *my* respect."

Lady Catherine drew herself up, glaring imperiously down her nose at him.

He called out. "Jones!"

Once again, the door opened immediately. "Yes, Mr. Darcy?"

"Lady Catherine must leave us. Please assist her to make a speedy departure."

PART II

PROGRESSO
(PROGRESS)

CHAPTER TWELVE

IN WHICH JANE DISCOVERS HER VALUE

Meadowlark, at sea, May 2ⁿᵈ, 1816

My dear Anne,

At last we are nearing the end of our sea journey. The waters are considerably more benign here near the southern coast of France, and Lizzy is exceedingly grateful. She was so wretched as we made our way to Lisbon! Charlotte and I were terribly worried for her. She had barely begun to recover when we came into port, and so her farewell to Charlotte was not what she had hoped. I was relieved to see her regain her color after a few days' rest ashore in Gibraltar; for once she had no complaints of the carriage as we explored the city.

How extraordinary Gibraltar is! So many of the buildings are entirely new – Grandpa told us of the Great Siege that destroyed much of the city, only a few decades ago! – and it seems that neither the buildings nor the people nor the cuisine can determine whether their British, Andalusian, or Italian influence is the most prominent.

Of course, one can hardly miss the Rock itself. Lydia observed that it is like the cliffs at Dover, where the sheer enormity of the thing renders all around it insignificant. It appears to have existed since the beginning of time, and the full span of years that we tread upon the earth are as nothing in comparison. Lizzy teases me for such philosophical musings, of course; she says that Signor Rinaldi's going on endlessly about Plato has made me quite maudlin. But her twinkling eyes and her smile have returned, so I cannot be sorry to be made fun of.

Oh, Anne, I do so wish that you and Captain Wentworth were with us! I am quite discomposed when I consider Signor Rinaldi, and your sound counsel would be dear to me. He is so attentive, and his manners are so amiable that I find it the easiest thing in the world to converse with him. In that way he is like Mr. Bingley, but it is that very thought which makes me uneasy, for did Mr. Bingley not appear equally amiable and attentive? I felt sure of his affection for me, and yet he disappeared entirely once we removed to London! It was easy to suppose that family obligations must account for it during the Christmas season, but as months went by and circumstances required our true friends to declare themselves, I learned to doubt the sincerity of his regard. I think, perhaps, he merely toyed with me for his own amusement in Hertfordshire.

I am shocked at myself to see those words in writing, my dear friend! Lizzy would congratulate me on entertaining such an uncharitable notion. She is forever insisting that it is impossible for everyone to be as disinterested as I, no matter how I may wish it so, and perhaps she is correct. But, oh! Is adversity the only means by which a woman may discover if a young man's affections are genuine? I should not like certainty to require suffering.

We make landfall at Livorno tomorrow, and thence to Florence for six weeks before traveling to Siena for the latter half of June. Signor Rinaldi and his sister have promised to show us all the most delightful aspects of the area, and perhaps with longer acquaintance I can determine what I truly feel for him. Give my very best to the Captain and our other friends, and wish me good fortune!

Your devoted friend,

Jane Bennet

Siena, June 1816

Elizabeth settled next to Jane, grateful for the breeze that blew gently through the open windows of the carriage. The early afternoon sun was so bright that it washed out the colors of the landscape.

"What a beautiful town San Gimignano is!" said Jane. "Thank you, Chiara, for insisting that we make the visit today!"

Elizabeth agreed. "I cannot say I understand the enthusiasm for building such tall towers atop a hill already so steep, but the effect is remarkable, certainly!"

Chiara Rinaldi laughed. "Oh, it is not so unusual that families should build great things to prove that they are superior to their neighbors. Can you imagine how the city appeared so many centuries ago, when there were more than seventy towers?"

"Like a forest of stone!" said her brother. "How do you feel, Miss Elizabeth? I hope you are not too fatigued."

"No, thank you, Signor Rinaldi. After walking so often in Florence these many weeks, I feel quite recovered and well able to manage the steep paths today."

"I am delighted to hear it." He turned his warm smile back to Jane.

Under pretense of observing the view down to the plateau as they descended the hill, Elizabeth studied him.

Jane had become acquainted with Marco and Chiara Rinaldi on the *Bonny Bess*, which had carried them from London to Lisbon. While Elizabeth had been miserably incapable of keeping anything in her stomach for the entirety of the ten-day voyage, Jane had proven an excellent sailor. Elizabeth had attempted to spend some time on deck as they passed the island of Guernsey on the third day, and begged Jane to speak of anything that might divert her mind from her mutinous stomach.

Jane told of the garrulous Scottish captain whose booming voice, high spirits and open flirtation had so overwhelmed her, and her gratitude toward the pleasing Italian siblings who spoke to her so kindly and diverted the captain's attention toward themselves at every opportunity. They were returning to Siena, having visited their eldest sister and her English husband for many months.

Chiara Rinaldi was a lively and pretty young woman of twenty-two, good-natured and friendly, with a disarmingly frank manner. Her brother Marco, at twenty-four, was exceedingly handsome. Wavy black hair framed a face with striking dark eyes and a patrician nose. His frame was fashionably lean, with narrow shoulders and strong, shapely legs.

He was well-educated and clever, and gave himself no superior airs; his family's modest fortune had been made in trade, and he spoke animatedly of the expansion that his brothers planned, in which he anticipated a role. He had easy, gentlemanly manners, with a ready smile and a gracious word for all, though his preference for Jane's company was clear.

When the Rinaldi siblings had announced their desire to accompany the Bennet family to Florence, shortly before the *Meadowlark*'s arrival in Livorno, Elizabeth noted the look exchanged by her grandparents and decided that a sisterly conference was in order. Ashore in Livorno, Elizabeth and her sisters had settled in with their chocolate and sweets on Jane's bed. Thanks in large part to Lydia's habitual disregard for subtlety, Jane had been persuaded to speak of her hopes and anxieties regarding Signor Rinaldi. As she did so, the truth of her disappointed hopes of Mr. Bingley had finally emerged.

Elizabeth had been grieved to learn that Jane had at first blamed herself for Mr. Bingley's abandonment, when she could no longer excuse it. She was surprised to hear Jane then suppose that Mr. Bingley's sisters likely had a hand in it, and perhaps even Mr. Darcy, for Jane was not naturally suspicious. But Elizabeth had been unspeakably proud when Jane declared – angry tears falling down her cheeks – that she could no longer absolve Mr. Bingley of treating her abominably; no matter the other influences, if he had truly loved her then he would have not have strayed from her side.

Elizabeth did not share Jane's belief that Mr. Bingley was selfishly careless with a woman's heart; that was his friend's defect. Her own opinion was that Mr. Bingley's lack of resolve lay at the heart of it, but in the end the cause did not matter. What mattered was that Jane was angry because she knew herself to deserve better treatment, and she was properly cautious of Signor Rinaldi's attentions. Half the night was gone before the sisters finally slept, curled all together in Jane's bed.

Signor Rinaldi's attentions had proven consistent, however, and increasingly ardent. He behaved with affable gentility toward other young ladies, many of whom were quite determined to attract his notice, but his warmest smiles were reserved for Jane. Chiara had commented to Elizabeth that she had never seen her brother so enamored of any lady. And when her brother had invited the Bennets to dine with his family this evening, telling Jane that his mother especially wished to meet her, Chiara gave Elizabeth a very significant look.

Now, as the carriage wound along the road to Siena, Jane had his undivided attention. He had determinedly withstood Jane's placid reserve for weeks and she smiled infinitesimally whenever his hand brushed against hers, which was often. Signor Rinaldi had closely observed her sister and it seemed he had learned to interpret her subtle shifts of expression, for he smiled in response.

Jane dressed with great care for the evening in her finest blue muslin gown. She begged Elizabeth to style her hair; Elizabeth said nothing as she carefully pinned a half-dozen tiny golden braids into place but could not suppress a smile when she caught Jane's expression in the mirror.

"Oh, do stop that, Lizzy."

"I do not know how you expect me to keep my countenance, Jane, when you appear equal parts elated and terrified!"

"It was less nerve-wracking to meet the Countess of Matlock! I saw the look Chiara gave you when he mentioned his mother. What if she dislikes me?"

"Then she is an unnatural creature indeed! Who could not love my dearest Jane?"

Jane smiled nervously. "He said much the same thing, but Chiara told me that their mother has very high hopes for him."

Elizabeth met her eyes in the mirror. "Jane, her opinion only matters if you truly believe that he is the one man with whom you wish to live for the remainder of your days." She smiled impishly. "And, of course, if you do not choose to drag him back to New York."

"Oh, Lizzy!" Jane covered her face with her hands. "That is just the thing! He seems everything amiable and good, clever and devoted, but something stills my tongue. I have no wish to say 'no,' but I cannot yet say 'yes'."

"Then let this evening guide you. Could you be happy to be a part of his family? Because if I am any fit judge, unless you *do* drag him back to New York then you shall have no choice in the matter!"

The Rinaldi family was large – Marco and Chiara were the youngest of eleven siblings, and the only ones to remain unmarried – and dinner was a crowded, boisterous affair.

Signora Rinaldi presided over the table like a queen. She plied Jane and Elizabeth with more food than they could possibly eat, all the while praising Lydia's robust appetite. She asked Jane endless questions in rapid-fire Italian, speaking far too quickly for Elizabeth to make out even half of what she said, and studied Jane's anxious responses with sharply appraising eyes.

Marco, seated across the table between two of his brothers, appeared nearly as anxious as Jane during this examination. He ignored his brothers' obvious ribbing and smiled encouragingly; Jane, meanwhile, gripped Elizabeth's hand tightly under the table and kept her attention on his mother.

Eventually, Signora Rinaldi stood and came around the table to where Jane sat. In the sudden silence she pulled Jane to her feet, took her face in both hands and planted a kiss on each of her cheeks. She spoke loudly and slowly, in an approving tone. *"Nessuna madre crede che una donna sia abbastanza brava per il figlio minore, ma sei una donna eccellente e molto bella."*

Elizabeth was grateful that she had taken care to speak so that the Bennets could understand. *It is likely true that no mother can believe any woman good enough for her youngest son,* she thought with amusement. *It is certainly true that Jane is an excellent and very lovely young woman.*

Marco's brothers clapped him on the back and his uncle loudly toasted Jane, who blushed crimson.

"What a triumph!" Chiara said in Elizabeth's ear. "Mamma was beside herself when Marco told her that he wanted to marry an American." Chiara looked at Jane thoughtfully. "She will have some difficulty becoming accustomed to the family, I fear. This is not even half of us, when you count the children of my brothers and sisters. And my brothers are already well on their way to being drunk."

Elizabeth had to agree. Jane was surrounded by the Rinaldi women now, all of them talking over each other, eager to give her advice or declare their approbation. Marco looked on with a wide smile, one of his brothers' arms around his neck as they downed several tiny glasses of a strong clear liqueur that Chiara called *grappa*. Jane smiled, but Elizabeth could see the effort it cost her to do so.

~ * ~

The following morning, both of Elizabeth's sisters accompanied her on her daily walk. They had fallen exhausted into bed immediately after returning to their lodgings the night before.

Lydia was keen to hear all Jane could say of Signor Rinaldi. "It is such a pity that he has no younger brothers," she sighed. "Though I suppose he may have nephews old enough."

Elizabeth was no less eager to hear Jane's thoughts but could see that Jane was not yet ready to share them. She directed a quelling glance at her younger sister. "I declare," she said, "that I have never before seen a place so entirely uniform in color."

Jane smiled. "Indeed, it is quite remarkable. It puts me in mind of Samson."

"That great sorrel draft horse that Cousin Thomas brought to Longbourn last October?" Elizabeth looked with exaggerated thoughtfulness at the buildings they passed. "Do you know, Jane, I believe you are right. I am sure that Samson could be standing here in front of us and we should never see him, so well would he be camouflaged."

"Oh! La, Lizzy, you are ridiculous," said Lydia, rolling her eyes. "Though it would be a laugh if it were true. Imagine if the Duomo were made of the same boring brick as everything else!"

They emerged from a side street into the *Piazza del Duomo*. The square was wide, fronted on three sides by red-brown buildings. The white marble cathedral, with its distinctive black-striped sides and intricately carved façade, gleamed in the morning sun.

Marco and Chiara had told them proudly of how the Sienese citizens paid for the Duomo themselves in the thirteenth century. When Elizabeth had asked about the great unfinished wall that jutted out from the southeastern side of the cathedral, Chiara had shrugged.

"Siena was once a great city, nearly as powerful as Firenze – *scusi*, Florence, you call it. After this Duomo was complete, Florence began to build one much larger. You have seen it; Brunelleschi's dome is a marvel. So the Sienese decided that they would expand their cathedral. But then the Black Death came."

The sisters made their way past the Duomo, continuing the wide circle that would see them back to their lodgings. They had walked only a few blocks when they heard a shouted conversation around the corner ahead. A man's voice came from the street, it seemed, while a woman's carried from above. Elizabeth could not help but listen, though she struggled to believe that she had understood correctly.

Lydia's urgent whisper confirmed that she had. "Lizzy, did she truly just say that he only desires to visit when she is in bed?"

"Hush, Lydia!" hissed Jane. "We should not be listening to this!"

"I do not see how we can avoid it," Lydia muttered. She clapped her hand over her mouth to stifle a laugh; Elizabeth did not know the term the woman had used to describe the man's wife, but it did not sound flattering.

"What do we do?" Elizabeth whispered to Jane. "Turn back, or go on?" They were nearly to the corner now.

"Turn back, I think."

Elizabeth nodded; all three of them were pink to the roots of their hair. They could hardly expect to walk blithely past as though they had not heard the argument.

Then they heard a new voice. *"Zio Lorenzo! Siamo fortunati a vederti così presto!"*

Jane stopped dead, the color draining from her face. Lydia's eyes grew wide and her mouth dropped open. Elizabeth's mind idly offered up a translation – *"Uncle Lorenzo! We are fortunate to see you so early!"* – moments after she recognized the speaker. She looked instantly to Jane, who seemed frozen to the spot.

Lydia ran to the corner of the building and peered around. A minute later she hastily straightened to avoid colliding with the person rounding the corner from the adjoining street.

ALEXA DOUGLAS

"I thought I saw someone hiding here," said Chiara Rinaldi, her eyes twinkling. "How fortunate! Marco and I were just on our way to call on all of you."

Jane smiled with some difficulty; her voice sounded strangled. "Indeed! We often walk out in the mornings, but we were on our way back."

Chiara looked at her curiously. "Jane, are you well?"

"Yes. Quite."

"You are such a ninny, Jane," said Lydia, rolling her eyes again. "Chiara, that man in the street is your uncle, is he not? We met him last night at dinner?"

"Yes, my uncle Lorenzo."

"And the woman on the balcony..." Even Lydia, Elizabeth was pleased to see, could not quite finish her sentence.

Chiara smiled. "His... oh, how do you say it? I do not recall the word. The woman he beds, who is not his wife. We do not speak of her among the family, of course," she said with a shrug. "It would be disrespectful to Zia Antonella."

Marco's voice could still be heard, speaking casually with his uncle just around the corner. Both men laughed.

"His wife *knows* that he keeps a mistress?" Lydia asked in a stage whisper.

Chiara nodded. "That is the word! Thank you. And yes, of course she knows." She looked at each of them in turn, bemused. "Do not men keep mistresses in America?"

Jane stared at her. Even Lydia seemed unable to think of a suitable response.

Elizabeth roused herself. "Yes, I believe some do, though it is meant to be a secret. It is a violation of a holy vow, after all."

"Oh, you must not fool yourselves," Chiara said with a wave of her hand. "No man can keep to only one woman. It is unnatural. Every man has a mistress, though perhaps some hide it, to show respect to their wives."

"My grandfather has no mistress," Lydia said. "He loves Nanna!"

Chiara gave her a pitying look. "Love has little to do with it."

Marco Rinaldi came around the corner in search of his sister, a grin on his face. His smile faltered when he saw Jane, who drew herself up and looked at him with a cold, distant expression.

Elizabeth was reminded, suddenly, of Mr. Darcy.

"Jane?" said Signor Rinaldi. "What troubles you?"

"Is Antonella's fate to be mine as well? I assume, from what Chiara says, that your mother and aunts and sisters all know the names of their husbands' mistresses, but do not speak of it amongst themselves."

108

Signor Rinaldi looked between Chiara and Jane, nonplussed. "Jane, dear heart, I—"

"I do not give you leave to address me so familiarly." Jane's voice was a whip. "When will it happen? When I am increasing, or after the babe comes? Or perhaps even before then?"

"Jane! Yes, a man often takes a mistress when his wife is increasing. Why does this upset you so?"

"You believe a woman must be *contented* that her husband exposes her to dishonor and disease?"

He shook his head. "I do not understand. Please, Jane—"

"I am Miss Bennet to you, Signor Rinaldi. You may understand this: I am now able to give you an answer to your proposal. I will not marry you. I will not bind myself to a man who dishonors his vows. And I will not see you again. Good day, sir."

Jane stalked past him, head high. Elizabeth caught Lydia's arm and rushed after her.

Signor Rinaldi followed, calling out, "Jane! Jane, please stop!"

Lydia pivoted on a heel, pulling out of Elizabeth's grasp. Signor Rinaldi drew up short, startled, just in time for Lydia to pull back her arm and punch him square in the face. He reeled back, blood spurting from his nose.

"Are you deaf? She is Miss Bennet! And she does not want to talk to you. Now go away!" Lydia looked at Chiara. "Take him and go home. We shall not see you again."

Lydia followed Jane with rapid steps, opening and closing her hand.

Elizabeth ran after her. "Lydia! How did you—"

"Grandpa taught me," Lydia said, nonchalant. "It hurts more than I thought it would, though."

Elizabeth shook her head in amazement but could think of nothing to say.

Lydia, however, had no such difficulty. "I do not know which is worse," she said. "Men who do not respect their wives, or the women who permit it."

CHAPTER THIRTEEN

IN WHICH GEORGIANA GETS HER WAY

Darcy House, London, 2nd May 1816

My dear Mother,

I hope this finds you and Father well, and my sister safely delivered of a healthy babe. I imagine Arthur is making a nuisance of himself; he was never one to tolerate waiting. You were wise to insist that Father accompany you, to keep Arthur out of the way while you and Margaret attend to the important work.

You shall be glad of your absence from Matlock House when I tell you of the happenings of the past two days. It began with a very successful dinner at the Gardiners', where Georgiana managed to overcome her anxieties and even Darcy behaved like a properly sociable fellow. Then came Aunt Catherine to breakfast, descending on Darcy House like a Fury to insist that Darcy make good on her demand that he marry Anne. He flatly and rather forcefully refused, but it was not until she insulted Miss Bennet that he threw her out of the house.

Father shall certainly receive a strongly-worded missive in the very near future, but you may assure him that there is no need for him to take his nephew in hand; Aunt Catherine's behaviour was appalling, and she remains the only person unable to see how ill-suited Darcy and Anne are.

I am most impressed with Georgiana. It is easy to forget that she is nearly seventeen; she says little but it appears she sees much, and her acquaintance with the Miss Bennets and Mrs. Wentworth has greatly improved her understanding. She has divined the state of Darcy's heart, and her opinion on the matter is much the same as ours. She consulted me on the scheme she has concocted, and when you are of a mind to instruct her on tactics and strategy, you shall find her an eager and able student.

We have determined that she shall deploy her battalion in a few days' time, and I am to assist in shoring up the rear guard. When next I write, I hope it shall be with news of a successful campaign. In the meantime, give my best to Father and Arthur, kiss Margaret for me (and the babe, when he or she deigns to make an appearance), and take a kiss for yourself.

Your loving son,

Richard

London, May 1816

Darcy had just finished his instructions to Lady Catherine's steward and was beginning a letter to his cousin Anne when he was interrupted by a knock on the open door of his study. Georgiana stood in the doorway. He set aside his correspondence and bade her enter; she perched on a chair in front of his desk, hands clasped tightly in her lap.

"Fitzwilliam, I have been giving Aunt Catherine's visit a great deal of thought, and I have come to a difficult conclusion."

"Please, Georgiana, pay no mind to what she says. Her opinions are forcefully stated, but they are hers alone."

"I do not believe they are, or at least not entirely. But please, let me say this; if you stop me, I am not sure I shall be able to explain it properly."

He nodded, wondering what this was about. *How can she credit anything Lady Catherine says?*

Georgiana took a deep breath and lifted her eyes to his. "I am not prepared to face the *ton*. I shall be of age to come out in little more than a year, and while the year past has been… instructive… the greatest lesson I must take from it is that my every word, expression, and action shall be watched and judged without mercy."

He nodded again slowly, frowning.

"I have no true friends among my own class, Fitzwilliam."

He started. *What? How can she say so?*

"You must forgive me for speaking so plainly, but it is important that you understand. The girls at school were at best distant, at worst cruel. I believe that is why I delighted so in Elizabeth and Jane's friendship, and—" she looked down – "why I was so ready to believe that George loved me."

Darcy kept the scowl off his face; his anger was not directed at Georgiana. He gave her what he hoped was an encouraging look.

Georgiana smiled gratefully. "Aunt Catherine was, as you say, forceful in expressing her opinion of those I do call friends. I shall undoubtedly face the judgment of the *ton* for maintaining ties to those in trade. I know that you and Aunt and Uncle and Richard shall do all in your power to protect me, but you cannot silence the criticism. I shall not be able to hide behind you in any event, particularly among ladies my own age."

Darcy anticipated the request that he was certain would follow this speech. "If you wish to delay your coming out, Georgiana, you must know I shall support your choice."

She surprised him, however, by shaking her head. "No, Fitzwilliam. I should merely be continuing to hide. That will not do; I must prepare myself. I must learn to be stronger." Her hands balled into fists. "When Aunt Catherine said those terrible things about the Gardiners, I wanted to shout at her, but I could hardly find my voice. I cannot allow myself to be silenced when I have no cause for shame, but I need practice and I need my friends to help me." She looked at him hopefully.

Darcy felt the bottom drop out of his stomach. *Surely, she cannot be suggesting… no, that is madness. But who can she mean?* He thought over their acquaintance. "Mrs. Wentworth? Or… Miss Kitty Bennet? Do you wish to travel to Hertfordshire? I am certain that Bingley will have no objection to opening his house to us."

She smiled at him fondly. "Nay, brother. You know perfectly well that I speak of Elizabeth and Jane."

His heart stopped in his chest. *She knows. How does she know?*

Her smile became sad. "I know that your acquaintance with Elizabeth has been… complicated," she said softly, "but I believe she will see what an excellent man you are, given time and opportunity. Besides," she said more firmly, "Elizabeth and Jane are the only unmarried ladies of my acquaintance who are already out in society and who I feel I can trust."

Darcy considered this. He recalled Elizabeth at Netherfield, accusing him of keeping his sister in a gilded cage. And given what Georgiana had just told him, the accusation was well founded. Not for the first time he experienced a brief, painful longing for his mother. She would wish her daughter to be prepared to enter society, and he had made a mess of it.

"What are you suggesting, Georgiana?" He spoke quietly; he both hoped and feared to hear his most secret wish spoken aloud.

Georgiana rose and came around the desk, taking his hands in hers. "I suggest that we join the Bennet family on their Italian tour."

She said it. He forgot to breathe.

"Travelling outside England shall provide endless opportunities for us both, brother! We shall be required to make new acquaintances and follow unfamiliar customs, which shall of course be terrifying—" here she squeezed his hands tightly, even as he squeezed hers – "but Richard is right. We shall neither of us escape our loneliness if we remain as we are."

Darcy stared through her, unseeing. *How does she know these things?*

He had barely admitted his loneliness to himself, and only Richard knew of his feelings for Elizabeth. He did not think his cousin would betray a confidence, which meant that he was doing a shoddy job indeed of keeping his feelings private. He had battled the urge to chase after Elizabeth for a month now, and here was his sister, suggesting he do just that.

Can I agree to this? What would Father have said? More to the point, what would Mother have said?

"Fitzwilliam," Georgiana said quietly, pulling his attention back to her. She knelt so that their eyes were nearly level. "If I am to succeed, I need to be away from the *ton*, and I need Elizabeth to help me." She bit her lip. "And I think… I think, maybe, so do you."

It was the expression in her eyes that broke him. She was asking him to take care of her, and she wanted to take care of *him*.

He stood, hugging her tightly to him as he had not done since she was a girl. She wrapped her arms around him and he kissed the top of her head, blinking back tears. "You are right," he said, his voice ragged. He cleared his throat. "I do. We both do."

Georgiana's face shone with excitement and affection. *She looks so like Mother…* but Mother was not here, and neither was Father. It was only the two of them, and he must do what he thought best for them both.

"We have a great deal of planning ahead of us, you know," he said with a smile. "I suppose you have their itinerary already?"

"Of course, brother," Georgiana said happily. "If we move quickly then we should be able to meet them in Siena in time for the *Palio*."

~ * ~

Fitzwilliam is not nearly as surprised as he should be, Darcy thought. "You knew already," he said.

"I confess I did," Fitzwilliam said easily, leaning into the plush green velvet of the wingback chair. Darcy had taken a private room at White's to discuss the plan with his cousin; he wanted none of the servants to hear of it yet. Fitzwilliam sipped his whisky. "Georgiana sought my advice before she approached you."

"And what did you tell her?"

"Only that her idea and her reasoning were sound, and that I would support her if you balked." He gave Darcy a frank look. "I gave away none of your secrets, old man. She discovered your affection for Miss Bennet entirely on her own."

Darcy shook his head wonderingly. "Who else knows?"

Fitzwilliam smirked. "My mother, of course, but it shall come as no surprise that she did the sum correctly long ago. None other, unless Georgiana has spoken of it to Mrs. Wentworth."

"She has not; too awkward, she says, as Mrs. Wentworth is also a friend of the Miss Bennets."

"And you agreed to the scheme, I see."

Darcy raised his brows in question.

"You are entirely too calm to be undecided or against it, Darcy. I can only assume you have asked me here to discuss the details."

Darcy grinned ruefully; trust Fitzwilliam to be a step ahead of him. *Well, perhaps I might surprise him yet.* This was, after all, why he had asked Fitzwilliam to meet him at White's. "I wondered," he asked casually as Fitzwilliam lifted his glass to his lips, "if you would consider resigning your commission."

Fitzwilliam spluttered and coughed; Darcy thumped him on the back. Whisky sloshed as Fitzwilliam set down his glass sharply and looked at Darcy, stunned.

"What did you say?"

Darcy grinned. "We shall likely be gone for a year, Fitzwilliam. I have recently made several improvements at Pemberley that require shepherding to ensure they succeed, and I wished to make several more in the coming year. I should not like to let them languish because I am overseas, and I trust no other to see it done."

"Damn you, Darcy, you know how I feel about handouts from you."

"What gives you the notion that I offer a handout? You have said on several occasions that you should resign if any other eligible means of support existed." He regarded his cousin seriously. "This is an advantageous business proposition for us both, Fitzwilliam. I shall expect you to be as involved in the management of the estate as I am, which is not – as you once observed – a life of leisure. My other properties also require management. I intended to tour Cargen Hall this summer, for example."

"You expect me to go to Scotland as well? Are you mad?"

Darcy continued as though his cousin had not spoken. "You shall have a salary equivalent to what you currently draw, plus expenses. You have invested wisely for over a decade; I trust you shall continue to do so. By the time I return, you should have the means to purchase your own property and the knowledge to manage it."

Fitzwilliam sat back, frowning.

"Or you could marry Anne," Darcy said, grinning wickedly. "Once Aunt Catherine believes me to be beyond her reach, she shall look to you. Rosings is an excellent property, and you and Anne would suit admirably."

Fitzwilliam's retort was cut off by the opening of the door. Darcy was sorry to miss it; judging by his expression, it would have been entertaining.

"Bingley!" Fitzwilliam shook Bingley's hand vigorously. "Delighted you could make it!"

Darcy gave Fitzwilliam a friendly glare. "I see you gentlemen have chosen to gang up on me."

"Not at all, Darcy," said Bingley, with his usual cheer. "I am just arrived to town and Fitzwilliam invited me to dinner. He said that the conversation might be of interest."

"Indeed," said Darcy, forestalling his cousin's reply. "I have just been offering him the opportunity to manage Pemberley on my behalf."

Bingley gaped at him. "What?" He took in Darcy's grin and Fitzwilliam's discomposure. "Clearly, I am behind events. What is all this about, Darcy?"

"I am taking Georgiana to Italy for perhaps a year. We hope to join the Bennet family on their tour. In my absence, I need a man I trust implicitly to manage my properties."

Bingley studied Darcy carefully. "Is it wise to seek out the Bennets? We have not met in some time, I know, but I understood that you and Miss Elizabeth were… not on speaking terms."

Darcy grimaced. "Indeed. I was entirely at fault and am grateful that my cousin persuaded her to speak to me again before she sailed. I owe him a very great debt for her restoration to society." He looked at Fitzwilliam. "I tell you again, cousin: I offer no handout. Whether I succeed in winning her affections or no, I have a debt to repay."

Bingley's eyebrows shot up. "Wait... winning her affections?" Understanding bloomed in his countenance. "She was the lure that brought you so often into society last December, then?"

"She was, and I could not possibly have made a greater arse of myself if I had proposed marriage to her." He sighed. "Georgiana wishes to travel to Italy to broaden her understanding of the world and learn to handle the ladies of the *ton*, with her friends' assistance. I go in hopes of becoming a man that Elizabeth can respect and earning her forgiveness, if not her love."

Their conversation was halted by the arrival of the meal. When they were alone again, Bingley looked speculatively at Fitzwilliam. "Why am I here, then?"

Fitzwilliam shrugged. "I thought I might need reinforcements to convince Darcy to go. I underestimated Georgiana, it seems."

There was a brief silence. "Darcy," said Bingley with an embarrassed look, "was Jane Bennet well when they left?"

"You are still attached to Jane Bennet?" Darcy said, astonished.

Bingley nodded, flushing.

"I must confess, Bingley, I had no idea. You left London before Christmas; when you did not return, I believed your attentions must have been captured elsewhere."

Bingley shook his head. "We went to Scarborough for Christmas, of course. Then Caroline heard from Miss Elliot about your... well, about what happened at your aunt's New Year's Eve gala, and that society had shunned the Bennets."

"All true," said Fitzwilliam. "Which is why my mother and I, and our friends in the Navy, spent the next three months restoring their reputation."

"Truly?" Bingley hesitated. "I wanted to rush back to town when I heard of it. To see Jane and assure her that I had not forgotten her. Apologize for my neglect of her in December. But Caroline insisted that we must not return, for if we were to be seen associating with them – or even with you, Darcy, after you left – it would sink us. I did not hear that they had been restored to good society."

Darcy's brows lifted in surprise. Miss Bingley had been a careful gatekeeper of information, but if he were honest with himself, he had been a negligent correspondent. "I apologize, Bingley. I never thought to tell you of it. I believed that you had forgotten about Miss Bennet."

"Nay, though I thought it likely that she had forgotten about me. Caroline was certain that she felt nothing for me, and you gave me no encouragement, Darcy."

"You never asked my advice, and I do not consider it my place to insert myself into your romantic affairs unless you are headed for clear disaster." Darcy gave Bingley a meaningful look. "Even when I am importuned to do so."

Bingley started, looking at Darcy and then to Fitzwilliam in confusion. Both men merely looked at him expectantly, waiting for him to puzzle it out.

The flush of anger that suffused his countenance was not long in coming. "Caroline," he spat.

"Aye. I did not think to warn you against her," Darcy said. "It appeared that you had the measure of her behaviour toward Miss Bennet in Hertfordshire. And had you sought my counsel I could not have advised you. Miss Bennet, as I have since learned from Georgiana, has a great capacity for keeping a serene countenance, whatever her feelings." He sighed and shrugged helplessly. "As for her state in March, I can say only that she was unattached. I know not what her feelings might be toward you."

The room fell into silence as they ate, Bingley and Fitzwilliam each contemplating Darcy's words. Eventually, Bingley put down his knife and fork and sat straighter in his chair.

"What think you of my chances with Miss Bennet, Darcy?"

"I could not begin to guess, but they can be no worse than mine with Miss Elizabeth." He smiled wryly. "I know exactly what she thinks of me, after all."

"Would you object to a third in your party?"

Darcy's smile became genuine. "No indeed. I believe Georgiana would welcome your company as well. Have you decided to risk it, then?"

"I have. I shall give up Netherfield and deposit Caroline with our aunt in Scarborough. Hurst can approve a marriage settlement, should the need arise, but she deserves no consideration from me. I should appreciate your advice on instructions to my solicitor for the management of her funds in my absence."

"I shall be happy to assist you."

Bingley grinned. "When do we leave?"

"The twenty-seventh of May. We shall sail to Calais and travel overland to Marseille, and thence take ship again to Livorno. From there it is but two days' journey to Siena. Barring unforeseen complications, we should arrive shortly before the *Palio*."

"And what is the *Palio*?" Bingley looked embarrassed again. "I confess, I know nothing of Italy."

"I know very little myself. Georgiana has been an eager teacher. She tells me that the *Palio* is a horse race that the Sienese hold in their largest square, in front of city hall, twice each summer. The neighbourhoods all compete, and victory brings great prestige. The Bennets are there to see the *Palio* on the second of July and shall travel south not long after it is done."

"That leaves little enough time for preparation, then."

"Indeed. A great number of decisions must be made, and arrangements attended to." Darcy looked a question at Fitzwilliam. He hoped his cousin would agree, but he had already developed a contingency for Fitzwilliam's refusal.

Fitzwilliam smiled and raised his whisky. "I rather enjoy the idea of collecting on a debt from you, Darcy," he said. "I cannot say I would object to living a life of leisure for a year, either. And I am certain my mother will kiss you when I tell her that I am to be 'Mr. Fitzwilliam' again."

CHAPTER FOURTEEN

IN WHICH ELIZABETH AND DARCY GO TO THE RACES

Siena, June 30ᵗʰ, 1816

My dear Charlotte,

You shall think me repetitive and dull when I tell you that I am, once again, rendered speechless with astonishment. The week past has seen several such tableaux – you would not know your pert and clever friend Lizzy, I fear, for she has been quite unrecognizable in the face of so many extraordinary happenings! Though, in fairness, her sisters have been equally dissimilar to their ordinary selves.

First, of course, came the discovery of Signor Rinaldi's exceedingly cavalier opinions on matrimonial fidelity, and Lydia's pugilistic display. Her hand suffered some tenderness and bruising, but Signor Rinaldi fared worse! He came to entreat Jane to reconsider her refusal yesterday. A blotchy purple stain covers his nose and beneath his eyes, but he remains unable to comprehend that a lady might rightfully expect her husband to forego all other women. Jane soon gave over any attempt to make him understand, and peremptorily dismissed him from her sight.

She blames herself not at all, for which I am grateful; Jane so often takes the faults and failings of others onto herself! Grandpa asked if she wished us to leave Siena, but she declared that Signor Rinaldi's shameless behavior should not deny us our enjoyment of the Palio.

Shortly before dinner came the greatest shock yet: we were called upon by Georgiana, Mr. Darcy, and Mr. Bingley! They are just arrived in Siena and desirous of accompanying us on our travels! Georgiana insists that she wrote of their intention before they departed London, but the post is likely several weeks behind them. She was quite anxious that their intrusion was unwelcome, as it seems this voyage was undertaken at her suggestion.

The ostensible reason for their journey is to improve Georgiana's knowledge of the world and her comfort in society, though such an excuse hardly explains the presence of Mr. Bingley. He was quite unable to look away from Jane during the whole of the visit, which supplies a more creditable motive.

We were such an awkward and silent company, Charlotte! Jane said no more than propriety demanded to Mr. Bingley and gave the whole of her attention to Georgiana. It was all I could do to speak to any of them, for my thoughts were leaden. After my last conference with Mr. Darcy I cannot fathom that he should willingly seek out my family, and of course his manner was as grave and stilted as ever!

After perhaps ten minutes of such misery, with my grandparents and Lydia the only ones capable of carrying a conversation – though Mr. Bingley, to his credit, did attempt to seem interested in our adventures – Grandpa took Mr. Darcy and Mr. Bingley aside. When they returned, Mr. Bingley looked as though he had been chastised by Mrs. Okill; I have never seen a more thorough dressing-down than the ones our headmistress gave!

They are to dine with us tomorrow and shall join us to view the Palio, and then we shall decide if they may add their number to our merry band of Bennets. Shall we be as Chaucer's pilgrims, each vying to be the greatest teller of tales along the way? What, I wonder, shall prove the most remarkable – the tales we shall tell, or the one that is told of our journey when we return? I suppose I must endeavor to recover my powers of speech!

Yours ever,

Elizabeth

Piazza del Campo, Siena, July 2nd, 1816

It was not yet time for breakfast, but already *Il Campo* hummed with activity.

Elizabeth was grateful that her grandfather had procured lodgings that overlooked the piazza. Most of the spectators would fill the center of the space, inside the newly laid earthen track, so the advantage of watching the race from above was substantial. Banners representing each of Siena's neighborhoods hung from the walls of the *Palazzo Pubblico* – the great city hall which formed one side of the semicircular piazza – the smaller banners flanking the great *Palio* banner that lifted in the breeze.

It was hours yet before the race, though Elizabeth's eager anticipation had been overtaken by thoughts of Mr. Darcy. In truth, she had thought of little else since his sudden arrival with his sister and his friend.

Yesterday's dinner had begun in nearly as stilted a fashion as their visit the day prior, but Nanna and Grandpa had determinedly engaged the young people in conversation. Georgiana had made a sweetly impassioned plea to Elizabeth and Jane, detailing the reasons she had sought their particular assistance, and her earnest expressions of friendship nearly made Elizabeth ready to tolerate Georgiana's brother for her sake alone.

Mr. Darcy spoke to Elizabeth's grandparents with greater ease and cordiality than she knew he possessed. He had looked at Elizabeth sympathetically when Nanna spoke of her wretchedness on the *Bonny Bess* but said little to her directly. Mr. Bingley, meanwhile, bore Jane's persistent repression of his attempts at conversation with admirable composure; her replies were nearly too terse for civility, but he accepted these with polite solemnity.

After dinner Elizabeth had persuaded Georgiana to play a duet. Elizabeth could feel Mr. Darcy's eyes on her, but his countenance remained inscrutable.

He had looked uncommonly handsome, with dark hair curling around his collar and pale gray eyes made dusky by the deep sapphire hue of his coat. When he approached the pianoforte, Elizabeth noticed how the coat seemed to cling to his body. It emphasized the unfashionable breadth of his shoulders and chest, which tapered to a narrow waist. His long legs brought him across the room in only a few strides, well-fitted trousers revealing ridges of muscle as he moved.

She knew he was handsome, of course, but his manners had been so offputting that the details had made no impression on her. She was greatly discomfited to recognize her interest in them now, particularly when neither his behavior nor her opinion had improved.

So piqued was she that she could not resist baiting him. "Do you come in all this state for a particular purpose, Mr. Darcy, or is intimidation a goal in itself?"

Georgiana looked on open-mouthed, but Mr. Darcy only smiled. Smiled! "I know you find amusement in professing opinions which are not your own, Miss Elizabeth."

"Your brother would teach you not to believe a word I say," Elizabeth said to Georgiana, who giggled. "Uncharitable of him, is it not?"

Georgiana smiled sweetly. "It is indeed, brother, when I know you merely wished to beg the favor of a particular song."

Mr. Darcy's brows had risen, but his smile remained. "Have you anything by Handel among your selection of music?"

"Sadly, no. We have only Mozart, Vivaldi, and Rossini, and several songs by Italian composers with whom I am unfamiliar."

"Then I am at your mercy, dear sister; pray choose what pleases you."

Elizabeth looked up at him. "Do you not find it singular that none of the most brilliant composers were born to the upper classes? What is it, think you, that prevents the wealthy and titled from achieving greatness in musical pursuits?"

"I have never given it any consideration," he said, surprised. "What cause have you to believe that a preventative measure exists?"

"The upper classes have produced men with genius in oratory, law, finance, strategy, philosophy, science… need I go on? How not music, then, or art?"

Georgiana threw up her hands. "Lizzy, I can find nothing else I know! You play so well on first sight, will you choose something? I shall turn the pages for you."

Elizabeth chose an operatic farce by Rossini; she had heard of *The Silken Ladder*, at least! She placed her fingers to begin the overture and looked curiously at Mr. Darcy.

"I have no answer for you, Miss Elizabeth. I can think of no explanation which satisfies me. What is your own opinion?"

"I can imagine two possibilities. The first is that genius *does* exist among the upper classes but is not encouraged, because the life of a musician is one of poverty and servitude in the courts of nobility."

Mr. Darcy nodded thoughtfully.

"The second is that genius has become a casualty of intermarriage. I am certain you know that breeding animals with limited stock results in the promotion of undesirable traits and the loss of desirable ones over generations." She arched an eyebrow at him. "Perhaps the same thing has happened among the *ton*, as they permit themselves to marry only within their own sphere."

Without waiting for his response, she began to play. He retreated, his countenance grave, and said not another word to her for the remainder of the evening. She had counted it a victory, but this morning it felt hollow.

Elizabeth was pulled from her thoughts when Jane joined her on the settee. The two of them had stayed awake late into the night; Jane's confusion and anger at Mr. Bingley's sudden appearance required a great deal of discussion. Filled as she was with disappointment and contempt following the revelation of Signor

Rinaldi's questionable character – despite his uniformly charming manner – Jane deeply distrusted Mr. Bingley's motives.

She had proposed several shocking explanations for his reappearance that would, in other circumstances, have caused Elizabeth to cheer, if only because such suspicions lessened the likelihood of her sister's being imposed upon. Last night, however, Elizabeth had only been grieved to see how deeply Jane had been wounded. They had finally resigned themselves to sleep, with no better understanding than when they began.

This morning they spoke of inconsequential things until Nanna joined them, a servant following with three cups of *espresso*. Elizabeth had become quite fond of the strong coffee, but Jane found it too bitter without the addition of a generous measure of hot, frothed milk. They sipped in congenial silence for a time before Nanna faced them, her expression serious.

"We have a decision to make today, girls. Shall we travel with your friend and her troublesome companions? I do not ask for your opinion now, nor do I seek for you to share a confidence you would rather keep."

Elizabeth met Jane's eyes. *Were the question only about the gentlemen, there would be nothing to decide.*

"Jane, my dear," Nanna said, "I know you mistrust Mr. Bingley, and he has much to answer for. I advise only that you consider the possibility that his behavior has been feckless rather than cruel. Cruelty certainly merits rejection. But you cannot yet know which is the explanation for his neglect."

Jane frowned thoughtfully at the cup in her lap. None of her suspicions had been so benign, and Elizabeth had not wanted to diminish the righteousness of Jane's feelings by suggesting such a motive.

"Lizzy," Nanna continued, "When last you saw Mr. Darcy, you told him that you could not accept an apology which his conceit made insincere, and you were right to do so. Yet he brings his sister to Italy because *her* esteem for you is so great! I fancy that I see discomfiture, rather than disdain, in his countenance. Perhaps he has taken your remonstrance to heart; only time may tell."

Elizabeth bit her lip. *Mr. Darcy cannot feel only disdain for me; after all, did he not confess his admiration and regard?* Her refusal to accept his apology must certainly have done away with any such tender feelings! Yet here he was, with Georgiana. *He must not hate me, at least.*

She had told no one, not even Jane, of his confession. She had been so confounded by his professed admiration that even now she could not determine her own feelings about it. On the one hand, it was not a compliment to be admired by a man she disdained. On the other, Mr. Darcy was notoriously uninterested in the young ladies of the *ton*. To be singled out for his notice did gratify her pride, particularly given that her distinguishing feature – her ready and exceedingly well-educated wit – was far less likely to draw notice and compliment than her sisters' beauty.

Could it be that I notice his attractions now only because I know myself to be attractive to him? How vain and shallow she must be, were it true! She resolved to observe his behavior today with as generous an allowance as she could grant before deciding if she could suffer his company for what would likely be several months at least.

~ * ~

"Oh, Elizabeth! I thought I should never find a flag for the Unicorn contrada; but look! I know not how my brother managed it!" Georgiana entered the salon with a grin, waving a blue-bordered orange and white silk flag above her head.

Each of the Bennets had chosen a different contrada – the Sienese term for a neighborhood – to support for the race. *"A little friendly competition adds spice to the adventure,"* Grandpa had said the previous week, as they perused the bright flags at a nearby shop. Lydia had explained the scheme to Georgiana, who was immediately taken with the notion of choosing her own flag but despaired at finding one with so little time remaining before the *Palio* began.

"Our landlord has proven to be a very useful fellow," Mr. Bingley said. "His cousin sells them, it seems." He held up his own red and white flag. "I quite like my Giraffe, with his great long neck."

"And naturally Fitzwilliam chose *Lupa*, because our landlord's contrada is *Lupa*," Georgiana said with a fond smile.

Elizabeth's flag was a duplicate of Mr. Darcy's: black and white, a single edge bordered with orange, and the She-Wolf – symbol of proud Siena – emblazoned at the center. She caught Mr. Darcy looking at the silk in her hands; he flushed and bowed an acknowledgement.

"It seemed the proper thing," he said stiffly. "He gave me to understand that support for one's contrada is a very serious business in Siena."

"I suppose it must be, if one is Sienese," said Lydia. "As I shall never live here, I simply chose what I liked. This Eagle with two heads is strangest bird I have ever seen! I am sure it shall bring me good fortune!"

"And to the victor shall go the spoils," said Mrs. Bennet, bringing forth an exquisite lace shawl. "Burano lace for the lady – or the lady of the gentleman's choice – whose horse crosses the line first."

There were feminine gasps; none of them had suspected that a prize was in the offing, and the shawl would be sure to draw envious gazes. Elizabeth met Lydia's competitive stare with a saucy grin. To compete when neither of them could have the slightest impact on the outcome was farcical, but it had ever been thus: Lydia and Elizabeth were the competitors, Jane the moderator.

Feeling other eyes upon her, Elizabeth found Mr. Darcy observing their unspoken exchange with amusement; their eyes met, and he lifted his flag as though in solidarity.

Elizabeth glanced away. What perverse chance had led him to choose the same contrada that she had selected? And what gave him the right to act as though this somehow made them allies?

You promised to judge him fairly, she told herself sternly. *He is not mocking you.* She was saved the discomfort of further self-examination by a trumpet fanfare, announcing the ceremonies which preceded the race.

The entire party moved to the balcony to watch the procession, and Elizabeth allowed herself to enjoy the spectacle. The breeze had stiffened and lifted each contrada's flag as men in garb from several centuries past strode around the piazza, holding their banners high. The jockeys followed, each dressed in his contrada's colors.

The horses approached the starting line, to the left of the balcony on which Elizabeth's party stood. Jockeys shoved at each other as they waited for the last horse to enter, which would begin the race. They became increasingly restive as the seconds ticked by, horses bunching together toward the inner part of the track. The spectators nearest the start line chanted, demanding that the race begin: *"Inizio! Inizio! Inizio!"* The chant soon spread, and before long the piazza echoed with it.

There was now a wide space at the outside of the track, Elizabeth saw. Finally, the last horse – its jockey dressed in the orange and white of the Unicorn – stepped onto the track and moved smartly forward to fill the gap. The rope was dropped and ten horses sprang forward, jockeys whipping their mounts into a gallop.

Elizabeth held her breath as they made the first sharp turn, the Unicorn maintaining a slight lead through the corner but losing it as the horses to the inside surged ahead on the straight. The field began to bunch together as they passed the *Palazzo Pubblico*, crowding toward the outside of the track. Elizabeth's entire party waved their flags and shouted encouragement as the horses rounded the second sharp corner and thundered beneath them, racing toward the starting line to complete the first circuit.

Mr. Bingley peered after them. "I say! Are those fellows riding bareback?"

"Oh yes," Lydia said. "It is one of the rules. The horses wear only a bridle, and the jockeys draw lots to assign horses. The jockeys are even permitted to knock each other off or whip the other horses."

The racers were again rounding the first sharp turn. Georgiana gasped as the Giraffe was crowded roughly toward the inside of the track and its jockey fell into the dirt. The man ran across the track and leapt up onto the stone rail, whooping as he watched his horse – no longer burdened with his weight – gain on the rest of the riders.

"Oh! Bad luck!" Mr. Bingley cried. "I am well out of it now, I daresay."

"Not at all, Mr. Bingley," Elizabeth said. "The horse which crosses the finish line first after three laps is the winner, whether its jockey is astride or no."

The field had stretched out considerably by the third time they passed the *Palazzo Pubblico*. Elizabeth was thrilled to see her *Lupa* in the lead, Lydia's Eagle keeping pace only a foot or so behind.

Lydia leaned far forward, waving her flag with arms wide, blocking Elizabeth's view. Elizabeth pushed her sister's arm to the side, cheering and waving her own flag.

The Eagle's jockey shoved at the She-Wolf's; the men grappled with each other as they approached the turn.

Lydia snatched Elizabeth's flag. Elizabeth grabbed for it, but their hands struck together with a resounding smack. Lydia yelped in pain and the flag fell.

The She-Wolf and the Eagle rounded the corner at full gallop, their jockeys still locked together as each tried to unseat the other.

Elizabeth watched helplessly as the black and white flag drifted toward the track. A stray gust caught it and the crowd let out a collective gasp as it blew straight into the face of the Eagle's jockey.

The man jerked back reflexively, maintaining his hold on the She-Wolf's jockey. They fell backward into the dirt, rolling and scrambling to the railing. The other jockeys pulled their mounts sharply to the inside to avoid trampling the fallen men, who were already coming to blows.

"Look!" Georgiana cried, pointing to where the two riderless horses still galloped neck-and-neck at the head of the pack. At this distance Elizabeth could not distinguish the black and white bridle of the She-Wolf from the yellow and black of the Eagle.

She watched them cross the finish line together, heart hammering in her chest. She realized that she had been holding her breath when the black and white flag of *Lupa* was lifted high and she drew in a lungful of air to shout in triumph, arms flung above her head.

The noise in the piazza was deafening.

"Miss Elizabeth," Mr. Darcy shouted, "it seems that yours is the hand of Fortune. I must congratulate you."

Elizabeth laughed and dropped a playful curtsy as the others applauded. The spectators below pointed her out, *Lupa* supporters cheering.

Grandpa lifted her hand and bellowed, *"La Fortuna!"* The cry was taken up by the crowd. Soon *"Lupa! La Fortuna! Lupa!"* could be heard making its way across the piazza.

Her color high, Elizabeth smiled and waved to the crowd below. The cheering suddenly grew louder, and Elizabeth turned to see Mr. Darcy holding his *Lupa* flag high with both hands. He bowed deeply, presenting it to her with exaggerated ceremony. She took it from him with equal formality and held it up, waving it for the crowd to see and smiling until her cheeks ached. The others filtered inside, leaving her alone above the boisterous crowd.

Finally she left the balcony, relief flooding her as she dropped her arms and allowed her face to relax. Mr. Darcy proffered a cool glass, which she accepted gratefully. She looked at him thoughtfully, lips twitching with amusement. "I had no notion that you were so fond of spectacle, Mr. Darcy."

A boyish grin crossed his face. "I am quite as astonished as you, Miss Elizabeth. Though I do not suppose I should have enjoyed it nearly so much, were I the one whose every expression produced such cheers."

Elizabeth blushed at the warmth in his gaze. She held out his flag, but he shook his head. "Nay. *La Fortuna* must have a symbol of her triumph, and I believe that yours was left in a pitiable state. I insist you keep it."

Nanna approached, eyes twinkling as she looked between them. "You have well and truly earned this, my dear," she said, draping the lace around Elizabeth's shoulders. "Though in fairness, if we are to believe that your flag influenced the outcome, I suppose Lydia has earned a trinket as well."

"Nay, I shall accept no prize for losing," Lydia said petulantly. "Better to be last than second, they say."

Nanna gave her a stern look. "You have none but yourself to blame, Lydia. Your behavior was very unsporting."

Lydia sighed. "I am sorry, Lizzy. It was wrong of me to take your flag from you."

"You are quite forgiven, Lydia," Elizabeth said, moving to embrace her sister.

The rest of the evening passed pleasantly enough. Elizabeth played the pianoforte at Mr. Darcy's request. He listened attentively, seated at his ease by Georgiana while Jane permitted herself to speak to Mr. Bingley. Her countenance was serious but not so forbidding as it had been, and Mr. Bingley looked to be grateful for whatever notice she was willing to bestow.

Outside, the sounds of drunken revelry could be clearly heard. Elizabeth begged Georgiana to remain with them for the night, that her brother need not worry for her safety as the gentlemen returned to their lodgings; the invitation was gratefully accepted.

Mr. Darcy and Mr. Bingley had no sooner gained the street than a shout of recognition was heard, and a man's voice said loudly, *"La Fortuna! Lei è bella, no?"*

"Lei è molto bella," came a hearty baritone in reply.

Elizabeth blushed – it was not done, to bandy words about a woman's beauty in the streets! – and blushed again as she belatedly realized that the baritone belonged to Mr. Darcy.

"Viva La Fortuna!" he shouted. The men in the street took up the cry, which finally faded as they moved away.

"Well, my dears?" said Nanna.

Jane frowned at her lap for several seconds before giving a single tiny nod; Lydia merely shrugged. Georgiana clasped her hands tightly under her chin, eyes bright and hopeful.

Elizabeth laughed. "We shall be happy to have you as a traveling companion, Georgiana," she said, to the other girl's delighted squeal.

Nanna gave a satisfied nod and bade them all good-night.

CHAPTER FIFTEEN

IN WHICH DARCY DIRTIES HIS HANDS

Orvieto, 14ᵗʰ July 1816

Fitzwilliam—

 As I walk through the streets of this city, I am reminded of your infernal habit of beginning any discussion of a place with a consideration of its defensive advantages. I imagine that you would like Orvieto exceedingly. It sits atop a high hill accessible only by a single narrow, winding road, with sturdy outer walls and an excellent view of the surrounding country. The Etruscans added yet another feature that would please you: they dug so many caves beneath its surface that a man might easily lose his way below the ground. Bingley has nearly done so, on more than one occasion.

 Our travelling companions are quite taken with the city. In particular, we find ourselves often in the Piazza del Duomo. It is the scene of many a local gathering and Elizabeth and Miss Lydia return daily, sketchbooks and pencils in hand. Miss Lydia is an accomplished painter, while Elizabeth's talent runs to detailed charcoal sketches. I cannot wonder at their enthusiasm; this Duomo fairly begs to be painted, so pleasing is its façade, and the varied groupings of people in the piazza "add to the picturesque," as Miss Lydia likes to say.

 Georgiana is often in company with the two eldest daughters of the Bianchi family, whose home is not far from our lodgings. Their father is a violin-maker, so when they came upon us shopping for new music they eagerly recommended several Italian composers. I must own that Georgiana was initially quite overwhelmed by them, as they have much in common with Miss Lydia – garrulous, open, high-spirited girls – but they are well-mannered and generous, and Georgiana has exerted herself to befriend them. With her old friends and her new, she is happy here.

Speaking of her old friends: Georgiana tells me that the Misses Bennet were given the opportunity to send us on our merry way when we intruded upon them in Siena. I believe Jane Bennet would happily have done so on first sight of Bingley. When I observed them together in Hertfordshire I could not be certain of her regard for him, so serene was her countenance, but her current disapprobation is impossible to miss. Bingley bears it well; her suspicion pains him but his attachment has not wavered.

You are surely cursing in frustration that I have barely spoken of Elizabeth. In truth, I cannot discern her feelings. She is often reserved – nay, even guarded – in my presence. Her wit does occasionally show itself, but to my chagrin its target is usually my own past words and behaviour. You need not tell me that I am being pierced by my own sword; Bingley has missed no opportunity to point out that my discomfiture at being the frequent object of Elizabeth's grave and silent observation is no worse than what all of society suffers when in company with me.

There is to be a festival at the Piazza del Duomo on Friday; perhaps there shall be some opportunity for Bingley and me to improve our standing in the eyes of the Bennets. I pray, at least, to avoid unmitigated disaster.

– Darcy

Orvieto, 19th July 1816

Darcy sipped his espresso, observing the dancers from a small table at the edge of the *Piazza del Duomo*. It was late, past ten o'clock, and the revelers showed no signs of slowing. The others of their party, save Mr. and Mrs. Bennet, had been persuaded to learn several of the local dances and were now leaping energetically alongside the eldest Bianchi siblings. Even Georgiana had lost her usual reticence under the influence of lively music and eager companions, but Darcy's eyes were inexorably drawn back to Elizabeth.

It had been many months since he had seen such gaiety in her countenance. She was flushed with exertion, bouncing curls burnished gold by the firelight and amber eyes glowing with merriment. She wore a simple white blouse with an embroidered neckline and skirts above the ankle in the Italian style, a deep red overskirt split to reveal a pale green underskirt.

Darcy found himself unable to breathe properly as she performed the leaping step particular to the dance, one hand on her outthrust hip while the other lifted her overskirt high to the opposite side, a coquettish grin lighting her features. The man dancing at her side clearly appreciated the effect; Darcy briefly envisioned punching him in his grinning mouth.

Such pleasant musings were interrupted by the arrival of Mr. Bennet, who angled his chair so that he could observe both the dancers and his wife. Mrs. Bennet had joined a group of matrons several tables away, all talking and laughing over each other with great animation. Darcy could not conceive how they were able to sustain a conversation.

"I know not how she does it," said Mr. Bennet, following his gaze. "For fifty years I have looked on in wonder as she adapted to every society, whether high or low, reserved or lively."

"A singular talent. I could say the same of my cousin Richard, but none other of my acquaintance." Darcy recalled his last weeks in London, spent among those whose society he would never have sought on his own. "I daresay most people are discomfited by those who are unlike themselves."

"Very true, Mr. Darcy. My father was wealthy by the time I was old enough to be aware of such things. I consider myself to be liberal-minded and no different in essentials than any other man, but I am acutely aware of my status when surrounded by those who lack my advantages."

Darcy grimaced. "It shall come as no surprise that I was raised with no such liberal-minded philosophy. How came you by such a belief?"

"My mother." Mr. Bennet smiled as though he were sharing a great secret. "Men fancy themselves the superior sex, but women hold the true power. My mother formed me, and it was for love of Esme that I became the man I am now."

"I daresay your mother was also a singular woman, if you credit her with your formation."

"She was, at that. My parents met and fell head over heels in love on the ship to New York. He was the third son of an insignificant country gentleman, she the eldest daughter of an Irish blacksmith. They were married by the captain when they were still three days from New York Harbor. They started out with nothing but each other, but they would not be gainsaid."

Mr. Bennet smiled broadly. "My mother was an unstoppable force. She had little education before she married, but she was whip-smart and took it upon herself to learn everything she could. She was an excellent teacher, too. She advised me when I set up my sidewalk business selling cold water as a boy, you know."

Darcy chuckled, recalling the story. "I had not heard that detail."

"My mother took after her Da," Mr. Bennet went on. "Granda had no formal education, as he would tell you himself, but he understood people. His customers would follow him anywhere, and did, until he died. He taught my mother how to read people and inspire loyalty, and she taught me."

"That is quite extraordinary," Darcy said. "My parents would not have believed such a thing possible."

Mr. Bennet gave him a significant look.

"No," Darcy acknowledged, "I would not have believed so either until very recently."

He thought of his own mother. He had seen her smile, but he had never known her to be happy. Lady Anne had inhabited Pemberley like a wraith, shunning the *ton* and their insincere sympathy for her inability to bear another child, never quite able to mask her fear when she was increasing or her despair when she was brought to bed months too early. As a boy he often found her in Pemberley's cemetery, laying before the grave markers of the babes who died shortly after birth, struggling to breathe.

Darcy himself had been a small and sickly infant, Mrs. Reynolds had told him, not strong enough to walk until well after his first year. His mother had doted on him excessively: she insisted that he was brilliant, special, better than other children. She taught him to take great pride in his name and lineage; his cousins were the only playmates she considered good enough for him, though on one of the rare occasions that his father intervened, she had grudgingly agreed that he might play with Wickham when his cousins were absent. George Darcy's desire that his favoured godson should be his only son's companion had become too persistent to ignore.

His mother's excessive praise and protectiveness had, indeed, formed him. *I was taught to value family above all else and never questioned my superiority. Naturally I saw no need to learn the trick of moving easily in society.*

Mother had not wanted to send him to school, Darcy remembered – fearful that some evil might befall him – but Father had stood firm. His father ensured that Darcy understood his duty and received the education befitting his station, but Darcy had been awkward around other boys; it was entirely due to Fitzwilliam that he had any companions at all. By the time he had entered Cambridge he no longer attempted to fit in. Only Bingley had ignored his resolute standoffishness long enough to befriend him.

"And what of your wife, Mr. Bennet?" he asked, eager to evade such discomfiting recollections. "I recall that her father managed your New York office."

Mr. Bennet's eyes turned to his lady with great fondness. "Esme was fifteen when I first saw her. She was beautiful, confident, and sassy. Dear Lord, the mouth on that girl." He chuckled, shaking his head. "I told my mother about her and the first thing she said was, 'You cannot marry that child before she is eighteen.' But I could hardly allow another man to steal her heart, so I befriended her brothers and made myself a fixture in their home."

He flashed Darcy a conspiratorial grin. "Her father knew what I was about, of course, but so long as I behaved myself and she did not object, he permitted it."

"I take it she did not object."

"No, but Esme will talk to anyone. Even then I often came across her in town, deep in conversation with someone she had only just met. Washerwomen, nannies… a chimneysweep once. The upper-class girls meant to shun her at school, but they could not withstand her determination to befriend them. The secret, she says, is curiosity without judgment. Esme will tell you that people want the same things. They want to be secure, to be loved and valued, to do something meaningful with their lives, and for their children to be healthy and safe." He shrugged. "We are all the same, in essentials."

Darcy was spared the necessity of formulating a response by the arrival of the dancers, including the Bianchi siblings. Teresa and Isabella, twenty and eighteen respectively, were Georgiana's particular friends. Their brother Matteo, at seventeen, was the eldest son.

Georgiana came directly to him, bouncing lightly on her toes. "Oh, brother! I have had such fun this evening! Thank you for permitting me to join the dancing."

Isabella Bianchi caught her arm. "She dances with the grace of a butterfly," she said. She smiled at Georgiana. "But you must practice every day if you are to dance the *trescone* at my wedding and still have your strength for the *saltarello*!"

"I shall practice very diligently, I promise! I should not wish to disappoint the bride!"

Darcy lifted a brow; this was the first he had heard of a wedding.

A loud shout echoed from a nearby street. *"Fuoco! Fuoco! Le stalle sono in fiamme!"* A short middle-aged man ran into the piazza. *"Aiutate! Le stalle sono in fiamme!"*

Fire! Darcy looked in the direction from which the man had come and saw the telltale signs of light above the rooftops. Too much light.

"Papà!" shouted Matteo Bianchi, and the older man turned.

Relief crossed Signor Bianchi's features for a moment. He shouted again, fear in his voice. *"Devi venire! Il fuoco si sta diffondendo alle case!"*

Matteo paled and sprinted to his father, closely followed by his sisters. The piazza was nearly empty; most of the townspeople had already disappeared in the direction of the distant glow.

"Did he say that there is a fire?" Georgiana asked.

"Yes," Miss Bennet said. "The stables are on fire and it is spreading to the houses."

"Oh no! What can we do?"

Mr. and Mrs. Bennet had a brief wordless conversation; he nodded.

"We do whatever needs doing," Mrs. Bennet said. "Come, girls." They all followed her in the direction the townspeople had gone.

The fire had already claimed the stable and several houses on either side. There were people everywhere: bucket brigades had been organized and the men were concentrating their efforts on the homes not yet engulfed in flames, attempting to prevent the fire from spreading further. Some of the women had begun to arrange food, drink, blankets and bandages. Others carried small children and led older ones away from the endangered homes, toward the center of town.

Georgiana gasped. "That is the Bianchi home!" She started toward a nearby building; the eastern side of the roof was burning and appeared to be in danger of collapsing inward.

Darcy held her back. "Georgiana, stop! I cannot allow you to endanger yourself. Look around you; there are easily a hundred people here, already attempting to douse the fire. We do not know the city or the people, and we do not speak the language fluently. We would do better to remain out of the way; we should only interfere and slow them down in our efforts to be of assistance."

From ahead of him came a loud snort. "A pretty excuse."

Darcy looked up from Georgiana's mutinous expression to see Mr. Bennet's disdainful gaze sweeping away.

"Dearest Grandpa," Elizabeth said, her tone dripping with scorn, "we must not be too hard on these fine English gentlemen. How could they hold up their heads in society, were they to sully their hands by the performance of *work*?"

Mr. Bennet smiled with dark amusement. "Indeed. Fortunate, then, that we Americans are made of sterner stuff." He paused only to kiss his wife's hand before setting off toward the men with the buckets.

Bingley, whose look of pained indecision had been transformed to furious resolve by Elizabeth's mockery, followed him without a backward glance.

Mrs. Bennet and her granddaughters strode toward the women with the food and bandages; Georgiana wrenched her arm out of Darcy's grasp and ran after them. Furious, Darcy followed. He was only steps away when the ladies were stopped by a frantic Signora Bianchi.

"*Miei bambini!*" she cried. "*I miei bambini sono ancora in casa!*" She rushed at Darcy, grabbing the lapels of his jacket into her fists. "*Per favore, Signore, devi aiutare! Trove i miei bambini!*"

Miss Bennet spoke urgently, just as his sluggish mind grasped what the woman was saying. "Mr. Darcy! There are children still in the house!"

Darcy felt as though he had been punched in the gut. *Please help*, she had begged. *Find my children!*

Miss Bennet asked the woman several questions in rapid Italian. "The two youngest children, she says. Luca is two and Stella is five. Their Nonna told them to hide beneath the stairs. She was overcome by the smoke and was only just now able to tell Signora Bianchi."

Darcy met Signora Bianchi's terrified gaze. He nodded firmly and took off at a dead run toward the Bianchi home, bellowing Bingley's name.

"What is it, Darcy?"

"Who is in charge here?"

"The builder there." Bingley indicated a burly man with plain, broad features and work-roughened hands.

Darcy accosted the man. "*Scusi, Signore. Devo entrare in casa. Ci sono bambini dentro!*"

"*Che cosa? Cosa ha detto?*" Matteo Bianchi turned, bucket dropping from his hands. *What did you say?*

"*Luca e Stella sono dentro, sotto le scale.*"

"Did you say there are children in there? Under the stairs?" Bingley asked, aghast.

There was a loud crash. A plume of soot and charred shingles flew into the air. The sagging roof of the Bianchi home had finally given way; the eastern half had fallen in, one large beam punching a hole through the floor. What remained of the roof still glowed dully above.

Darcy's heart nearly stopped in his chest. Panic crossed Matteo's face and he instantly ran for the door; Darcy, Bingley and the builder followed.

The builder grabbed the boy's shoulder, gripping hard when he tried to pull away. *"No, Matteo! Andiamo insieme, e stiamo attenti."* He looked at Darcy. *"Capisce?"*

"Sì." Darcy understood. "We go together, and be careful."

The builder led the way, testing the door and observing the ceiling before he crossed the threshold. Darcy understood the man's caution, but it took all his self-control to keep from barreling past him into the house.

We must find the staircase. He looked at Matteo. *"Dove sono le scale?"*

Matteo pointed across the room to where a hallway led to the back of the house. As they neared it Darcy could see that the far wall supported the staircase, or what was left of it. The top section had caved in, lanced by the fallen roof beam.

Darcy looked in vain for a door to the storage area beneath the stairs. *"Matteo, c'è una porta?"* Is there a door?

"Oh! Sì!" Matteo stepped past the builder, bending to open an angled door no more than four feet at its tallest point. *"Luca? Stella? È Matteo!"*

The door was wedged closed. The builder yelled, *"Aspetta!"* – Wait! – but it was too late.

Matteo yanked hard and the door opened, showering the hallway in debris as the wall crumpled. Darcy leapt back, registering the faint sound of screaming children. Matteo fell, holding his head.

Bingley leaned over him. "He's bleeding, Darcy. He appears to have been struck by something."

"Here." Darcy handed Bingley his handkerchief. "Get him outside."

The builder looked behind the door; there was not room to squeeze in, and it was too dangerous to move the rubble. He pulled a sledgehammer out of a loop on his belt. Yelling at the children to stay where they were, he took the hammer to the wall, opening a section beneath the short flight of stairs that rose to the landing.

Darcy removed his jacket; it would only hamper him. Kneeling, he put his head and shoulders into the hole. He called out, using the soothing tone he reserved for skittish horses. *"Luca. Stella. Sono il signor Darcy. Venite da me."* Come to me.

"Dov'è Matteo?" Stella, asking for her brother.

"Va bene, piccolo; Matteo è fuori. Venite." All is well, little one; Matteo is outside. Come.

He heard movement and waited until he could see a small face. Reaching forward, he carefully pulled Luca out. Stella crawled out behind her brother. Darcy lifted the trembling children into his arms; making haste for the door, he exited the house to find the entire Bianchi family waiting anxiously around Matteo.

The children cried out and their mother enveloped them in a tight embrace. Darcy pushed a hand through his hair. "What else is there to do?" he asked, turning back to the burning buildings.

They worked through the night. Darcy took a turn at the bucket brigade, helped wedge a support beneath a sagging beam, and searched the rubble for survivors. As dawn broke, they were clearing debris from the streets. The fire was out and the remaining buildings safe; once the streets were navigable, the builder called a halt.

Darcy was exhausted, filthy, and starving. He and Bingley made their way to where the ladies served a simple meal of bread, cheese, grapes, and fresh water. Elizabeth and her younger sister were there, but he could not see Georgiana. He looked around, suddenly alert.

"Mr. Darcy," Elizabeth called out to him.

He turned his head slightly, eyes still seeking his sister.

"Have no fear, Mr. Darcy. Georgiana is well. She returned to our lodgings several hours ago with Jane and Nanna."

He looked at her properly then, heaving a great sigh of relief. Her face and clothes were soot-smudged, her curls drooped and there were dark circles under her eyes, but she smiled – a genuine smile, carrying no trace of mockery or contempt – and offered him a colorful ceramic plate piled high with food.

"Please," she said. "It has been many hours since you last took any refreshment."

He took it, giving her a tired smile in return.

~ * ~

It was midafternoon before Darcy rose from bed; he had slept through the bright, hot midday without so much as stirring. He entered the sitting-room to find the ladies gathered, along with Mr. Bennet. The older man appeared drawn, as though he had slept little, but his eyes were as sharp as ever.

"I owe you an apology, Mr. Darcy. I am not too proud to admit when I am wrong. You may have been late to enter the fray, but you worked as hard as any man there."

"You were not wrong, Mr. Bennet," Darcy admitted. "My intent was to escort my sister to our lodgings. I am ashamed to say that it was only Signora Bianchi's fear for her children that persuaded me to stay. Once I was there, I found I could not leave."

Mr. Bennet shrugged. "It matters not. In the end you stayed, and you were a great help to these people."

Darcy shook his proffered hand. "Call me Darcy, if you would, sir."

"I shall be pleased to do so. Call me Bennet."

When they were all assembled, they returned to the scene of the fire. More work had been done while they slept to remove debris and stabilize the most dangerous structures, including the Bianchi home. Signor Bianchi stood next to the builder, who gestured toward the ruined eastern side of the building.

"Signor Darcy!" Matteo Bianchi hurried toward him, carrying his jacket from the night before. He had left it in the Bianchi home, he realized. He was reaching for it when Signora Bianchi shooed her son out of the way. Before he knew what was happening Darcy found himself bent forward, his jaw cradled firmly in Signora Bianchi's hands as she kissed his cheeks with enthusiasm. She held on, clearly thanking him effusively, but speaking so rapidly that he could make out perhaps one word in three.

She released him only for Signor Bianchi to envelop him in a bone-crushing hug, weeping openly and saying something about his children's safety. Teresa Bianchi came forward carrying Luca, who reached out for Darcy. The young woman promptly handed him the child and Luca wrapped his arms around Darcy's neck, laying his small head on Darcy's shoulder.

He looked to Bingley in confusion. Bingley laughed, thumping Signor Bianchi heartily on the back. "Darcy, you look as flummoxed as I have ever seen you! They are thanking you, man! Be gracious for once."

Stella stepped from behind her sister's legs, shyly holding up his now-clean handkerchief and a flower. Kneeling to take them, he thanked her very politely.

Signor Bianchi scooped up his youngest daughter. Eyes still brimming with emotion as he regarded the boy in Darcy's arms, he indicated his home and the other children as he spoke. Darcy could not quite catch his meaning, though he heard the word *"famiglia"* several times.

His difficulty must have been evident, for Miss Bennet stepped forward. "Mr. Darcy, you are now considered family. You are to treat the Bianchi home as though it were your own – once it has been repaired, of course."

Signora Bianchi patted Darcy's cheek and spoke rapidly, indicating her eldest daughter. The girl blushed, eyes on the ground.

Miss Bennet's mouth quirked up ever so slightly. "I am bidden to tell you that Teresa is as yet unpromised, should you be in want of a wife."

Bingley barked a laugh and clapped his shoulder; even Georgiana tittered behind her hand. Fortunately, Elizabeth stood out of his line of vision. He could not have borne to see her laughing at him. Darcy's face was aflame, and he could not think of a thing to say other than, *"Grazie."*

He looked helplessly at Miss Bennet, who took pity on him. She graciously explained that, while he was exceedingly grateful and Signorina Bianchi was quite lovely, he would not think of taking her away from her family. Eyes twinkling, she added that Luca appeared to have claimed Darcy for his own, in any event.

Everyone laughed, even Darcy. He looked down to see that Luca's eyes had drifted closed. Signora Bianchi offered to take him, but Darcy declined. He found he rather liked the weight of the boy in his arms.

At Mr. Bennet's suggestion the entire group made their way to the *Piazza del Duomo*, to take a meal at the charming café on its northern side. The cathedral came into view, its façade warmed by the late afternoon sun.

Darcy stopped, his breath caught, as though seeing it for the first time. He took in the gorgeously carved bas-reliefs covering the cathedral's marble base and the large latticed circular window high above the central door. The great golden mosaics above each of the doors and below the roof shone brilliantly.

"Extraordinary," he breathed.

"Indeed, Mr. Darcy." Elizabeth's voice broke into his reverie. She stood beside him, her hands crossed over her heart. "The mosaics celebrate Mary, you know. I think, perhaps, she was watching over all of us last night." She glanced up at him with a small smile and moved on, catching up to her sisters.

Darcy followed, smiling, the unfamiliar feeling of hope rising in his chest.

CHAPTER SIXTEEN

IN WHICH HAPPINESS COMES IN WAVES

Napoli, August 2nd, 1816

Dearest Charlotte,

It is an extraordinary thing to be adopted, particularly when one is not properly an orphan! There is no mistaking it, however; we have all been definitively claimed by Signora Bianchi, and thus by the entire Bianchi family.

The week after the fire saw a veritable whirlwind of activity. Between preparations for Isabella's wedding and repairs on the homes that burned, there was sufficient work for a score of women and twice as many men. The townspeople threw themselves into it with great determination, and we worked alongside them. Jane and I sewed until our eyes crossed, and Georgiana and Lydia arranged endless flowers and ribbons and lace.

And oh, Charlotte, the cooking! Were it only for my mother to decide, you know I should never have seen the inside of a kitchen, so I must be grateful to Great-Grandma Bennet for insisting that we learn something of the culinary arts. Nonna Bianchi took the ladies under her wing – even Georgiana, who has never so much as browned toast in her life! – and taught us to make a half-dozen different types of pasta with sauce, how to roast boar, and the secret of a delightful lemon cake that I would happily eat at every meal!

The men, meanwhile, were building. I would not have believed that an English gentleman could be publicly parted with his waistcoat and jacket under any circumstance short of grievous injury, but we have seen Mr. Darcy and Mr. Bingley in shirtsleeves so often over the two weeks past that it has nearly lost its ability to shock us! The men built a lovely pergola for the wedding, patched the roof and repaired the staircase and the upper floors of the Bianchi home, and rebuilt the stables. Had I not seen the buildings rise with my own eyes, I should have insisted that they were magicked into place, so quickly did they appear!

Isabella's wedding was not at all like an American or English affair. The ceremony included a Catholic Mass, and the party lasted until the wee hours of the morning. There was food enough to feed an army and my feet are yet sore from dancing! Even Mr. Darcy was not permitted to sit out the revels. He fancies himself formidable and is quite used to his own way, but no man refuses an Italian mother! I shall not soon forget Georgiana's expression at seeing her curmudgeonly brother bullied into dancing the trescone!

I am most grateful to my new Italian mamma for passing on a remedy for stomach ailments. Candied ginger worked delightfully to ease my wretchedness on the seas between Civitavecchia and Napoli. The remedy also came with exceedingly detailed advice to Jane and me on the subject of marital relations and childbearing; Mamma Bianchi rightly assumed that our own mother had said nothing of this, and her insistence that young ladies should not be left in ignorance was gratifying.

Less pleasing was her stern admonishment to cease toying with the hearts of Mr. Bingley and Mr. Darcy and marry them forthwith. Jane attempted to explain, but the dear woman simply waved her away. She said, "Men are impossible. Marriage is impossible. Life is impossible, and yet we live anyway. You find a good man, my girls, and you get on with it." I thought instantly of your determined pragmatism. (Did I mention, my dear friend, that Mamma Bianchi's Christian name is Carlotta? Fate shows her hand again!)

Mamma Bianchi's final piece of wisdom was to avoid Rome just now, as the city shall be empty of all who have the means to travel to the sea for the month of August. Thus we are off to Amalfi, where they make some of the finest paper in the world. I shall be sure to send you a parcel of blank sheets with my next letter!

With great affection,

Elizabeth

Amalfi, August 1816

"Oh, Fitzwilliam! We are truly to spend a month here? How glorious!"

"Indeed, Georgiana. We must remember to send Signora Bianchi a gift in thanks for her recommendation."

Elizabeth was entranced. The ferry from Napoli had taken them past a dozen seaside towns, though Amalfi was the most charming yet. Brightly colored buildings rose high above the vivid blue water, tucked into the terraced hillside. People strolled along the beachside walk and ladies cavorted in the calm waters behind a protective sea-wall. Boats large and small plied the harbor, and the masts of several pleasure vessels bobbed next to a nearby pier.

The travelers soon set out to explore the town. Jane and Mr. Bingley walked companionably together; Jane had shared no details, but the past month had produced a substantial thaw in her demeanor. The entire party watched the two of them together with great interest, while trying very hard to look as though they paid them no attention at all.

Poor Jane. She so hates to be the center of attention. Elizabeth noted her own satisfied smile mirrored on the faces of the others. *I suppose Mr. Bingley should get on with it, so we may all be captivated by something else.*

Jane took Mr. Bingley's arm as the street rose steeply ahead of them, and Elizabeth caught a snippet of their conversation: Jane was describing New York City, which stood in stark contrast to the various towns they had visited in Italy. They turned into another narrow street, which widened suddenly into a piazza as it descended toward the sea. A steep staircase of plain gray stone formed much of the east side of the piazza; Elizabeth's eyes followed it up and she halted, staring in astonishment.

Amalfi's cathedral perched atop the hill. Its façade was like nothing she had ever seen: intricate Moorish arches and a mosaic pattern of stone, which alternated black and warm golden tan in the bright sun, gave the church a distinctly Eastern appearance. The blocky bell tower ended in an elegantly decorated column which hid the bells behind more Moorish arches.

"Oh, why did I not bring my sketchbook!" Lydia groaned.

Elizabeth nodded; she could hardly wait to draw this building.

"We shall be here a full month, my dears," said Nanna. "There is yet plenty of time. Perhaps we should see about acquiring some paper." She pointed at a shop across the square and Lydia eagerly led the way.

Mr. Darcy fell in beside Elizabeth. "I am curious about how one would convey the manner in which the bricks seem to glow in the sunlight with only charcoal."

She turned to look again at the cathedral. "Such a feat would require more talent than I possess. I shall use pastels. I keep them on hand for just such a subject, when charcoal is insufficient."

The Gallo *Cartoleria* boasted some truly remarkable papers, however. Elizabeth seized one and held it up. "See here, Mr. Darcy, this marbled paper is perfect! The colors are so subtle, and just the shade of the Duomo at this time of day. I need not use my pastels after all!"

"We call our Duomo the *Cattedrale di Sant'Andrea,* and the way it looks in the afternoon sun was the inspiration for that paper," said a young woman in heavily accented English. "We make smooth paper, for ink or charcoal. Also rough paper, for pastels. Which do you prefer?"

"The smooth, please," said Elizabeth. The young woman placed a thick envelope into her hands. "You make this paper?"

"*Sì.* I am Francesca Gallo, and my family has made this paper for generations. We also make plain paper – very high quality, for writing – but we are known for the marbled papers." She gestured at the wide selection, in a veritable rainbow of colors. "We are inspired by the world around us. For example – *scusi,* I cannot help but notice that the color of your eyes is remarkable." The girl was looking intently at Elizabeth's eyes. "May I see them in the sunlight?"

Amused, Elizabeth walked to the window; people had stared at her eyes for as long as she could remember, but rarely with this open display of enthusiasm. Lydia and Mr. Darcy followed.

Miss Gallo looked closely at Lydia. "You are her sister, *sì?*"

"Yes, I am."

"Then you have seen her eyes for years, but most people do not truly *look* at what is around them. Look now; what colors do you see?"

Lydia stared at Elizabeth for a long moment. "Amber, mostly, though I see gold and even some copper when she turns her head toward the sun. And there is a dark brown ring surrounding the amber."

Miss Gallo grinned. "*Esattamente!* We shall make a special paper for you, Miss…"

"Elizabeth Bennet. You certainly need not go to the trouble!"

"No trouble at all; it will be a pleasure! Would you like to see how it is done?"

"Oh, yes! *I* should like it above all things!" Lydia bounced in her eagerness.

"I am certain we should all like to see how the marbled paper is made," Elizabeth said. "Will it be a difficulty, to have so many strangers looking on?"

"No, Papà will not mind if we are careful. Come, I will show you."

~ * ~

The following month flew by. On a lazy afternoon, Elizabeth sat at a table on the edge of the beach. She had a delightful view of the water and the nearby pier, the masts of many small boats bobbing gently. She frowned at her sketch-book; she had been struggling with this drawing for the better part of an hour. *How does one capture the movement of the water as waves break upon the shore?*

Nanna and Jane approached from the direction of the town. "You were quite fortunate to find a table so well-shaded, Lizzy," Nanna said, seating herself beside Elizabeth. "The cartoleria is not far to walk, but at this time of day I am glad to be out of the sun!"

Elizabeth laughed. "This table is dearer than a seat at Lady Matlock's gala! I dared not join Georgiana and Mr. Darcy on their walk along the shore, for fear of having nowhere to sit afterward. I have fended off three English ladies in the past half-hour!"

"Were they the Mrs. Wentworth sort or the Lady Middleton sort?"

"Worse even than Lady Middleton! Two of the Miss Bingley sort and a Miss Elliot!"

Nanna chuckled. "Well, you need no longer defend our position alone, for I shall not be moved from this spot." She handed Elizabeth a card. "Lydia asked that I bring this to you."

Lydia had visited the Gallo Cartoleria nearly every day over the month since Francesca Gallo's demonstration of paper-marbling. That first day they had gathered around a tray of shallow water, fascinated as Signorina Gallo dragged a thin reed through the ink floating on the water's surface to create an elegant pattern that adhered instantly to the paper. Each of them had taken a turn, though Lydia was particularly keen to experiment. On subsequent visits, with some trial and error, Lydia had begun to create pictures with the ink: this image was a collection of sunflowers against a green marbled background.

"Oh!" Elizabeth cried. "This is her best yet! She shall soon be begging Grandpa for a portable paper studio to carry with us to Rome, I daresay."

Jane smiled fondly. "She has done so already, Lizzy, and he means to indulge her. He was discussing the necessary supplies with Signor Gallo when we left the shop."

"That is only a small part of it, Jane," Nanna said. "He means to import their paper, too. Your dear Mr. Bingley has taken quite an interest; he was most attentive during the negotiation."

Jane no longer attempted to deny her claim to Mr. Bingley's heart. He appeared to court her more assiduously than he had done even in Hertfordshire, but though she clearly received his attentions with pleasure, she kept her own counsel on the matter. Indeed, she was often pensive and carefully noncommittal when his name was mentioned.

"It can only be to his benefit to observe Grandpa's skill at negotiation," Jane said. "Do you think that marbled paper shall be popular in New York, or is it to travel only as far as England?"

"Oh, it shall do very well in New York."

Elizabeth returned to her sketch. Jane had spoken often of New York since their arrival in Amalfi. She had developed no more fondness for England than had Elizabeth during their months there, but this longing for New York was new.

Perhaps Jane's homesickness is due to the necessity of choosing between the man she wishes to marry and the home she loves. Elizabeth privately believed that Mr. Bingley and England was a far better choice than the alternative. She had contrived to mention Mr. Pringle's name at dinner the previous evening, when the conversation had again turned to New York.

Jane's look of wistful nostalgia had sobered at once. Elizabeth had been obliged to explain to the gentlemen that Mr. Pringle was the presumptive heir to the Bennet-Janssen shipping empire, in the absence of a male relation willing to assume the mantle. Mr. Bingley offered his condolences on the prospect of seeing the company fall outside family hands; Nanna had winked at Elizabeth.

Georgiana and Mr. Darcy now came into view, heads turning at a shout from the captain of a small sailboat coming up alongside them. Mr. Darcy secured the line the man tossed and lent him a hand up to the pier, looking for all the world as though he had done it all his life. They chatted affably as they walked ashore, where they were joined by Grandpa and Mr. Bingley.

Elizabeth considered Mr. Darcy. His manners had improved considerably over the two months past; he was often congenial, particularly within their small group. He also appeared easier among strangers, though this only held true with

Italians. Amongst the few other English tourists in Amalfi, Mr. Darcy was as unbending as ever.

As for his manner toward herself, Elizabeth knew not how to interpret it. Mamma Bianchi had insisted that he admired her, though Elizabeth felt that his behavior could not possibly be mistaken for courtship. He was no longer silent and standoffish, true, but neither was he tender or devoted; rather, he was cordial and gentlemanly, often engaging her in spirited debates. She thought, perhaps, that they were becoming friends.

Mr. Bingley bounded up to the table, the others following at a more sedate pace. "Darcy has hit upon a capital idea! Our new friend there has a sailboat and is willing to take us out this evening to see the sunset from the water. There is room for all, though it might be a bit snug. Who shall join me?" He looked eagerly at Jane. "Do say yes, Miss Bennet!"

"It would be a pleasure, Mr. Bingley," said Jane with a demure smile.

"Miss Elizabeth? The sea is very calm this afternoon."

Georgiana give a tiny shake of her head. Elizabeth looked between Mr. Bingley and Mr. Darcy, mind whirling. *Can it be that Mr. Darcy is as conniving as any matchmaking mamma?*

Elizabeth put on a regretful expression. "I confess that I cannot look forward with pleasure to even so brief a time aboard, with our ship's departure for Rome only a few days hence, Mr. Bingley. But on no account should my desire to remain on land prevent anyone from enjoying the scheme."

"Mr. Bennet and I shall be delighted to join you," Nanna said. "I have so many questions about sailing, and I cannot bear to pass up the opportunity to put them all to a man who cannot run away!"

On return to their lodgings Mr. Darcy excused himself to attend to his correspondence. Lydia returned from the cartoleria, wild to know Elizabeth's opinion on every detail of her portable studio.

"Oh, la!" she said to Mr. Bingley's invitation. "What is a sunset? I am sure I have seen ever so many from the deck of a ship by now."

Elizabeth suppressed a grin; hopefully Jane had not noticed Lydia's giggle at the end of that speech. *Now it is time for Mr. Darcy and Georgiana to bow out.*

She had expected Georgiana to claim fatigue or illness, but such theatrics proved unnecessary. Mr. Darcy came into the room, his expression grave. Elizabeth's amusement soured; she did not believe Mr. Darcy to be a capable actor.

"I must apologize, Bingley," he said. "Georgiana and I must forego the pleasure of the cruise this evening. I have received some news from home which concerns us both, and which shall require some discussion before we may decide on a course of action. Pray excuse us."

There was a brief silence after they departed. Elizabeth looked at the clock. "Mr. Bingley, if you are to be on the water before the sun dips below it, you must go now."

"Perhaps we should postpone our outing," he replied, frowning. "I hope Darcy's news is nothing too serious."

"We know nothing as yet," said Elizabeth, "so for now we may do naught but wait. You may do that just as well on the water as on land, and far more pleasantly, I wager."

"Lizzy is right. It is useless to sit here and fret," said Jane. "Mr. Darcy did not ask us to delay, after all."

Jane's endorsement was all that Mr. Bingley needed, and the party of four set off.

"Well, Lizzy," said Lydia, "we may as well pass the time by doing what we said we were going to do. I truly do wish to show you the plans for the studio. I only hope Mr. Bingley is not so daft as to go the whole evening without proposing!"

"Have no fear, Lydia. Even if Mr. Bingley is too daft to take advantage of such a carefully orchestrated opportunity, I have little doubt that he will soon find some means of speaking to Jane."

Elizabeth's concern was for Georgiana; the need to "decide on a course of action" suggested that she and Mr. Darcy might return to England rather than journey to Rome with the rest of them. She did not wish to look too closely at her distress over the idea. *It is Georgiana's company that concerns me; Mr. Darcy can do as he pleases.*

A few hours later Elizabeth sat, curled into her bedroom chair in her night rail and robe, a book laying unseen on her lap. The sailing party was to dine at a café on returning to shore, and Mr. Darcy and Georgiana had not emerged from their conference. She and Lydia had retired early after a quiet meal and a lively discussion of Lydia's ever-expanding dreams of establishing her own paper studio in New York.

Without the distraction of conversation, Elizabeth's mind insisted – quite against her better judgment – on speculating. *What might be Mr. Darcy's news, to cause him to look so? What might he decide to do? I cannot expect that he will give Georgiana's opinion equal weight in such a matter.* And, most disconcerting, her mind ignored her attempts to lie to herself. *Naturally I would miss Georgiana, but why does the thought of Mr. Darcy's departure trouble me?*

It was nearly midnight when her swirling thoughts were interrupted by a knock at her door, which opened to reveal Jane – still fully dressed – with windblown hair, flushed cheeks, and the most elated expression that Elizabeth had ever seen on her sister's usually serene face.

Jane caught her up in a tight hug. "Oh, Lizzy! I am so happy! It is too much; it is too much! Oh, why cannot everybody be as happy as I am!"

CHAPTER SEVENTEEN

IN WHICH DARCY SECOND-GUESSES HIMSELF

Rosings Park, Kent, 4ᵗʰ July 1816

Darcy,

I have never given much thought to the significance of this date, though I imagine our friends the Bennets are keenly conscious that today is the anniversary of their country's declaration of independence from England. I mention it because I have momentous news, which materially affects the independence of one who is dear to us both.

Two weeks after you left England, an express reached me at Pemberley. It was from Anne; her mother had suffered a fit of apoplexy and could neither speak nor move the limbs on her right side. The physician that our aunt employed is a hack, which Anne knows well. She begged me to send yours, and to come myself to Rosings.

I traveled with all possible speed. When I arrived, Aunt Catherine was awake but uncomprehending and incomprehensible, try though she did to speak. Her resentment had gone, and what remained was confusion and frailty. Anne remained admirably calm in the face of such a fearful event, but Mr. Collins's dire pronouncements were more than any of us could bear. I very nearly threw him bodily from the house, Darcy! Bless Mrs. Collins; she spirited him away before I could get my hands on him.

The physician was perhaps eighteen hours behind me, but sometime in the night our aunt became entirely insensible. By the time he arrived her breathing had become erratic. He waved a candle in front of her eyes and declared that there was nothing he could do – there was bleeding into the brain, and the pressure had done irreparable and inevitably fatal damage. She died later that morning.

You are wondering why I did not write immediately. I meant to, but Anne would not have it. She insisted that your journey was far more important, and she was quite as fierce as her mother ever was! Besides, there is nothing you could have done here which cannot be managed by myself and my father.

I am also to assure you that you are in no way to blame for any of this. Our aunt was enraged at what she viewed as your "abandonment," but Anne rightly points out that her mother lived in a perpetual state of outrage. Your physician's opinion is that no attack of fury was responsible; he blames a weak blood vessel in the brain.

It has now been three weeks. The rites are over, the will is read, and Anne is mistress of Rosings. Aunt Catherine left her in a sorry state of ignorance regarding the management of her estate – even I, with my paltry knowledge, am Solomon in comparison! I have remained at Rosings to assist her; we have had several meetings with her steward and made a tour of the property. It will please you to hear that the instructions you sent have been followed to the letter, and Anne has been most diligent in endeavouring to learn what she must know.

Pemberley continues to thrive; I have been in close correspondence with your steward, and Father made a visit to view the improvements with his own eyes. He sends his hearty approval. Anne is therefore the project which occupies me. She seems not to know how to behave, without her mother's domineering presence.

It puts me in mind of Georgiana, but where Georgiana is still young and has many excellent friends to guide her, Anne has spent twenty-seven years in comparative isolation. In desperation I have invited the Wentworths to Kent. Mrs. Wentworth, as you know, is the most excellent creature to walk the earth; if any person can befriend and guide our cousin in her new role, it is she.

I also entreated your physician to examine Anne, and while she does have weak lungs – illness and exertion make it difficult for her to breathe – there is nothing much the matter with her that fresh air and exercise cannot cure. He established a strict regimen of walking, and already she appears in greater health.

As for you and Georgiana, you must not think of returning early, solely on our account. As I write this, you are doubtless still attempting to accustom yourself to being in daily company with Elizabeth Bennet. By the time it reaches you, God knows where you shall be, and whether she has come to look on you with affection. I hope that she does, but even if it is not yet so, I entreat you to remain with her. Return to England only if it is necessary for some other reason.

Be assured that we are all well. Anne and my parents send their love, and we all look forward to hearing news of your adventures. Kiss Georgiana for me and give my best to Bingley and the Bennets.

— R. Fitzwilliam

Amalfi, 6th September 1816

Darcy set down Fitzwilliam's letter. By now he had read it so many times that he had committed it to memory, though he was no closer to understanding his own conflicted feelings about its contents.

When he had first read it the previous evening, he felt only stunned disbelief. Suddenly, no contrivance was needed to cry off the sunset cruise. He had registered the worried faces of his friends only dimly; it was Georgiana's anxious expression that had forced his mind into action.

Her initial shock was equal to his own, but she recovered more quickly. When he would have taken full responsibility for the apoplexy which ultimately claimed his aunt's life, she categorically refused to permit it. She had repeatedly returned his attention to his cousin's letter; when he persisted, she snapped at him.

"Fitzwilliam," she said, "you may rightly regard yourself as a powerful man, but even you are not God. You cannot strike down your family from afar!"

Her words had silenced him for a full ten minutes. Never before had he considered the hubris required to believe himself solely culpable for such a thing. He realized that his impulse to return immediately to England was borne of the same fruit, and Fitzwilliam had anticipated this. Had not his cousin gone to some pains to assure him that all was well in hand?

And surely, if he was honest with himself, Fitzwilliam was far better suited to assist Anne through these early, difficult months. His cousin's impulse to call for Mrs. Wentworth, rather than his own mother, was a stroke of genius. Anne Wentworth was a gentle, capable soul, far less likely to intimidate their fragile cousin. *Though perhaps not so fragile,* he thought, recalling Fitzwilliam's words.

He was deeply discomfited by another emotion, about which he would not have spoken to any other creature had Georgiana not confessed it as well: relief. They would never again be required to contend with their aunt's officious and infuriating manner of ordering the lives of all those in her sphere. *Anne must also feel some measure of relief. Her mother has shaped the whole course of her life, after all.*

And, he realized, had Aunt Catherine been aware that she could no longer communicate her wishes nor even move without assistance, she must have been exceedingly miserable. In such a case, her death could even be viewed as a kindness.

After a great deal of painful discussion, Darcy had felt honour-bound to suggest returning to England, despite his cousin's entreaties. He had not been surprised when Georgiana rejected the notion. She pointedly reminded him that nearly three months had passed since their aunt's death, and that another month at least would be required to see them home.

"Richard is right, Fitzwilliam," she had said. "There is nothing for either of us to do there. If we return now, we shall be of no meaningful assistance to Anne, and we shall both miss Elizabeth dreadfully. Pemberley shall always delight to have its master in residence, but otherwise I see no benefit to such a course."

Against such a well-marshalled argument, Darcy could not contend. They had both retired early, but he slept fitfully and was yet uneasy this morning.

Perhaps there shall be happy news at breakfast. Bingley, at least, appeared likely to have his dearest hopes gratified.

They were not to be kept long in suspense. No sooner were they all assembled than Mr. Bennet stood, looking profoundly satisfied, and announced, "Let this day be one of celebration. Our dear Jane has consented to marry Mr. Bingley."

Georgiana and Miss Lydia cried out in delight. Elizabeth – clearly already party to this news – embraced Bingley as a brother, and Darcy offered his hearty congratulations.

"Now, children, pray allow me to continue," Bennet said with mock sternness. "The happy news is not yet fully told."

Elizabeth looked a question at her sister, whose countenance radiated excitement and pleasure.

"The Bennets are doubly blessed this day. Not only do we gain a husband, grandson, and brother that any family would be proud to claim, but Bennet-Janssen gains its next chairman and majority shareholder." Bennet grinned at Bingley. "For all that you claim to be an Englishman to your last breath, my boy, we shall make a New Yorker of you yet!"

There was a collective gasp. Darcy sat, thunderstruck, staring at his friend.

Miss Lydia recovered first. "Truly, Mr. Bingley? You are to live in New York with Jane and take over the company?"

"Indeed, it is true. And you must call me Charles; we are to be brother and sister, you know."

"Oh, Charles! Thank you! Lizzy – oh, Lizzy, we are saved! I cannot believe it!" She clapped her hands, bouncing. "Goodbye, Mr. Pringle, you wretched old prune! My dear brother, I could just kiss you!"

"You must wait your turn, Lydia," said Elizabeth, grinning widely. "I do believe Jane has earned the right to go first."

Miss Bennet and Bingley both coloured at this, but then Miss Bennet kissed his cheek with an impish smile.

Miss Lydia strode purposefully to her soon-to-be brother. Instead of kissing him, however, she took his hand and shook it as firmly as any man. Her family laughed. So did Bingley, once he got over the shock of it.

"My dear Charles," Elizabeth said, "this is glorious news. We are, indeed, doubly blessed. You cannot know the depth of our gratitude."

Georgiana looked at Darcy, confusion written on her features. Darcy could only shrug.

"It is I who am grateful," said Bingley. "I must thank Providence for allowing me to become part of your family. But we must do something to celebrate; I can sit still no longer! Jane, dear, what activity shall we enjoy this morning?"

"I believe I should like to go sea-bathing. It is so much more pleasant to sea-bathe here than it was in England – the water is so pleasant and gentle! – and it shall be my last opportunity for a great while."

The idea was loudly seconded, and the entire party promptly set off. Darcy lagged behind, so lost in his own thoughts that he startled at Elizabeth's voice beside him.

"Pray, forgive me, Mr. Darcy," she said. "I have no wish to intrude upon your private reflections."

"Nay, Miss Elizabeth, I was woolgathering. Do continue."

"I was only thinking that in all the excitement of the morning, we have neglected you in your distress. You are well, I hope?"

Darcy looked at her, momentarily unable to speak. Her expression of kind solicitude never wavered; it felt like a soothing hand, stilling the turbulence of his thoughts. Without making the conscious decision to do so, he found himself telling her about his aunt's death, their final confrontation in the breakfast-room at Darcy House, and the nagging sense of guilt that he could not but feel, despite his sister's and cousin's best efforts to exonerate him.

She nodded, thoughtful. "They certainly mean well," she said at length, "but I believe they must be entirely mistaken."

"What?" He was so surprised that he halted in the middle of the street.

"Mr. Darcy," she said, taking his arm and leading him to the promenade. "Surely a gentleman of your understanding cannot be in error. Consider: your aunt did not, perhaps, handle life's irksome experiences with the sort of effortless grace which is always expected of ladies, but what of that? Was it not your pugnacious refusal to agree to her request that turned her fairly purple with rage? I must say, her anger is understandable. I am sure there is no more infuriating creature in all the world than a recalcitrant nephew."

Darcy stared. The words were absurd, but her mien was grave and earnest. *Can she be joking?*

She shook her head sadly. "A loving mother wants only what is best for her child. When she cannot beg, bully, or bribe a mere stripling of a boy into marrying her beloved daughter, naturally it affects her. She must certainly dwell on it, and the blood must pound in her head most fearfully."

A smile tugged at his lips. He opened his mouth to speak but she held up a hand, shaking her head firmly.

"Nay, Mr. Darcy, you need not say another word. You have convinced me utterly. How was her brain to suffer without grievous injury the assault of a word as terrible as '*no*'?"

He could not help it; he laughed. It was out of all proportion, but once he began, he found he could not stop. Elizabeth fought to maintain her serious expression, which only set him off again. Soon he was shaking with full-throated laughter. After some time, he became aware that passersby were staring; he controlled himself with an effort, still chuckling.

He met her dancing eyes. "Thank you, Elizabeth. Your point is well taken."

She coloured slightly. "You are very welcome, sir. I must join my sisters and Georgiana now; they have surely been wondering what has become of me."

He watched her go, heading for the protected cove where the ladies seabathed. He turned the other way and walked to the men's bathing area, where he found Bingley already in the water. Bennet reclined in a shaded beach chair; he looked curiously at Darcy but said nothing.

Darcy hired a bathing-machine and stripped out of his clothes in the cramped, hot quarters. The attendant rolled the wheeled cabin into the sea and Darcy emerged, gratefully allowing his nude body to sink into the cool water. He swam out to where Bingley floated, past the breaking waves.

"I say, Darcy, what kept you?"

"My self-importance required skewering," he said blandly, floating on his back. "Elizabeth obliged me. Her wit is exceedingly satirical, did you know? I had a great laugh at myself and I now feel quite at ease."

"Are you sure you are quite well? I cannot recall ever hearing you make such a speech."

He smiled. "I am well, Bingley."

"Are you not going to lecture me on the follies of taking up residence in America and devoting myself to a life of trade?"

Darcy sobered at Bingley's uncertain expression. "I was greatly surprised, as you no doubt observed. It is not what your father wished for you."

"No."

"Why do it, then?" Darcy found that he was genuinely curious.

Bingley paused before answering. *No doubt expecting my disapprobation*, Darcy thought.

"Jane does not wish to leave New York. I assumed at first that she must move to England, were we to marry. Then I spent a great deal of time talking with Bennet about his businesses. Did you know that they are also heavily invested in real estate? Two of his other children – the twins – manage that. Margaret handles the legal and financial aspects, and Andrew is the born salesman."

"His *daughter* handles the business, did you say?"

"Yes. He believes that Elizabeth is quite capable of running the shipping company, but her father won't hear of it. He insists that one of his daughters marry the man who will inherit."

Sudden realization struck. "Mr. Pringle, was it?"

Bingley laughed. "*Was*. Past tense. The man is of an age with their father, Jane says, deadly dull and disrespectful to women besides."

"Little wonder, then, that Miss Lydia was so ecstatic to hear your news this morning." Another thought occurred. "If this Mr. Pringle was their father's choice, how is it then that you shall supplant him?"

"Bennet is still the chairman and majority shareholder," Bingley said. "His son is the chief executive, but ultimately the decision is Bennet's to make."

"I do not envy you the political quagmire that awaits you, then."

Bingley grimaced. "Indeed. I do believe, though, that the reward shall be worth the effort."

"It was the promise of trade, then, that convinced you?"

"It was certainly enticing. What convinced me, though, was that when Jane asked what I love about England, I could think of nothing I love so well as her." He shrugged. "I have no estate, and I can certainly content myself with seeing my relations every few years. And with all respect, Darcy, I find the life of a gentleman quite difficult."

Darcy was intrigued. "How so?"

"It wants structure. I am always flitting about, trying to find something to occupy me. And a ridiculous amount of importance is placed on things of very little merit. In trade, at least, a man earns respect by his own efforts."

Darcy considered this. He had not been above splitting wood or patching a tenant's roof at Pemberley, much to his father's chagrin, but he had never done such hard manual labour in his life as during those last weeks in Orvieto. He had spent his days hot, thirsty and half-dressed and ended them dirty and sore, his hands blistered and bleeding. But he had felt real pride when he saw the Bianchi home restored. It was much like the pride he felt in knowing his tenants prospered, but it had a more tangible quality. And he was certain that exceedingly few men of his class had any such experience.

"I can find no fault in your reasoning, Bingley," he said at length. "I expect you and Miss Bennet shall be quite happy."

Bingley appeared to study him for a moment, before deciding that he was sincere. "Thank you, Darcy."

~ * ~

Darcy was in the dining-room nursing a glass of port when Georgiana found him.

It was very late. Most of the party had already sought their beds, but Darcy found himself unable to rest. His thoughts were too unsettled, though now for an entirely different reason than the previous night.

During dinner he had listened as the Bennet sisters enthusiastically detailed what Bingley must see and do in New York when he arrived. Elizabeth's face was animated as she spoke of her home, and her amusing anecdotes made even Darcy wish to visit.

Afterward Darcy had retreated to a chair in the corner of the drawing-room with a book. An astute observer would have noted that the pages never turned, however, and he had escaped to this room shortly after Mr. and Mrs. Bennet had retired. His thoughts returned, again and again, to Bingley's decision. Why had it stunned him so?

Because I cannot envision making it myself.

It had never occurred to him that Elizabeth might wish to remain in America; he had simply assumed that she would marry him and come to love Pemberley as he did.

And if she does not? What if, when pressed, she finds that she loves her homeland more than she loves me? Indeed, can she ever love me at all?

They had traveled together for over two months now, and he saw no sign that she returned any part of his regard. He had made an effort to amend that part of his character which most affronted her – his improper pride in the merits of his own class – and the only effect that he could see was that she no longer appeared to actively loathe him.

"What troubles you, Fitzwilliam?" Georgiana's voice was soft. She was in her night rail and dressing gown, hair in a long braid down her back.

Darcy was struck again by how very much she resembled their mother; at just seventeen, she was no longer the fragile girl who had been so bereft when their father died.

"I begin to think that I am a fool to be chasing after Elizabeth," he said. "She has no love for England or any of its society, myself included. Even were she to feel some affection for me, with Pemberley to look after I could hardly make Bingley's choice. How am I to win a lady who wants none of what I have to offer?"

Georgiana regarded him gravely. "Why do you believe that you have naught to offer her?"

"Did I not already explain? She wants none of my money, my position in society, nor my property. She believes she has my contempt, and why should she desire that?"

"Fitzwilliam. You must cease this self-pitying nonsense."

Darcy bridled; he had never heard her speak in that tone to anyone, much less to him.

"Listen to yourself," she went on. "I assure you that if she desired your money, your position in society, or your property, she would most certainly have your contempt." She fixed him with a challenging look. "Do you mean to tell me that, after two months spent in daily company, you know nothing of what makes Elizabeth happy?"

Darcy gaped at her. "Well…yes. No, I mean. I do know several things she enjoys."

Georgiana lifted a brow. "That is a start, at least." She sighed and took his free hand in hers. "My dear brother, I have no doubt that Elizabeth could make you happy. But if you make no efforts toward *her* happiness, she shall have no reason to do so. You must seek to learn not only what Elizabeth enjoys, but how she responds to the behaviour of others. What makes her laugh? When does she express affection? When is she sad or angry? When you understand what causes her to feel happy and loved, you shall find that you have a great deal to offer."

Darcy waited, but she said no more. "Can you not tell me what that is? Or perhaps you will not."

She shook her head. "You must discover it for yourself if your behaviour is to be genuine. Elizabeth cannot abide falsity."

"Indeed. She made that abundantly clear in London." He sighed. "So I must seek to know her better; not only her likes and dislikes but her joys and sorrows."

At her nod, he gave her a wry smile. "When did you become so wise?"

"When you encouraged me to spend time with so many wise friends." She squeezed his hand. "Will you hear one more piece of advice, Fitzwilliam?"

"Gladly. This day and night have proven that I should not be permitted to think on these subjects entirely on my own."

She kissed his cheek with a fond smile. "I thank you, then, for your faith in my counsel." She sobered. "We are likely to meet with far more of our countrymen in Rome than we have elsewhere. I have noticed that when we encounter other Englishmen here, you behave very much like your old self."

"Insufferably silent and disdainful, I suppose."

"Precisely. You must try to be sociable. Even when your silence is only due to disquiet, Elizabeth is likely to see it as pride."

"You know how I despise the barbed pleasantries and endless machinations of our set. I shall make an attempt, but I am not our cousin, or Bingley, to be affable with such people."

"Look to Mr. Bennet for your model, then. He seems to strike an admirable balance."

Darcy nodded slowly. "He does. Perhaps I shall ask him how he manages it."

CHAPTER EIGHTEEN

IN WHICH DARCY SEES THE LIGHT

Piazza di Spagna, Rome, 26ᵗʰ September 1816

Fitzwilliam—

We have been two weeks in Rome and have barely scratched its surface. This city is vast, labyrinthine, and humbling, particularly when one is among the ancient sites. After all, Rome had been an established city for centuries by the time the Colosseum was constructed – only a few decades after the Roman invasion of Britain! Bingley and Miss Bennet in particular are wild for ruins; we were nearly forced to drag them bodily from the Forum yesterday so that we might keep a dinner engagement.

Unlike our previous destinations, Rome hosts a sizable community of British citizens. In the main, these are wealthy families who have flocked to warmer climes now that Napoleon's wars are over. The Darcy name opens doors even here; within a day or two of our arrival we were receiving invitations, though some clearly regretted the impulse to include our party when they were introduced to our American friends. Nor have they been reticent in expressing their contempt.

The Bennet ladies suffer the worst of it: snickering behind fans, conversations that suddenly cease when they appear, and the like. A few matrons have been so bold as to compliment my forbearance for travelling in such low company. One, a Mrs. Kingsley, did not even have the courtesy to lower her voice, with Elizabeth not ten steps distant! I could conjure no response to such appalling behaviour. I attempted to apologize for my countrywoman, but – alas – Elizabeth remarked upon the pot calling the kettle black and left me at the billiard-room.

Mr. Bennet fares better. You will appreciate his advice on mingling in offensive company: "If I can, I discover one thing I can admire about a person, and cling to it. Failing that, I imagine them in a state of public undress." I have endeavoured to put this into practice and am startled by my success. Just today, Bingley ventured to predict that my days of being a "glowering barnacle on the wall of every drawing-room in society" may be at an end.

A very few months has wrought such a change inside me – was it only April when I was spouting nonsense about it being a degradation to marry Elizabeth? – that I can no longer hear my own opinions reflected in those of my countrymen. Indeed, the English have begun to treat me with the same contempt they show the Bennets. It is delightful to enter a room without being marked as an object of prey!

I now prefer those with more open attitudes and demonstrative temperaments. Paolo Alessi, for example, reminds me greatly of you; he is the eldest son of a prominent Venetian family and shares your friendliness and insouciant wit, but also your pragmatism and determination. He has agreed to aid my current campaign, which is to persuade Elizabeth that I have left the stain of pot and kettle behind me. Perhaps, between us, we may endeavour to equal your success in the field.

— Darcy

Rome, October 1816

The day was rainy and cold; Darcy was grateful that their party had chosen to visit the museums on the Capitoline Hill. Viewing the collection had taken the whole of the afternoon: the rooms were large, each overstuffed with paintings and sculptures, the ceilings covered with frescoes. Most of the group had wandered ahead, but Darcy stood with Paolo Alessi before a bust of Emperor Commodus. The sculpture portrayed a curly-haired, bearded man with a lion's pelt draped over his shoulders, the lion's great mouth with its sharp teeth perched atop his head.

"The good Emperor gives new meaning to the term 'pretentious'," Darcy said. "Portraying himself as Hercules is quite a stretch, given his lackluster abilities."

"*Sì*, the Romans had quite a flair for self-worship," said Paolo. "This is nothing, though, in comparison with Nero. Recall that he commissioned a statue of himself so large that the amphitheatre next to it was nicknamed the Colosseum in reference to the statue." He smiled at an elegantly dressed middle-aged woman who approached as they spoke. "Men have been exaggerating their prowess for centuries; would you not agree, Your Grace?"

"A statement with which no woman could possibly disagree," she said.

The woman was Duchess Rutherford. Though already in her middle forties she was still handsome, slim and impressively buxom, with occasional glints of silver in her caramel-coloured hair. Married while still quite young to the duke, then in his fourth decade of life, she had been quietly exiled from England when the rumours of her extramarital exploits became too numerous to ignore. She had been holding court in Italy for a decade.

This was a fortuitous meeting, Darcy realized; the duchess was, for all intents and purposes, the *grande dame* of English society in Rome. To be approved by her was to be welcomed – nay, sought after – elsewhere. She introduced them to her dear friend Lady Whiting, a very respectable English widow who had decamped to Italy following the death of her husband.

The duchess's speculative gaze raked over Darcy, evidently pleased with what she saw. "I am fascinated by the sight of an English gentleman condescending to befriend a Venetian. How did you become acquainted?"

"We met at the fencing club, *madama*," Paolo said. "I was foolish; I told the fencing-master that he must find me a more worthy opponent than these young Roman *zerbinotti* – ah, what is the English–?"

"Popinjays?" the duchess asked.

"*Esattamente!* Young fools with loud mouths and flimsy swords. Three days later, he introduced me to this man." He nodded at Darcy, who flashed a predatory smile in return. "Now I am the *zerbinotto*. It is well that I have a forgiving heart, for what man likes to have his pride fed to him like a jellied eel?"

The duchess's eyes danced with amusement. "He is a proper Englishman, then; they can afford to condescend when they know themselves to be superior."

Paolo laughed. "Indeed! The English exclaim over our art and history, but when they meet an Italian they look as though they are sucking on a lemon. Darcy here surprised me, though. He is easier with my countrymen than his own."

"How singular!" said Lady Whiting. "Of course, the English typically find Americans even more distasteful than they do Italians, but I understand that you travel with a party of Americans, Mr. Darcy."

"Yes, the Bennets of New York. My friend Charles Bingley is engaged to Miss Bennet, and she and Miss Elizabeth are my sister's particular friends."

"I should have imagined that a man with your reputation would find such company very trying."

Darcy coloured. "I confess I did, when I first knew them in Hertfordshire. Longer acquaintance and the close companionship of shared travels has altered my opinion."

"One does not often hear that shared travel *improves* a man's opinion of his companions," Duchess Rutherford said. "Pray, in what manner?"

"I have developed a keen appreciation for their forthright honesty and habits of industry. Disguise and indolence of every sort are my abhorrence. The *ton* is regrettably thick with both."

"Then you must understand my love of Italy. Pray, do tell us more about the Bennets. I have heard only the prevailing English sentiment."

"Mr. Bennet is an excellent man. He is a brilliant businessman, as was his father before him, and his wife and granddaughters are clever and well-educated. The family moves in the first circles in New York, but when the neighbourhood near our lodgings in Orvieto was aflame, not one of them gave a second thought to lending their hands to the task of dousing the fire and caring for the towns-people."

At the ladies' exclamations, Darcy told the tale. "The Bianchi family was exceedingly welcoming and generous," he finished. "I believe it was that night, and the weeks that followed, that taught me to fully admire those qualities in my American – and Italian – friends that I had previously disdained."

"How very remarkable," said the duchess. "I must meet these paragons for myself."

"I shall be happy to introduce you. I believe they are just in the next room." Darcy led the way, coming face-to-face with Elizabeth as he crossed the threshold. Her gaze was surprised, assessing – as though she were seeing him anew.

"I thank you for your kind words about my family, Mr. Darcy," she murmured as they made their way to where her grandparents stood.

"It is no more than the truth, Miss Elizabeth."

Introductions proceeded with all the usual civilities, and the two ladies joined them for a time as they continued through the museum. The entire party stood before a portrayal of *The Rape of the Sabine Women* for long minutes, the gentlemen silent as the ladies viewed it with varying degrees of horror and fury.

"Why are the women being taken?" Georgiana asked.

"Legend has it that the newly-founded city of Rome was populated almost entirely by men," the duchess said. "The Sabine men would not permit their daughters to marry the Romans, so the Romans abducted the women instead."

"The artist's sympathies appear to be with the women," said Miss Lydia. "See how the anguish in their faces is rendered with such care! And this small boy is furious! Perhaps it is his mother or sister being carried off."

"The abduction and rape of women in war is one of the oldest stories there is," Mrs. Bennet said grimly. "It happens to this day. Legend also says that the Sabine women were given all the rights of honorable wives by their Roman captors, but many women are not so fortunate."

Elizabeth lifted a brow. "One could argue that marriage – for a lady – is not so very different even now. Many ladies may choose the man who shall remove them from their home and all they have known, but by no means all. And a lady is under the power of that man, for good or ill, for the remainder of her life."

Darcy was astonished. He had never considered that a lady might object to marriage in its own right. He saw his astonishment mirrored on Bingley's face, and even Georgiana's, but Bennet merely looked at his granddaughter sadly.

"Perhaps not all their lives," said Lady Whiting. "A woman may become independent after marriage."

"She must inevitably suffer to do so," added Duchess Rutherford, with a significant look at her friend.

Elizabeth coloured. "I am sorry, my lady. I have no wish to cause you pain."

Lady Whiting shook her head firmly. "Nay, my dear. I may speak of my husband now without distress. Nor should you be ashamed to desire that a woman's lot might be better than dependence and – should she be bound to an intemperate man – wretchedness and fear."

"Our lot need not be so, Lizzy," Miss Bennet said quietly. "Consider Aunt Margaret. She sits at the helm of a highly successful business and is married to a wonderful man."

Elizabeth looked dubious, but she said nothing more. The duchess, who had never crossed the Atlantic, turned the subject by inquiring with great interest about America generally and Elizabeth's Aunt Margaret particularly. She was fascinated by Mr. and Mrs. Bennet's descriptions of American society and the beauties of the countryside; she soon declared her desire to make a visit.

"I shall make my first visit next year," said Bingley with a wide grin. He eagerly described his plans to make his home there with Miss Bennet, to Duchess Rutherford's evident delight.

Elizabeth grinned at him, her wit already restored. "Shall we truly be able to pull you and Jane away from all these glorious ruins?" She leaned close to the duchess and Lady Whiting, as though sharing a secret. "Were dear Jane not so particularly attached to home, I fancy they would travel the world together with an ever-growing circus of children, in pursuit of ancient sites and precious relics to dig out of the ground."

There was general laughter; even Miss Bennet allowed that Elizabeth's conjecture was not far from the truth. Miss Lydia hurried to Elizabeth's side, her countenance filled with excitement.

"Lizzy, you are absolutely brilliant!" she whispered. "You have given me such a wonderful idea for a painting to give to Jane and Charles when they marry. What colour do you suppose Jane would like the tent to be for their tour around the world?"

~ * ~

Three weeks later Darcy reclined at his ease in Lady Whiting's music-room, entranced by the scene before him. His seat was carefully chosen so that he could see both ladies seated at the pianoforte. Together they made a study in contrast: Elizabeth in ivory and gold satin, her dark curls secured by mother-of-pearl combs, and Georgiana in sapphire velvet, a matching ribbon threaded through her fair hair.

He was immeasurably proud of Georgiana. She had ever been too anxious for public display, but with Elizabeth beside her she appeared calm and poised. The two of them had developed a great fondness for Rossini during their travels, and they particularly delighted in this opera: *Tancredi* was singular in that its title role, though a man, was written for a woman's voice. Elizabeth's rich contralto soared, contrasting with Georgiana's delicate soprano as doomed lovers Tancredi and Amenaide sang in fearful anticipation of the dangers to come.

Darcy could hardly breathe, watching.

The performance finished to resounding applause. Duchess Rutherford's approval of the Bennets had markedly improved their social standing, and Elizabeth and Georgiana were soon surrounded by admirers.

"Without doubt the most enjoyable performance of the evening," Bingley said.

"I could not agree more." Philippa Kingsley insinuated herself next to Darcy with a fawning smile.

Darcy frowned. He had been assiduously avoiding the Kingsleys since that evening when Mrs. Kingsley had so flagrantly insulted Elizabeth. With acceptance of the Bennets had come a renewal of his desirability, however; he once again felt himself a fox evading the hounds.

Miss Kingsley's too-thin frame was exquisitely garbed, patrician features framed by black curls. She had exhibited first this evening; her Mozart concerto was technically excellent but soulless to Darcy's ear. She was trailed by her cousin Annabelle Cooper, Sir Robert Kingsley's niece and ward.

Sir Robert's sister had died impoverished and pox-ridden, or so went the gossip. Her daughter Annabelle, now twenty-five and without face or fortune to distinguish her, was very nearly on the shelf. She stood next to Elizabeth, rolling her eyes in amusement at her cousin's excessive praise of Georgiana. "You were both delightful," she said, smiling with genuine warmth at Elizabeth and Georgiana.

Miss Kingsley pointedly ignored her cousin. She turned her admiration on Darcy, showering him with so many superlatives that he was tempted to roll his eyes as well. He caught Bingley's smug expression and smiled broadly.

"I say, Bingley, you must introduce Miss Kingsley to your sister. I daresay they would get on quite well."

"Oh, indeed, Charles!" Miss Bennet smiled at her alarmed fiancé with an enthusiasm so unlike her usual serenity that it could only be fabricated. "Have you been to Scarborough, Miss Kingsley?" She casually inserted herself next to Miss Kingsley, allowing Darcy to move away.

Darcy spoke in a low voice to Elizabeth. "Pray tell your sister that I owe her a large debt of gratitude for rescuing me just now."

She flashed him a grin and drifted away with Georgiana and Miss Cooper.

Darcy took a seat next to Bennet, among a group of older men debating the applications of the steam engine. Miss Kingsley was unlikely to attack him here, but he now had an excellent view of the Roman dandies stalking Elizabeth around the room. Seething and ready to pummel the lot of them, he watched as she skillfully evaded them all. They flirted and cajoled and leered at her, mocking each other mercilessly whenever she delivered a witty retort.

At length she appeared at her grandfather's side, looking wild-eyed and hunted. Darcy immediately vacated a space between himself and Bennet. Elizabeth dropped into it with her back to the corner, hidden by the knot of men who stood to acknowledge her.

"Please, gentlemen, do not halt your discussion on my account," she said. "Indeed, if I may be permitted an opinion, I look forward to the day when steam-powered locomotives may be the means of conveying travellers across the great distances of our country, rather than hauling only coal and timber."

"Ha! Bennet, you have addled your granddaughter's brain," barked Sir Robert Kingsley. "Steam engines cannot be made sufficiently reliable for a traveller's needs. Horses shall always be the superior means of carrying a man from one place to another."

The debate continued, but Elizabeth spoke only to Darcy. "I begin to understand your use of the fox as a metaphor. I must thank you for the kind offer of a seat in your den."

"Not at all. There is no surer means to the destruction of amorous intent than a discussion of the path of industry. Be assured, madam, that between myself, your grandfather and Bingley, we are prepared to shield you with patent law and mechanical engineering at a moment's notice."

She laughed in delight. "If there were only a topic on which young ladies could converse that was equally capable of defeating the feminine hordes. I should like to be able to return the favour."

"You must be the judge of whether any such topic exists, but failing that, I rather think that we have hit upon an acceptable substitute. Think you that steam engines may pull carriages in time?"

She did, and they spent a pleasant ten minutes in private discussion. Elizabeth was animated and exceedingly well-informed on the subject. Darcy listened attentively, asking several detailed questions. By the time he declared his confidence in the correctness of her conclusions, she had lost the wild-eyed expression.

She favoured him with a look that was at once skeptical and hopeful. "You are truly swayed by my opinion?"

"I am swayed by your superior information and your excellent reasoning," he said matter-of-factly. "I shall instruct my factor to inquire into the possibilities for investment in locomotion and railways, though I suppose I might simply ask your grandfather about his investments."

She coloured faintly and looked away, not quite hiding a giddy smile that warmed him to his toes. Suddenly her expression soured.

Darcy followed her gaze to the pianoforte, where Georgiana stood with Miss Kingsley and Miss Cooper. Miss Kingsley appeared to be pressing

Georgiana to play again; Georgiana was shaking her head, her discomfiture plain. Darcy's jaw clenched reflexively.

"Annabelle cannot protect her alone," Elizabeth said.

He looked at her, surprised.

She smiled faintly. "I think you would approve of Miss Cooper as Georgiana's protector, but Miss Kingsley is a formidable adversary."

"Indeed." He prepared to stand, mouth pressed into a grim line.

She rested her hand briefly on his knee. "Nay, please allow me. It is my turn, after all."

He sat back, stunned at the casual intimacy.

Her chin lifted in determination. "Once more into the breach, as the colonel would say." She approached the group with an apologetic smile, deftly disengaging Georgiana with a nod in Darcy's direction.

Miss Cooper gestured to the pianoforte with a look of entreaty. Miss Kingsley wore a challenging expression; even from his seat, Darcy could see that her next remark was cutting. Elizabeth merely smiled and sat down to the instrument as Georgiana joined him.

A hush fell as Elizabeth began a slow, somber ballad, her voice and mien the picture of grief. After the first verse Darcy finally recognized the words. It was a passage from *The Lady of the Lake*, though he had never heard it set to music.

By the time Elizabeth reached the final verse, the room was silent but for her:

> *"Like the dew on the mountain,*
> *Like the foam on the river,*
> *Like the bubble on the fountain,*
> *Thou art gone, and forever!"*

Silence hung in the air as the last note slowly faded. Georgiana was not the only lady to stifle a sob; Darcy swallowed past a lump in his own throat. Finally someone began to clap, and instantly the room rang with applause.

Lady Whiting approached the pianoforte, wiping at her cheeks. She embraced Elizabeth and closed the instrument. "Following such a performance we must recover our spirits with libations and wit," she said, "but we must give Miss Elizabeth a moment to compose herself before she is fit for laughter."

Elizabeth left the room through a side door, Miss Bennet wordlessly following.

"I have never heard her play that," Georgiana said. "It nearly broke my heart!"

"She played it at her cousin's funeral," Bennet said quietly. "Julia was eleven, Lizzy seventeen; they were very close. I have not heard it since."

"What did Miss Kingsley say to her?" Darcy asked.

"She said that Elizabeth might play whatever she wished; that nobody would pay her any mind," Georgiana said.

Bennet chuckled. "Some people have not the good sense to know when they are already beaten."

Perhaps ten minutes later they were approached by Lady Whiting. "Mr. Darcy," she said, "I wonder if you might do me a favour. The dear, obstinate duchess is determined that Miss Elizabeth's song was not *The Lady of the Lake* at all. May I entreat you to fetch my copy from the library? You should find it on the shelf to the right of the fireplace."

Darcy raised a brow at Duchess Rutherford; as machinations went, this was entirely transparent. She shrugged minutely and returned to her conversation.

"I am pleased to be of service, Lady Whiting."

The library appeared empty when he found it, but he soon discovered Elizabeth and her sister seated on a high-backed divan before the fireplace. Both looked to have recently been in tears. He apologized for disturbing them and explained his putative errand.

"In truth, however, I believe the duchess meant to give me an opportunity to see to your well-being. Is there anything I can do for your present relief?"

Elizabeth gave him a small, grateful smile. "Nay, Mr. Darcy, I thank you. I believe I need only a few minutes more to compose myself and restore my complexion before returning to the music-room."

"Then I shall carry out my errand and leave you in peace. First, however, may I say: you have my deepest condolences on your loss. That must have been a difficult piece to play; I stand in awe of your fortitude."

At her quiet thanks he turned to the bookshelves, readily finding the volume he sought. He was turning to depart when the door opened and Miss Kingsley slipped inside the room.

"At last we may have a private word, Mr. Darcy," she said.

Darcy signaled Elizabeth and Miss Bennet to remain where they were with his hand held low, hidden from Miss Kingsley by the divan.

"I cannot imagine what we might have to discuss, Miss Kingsley."

"Why, the terms of our marriage! We are alone here, and I am hopelessly compromised. I trust that you shall do all that is required."

Darcy drew himself to his full height and allowed his expression to fall into its old disdainful pattern. "I shall do no such thing, madam."

He had only time enough to see her self-assured triumph melt into aggrieved bafflement when the door opened again, admitting Miss Cooper.

"Ah, Philippa, here you are," she said, taking in Miss Kingsley's expression. "Your father is hard on my heels; I advise you to leave Mr. Darcy to his errand and depart the library at once. You may say you left the music-room to refresh yourself and were only just returning."

Miss Kingsley rounded on her. "Annabelle, you scheming hoyden! You cannot possibly believe that Mr. Darcy wants *you*. I demand you leave this instant!"

The door flew open, banging against the wall. Sir Robert was framed in the doorway, glaring thunderously at his daughter.

Miss Kingsley's countenance instantly transformed. "Papa! What brings you here? Annabelle and I were just helping Mr. Darcy search for a book."

Sir Robert took her firmly by the arm. "You need not feign innocence, Philippa. I have already told you that if you attempt to compromise the honor of a gentleman, I shall find you an acceptable husband forthwith. Mr. Darcy shall not be that man, however; his friendship with those Americans would bring shame upon our family. No offense intended, sir. I merely state fact." He propelled his daughter from the room.

"None taken," Darcy said with wry amusement. He grinned at Annabelle Cooper. "I thank you for your timely intervention, madam."

"I should fancy myself Perseus come to slay the Gorgon," she replied with a saucy smile, "but I am sure you needed none of my help. Indeed, I shall carry with me like a treasure the image of Philippa's countenance after you flatly refused her. Good evening, sir." She gently closed the door behind her.

After a moment Darcy said into the silence, "You are correct, Miss Elizabeth. I wholeheartedly approve of Miss Cooper."

Elizabeth and Miss Bennet rose from the divan wearing matching expressions of astonishment. "That was a lucky escape," Elizabeth said. "I am sorry not to have seen it, though! I so desperately wanted to peek!"

"Why did you wish us to remain hidden?" Miss Bennet asked.

"There was no cause to make you a target for Miss Kingsley's rancour. She was unlikely to be gracious when denied. And as much as it is considered un-gentlemanlike to disappoint a lady...."

"You must not concern yourself about Medusa's delicate sensibilities, Mr. Darcy," Elizabeth said. "I only pity the poor man her father shall bribe to wed her."

"Lizzy!" Miss Bennet's laughter belied her rebuke.

Darcy grinned. "Only imagine, though, the impressive statuary garden they shall have." He offered an arm to both ladies.

Elizabeth's eyes twinkled merrily. "I do hear that the Grecian aesthetic is all the rage."

They returned to the party, laughing companionably.

CHAPTER NINETEEN

IN WHICH ELIZABETH HAS A REVELATION

Piazza di Spagna, Rome, November 1ˢᵗ, 1816

My dear Charlotte,

Our time in Rome has provided quite an education! Quite aside from the ancient sites and glorious art, we have discovered that young ladies must leave the house armed with witty and cutting remarks in order to deflect the attentions of impertinent young men. The Romans call it "Il Gioco," as though it were the only game that existed. Even Georgiana has been forced to develop a talent for it, though dear Jane cannot bring herself to utter the bawdy, insolent comments that are most successful in causing a group of pursuing young men to call off the chase.

I would never say this to Mr. Darcy, but Il Gioco has been good for Georgiana. She came to Italy to learn to hold her own among the ton, and these appalling young Roman men have achieved in the space of a few weeks what I have not succeeded in teaching her in many months. Mr. Darcy has not witnessed the cleverness of her retorts – impertinent young men do not follow the ladies who are escorted by gentlemen – so he has observed her vastly improved confidence but does not know quite what to make of it.

Lydia, of course, has little difficulty with Il Gioco, despite being only sixteen. Her talent for snappy insults aside, it seems my mother was more farsighted than I dared hope: Lydia is far better company than when we departed home. I cannot imagine her character would be so improved if she were still among her wild and thoughtless friends. All she required, it seems, was a task sufficient to consume the greater part of her passion. In Hertfordshire it was our cousin Tommy. In Amalfi, the marbling of paper.

Since the announcement of Jane and Charles's engagement, she has campaigned for Grandpa and Nanna to give a masked ball; thus far her entreaties have been unsuccessful, but she perseveres!

Now to your most particular inquiry. Has my heart yet changed toward Mr. Darcy? It has, but perhaps not in the manner you hope. He certainly gives the appearance of having changed – he is easier in company, less disdainful, and I have glimpsed hints of humor in him. But if incivility is the very essence of love – leaving us so engrossed with one that we neglect all others – then I must I conclude I do not love him, for I find I can readily be civil around him. There is no comparison with Jane and Charles! None of us can hope to hold the attention of either for long when the other is near – and the other is always near!

With your example and Jane's before me, I am determined that I shall not marry unless I am first made exceedingly rude. If Nanna sees fit to deliver me a stern lecture about my inability to attend to anybody except The Man Himself – whosoever he might be – I shall know that I have, at last, discovered the one who must be my husband!

With greatest affection,

Elizabeth

Rome, November 19th, 1816

Elizabeth and Georgiana walked together to where Mr. Darcy awaited them at the *Fontana di Trevi*. He gazed idly at the fountain's intricately carved marble figures, a small wrapped package in one hand.

"You shall certainly find a delightful gift for Jane's birthday very soon, Lizzy." Georgiana's tone held not a hint of doubt. "Besides, there are two weeks yet."

Elizabeth smiled. "Your confidence, though perhaps misplaced, is heartening. It appears your brother has had better luck than I, however."

Mr. Darcy lifted the package he carried. "Yes, I found a book that I think Matteo will greatly enjoy."

"Fitzwilliam," Georgiana laughed, "I declare you have already bought half of Rome for the Bianchi family!"

"I am merely being a dutiful elder brother."

They set off toward their lodgings. "I daresay the Bianchi family has never had such a Christmas as they shall this year," Elizabeth said.

"And every year after, if my brother has his way. At this rate they shall soon require a larger house!" Georgiana affected a look of innocent curiosity. "Are we to return to Orvieto so that you may add another storey with your own hands, Fitzwilliam?"

Mr. Darcy gave her a look of mock indignance. "From whom did you learn to make sport of your devoted brother? It was not he, I am sure!"

"Why, from my dear friend Elizabeth, of course! Fear not, for she has also taught me to make sport of myself."

Elizabeth grinned. "I highly recommend it, Mr. Darcy. If you laugh at yourself, we shall all find it far more difficult to laugh at you."

"You presume that others are in the habit of laughing at me."

"Only where you cannot hear them," Georgiana said, patting his arm fondly. "One does not remove a stubborn barnacle from its spot by teasing it. Such a strategy only makes it cling ever more tightly."

Mr. Darcy lifted a stern brow, but there was a ghost of a smile on his lips.

Elizabeth nodded sagely. "She is quite right, you know. One may only tease successfully where there is genuine affection on both sides. Else it is merely cruelty." She gave Georgiana a serious look. "The ladies of the *ton* play such verbal games. You must not stoop to cruelty, my dear, but humor may be your ally. If you can make sport of yourself without diminishing yourself in the process, you shall not be the target of any lady's jibes for long."

"Not in my presence, perhaps, but there might always be cruel remarks in my absence. Particularly if a lady seeks to improve her social standing."

"Ladies worth knowing shall understand with whom their loyalties should lie," Mr. Darcy said darkly.

Elizabeth cocked her head at him, curious.

The look he gave her was conscious. "A clever and generous friend is far superior to one who is cleverly vicious." He glanced at her again. "Whatever her standing."

Elizabeth could not quite mask her surprise. She trailed her companions, deep in thought.

She had never expected to hear her own philosophy from his lips. True, he now behaved with greater amiability in society, but that society consisted of the wealthy and privileged. He spoke with admiration of Bingley and her family, despite their connections to trade, but she had assumed he made exceptions for those he knew well.

Has he ever displayed genuine warmth and respect for any who were not, by any definition, his social equals? She could think of only one instance. *The Bianchi family.*

Mr. Darcy's efforts to distance himself had been overcome by their determined refusal to permit his brooding silences and standoffish manners. In the end he seemed at ease among them: he bore their good-natured teasing with admirable grace and hugged them all when it came time to depart Orvieto. He had even kissed Mamma Bianchi on the cheek! Now he was buying them each a thoughtful gift for Christmas.

They truly became his family, she realized. For a man with so few relations, raised without demonstrations of affection, how might that change his view of the world?

Her attention was diverted by movement in a shop window. Calling to her companions, she watched as a miniature hot-air balloon raised and lowered by means of a pulley and a complicated set of counterweights. The balloon was exceedingly detailed, down to the tiny man in goggles and a tweed jacket holding onto the rigging and the shaggy black dog standing with paws on the basket's edge, pink tongue wagging. Georgiana exclaimed delightedly and even Mr. Darcy seemed charmed.

Elizabeth took in the rest of the window display: miniatures of all sorts, all made with a touch of whimsy. "This is just the thing! I shall surely find a gift for Jane here."

She had taken only a few steps into the shop when she was captivated by a miniature desk, perhaps six inches wide. Tiny bound volumes of *Much Ado About Nothing*, *Twelfth Night*, and *Romeo and Juliet* were stacked on one side, while a half-burned candle and a human skull were set on the other. In the center, a quill and inkwell sat next to a piece of parchment inscribed with "Act III" and "Hamlet: 'To be or not to be,'" as though the playwright had merely stepped away for a moment. *Georgiana will adore this,* she thought.

"Miss Bennet! You must see this," came Mr. Darcy's voice.

He stood across the room, where a shelf held full-size books. The excitement in his countenance was so unusual that Elizabeth went over to him without hesitation, burning with curiosity.

"Look at this," he said, indicating the shelf in front of him.

Between two of the books Elizabeth saw a depiction of the *Palio* in Siena: ten tiny horses raced around *Il Campo* on a track sandwiched between hordes of spectators, the banners of every contrada hanging from the walls of the *Palazzo Pubblico*. The scene was self-contained, as though in a box whose side had been carved away. It was as wide as several books together.

"How clever!" she exclaimed. "Are they all meant to be tucked into bookcases?" There were several others on the shelves below, each depicting a different scene: Pisa's leaning bell tower, St. Peter's Basilica, even the Duomo in Florence, its great dome rising above the other rooftops.

"It seems to be so," Mr. Darcy said. He pointed to one she had not yet seen. "I thought perhaps you would like that one for your sister."

The box showed the ruins of the ancient Roman Forum, with its crumbling temples to either side and the Arch of Septimus Severus in the background.

"You are quite right, Mr. Darcy. Jane shall adore it." Elizabeth stood and beckoned to the shopkeeper, who took the box from the shelf with careful fingers.

"I am pleased you agree, Miss—" Mr. Darcy's voice cut off suddenly.

Elizabeth looked back at him, alarmed. He knelt to look at a shadow box on the lowest shelf, his expression reverent.

"Oh, Elizabeth," he breathed. "It is absolutely perfect." He glanced up at her. "Hold, let the shopkeeper set it on the counter, that you might see it better."

Elizabeth felt herself flush. This was the second time that he had used her Christian name, though he did not seem to be aware of having done so. The first, in Amalfi, followed her prodding him into unrestrained laughter. She steered her thoughts away from what it might mean.

The box showed the *Piazza del Duomo* in Orvieto. The Duomo's mosaics shone golden and the piazza was decorated for a festival. Several couples danced the *saltarello* surrounded by clapping onlookers, musicians nearby on a small stage. A painter sat to the opposite side of the piazza, the Duomo his subject.

Elizabeth was reminded forcibly of the night of the fire and a soot-smudged Mr. Darcy in his shirtsleeves carrying two small children from a half-ruined, smoking building. She thought of his expression the following day – the same warmth and reverence she saw now – when they came upon the glorious sight of the Duomo glowing golden in the afternoon sun. And of watching him dance with Mamma Bianchi, laughing despite himself, at Isabella's wedding a few weeks later.

"It is indeed perfect." Her voice came out slightly hoarse, her body suffused with warmth. She dared a glance at him; his eyes were on her, a tender expression there that she had never before seen.

The shopkeeper watched them with open enjoyment. Discomfited, Elizabeth focused her attention on making her purchase and then perusing the other miniatures. She could not suppress a smile when she overheard Mr. Darcy order a green balloon piloted by a dark-haired pirate girl with a blue parrot on her shoulder – clearly meant for Stella – but her mind was awhirl.

Can it be that he still admires me after all?

~ * ~

That afternoon the entire party, joined by Annabelle Cooper, strolled upon the great worn paving stones of the ancient Appian Way. It had taken them an hour to cover a single mile, so frequently did they stop to examine the crumbling tombs and monuments on the roadside. Hardly anything remained of most, but they all enjoyed the challenge of trying to make out the faded text. Mr. Darcy served as their translator, being the only one among them who recalled enough of his schoolboy Latin to be of use.

The weather was sunny and mild, perfect for an afternoon outdoors. The shadows stretched long by the time they found a suitable patch of grass for their picnic; Elizabeth and Lydia helped Nanna spread the blanket and set out their repast while the others examined a nearby tomb. The rear brickwork was damaged but the frontispiece was largely intact, marble bas-reliefs of interred family members prominently displayed in a line.

"The inscription marks this as the tomb of the Rabirii," Mr. Darcy said as he seated himself on the blanket. He was closely followed by Georgiana, Grandpa, and Annabelle. Predictably, Jane and Charles continued to inspect the tomb, deep in conversation.

"I can understand why the ancients would not want to bury their dead inside the city limits, but I do find it strange to see such great monuments lining one of the primary roads entering the city," said Georgiana.

"It is easily explained," said Annabelle. "Every prominent family is the same: they must ever declare themselves the wealthiest and most worthy by the size and extravagance of their monuments to themselves, but one must see a monument for it to be properly impressive."

"Oh dear. Perhaps you may advise me, Miss Cooper." Grandpa smiled slyly. "Is it too pretentious to erect a thirty-foot statue of myself in front of Bennet-Janssen's main office? I desire to impress but would not wish to overshoot the mark."

"It is, sir. It must be no greater than twice life-size if you wish to be thought modest. And only marble or bronze will do; it cannot be gold-plated."

Even as Elizabeth chuckled, knowing perfectly well that her grandfather had no such pretensions, it struck her that Annabelle was the only one among their number today who had not been born to wealth. *How many things that I take for granted must she find equally appalling?*

"Jane dear," called Nanna, "if you and Charles hope to share any of this meal, you must give over your speculations on the original size and decorations of the tomb and join us."

"We shall join you momentarily," Jane said distractedly. "Charles, look at these. Could these be nail holes? Do you suppose this entire frontispiece was sheathed in marble at one time?"

Bingley peered at the tomb. "Do you know, Jane, I believe you are right. Darcy, we need you! There is a very faint inscription here that is beyond my meager skill."

Mr. Darcy obligingly returned to the tomb.

Lydia rolled her eyes. "They are both incorrigible! I shall be painting for months at this rate! Nanna, do you suppose four paintings would be too many for their wedding gift?"

"Four would make an elegant arrangement, but I should certainly not advise you to paint any more than that."

"What are you painting, Lydia?" Annabelle asked.

"Jane and Charles and a growing brood of children and animals, touring the ancient sites of Rome with their great striped circus tent," Lydia said in a grinning whisper. "Lizzy gave me the idea."

"She has already painted the Colosseum, the Forum, and the Baths of Caracalla," said Elizabeth. "Are there three children or four in the most recent?"

"Four children, a dog, a cat, and a peacock," said Lydia.

"Then perhaps six children this time?" said Elizabeth.

Annabelle grinned. "And a monkey!"

"The children shall be playing their games on the great paving stones while their parents examine this very tomb," said Lydia. "And the monkey must be perched atop it, of course."

Their conversation ended of necessity, as Jane and Charles had finally completed their examination of the tomb and joined the rest of them, Mr. Darcy in tow.

"It is quite a modest tomb, particularly compared with some of the others we have seen, though far better preserved than most," said Jane.

Charles nodded. "I can certainly imagine many members of the *ton* turning up their noses at so nondescript a family memorial. I imagine the ancient Romans were much the same."

"Speaking of the *ton*," Lydia said, "may we not seek more pleasant society and occupation than their parties here in Rome?"

"Lydia, dear, you must give up this notion that we shall have a masque for our engagement," Jane said with exasperated fondness.

"I have done, Jane. I propose that we travel to Venice. Signor Alessi says that there are far fewer of the English there."

"You know that we intend to travel to Venice in January," said Nanna. "What reason have you to make the journey now?"

Lydia shrugged. "While today has been very pleasant, I confess I have had my fill of ruins and even more of the English – present company excepted. I long to see the canals, and the homes that seem to grow out of the water, and of course *Carnevale*."

"*Carnevale* was outlawed by the Holy Roman Emperor nearly two decades ago, Lydia," Grandpa said. "Venice remains a part of the Austrian empire."

"The people still celebrate privately. Signor Alessi told me that many families hold fancy-dress balls during the *Carnevale* season. I should dearly love to see one!"

"My family shall be traveling to Venice next month," said Annabelle, "and I am certain that my aunt intends for us to attend at least one such ball."

"If you are to be in Venice in February, you must! Signor Alessi told me that the balls in Venice are delightful affairs. Perhaps we may attend one together!"

Elizabeth thought that perhaps Lydia was most swayed by Signor Alessi himself. Though not handsome, he was rakish and charming in much the same manner as Colonel Fitzwilliam. Elizabeth saw no real cause for alarm – Signor Alessi showed no preference for her sister, and Lydia was not behaving as she had with Mr. Wickham – but she resolved to observe Lydia more closely.

"Are these sentiments shared by all?" Nanna asked.

Jane spoke first. "I could spend years poking around the ruins, but I have no objection to a longer stay in Venice if the remainder of our party prefers it. I have enjoyed the society in Rome no more than that in London."

Charles seconded Jane's sentiments. "I never thought to be grateful to a person as scandalous as Duchess Rutherford, but had she not welcomed you all I might have called out Sir Robert Kingsley for his wife's rudeness."

Mr. Darcy nodded vigorously; Georgiana murmured her agreement.

"You agree, Mr. Darcy?" Nanna asked.

"I do," he said. "The duchess likes you all, and I believe Miss Elizabeth did away with much of the general prejudice at Lady Whiting's musical evening, but otherwise the behavior of my countrymen toward your family has been unpardonable. I shall be glad to be rid of it."

"Lizzy?" Nanna asked.

"Two months in Rome is quite enough to satisfy me," she said. "Venice has long been the jewel of Europe, and I confess that I share Lydia's enthusiasm to see *Carnevale*, even if it is in hiding."

Lydia beamed at her, but Elizabeth's eyes were on her grandparents as they held one of their wordless conversations. Elizabeth idly wondered how many years they had been married before they gained the ability to come to an accord so swiftly, using only the most subtle movements of eyes and mouth.

Grandpa addressed them all. "We have several commitments in the next two weeks, the last of which is Jane's birthday. We shall depart shortly thereafter and arrive in Venice before Christmas."

Lydia cheered, clapping her hands together excitedly. "*Carnevale* is in February. I must begin sketching costumes at once!"

CHAPTER TWENTY

IN WHICH DARCY FACES THE TRUTH

Piazza di Spagna, Rome, 7th December 1816

My dear Anne,

I just received your letter; how delightful, that you shall join the Captain when he sails for the West Indies! I know little of Bermuda. I wonder, is it like Amalfi in the summer? It was so excessively hot! You may be in the Indies even as I write, and I am eager for your descriptions.

We depart two days hence for Venice, and I am relieved at the prospect of leaving behind the wretched young Roman men. How grateful I am that Elizabeth has been always with me! Her example has taught me to hold my head high and answer rudeness with wit – I am, as a result, more sanguine about my coming-out next year than I believed possible – but it is exhausting!

I should like to see Elizabeth properly in love, but she has laughed off the attentions of easily a dozen young men. I believe she fears the inescapable dependency of a wife. How could she not? Her grandfather has always encouraged her intellect and her passions are often unladylike. She might seek a husband who shall not oppress her; instead, she attacks the subject with wit or avoids it altogether.

How I miss your wise and gentle counsel! I cannot discuss this with Elizabeth's family, so I must shift about for myself. I do recall your admonition, however; you would say that all persuasion must come from her own heart. If only it would persuade her to love my brother! Fitzwilliam loves her; more, he truly esteems her. His mind is the equal of hers, and he now appears capable of understanding that even a lady in his care may thrive only on her own terms. Besides, I so desire to have her for a sister!

180

I have invited Elizabeth and Lydia to travel in our carriage. Mrs. Bennet gave me a very shrewd smile when I asked; nothing escapes her, it seems! Fitzwilliam has thus far hidden the strength of his attachment, but five days in close quarters shall provide ample opportunity for him to demonstrate his regard! My only real misgiving is that Lydia and I, despite being of an age, have so little in common that we rarely have anything to say to one another. I shall make an effort for Elizabeth's sake, however; wish me good fortune!

Ever your grateful friend,

Georgiana

Traveling from Rome to Venice, Italy, December 1816

Darcy gazed out at the ancient road. The carriage was well-sprung, but they all bounced uncomfortably across the worn, uneven paving stones. They had left Rome behind only a half-hour ago; it would be an exceptionally long journey if the road continued so.

Elizabeth sat across the carriage. It was largely in deference to her sea-sickness that they went overland to Ancona before taking ship for Venice, though it also saved them three days' travel. Her skin glowed in the morning sun, bobbing chestnut curls framing eyes that gleamed more gold than amber in this light. She was dressed simply, though a discerning eye would recognize the quality of fabric and tailoring that bespoke wealth. Her coat was burgundy, an unusual choice for a lady's garment, paired with fawn-coloured gloves and bonnet. She held a book in her lap, not yet opened; hardly surprising, given the jostling they had been subjected to thus far.

Darcy was determined that they should not pass the morning in silence. "Miss Elizabeth, perhaps you might aid me. I have been considering our journey. If the Romans could build straight, flat roads across the continent over two thousand years ago, it should be a simple matter to lay track for a steam-driven locomotive. How long, do you suppose, might this journey take if our carriages were hitched to such a machine?"

Her eyes lit with interest. "An excellent question! What speed may a locomotive travel when pulling a carriage? Twice that of a coach and four, perhaps? Its progress would not be halted by rain, and one need not stop as often to re-supply fuel."

Her eyes brightened, head tipped to the side and a smile playing at the corners of her mouth. He nearly missed her next words, so captivated was he by the expression.

"If one fitted up the carriages with a mess and sleeping berths as one finds aboard ship, one would hardly need stop at all."

He was caught by her idea. "Think you to travel through the night?"

"Certainly, provided adequate light to see that the track ahead is clear."

"I had not considered that such a light could exist. If it did… I do not suppose you know the distance between Rome and Venice?"

"The driver told me it was roughly three hundred twenty-five miles." She thought for a moment. "Twenty-two hours of travel is certainly a long day. More likely two days, with necessary stops. But there should be no danger of seasickness!" she laughed.

Darcy was impressed; he knew no other lady who could do such swift mental calculations.

"Lizzy, I shall never comprehend how you go on so about steam engines," said Lydia. "How are Georgiana and I to carry on a conversation with you two shouting across the carriage?"

"Well, I am delighted by the prospect of a weeks' travel accomplished in only two days," Georgiana said.

Lydia shot her a meaningful glare.

"But I confess it is quite difficult to hold discourse on a second topic when one is seated across," she added. "Elizabeth, might you and I change places for a time? You needn't worry; my brother is a gentleman. I wish only to speak with Lydia about the costumes she is designing."

Darcy glanced sharply at his sister; she flushed slightly. *She does recognize the impropriety of her suggestion, then. Of course, who am I to look a gift horse in the mouth?*

Elizabeth pressed her lips together and looked from Georgiana to Darcy.

"It is not strictly proper, but the argument has merit," he said. "You have my word that I shall give you no cause to repent."

She regarded him steadily for several seconds. "After we stop to rest the horses, then," she said. A corner of her mouth quirked up. "Which one need not do when one's carriage is pulled by locomotive."

Lydia sighed dramatically. "Oh, Lizzy!"

Elizabeth was quiet as Darcy settled himself next to her in the carriage after luncheon, her downcast eyes nearly hidden by her bonnet. After several minutes of silence Georgiana raised the subject of costumes, and Lydia pulled out her sketchbook. Soon the two were deep in conversation. Elizabeth had yet to speak a word.

"Are you well, Miss Elizabeth?" he asked. He was rewarded with a better view as she favoured him with a faint smile.

"I am, sir. A trifle fatigued, perhaps."

He felt a brief stab of disappointment. As he observed the colour in her cheeks, however, reason reasserted itself. *She is shy,* he thought. *Perhaps she is not unaffected by me after all.*

He resolved to set her at ease. "Shall I read aloud? You may listen or ignore me at your leisure."

She smiled. "I shall be happy to listen, so long as I remain awake."

He pulled Galland's *Les Mille et Une Nuits* from his bag. "Know you the story of Scheherazade and the Thousand and One Nights?"

He had purchased the book to read to Georgiana when he was home for the summer five years and a half ago. They had never finished it; Father died after Darcy had been at Pemberley for only a few weeks. Darcy had entirely forgotten it until Georgiana suggested they read it together on the journey to Siena. It had delighted them both, and he was now eager to share it with Elizabeth.

"A little," she said. "Our governess forced me to read a few stories when I was slogging through French. I quite enjoyed them once I had worked out the translations."

He raised an eyebrow. "Shall I attempt to read in English?"

She laughed. "Thank you, but that shall not be necessary. It was a difficult battle and not without scars, but I emerged victorious. You may proceed *en français.*"

Scheherazade and her stories filled the next several days. They captured Elizabeth's lively imagination and prompted many a thoughtful discussion. Darcy enjoyed these even more than the stories; Elizabeth was clever and persistent, challenging him to consider perspectives entirely different from his own. With her mind engaged, her discomfort sitting next to him vanished; the miles passed more quickly than he had thought possible.

On the afternoon of the fourth day, he looked up from "The Three Apples" to find Elizabeth deep in thought. She started suddenly as she noticed his steady regard.

"Forgive me," she said. "I was considering the enthusiasm for executions in so many of these tales. Why should the vizier's life be forfeit for failing to solve a murder in three days?"

He frowned. "That does seem excessive, even as a source of motivation. The most likely result of such an edict is that an innocent man is accused."

"Naturally! A poor man or a slave, I should imagine; a man with no resources cannot defend himself. Of course, women are equally defenceless, and Scheherazade's husband is the most bloodthirsty of the lot."

"You think him bloodthirsty?"

"Do you not? By the time she marries him he has executed every virgin in his kingdom, save she and her sister, and they were spared only because they were the vizier's own daughters."

"His experience has taught him to mistrust the fidelity of women." Darcy was not certain why he defended the king, other than to see the answering fire in Elizabeth's eyes.

"Think you that this merits execution? I will allow that the faithlessness of his first wife leads him to a very natural prejudice against women, but there is nothing natural about his decision to kill each of his subsequent wives the morning after he weds them."

"Prejudice may be natural, but it is not rational. It excuses – nay, encourages – behaviour that is appalling to the disinterested observer." He grimaced. "As I have learned, to my shame."

Elizabeth's gaze was probing. "One may correct one's behaviour without any alteration to the underlying prejudice, when sufficiently driven by self-interest." She glanced meaningfully at Georgiana before returning her eyes to Darcy's face. "The king did not spare Scheherazade because he believed her to be faithful. He wished only to hear the end of her tale."

Darcy felt pinned in place. He could not fail to understand her meaning. His own improved behaviour had not gone unnoticed, but she was not yet confident that his motives were just.

"In the end," he said, "the king learned to trust her."

"Yes, after she toiled for a thousand nights to remain intriguing enough to be allowed to live. And after he had already murdered a generation of young women."

He sat back, alarmed. *Does she feel that she has been repeatedly forced to prove her worth? Have I been so destructive?* He chose his next words carefully.

"The cure for prejudice, I find, is repeated exposure to the truth. Scheherazade was too compelling to be dismissed, and thus the king could never convince himself that his prejudice was correct when applied to her." A rueful smile tugged at his mouth. "The king was foolish and remarkably stubborn. Had he been a more generous man, he might have seen the truth sooner. Indeed, he might never have cherished such a prejudice at all."

He paused for a moment, gathering his courage. Elizabeth's gaze was unnervingly direct, but he fancied he saw a softening there. Knowing that his words must be circumspect, he allowed his eyes to reveal what he felt. "In the end, however, his heart was changed for the better. And it was his regard for the extraordinary woman with whom he shared his days that eventually forced him to understand his folly."

Elizabeth's eyes widened and a flush crept up her neck. She made no reply.

Darcy's heart thudded in his chest as she lowered her head, lower lip captured between her teeth. He wanted desperately to touch her but forced his hands to remain still, silently willing her to look at him. When she glanced up through her lashes he felt himself smile, and the answering faint upturn of her lips stole his breath.

The carriage jostled as the driver turned into a cobbled lane. Darcy could not decide if he was more aggrieved or grateful for the distraction.

He heard a giggle. Georgiana and Lydia hastily buried their noses in Lydia's sketchbook, but they had clearly been eavesdropping. *It would hardly do to ask for her hand with those two looking on,* he admonished himself. *Perhaps we may speak privately later.*

Elizabeth would desire a walk once they reached the inn. He was delighted to see a small garden to one side of the yard, but it was not to be. As he assisted her from the carriage and pointed out the charming spot, Jane claimed her sister for that very purpose.

With an inward sigh, Darcy bowed and set off down the cobbled lane; he could not begrudge the sisters their time together. He swiftly walked the length of the town, disquietude giving force to his long strides. He hardly noticed anything he passed, so absorbed was he in his own thoughts.

Should I declare myself? No; not yet. Elizabeth had seemed surprised, he realized, by his confession of regard, veiled though it was. Her reaction had been promising – he let out a great sigh of relief as he saw again in his mind's eye the first tangible proof that she might respond favourably to his suit – but perhaps, in his attempts to be circumspect, he had disguised his attachment from its object.

He walked more slowly back to the inn. *No, to declare myself now would be precipitous. She needs to be sure not only of my affection, she needs to be sure of me.* He recalled her admonition at the Netherfield ball, so long ago, that proper behaviour could mask a defective character; indeed, had she not just implied that she suspected him of continuing to harbour the same prejudices that led him to demean her in the first place?

She must know my mind before she will accept my heart. The notion did not frighten him half as much as it might have. *But how may I go about it?*

He was pulled from his thoughts by a familiar laugh. Ahead he spied his sister and Lydia, heads together, giggling as they peered into a shop window. They did not appear to have seen him. He hung back, curious.

"I cannot understand half their conversation," Lydia was saying. "Lizzy was always head and shoulders above me and Jane. Grandpa has been sneaking her books since she was little, you know. I long ago gave over listening to her, and your brother is equally bad!"

"He is! Fitzwilliam has always given me such encouragement that until now I believed myself very well educated. Perhaps it is merely that I have never heard him speak so philosophically, but I feel quite unequal to the conversations he and Elizabeth have had these past days!"

Lydia grinned. "There is one subject in which we both have the best of her, I think. I cannot comprehend how she can be so ignorant of her own regard for your brother!"

"I was not certain of her feelings before, but after today I have no doubt," Georgiana said. "How can we persuade her to see it? Perhaps their costumes should be more clearly paired? Your idea of Zeus and Fate is brilliant, but very subtle."

"Yes, and that pairing is not one of love; it speaks of her power over him. Back to the drawing board I go! But what of you? Do you know a duet that would serve? Lizzy must be the one singing about secret love, of course."

"Oh, certainly! Though it would be so much simpler to choose a duet between two lovers and convince my brother to sing. He has an excellent voice, you know, for all that he hates display."

Darcy's smile vanished. *Surely she would never ask such a thing!*

Lydia laughed. "I shall eat my bonnet if ever I witness the forbidding Mr. Darcy sing before company!"

"I shall hold you to it! Beginning with that enormous feather!"

Their voices were moving away. He looked around to see the two girls striding arm-in-arm.

"I say, Georgie," said Lydia, "now that you can string together more than three words when in company, I believe we shall have a great deal of fun together."

He waited several minutes before following. At the inn he found the whole party gathered in a snug private dining-room, all eyes on Elizabeth. She was seated near the fire, telling an amusing story with great animation. He thought again of Scheherazade, the clever young woman who slew her husband's prejudices, wielding his own fascination against him.

Looking into Elizabeth's dancing eyes, Darcy fancied that he understood the king.

PART III

CARNEVALE
(CARNIVAL)

CHAPTER TWENTY-ONE

IN WHICH ELIZABETH IS MORTIFIED

Palazzo Sforza, Rio de San Vio, Venice, December 26th, 1816

My Dearest Charlotte,

Merry Christmas to you and Mr. Lewis! Our holiday was delightful; we amused ourselves with books and games during the day, music and dancing in the evening. Nanna always invites the servants to join in the Christmas dancing, of course. The London servants could not be cajoled for anything to make merry with us, but the Venetians have no such reservations!

Our traveling companions were taken aback by Nanna's insistence that the servants all leave off their duties and kick up their heels. I expected Mr. Darcy to retreat to the corner of the room with his scowl firmly in place – what Charles has taken to calling his "barnacle position" – but he surprised me. After a bit of internal struggle over the notion of dancing on Christmas Day – and with the servants, no less! – he was quite gallant. He danced with all the ladies of our party and every female servant besides. He even appeared to enjoy himself!

In truth, Mr. Darcy's behavior has continually been a surprise these past weeks. After months of gradually lessening reserve, it is as if a floodgate has opened. He is all ease and friendliness and we spend a great deal of time in conversation about any number of topics (most of which are never discussed in the drawing-rooms of the ton).

It has also been exceedingly gratifying to see the change in his treatment of Georgiana. Far from the autocratic and overprotective guardian of old, he is now an affectionate and devoted brother. He solicits her opinion and even appears to trust her judgment more than his own at times! Of course, her growing poise and confidence has followed a genuine improvement in her understanding. I do not fear for her half so much as I did a year ago, Charlotte!

As for the city: Venice is unlike any I have ever seen. Paolo Alessi is Venetian, you will recall; he described it as a wealthy matron, past her best years but still beautiful. The comparison is apt: the palazzi that line the Grand Canal are unfailingly elegant, with a distinct air of faded glamor. Palazzo Alessi is one of the grandest; our rented palazzo is comparatively cozy. We have no garden – they are tiny, where they exist at all – and looking out to see watercraft going past the house has not yet ceased to be strange. Most astonishing: New York is far easier to navigate! It takes nothing at all to become completely turned around in all these narrow alleys and canals.

To my mixed consternation and delight, the Kingsleys have also journeyed here. The delight is entirely in the person of Annabelle Cooper, of course; the Kingsleys are as appalling as ever. Annabelle suspects that her uncle is brokering a union between his daughter Philippa and Paolo Alessi. (His threat to marry her off forthwith was not an idle one, it seems.) My sympathies over such a match are all with the gentleman, I fear. We are to attend a card party at the Palazzo Alessi for the New Year, which shall afford an opportunity to closely observe the couple. Let us hope that this proves to be the most compelling event of the evening; I desire no repetition of the dramatics of Lady Matlock's gala!

With many wishes of joy to you and yours,

Elizabeth

Venice, December 31st, 1816

"You wished to see us, Jane?"

In the mirror before her Elizabeth saw Lydia's head peering around her bedroom door, Georgiana just behind her. Jane bade them enter and placed the last hairpin in Lizzy's coiffure.

"Your hair looks smashing, Lizzy," Lydia said.

"As does yours, Lydia. That artfully messy look quite becomes you."

They had all dressed with care for their first Venetian evening party. Elizabeth's new gown was a shimmering blue-gray silk nearly the exact shade of Lydia's eyes, trimmed with dark gray embroidery to match the black pearls softly

192

glowing at her throat. The necklines this season were daringly low; she had been obliged to purchase a new corset and the result was an impressive décolletage. Jane had twisted her hair at the back of her head from her nape to her crown, leaving the ends to fall to one side in a cascade of spirals.

Lydia's hair was piled atop her head, curls hanging in every direction and framing her face in what only appeared to be haphazard fashion. She wore russet satin slashed with cream, which set off the classic strand of white pearls that had been her Christmas gift from their grandparents. This was the first evening party she had been permitted to attend and Nanna insisted on a more modest neckline; Lydia had pouted over it for days until Nanna informed her that permission would be withdrawn if she proved herself too childish to attend.

Georgiana was in cornflower blue satin with a heavily beaded hem, a large rectangular sapphire on a gold chain around her neck. Her hair was styled simply, with tiny pink flowers tucked into one side. Heaven knew where Mr. Darcy had procured them at this time of year; Elizabeth had seen no hothouses in Venice.

Jane was luminous as ever in a mossy green satin trimmed with deep green velvet, diamonds set to look like flowers at her ears and throat. Her head was adorned with a lattice of braids and ribbon, which brought attention to the diamond pins at her crown.

"I wish to put you both on your guard," Jane said. "Charles tells me that Paolo Alessi has a younger brother who you shall likely meet this evening. Dario Alessi is by all accounts handsome and charming, but also careless with the hearts of ladies. He surrounds himself with equally careless friends, and they are often out at all hours. Their manner of entertaining themselves is… well, not fit for the ears of young ladies."

"He sounds very like George Wickham," Georgiana said with distaste.

Jane nodded. "I have heard the term 'rake' used to describe him more than once."

"I should like to think that we have both learned better than to be taken in a second time," Lydia said, "but I thank you for the warning. We ladies must protect each other."

~ * ~

Elizabeth could feel Mr. Darcy's eyes on her as they passed beneath a graceful marble arch into the grand salon of the Palazzo Alessi. She dared not return his gaze for fear that he should see the blush staining her cheeks as she recalled his earlier expression.

Their party had assembled to depart the Palazzo Sforza at the foot of the main staircase. Jane and Elizabeth were the last to descend; they had been laughing over some trifle when there was an audible gasp from below. The sound came from Charles, whose eyes were glued to Jane. Mr. Darcy, following his friend's gaze, gaped at Elizabeth. Neither man appeared to notice Lydia and Georgiana's smothered laughter.

Cheeks aflame, Elizabeth had looked away in time to observe Grandpa's smile as he tenderly kissed his wife's hand. Nanna lovingly placed her palm to her husband's cheek. Elizabeth smiled; her grandparents had been in love for fifty years and made no secret of it, despite the dictates of propriety. It was an inspiration to all of them.

She had been obliged to stop on the last stair, directly in front of Mr. Darcy. He kissed her hand wordlessly, releasing it with obvious reluctance. The resulting flush had coursed through her whole body.

He handed her up from the gondola and stayed close among the press of people in the Palazzo Alessi's entrance hall. As they followed Jane and Bingley up the stairs he kept her closer than propriety ordinarily allowed, placing his free hand over hers where it rested on his arm. His jaw tightened as he took in the crowd on the first floor, but when he spoke his voice was deceptively casual.

"Miss Elizabeth, I must beg you to remain with me this evening. Paolo is very serious about his cards and Bingley is possibly the most careless whist player in the history of the game. I refuse to lose another shilling for want of a properly attentive partner, and you are the best whist player among us. May I rely on you?"

Charles grinned. "Indeed, Elizabeth, you must, for all our sakes. There is nothing more unpleasant than my friend here when he discovers that something he wishes to hold tightly has escaped his grasp."

Elizabeth blushed at the double meaning. She struggled to respond with her usual playful wit. "Have no fear, Mr. Darcy, I shall not abandon you," she said finally, eyes on his cravat.

The tension in his jaw relaxed. They entered the grand salon; the room had been set with nearly a score of card tables. Seeing only a few knots of people in the corners, Elizabeth realized that most of the guests must be in the hall. One of the nearest gentlemen proved to be their friend; Paolo Alessi greeted them with his usual enthusiasm. Miss Kingsley favored them with a chilly smile and a shallow curtsey, but Annabelle came forward with a sincere welcome and a kiss for each of the ladies.

"Please allow me to introduce my family," Paolo said, indicating the others. "My brother Dario and my sisters Giulia and Silvia. My parents are surrounded, I fear, but I shall introduce you when they have broken free."

Elizabeth examined the Alessi siblings. Paolo was twenty-seven and the fairest of the group, with light brown hair and hazel eyes. His face shone with good-natured warmth, but his nose was too prominent to call him handsome. He was of modest height, shorter even than Charles, but his brother was nearly as tall as Mr. Darcy.

Dario, at twenty-two, reminded Elizabeth forcibly of Marco Rinaldi with his dark, curly hair and snapping black eyes. He was devilishly handsome when he smiled; Elizabeth guessed that he had been wielding that grin since boyhood, to devastating effect.

Giulia and Silvia appeared so much alike that they might have been twins, though they were twenty and seventeen. Both were petite, pretty girls with olive skin, aquiline noses, and hair and eyes the color of chocolate.

A group so large must naturally fragment; Elizabeth was grateful to see that Georgiana and Lydia were pulled away by Giulia and Silvia, though Dario's eyes followed them. Jane and Charles chatted gaily with Paolo and Annabelle while Miss Kingsley stood in frosty silence.

Nanna pounced on Dario. Elizabeth nudged Mr. Darcy to follow as Grandpa moved deftly to block Dario's escape.

"Observe carefully," Elizabeth murmured at Mr. Darcy's questioning look.

Over the next several minutes, with her characteristic warmth and apparent guilelessness, Nanna got the young man talking. Before he quite realized it he had confessed – with evident chagrin – to his dissolute lifestyle and his cavalier behavior toward members of the fairer sex.

"Do not trouble yourself, dear," Nanna said. "Such boyish folly may yet give way to the wisdom of manhood, if you seek it."

Dario bridled and Elizabeth was forced to stifle a laugh.

"It may," Grandpa said, "though I must own that I have seen many a young man whose folly was beaten out of him after toying with a young lady who was by no means unprotected or friendless."

Dario made no response, regarding Grandpa warily.

"Do such men truly learn wisdom?" Mr. Darcy asked, before the silence could become awkward.

"Nay, not often." Grandpa shrugged. "Those that survive the consequences of their actions are rarely happy. They resent their wives and feel as though they have been cheated of some greater fortune."

Nanna playfully swatted her husband's arm. "Now dear, you must stop trying to frighten all the young men." She turned to Dario. "He rarely kills them outright."

Dario paled. He stared at Grandpa, whose benign smile contrasted starkly with his hard eyes.

"My husband takes great care of all those under his protection," Nanna went on, "though of course most young men can be reasoned with. But where are my manners? We have surely been keeping you from your friends."

Grandpa's smile never wavered; with a half-hearted apology, Dario Alessi fled.

Mr. Darcy laughed. "That was extraordinarily well played. You have my gratitude; I believe that Georgiana shall now be quite as safe as Miss Lydia."

"Let us hope that he tells his friends of his encounter with the murderous Americans," Elizabeth said.

"Have you killed many such men?" Mr. Darcy asked, still smiling.

"Three," said Grandpa, his expression deadly serious. "Rapists all. Four others met with accidents before I could call them out. My businesses are large and there are many families under my protection. No young lady should ever be forced to marry such a brute, be she highborn or low."

Mr. Darcy's smile fell away. "I wholeheartedly agree, sir." He registered Elizabeth's expression of fierce satisfaction. "This is clearly no surprise to Miss Elizabeth. Does Miss Lydia know of the extent of your protection?"

"She does. I have told each of my granddaughters on the day she turns twelve."

Mr. Darcy started. "Twelve?"

Grandpa smiled grimly. "You think that too young, perhaps, Mr. Darcy? I have learned that it is not. In one case, sadly, it was too late. But Lydia was not satisfied to rely only on the promise of my retribution, which is why she asked that I teach her to box."

"My Giulia insisted on learning to fence," came a new voice.

They turned to see a portly middle-aged man who bore a strong resemblance to Paolo Alessi and a tiny, elegant woman a few years his junior, whose dark curls and black eyes had clearly been passed to Dario.

"I hope you will forgive me," the man went on. "It is not often that a man puts the fear of God into my son; I wished to thank you. I am Giacomo Alessi and this is my wife Cinzia."

Grandpa made the introductions, pointing out the rest of their party across the room.

Elizabeth whispered to Mr. Darcy. "How is it that the entire family speaks English?"

"Signor Alessi insists that his children speak English, French, and German," he said into her ear. "Paolo tells me that his father's ambitions for them are far greater than Venice. Paolo has two other sisters, between himself and Dario in age, who are married to Austrian noblemen."

"My husband worries that Dario will do something foolish. He is a good boy," Signora Alessi was saying. "Headstrong and impulsive, perhaps, but what boy his age is ever cautious? His heart is always in the right place."

Elizabeth felt Mr. Darcy's gaze again and she looked up to see one brow raised over amused eyes.

Yes, here is a man who was cautious at twenty-two. She rolled her eyes briefly and turned back to the conversation, but not before she saw him smile.

~ * ~

Elizabeth was true to her word; she remained at Mr. Darcy's side for the whole of the evening.

While they conversed with Signor and Signora Alessi, the other guests had filled the salon. Mr. Darcy escorted her to the table where Paolo Alessi and Miss Kingsley waited; Elizabeth could feel tension building in the muscle under her fingers and observed that Mr. Darcy's jaw was again clenched, though his expression was bland.

He is discomfited by the crowd, she realized, *though he hides it better than before.* Suddenly his insistence that she remain with him made a great deal more sense. Notwithstanding the mortification caused by his transparent admiration, they had become comfortable with each other. She found that she wished to help him; as with his sister, she knew that her vivacity could ease his way.

She squeezed his arm and he looked at her instantly, surprised. She gave him a reassuring smile. He placed his hand over hers again, brow smoothing, and she felt his tension ease.

Over the whist table she and Paolo Alessi initially carried the conversation, though with a little effort she engaged Mr. Darcy's participation as well. Philippa Kingsley spoke in monosyllables; Elizabeth eventually ignored her. It was just as well, for Paolo was indeed a fierce competitor and the game required her attention.

Mr. Darcy was in good spirits as they sat down to dinner; he chose a place at the end of a table across from Georgiana and Annabelle. "I must thank you for your superior partnership, Miss Elizabeth. That is the first time I have bested Paolo at cards and I dearly hope it shall not be the last."

Listening with one ear as Georgiana recounted her triumph with Annabelle against Giulia and another girl, Elizabeth sought around the room for her family. Her grandparents were at the next table with Jane and Charles. Lydia sat next to Silvia Alessi and across from Dario and Giulia, near the head table where their hosts sat with the Kingsleys. Lydia was engaged in animated conversation, though Elizabeth could not tell from this distance whether Dario's attention favored Lydia more than his sisters.

Annabelle leaned forward. "Your sister was partnered with Silvia against Dario and his friend Vincenzo Rossi. Vincenzo is the sleepy-eyed one with the sandy hair, to the other side of Giulia. Lydia was quite the belle of the ball, too; just when it seemed that one of them had her full attention she would suddenly give it to the other, or to Silvia. I thought they should come to blows at one point."

Looking more closely, Elizabeth could see that Lydia was employing the same tactic now.

"Is she mad?" Georgiana asked. "Jane warned us not three hours ago!"

"Foolish, rather, I daresay," Elizabeth said. "It would be like her to flirt with both, merely to see how far her power went."

"She may quickly find herself in treacherous waters," Mr. Darcy said. "Perhaps you should speak to her. I shall speak to Paolo."

Elizabeth would have gone to her sister immediately had not the sound of ringing crystal silenced the room.

Giacomo Alessi stood with arms spread wide, one hand resting on Paolo's shoulder and the other on Miss Kingsley's. *"I miei amici, sono lieto di annunciare il fidanzamento di mio figlio Paolo con signorina Philippa Kingsley!"*

The applause was loud as Paolo bowed deeply over his new fiancée's hand. There were hoots of approval and raucous exhortations for a kiss which the lady resolutely ignored, icy smile fixed in place.

Elizabeth smiled and clapped with the rest, but she wondered at the match. "Does Paolo know what sort of woman he is taking to wife?" she asked Annabelle.

"He does, but he was persuaded by other considerations. Sir Robert has no heir. Paolo will make an honest woman of my cousin – until a son is born, at any rate – and Sir Robert will name him the heir to the baronetcy. They have been discussing plans to improve Sir Robert's holdings for weeks."

"Does Dario then become the heir to his father's fortune?" Georgiana asked.

Elizabeth had not missed the girl's surprised gasp at Annabelle's casual assumption of marital infidelity, but she recovered quickly.

"Yes, though he little deserves it, by all accounts," Annabelle said. "Keep Lydia well clear of him, Lizzy!"

Even as Elizabeth nodded, her grandmother was already in motion. Nanna gave her hearty congratulations to the happy couple and their parents before moving on to Lydia's table, adopting her most charming expression of apologetic insistence as she detached Lydia from the group.

Lydia's laughter carried easily as she took a seat next to Jane. "Dearest Nanna, I care not a fig for either of them. Though even you, Jane, must allow that Paolo's brother is very handsome indeed."

"That is precisely why I warned you, Lydia."

"A man must be more than merely handsome to catch my fancy. Those two were behaving like bantam roosters in a pit, so it amused me to set them at each other." She shrugged. "Do not fret, Nanna. I am sure I shall hardly have cause to speak to them again, and I shall be very happy to play with you. Grandpa may help me improve my strategy at *vingt et un*."

Elizabeth was relieved to see her concern mirrored in Mr. Darcy's countenance. Lydia might be safe for the remainder of the evening, but how were they to protect a girl who had not the good sense to recognize the wolf when he stood at her door?

CHAPTER TWENTY-TWO

IN WHICH DARCY REMAINS ON GUARD

Palazzo Sforza, Rio de San Vio, Venice, 23rd January 1817

Fitzwilliam—

The traditional beginning of the Carnevale di Venezia is now less than a fortnight distant, and it appears that Lydia's information was correct. While celebration of Carnevale – indeed, wearing a mask for any reason – is strictly forbidden, at least a dozen balls shall be held between now and 18th February. All are fancy dress balls with elaborate costumes and painted faces, by which the Venetians follow the letter of the law, if not its spirit. The commanding officer of the occupying Austrian force is himself quite enamored of such balls; so long as the officers receive invitations, the military looks the other way.

It is therefore no surprise that half the city has been invited to the engagement ball for Paolo Alessi and Philippa Kingsley. Worse, each guest is expected to represent one half of a famous couple. Georgiana informs me that she will ensure my costume meets with my approval; otherwise I have no say in the matter.

I hardly need tell you that I dread this event, and not only for myself. I discussed with Mr. and Mrs. Bennet the question of Georgiana and Lydia attending the ball at great length. We permitted it only because the Alessis are known to be a sensible, respectable family, the behaviour of their younger son notwithstanding.

We all have our eyes on Lydia whenever Dario Alessi appears, which is oftener than chance alone – or even common acquaintance – should dictate. His reputation precedes him, and it bears a strong resemblance to that knave Somerton's. He looks at her as a hound does a fox, and she is yet a month shy of seventeen – too young and foolish to recognize her danger, for all her greater maturity over the past months.

My unease grows as February looms, I confess. I shall be exceedingly pleased to be mocked as a querulous old man should nothing come of it in the end, but I cannot be easy. Mercifully, Paolo is not in love; he remains sufficiently clear-headed to check his brother's predatory behaviour.

In the meantime, I take some consolation in Elizabeth's generosity of spirit; we find ourselves very often in large parties and she invariably exerts herself to stand guard over our sisters even as she soothes my frayed nerves. If only I could find a way to speak to her! But privacy is a foreign concept in this city, and I cannot declare myself before an audience.

I shall write again soon; you are no doubt salivating to hear the details of my costume, and I grant you shall have ample opportunity to exercise your wit at my expense. Until then, cousin—

Darcy

Venice, 28th January 1817

"Oh, Fitzwilliam! I should like to buy everything in this shoppe! It is all so beautiful!"

Darcy chuckled. Georgiana's enthusiasm was certainly understandable; the glass creations were extraordinary. They were surrounded by vases and figurines, chandeliers and glassware – even jewelry! – all of it in every colour of the rainbow.

Lydia called out from the next room. "Georgie! Come look at these darling ear drops!"

"Ear drops shall certainly be a safer purchase than anything else," Elizabeth said as Georgiana hurried to find Lydia. "I daresay you are not keen to buy her a chandelier, Mr. Darcy!"

He smirked. "I suppose that depends on the chandelier." He moved slowly through the room, examining the items overhead. Some were exceedingly simple, others gaudy and ornate.

"Charles, I should very much like to purchase this vase for the drawing-room," Jane said. "It is so lovely!" It had a sturdy cobalt base, the color fading in delicate swirls to clear glass at its fluted mouth.

"Of course, my dear. You may choose whatever you like; I have no talent for such things."

"It is fortunate that my sister has excellent taste, Charles, or you should live to regret those words!" Elizabeth grinned. "What would you say if she had chosen this instead?" She nodded toward a nearly life-size rooster rendered in a discomfiting shade of orange.

Jane laughed. "Lizzy, I would never! It is hideous!"

"It is precisely because Jane has such excellent taste that I have no fear of such an appalling item being displayed in our home," Bingley said easily.

"How disappointingly sensible of you!" Elizabeth said. "What of you, Mr. Darcy? Have you chosen a chandelier for Georgiana yet?"

"I rather fancy this one." He pointed to a frothy pink thing above his head. It was massive, with frilled edges and elaborate curlicues, green glass rosettes on every conceivable surface.

Her eyes widened as she took it in. It required substantial effort to keep his countenance; she stared at him hard, a smile hovering at the edges of her mouth.

Bingley chortled. "I say, Darcy—"

"Bingley, you have already proclaimed your ignorance in matters of taste," Darcy said. "What say you, Miss Elizabeth?"

"Oh, I quite agree, Mr. Darcy," she said, all wide-eyed innocence. "It is exceptional. Are you certain that you would wish to relegate it to Georgiana's quarters, though? It is too large for a private suite, I think, unless her rooms are truly palatial. Something so grand rightly belongs in a ballroom, do you not think?"

Georgiana and Lydia appeared in the doorway, drawn by Bingley and Jane's laughter.

"What is so funny?" Lydia demanded.

"Mr. Darcy and I have been debating whether this chandelier would be better suited to Georgiana's rooms at Pemberley or its ballroom," Elizabeth said. "I am in favour of the ballroom, but Georgiana must be the judge."

Georgiana gawped at the thing and burst out laughing. "Lizzy, how can you even think of my wishing to have something so dreadful in my rooms?"

"You must not look at me, Georgiana. It was your brother who suggested it."

"Fitzwilliam!"

Her slack-jawed astonishment was too much. His reserve faltered and he joined the others in their hilarity.

"Lizzy, I must insist you stay clear of my brother," Georgiana said. "You are a terrible influence! I very nearly expired from shock just now!"

"Nay, I shall accept no blame for this jester's display! It is him you must punish. Dress him in motley for the ball; perhaps then he shall be persuaded not to prey upon his sister's delicate sensibilities."

Georgiana grinned, a wicked gleam in her eyes.

"You would not dare," Darcy said.

Bingley interrupted before Darcy could discover if Georgiana would rise to that bait. "I say, it is nearly noon! Jane dear, we must make our purchases now if we are to observe the clock toll the hour."

"Georgie and I shall await you outside," said Lydia, hauling Georgiana through the door.

Darcy smiled at Elizabeth. "As you have so little regard for my taste, madam, I must ask you to select something in my stead. Which chandelier would you choose for Pemberley's ballroom?"

"I am astonished that you have any ideas of furnishing a ballroom, Mr. Darcy," she said. "I was under the impression that you set foot in them only under duress."

"To be sure, I have made no effort to update it. After Georgiana's coming-out next season, however, it is likely to see some use. I believe it was my great-grandmother who last furnished it."

"Oh dear. I suppose I must aid you, then." She stopped beneath another massive chandelier. Its milky, translucent glass was dusted with shimmering gold and gave the appearance of wide, flat leaves propping up two tiers of candles. "This would be an excellent choice, I think. It is simple and elegant; you are not one for frippery or ostentatious display."

Darcy smiled. In no time at all she had selected the only chandelier in the shoppe that he could envision installing in his home. "I thank you. It is indeed far more suited to my taste."

She favoured him with a saucy grin. "You need not attempt to save face. It was obvious to all how desperately you wanted that pink confection!"

Outside she took his arm as naturally as breathing. They strolled toward the great astronomical clock at the other end of the *Piazza San Marco*, Elizabeth gaily abusing his abominable taste as he invented ever more ridiculous items with which to furnish his ballroom.

Suddenly the grin fell from her face. "That foolish, foolish girl. It cannot be a coincidence that he is here." Her narrowed gaze was fixed on Lydia, who stood beneath the clock tower flirting with Dario Alessi. Several of Dario's friends snickered nearby.

It was Bingley's wish to see the clock, Darcy thought. *Dario's presence here might yet be a coincidence. How could they have arranged it, otherwise?*

Georgiana, who had been absorbed by the clock, finally noticed her friend's absence and looped her arm through Lydia's. Following close behind, Jane favoured Dario with as chilly a greeting as Darcy had ever witnessed and steered her sister away with Georgiana.

Bingley casually stood in Dario's way. "As many times as I have seen this clock, I have never chanced to be here at noon. I could not miss the opportunity."

Dario grinned. "I have loved this clock ever since I was a boy. I was explaining it to Miss Lydia and she laughed at me for my – what is the word?"

"Obsession," Lydia said.

Bells began to chime. Bingley checked his pocket-watch. "Are those bells not early?"

"They are," Dario said. "The bronze bell ringers at the very top, you see? The old one rings the bells two minutes early, for the past. The young one rings them two minutes late, for the future. The clock numbers above the face will change when the *campanile* rings noon." He pointed at the tall bell tower across the square.

They all paused for several minutes to observe the clock's unusual workings. Dario enthusiastically explained the celestial mechanism of the clock face, extolling its usefulness to sailors.

Lydia spoke in a stage whisper. "Did I not say it before? He is obsessed!" At Dario's laughter she said, "Choose another topic, signor. Tell us of the balls and parties that will be held before the Lenten season begins."

"Ah! We do enjoy our parties in Venezia. There is wine and food and music and dancing until the sunrise. We laugh and tell many jokes after the children are abed," he said with a salacious grin. "There are costumes and duels and lovers' quarrels, and we are merry every night until it is time to be sober again."

"It sounds exhausting," Jane said.

Lydia gave an unladylike snort. "It sounds delightful! You are not yet in your dotage, Jane. You must have fun while you may."

"Be that as it may, Lydia," Elizabeth said, "we must take our leave. The gentlemen have an appointment this afternoon and it is past time we returned for our luncheon!"

Elizabeth studied her younger sister intently as the *gondoliere* guided them back to Palazzo Sforza. Darcy wished to reassure her, but what could he say? He must discuss these "coincidental" meetings with Paolo. His sense of foreboding was growing stronger.

～ * ～

"Bingley, how is it that you are not married to that lovely woman?"

"Jane wishes for both our families to attend. We shall marry after we return to England."

"You are almost as bad as Darcy! You English like to deny yourselves happiness, I think."

Darcy stripped off his jacket and waistcoat, ignoring Paolo. His friends had already given him no end of grief that he had, as Paolo had put it, "chased that woman across the whole of the country with nothing to show for it." Bingley had called him gutless and Paolo had instantly dismissed his desire for privacy.

He is right. It is a poor excuse. He was not certain what stayed his tongue, precisely. Perhaps it was the distaste he saw in Elizabeth's eyes when he spoke of England. *My happiness cannot rely upon her misery.* He untied his cravat.

"I shall not challenge him today, not with that great scowl upon his face," Bingley said. "I prefer to have a sporting chance."

Darcy glanced up; Bingley and Paolo regarded him with amused wariness.

"Then you must prepare to be defeated by me instead," Paolo said with a laugh.

They pushed through the door to the armory. The two were well-matched, though neither could best him.

Darcy grimaced. *What I would not give to have Fitzwilliam here to spar against!* A group of younger men entered the changing-room; Darcy paid them little mind. *She does not loathe everything about England, surely.*

"Why an eagle mask?" one of the young men asked.

Indeed, she has many friends there who esteem her greatly.

"The Montague crest is a gryphon," another said.

With my support – and my family's – few would dare snub her.

"A gryphon is not an eagle," the first man said.

Perhaps if she were to visit Pemberley. She cannot but be delighted by Derbyshire.

"A gryphon has the head of an eagle and the body of a lion, imbecile."

The last voice penetrated Darcy's consciousness. He turned, unsurprised to see Dario Alessi surrounded by his pack of young jackals.

"Well met, Signor Darcy."

"Signor Alessi."

"My brother says that you know how to handle a blade."

"I can hold my own."

"I have not had a proper match in weeks." Dario took a few confident steps, halting just a shade too close to Darcy. "Would you care to try your luck against me, old man?"

Darcy grinned wolfishly. *This shall do very well indeed.* "Are you so eager for a drubbing, *ragazzo*? Do not leave me waiting. I shall think you full of nothing but hot wind."

The jackals' laughter followed him as he entered the armory. He perused the blades for some time; the blade he preferred from his previous visit appeared already to be in use. Of those that remained, most were too short and he misliked the balance on many of the longer ones.

The door to the changing-room opened several more times. He caught occasional snatches of Dario's conversation, but his mind was again elsewhere.

"Where will you meet us?" ... "Lido." ... "Mestre, of course."

We need not spend long in London each Season. We neither of us enjoy the society of the ton.

Finally settling on a blade, he went in search of his friends. Bingley and Paolo were already warming up. The fencing-master offered to spar with him, that his arms might be limber for a proper match; for the next several minutes they traded touches back and forth, neither expending significant effort but their foils moving ever more quickly.

When they paused, Darcy saw that they had attracted an audience. Bingley grinned at the jackals who regarded Darcy with raised eyebrows. Several of Dario's friends cast worried glances at him, but Paolo rubbed his hands in delighted anticipation.

Dario slashed the air as he stepped onto the *piste*; he had not bothered to warm up, but Darcy was certainly not going to suggest it. *Let this zerbinotto strut and display his plumage. Fitzwilliam is right: overconfidence kills just as swiftly as incompetence.* He took his position, permitting disdain to show on his countenance.

The fencing-master signaled them to begin.

Dario proved to be a canny opponent, for all his braggadocio. He hung back where Darcy expected him to come on aggressively, feeling Darcy out. Dario was swift and strong, his reach nearly as impressive as Darcy's own; neither man made contact for more than a minute. Eventually, however, Darcy parried just a half-second too late.

Point to Dario.

Dario grinned and the jackals hooted. Darcy smiled.

At the next signal Dario came at Darcy immediately. Darcy's smile never wavered. He parried with little apparent effort and Dario's smug expression fell slowly away as he found himself unable to get near Darcy again. Dario was fast, certainly; but Darcy was faster, and the superior technician. Realization dawned on the younger man's face: he had been *allowed* to score that first point.

Expression turning swiftly to rage, Dario came at Darcy again. He was aggressive but unrestrained – his thrusts sloppy, his parries late. Darcy unleashed his own cold, controlled fury, forcing the younger man back with the rapidity and ferocity of his attack. Seconds later Darcy's foil bent, its tip firmly planted against Dario's chest.

Point to Darcy.

Both men returned to their places, breathing hard. Made wary by Darcy's assault, Dario resumed his attacks with greater control. Darcy pressed him, refusing to allow him a moment to relax; his arm would be cramping by now. As the seconds ticked by, Darcy allowed his own arm to drop just a bit too far.

Astonishingly, Dario fell for the ruse again.

Darcy sprang as Dario came forward, anticipating his thrust with a parry that sent the younger man's arm wide and planting the tip of his foil against Dario's chest a second time, moments before the fencing-master called the end of the match.

Dario scowled, face crimson. "Make a fool of me, will you?" He took a step toward Darcy, foil raised as his other hand closed into a fist.

"Fermati!" the fencing-master barked, stepping between them.

Darcy had not moved a muscle. "It is a fool who declares victory before the battle is joined."

"You shall regret toying with me, old man. 'This day's black fate on more days doth depend; this but begins the woe, others must end.'" Dario spun on his heel and stalked out, jackals trailing him.

"What is he going on about?" Bingley asked, looking at Paolo.

Paolo rolled his eyes. "He has been quoting *Romeo and Juliet* for weeks. Darcy, you are Tybalt. My fool brother means to take revenge for his wounded pride."

"Am I to expect a challenge, then? A proper duel?"

"I doubt it. Even Dario is not so stupid as that, after the humiliation he just suffered at your hand. Most likely he shall try to return the favour, make you appear foolish in front of others."

Darcy's wolfish smile returned. "He is welcome to make the attempt. He shall meet with rather less success than he envisions."

~ * ~

Bingley regarded a group of young ladies strolling along the canal as the gondola returned to the Palazzo Alessi. "I wonder, Darcy, do you think Paolo's brother might come at you through Georgiana, or perhaps Elizabeth?"

"Neither is foolish enough to put themselves in his power, Bingley."

"Ordinarily I should agree with you, but I have heard so many rumours of the licentious goings-on at these balls. If even half of them are true I should not want my sister in attendance, and she is twenty-eight! If Dario were to set his sights on either of them…"

Darcy's jaw clenched, but Paolo shook his head.

"I tell you it is not my brother's way; he would think it cowardly. Besides, Guilia and Silvia shall be very pleased to look after Miss Darcy, and I should be surprised if Miss Elizabeth requires anyone's protection. She is a fearsome creature."

Bingley laughed. "She is, at that."

"The lady who most requires protection is Miss Lydia," Darcy said. "Perhaps she should not attend."

Paolo shook his head again, slowly. "Unwise, I think, Darcy. My brother might take it into his head to call out to his Juliet on her balcony, with all the family away. And she is impetuous enough to permit it."

"She would be angry enough, certainly," Bingley said.

Darcy frowned. "Think you that she is safe from such display at the ball?"

"No," said Paolo. "But then it shall be theater, not seduction. They shall have a grand audience."

"Is she truly safer under the eyes of dozens of people?" Darcy sighed. "Paolo, you must speak to your brother. Speak to your father if Dario refuses to hear you. We shall guard Lydia, but your family must do their part."

"They shall, Darcy. We shall not fail you."

CHAPTER TWENTY-THREE

IN WHICH ELIZABETH LEARNS TO BE SCANDALOUS

Palazzo Sforza, Rio de San Vio, Venice, January 30th, 1817

My dear Charlotte,

The tension in the house has become a tangible thing. Leaving aside the far too frequent appearances of Dario Alessi, there is the matter of costumes. The Alessi's ball is less than a fortnight distant, and the costumes are set to be brought for last-minute fitting on Tuesday. This is the first sighting that any of us shall have, too! Lydia and Georgiana have remained resolutely silent on the details.

Between them they were persistent and persuasive, convincing the rest of us to leave the costuming in their hands. Had Georgiana not been involved I should never have agreed; Lydia is creative but she wants steadiness and judgment. We all trusted in Georgiana to ensure that our ensembles were appropriately modest, and we must hope that our trust was well placed! I have no doubt that my grandparents, and likely Jane and Charles, shall be in paired costumes. I worry that they shall place me in one that pairs with Mr. Darcy's, but I cannot determine if my fear is greatest that he would approve such a scheme, or that he would not! As you can see, the ambivalence of my feelings toward him continues apace.

There is also the matter of the ball itself. Even we ladies hear of the scandals that have arisen from such celebrations. It is such a contradiction! Venice is ruled by the Holy Roman Emperor, whose disapprobation for the indulgences of Carnevale is so great that it has been outlawed. The Venetians themselves are devoutly Catholic to a person. And yet... well, the indulgences of Carnevale are well-known for a reason!

Your faithful (and anxious!) friend,

Elizabeth

Palazzo Sforza, Rio de San Vio, Venice, January 31st, 1817

It promised to be a delightful afternoon. The gentlemen were again at the fencing club and Elizabeth's grandparents lunched with the neighbors, so the young ladies had the house to themselves. They were joined by the Alessi sisters and Annabelle Cooper; all were in high spirits.

"You must not be anxious about my brother's ball," said Giulia. "True, it is the time of Carnevale, but this party shall be positively dull in comparison to the rumors you have heard. Signor Kingsley has seen to that!"

Annabelle nodded. "My uncle's strictures have been a source of some consternation for poor Signor Alessi, I believe." Under her breath she added, "He wishes Philippa to have no excuse for the sort of antics which might end her engagement."

"I am sorry for my Papà but for myself I am pleased," said Silvia. "Mamma says that the ball shall be very English, and I have never been to an English ball."

"They are not so very different, Silvia," said Giulia. "The dances are the same, though the English are stricter about who may dance with whom, and of course they hardly look to be having any fun."

Annabelle laughed. "That is terribly unfair! It only seems so because Italians lack all restraint."

"On the contrary," said Lydia, "the English are such masters of restraint that it is a wonder any of you ever smiles at all, much less dances!"

"Perhaps if Americans had any understanding of subtlety, you would not leap to such a patently absurd conclusion. We cannot go about smiling willy-nilly; that would tarnish our image of perfect unflappability!"

They all laughed. In this company Elizabeth's penchant for poking fun at foibles was a shared source of pleasure. Georgiana asked if the Venetians favored the newer quadrille or the older cotillion dances and was pleased to learn that they were equally popular.

Annabelle rolled her eyes. "My aunt engaged a *dancing-master*, if you can believe it, to ensure that Philippa and I are 'proficient at all the dances expected of Venetian young ladies'."

"How ridiculous!" Giulia said. "He shall only teach the minuet, the cotillion and the quadrille, which you know."

"He may teach the *furlana* if you ask," added Silvia. "Every Venetian knows the *furlana*; it has been danced here for more than two hundred years, and it shall certainly be danced at the ball."

"Fie on the dancing-master," Lydia said. "Will you teach us, so that we may all learn?"

There was general agreement. The group spent the next quarter-hour going through the dance, Giulia calling the steps and Silvia clapping the tempo, which gradually increased with each repetition. They stood in a circle, hands clasped, stepping toward the center and back out. Hands on hips, each girl then placed the toes of her right foot forward and to the right several times before they paired up to twirl, elbows linked. The simple pattern repeated with slight variations; the dance was quick, but it was no more difficult than any other Elizabeth knew.

When they discovered that neither Annabelle nor the Alessi sisters knew the *saltarello* or the *trescone*, both of which they had learned in Orvieto, Lydia – who proved to be an excellent instructor – gave lessons in the traditional Tuscan dances.

After an hour, the ladies paused for refreshment. There was a challenge for the last lemon tart; a fierce duel with Nanna's knitting needles followed from which Annabelle emerged the victor, devouring her tart with exaggerated expressions of delight. Lydia draped herself across the divan, declaring loudly that she had been grievously wounded, which set them all to laughing again. Eventually the Alessi sisters departed with promises to visit on the morrow. Jane declared herself fatigued and went to take a nap.

"What shall we do now?" Georgiana asked.

Lydia favored them with a sly grin. "Shall we not return to our dancing? I wager I know a dance that none of you have yet learned!"

Georgiana looked confused. "What can you mean, Lydia?"

"The waltz!"

Elizabeth's was not the only gasp of surprise. "How can you possibly know the waltz? Mamma would never have permitted you to learn and Nanna would have given an earful to anyone offering to teach something so scandalous!"

Lydia's eyes sparkled with mischief. "Not if she knew nothing of it! Francesca Gallo taught me, in Amalfi. She danced with her brother Antonio and I with her brother Alessandro."

"Lydia! You should be ashamed of yourself!"

"Alessandro is ten years old, Lizzy! There was nothing unseemly about it!"

Annabelle interrupted before the argument could become heated. "Do you truly embrace your partner?"

"Yes," Lydia said. "Or near enough as makes no difference. I certainly would not dance the waltz with just any young man!"

Georgiana bit her lip. "Lizzy, you must be my partner. I shall only be entirely easy if you are with me!"

"Georgiana! How can you even think it?"

"Lizzy, they have been waltzing at Almack's for years! Even my aunt advises me in her letters that I must learn it eventually, for it has become commonplace among the *ton*."

Elizabeth's eyebrows rose in surprise.

"She speaks truly, Elizabeth," Annabelle said. "Think of it this way: you are a proper lady, but how delicious to know that you might be scandalous if you choose!"

"It shall be a lark, Lizzy," Lydia said. "You need never dance it again."

Elizabeth regarded each of their eager, imploring faces. *It is not as though I shall ever dance a waltz in a public place*, she thought. *Mr. Darcy would likely rather be hog-tied than be forced into such a display of intimacy, and no other man would dare ask.* She smiled faintly at the image of a hog-tied Mr. Darcy and Georgiana clapped, interpreting her expression as agreement.

"Very well, then," Elizabeth sighed, shaking her head. "But you must never breathe a word of this to anybody." She fixed her sister with a glare. "Promise me, Lydia."

Lydia rolled her eyes. "I promise, Lizzy, nobody shall ever know that you are so modern a female." She grinned and pulled Elizabeth to her feet. "Now, the dance begins with a promenade. You hold hands with your partner like so...."

~ * ~

Their grandparents and the gentlemen returned, and after supper the card tables were placed. Elizabeth and Mr. Darcy shared a loo table with Georgiana and Annabelle. Conversation flowed easily; Mr. Darcy proved very willing to be laughed at and was fully prepared to laugh at Elizabeth and Georgiana in their turn, joining forces on several occasions with Annabelle. They drew amused stares from the other table, so merry were they.

Eventually Georgiana declared herself parched; the sentiment was loudly seconded by them all.

"I believe the servants have set out refreshments on the sideboard in the dining-room. Shall I bring you some?" Mr. Darcy asked.

"Brother, unless you have grown another pair of arms like a Hindu goddess you shall never succeed in bringing refreshment for four," Georgiana said. "Come, we shall go together."

The moment they were out of earshot Annabelle leaned close and whispered, "You are a strange friend indeed, Elizabeth! When were you planning to tell me that you and Mr. Darcy have an understanding?"

"I was wondering the very same thing," said Jane, taking Georgiana's vacated chair.

Elizabeth colored. "There is no understanding. He has spoken to me of neither love nor matrimony."

"Do you need to hear words?" Annabelle asked. "I should think the fact that he cannot tear his eyes from you speaks loudly enough."

"Even I have seen it, Lizzy, and you are ever insisting that I am blind to every man but Charles!"

Elizabeth shook her head. "His admiration is clear enough. But it was only this past April that he declared to me that he could never marry one so far beneath his station! You recall it, Jane. How am I to interpret his behavior now if he refuses to speak? I dare not expect a proposal."

Jane's expression was serious. "I believe I can say with certainty that his opinion of our relative social positions has changed, Lizzy. But what are your feelings?"

"I—" Elizabeth sighed. "I am not certain. I confess I am increasingly attracted to him. I like this new, liberal-minded Mr. Darcy very much indeed."

"What then is your objection?"

"How can he possibly remain as he is now when he is once again surrounded by the *ton*? They are pernicious! I despise those people, Jane, as they do me. Given the choice I should not live my life among them!"

"Mr. Darcy despises them as well, I understand," Annabelle said.

"That has not prevented him from behaving like them in the past."

Annabelle squeezed her hand. "Lizzy, you fail to account for your own influence. In England he may have done so, but not in Rome and certainly not here! Besides, you are both fabulously wealthy. He has a great estate in the country, and you have family across an ocean. There are myriad reasons to avoid the *ton* and you shall have the means to do so."

Jane rose as she spied Georgiana and Mr. Darcy returning, trailed by a servant carrying a laden tray. "Annabelle is right. And when you do visit London, you have friends among every part of good society!" Jane's smile was filled with a predatory glee that Elizabeth had never seen. "You are one of the most indomitable women I know, Lizzy. If you were of a mind to do it, you could turn the *ton* on its head in a single Season."

Elizabeth studied Mr. Darcy, mulling her sister's words. Perhaps she could... but did she wish to?

CHAPTER TWENTY-FOUR

IN WHICH A MUMMER'S DANCE UNFOLDS

Palazzo Sforza, Rio de San Vio, Venice, 4th February 1817

Fitzwilliam—

What possessed me to trust Georgiana's assurances in the matter of costuming for this ball? Indeed, why did I agree to a costume in the first place?

The tailor has just departed, and even Bingley is fuming. Having seen only the costumes for the men I shudder to think at what must have been concocted for the ladies, because ours are very nearly unfit for proper society.

Bennet is to be Oberon, it seems, King of the Fae in <u>A Midsummer Night's Dream</u>. He wears a crown and a robe of rich purple silk embroidered in silver over a fine lawn shirt. Of the three of us, he is the only one who was not shouting at the tailor.

Bingley is Zeus. Originally this costume was meant for me, and Elizabeth was to be Fate – the only creature more powerful than the king of the gods. (It is anyone's guess how Jane Bennet shall be dressed, as Zeus's partners were many.) Bingley took one look at the loose one-shouldered toga which left his chest bare, paired with sandals and a lightning bolt to carry in his hand, and categorically refused to don it. After much shouting and hand-waving (by the tailor) they compromised on a sleeveless tunic under the toga and a gauntlet with a lightning bolt. Bingley also agreed to allow his beard to grow when presented with the alternative.

I have conceded to the elaborate costume beard. I am to be King Shahryar of <u>One Thousand and One Nights</u>, so the beard is thick and black with curled mustaches. I made no outward objection to the turban, the billowing trousers, or the slippers, but I could not accede to go bare-chested in only a sleeveless robe.

The tailor might have argued longer had I not the book with me. The illustrations all show the king in garments which, while loose-fitting, cover him from neck to ankle. I assured him that he could gild the thing as much as he liked, but that I must have a proper shirt. He also pressed me to wear a long, curving sword – as though I could dance with such a thing!

The only reason I agreed to any of this is that my identity shall be entirely disguised, and few of my countrymen shall be there in any event. Elizabeth attempted this morning to reconcile me to fancy dress; she encouraged me to think of it not as disguise but instead transformation, short-lived though it be. When the mirror shows me an Arabian king I might manage such a feat. If I am fortunate, Lydia Bennet has taken pity on me and dressed Elizabeth as Scheherazade. I shall write again after the ball. Until then, cousin—

Darcy

Palazzo Alessi, Campo San Samuele, Venice, 11th February 1817

Relieved of his greatcoat, Darcy turned to find Elizabeth. It had become his habit to escort her of an evening; tonight, he desired no other man to touch her.

Lydia had indeed taken pity on him. Elizabeth was glorious as Scheherazade: instead of a gown the modiste had made a corset of cream-coloured satin traced in gold that exposed a scandalous décolletage. It tucked into a crimson skirt that split from the wide sashed waist to reveal voluminous gold satin trousers and delicate gold slippers crusted with glittering red stones. There was also a short, sleeveless jacket with a high collar and open front, matching the skirt, and broad gold bangles about her upper arms and bare wrists.

Her hair was pulled loosely into a long braid down her back, threaded with crimson flowers; gold draped across her forehead and dripped from her ears. Her kohl-lined amber eyes glowed and her ruby lips curved into a seductive smile. She was exotic – intoxicating – and he suddenly found it very easy to imagine himself as the sultan, hopelessly enraptured by his beautiful, clever wife.

Next to Elizabeth's fiery beauty, her sister Jane appeared cool as marble. Dressed as Hera, she wore a demure toga-style gown belted with peacock feathers, and a peacock-feather headdress. Her hair was pulled up into a classic Greek style, and she and Bingley looked every inch the king and queen of the gods.

Mrs. Bennet was, predictably, Titania to her husband's Oberon. She appeared otherworldly in a gown of iridescent silver which only emphasized the gleam of her white hair. She stood next to Elizabeth, and Darcy was suddenly struck by how very alike they were. In Mrs. Bennet, he realized, he was seeing Elizabeth's future self.

He bowed over the older woman's hand. "You look remarkably lovely this evening, Your Majesty."

She laughed and patted him fondly on the arm. "I am very glad to hear you speak, my boy. I should not know you at all, otherwise!"

"I am crushed! I imagined that all must know King Shahryar."

"Whenever his lovely bride is on his arm, I have no doubt that all shall recognize him," she said. She winked at Elizabeth, who blushed.

"But who shall know your youngest granddaughter?" he asked. "The costume is extraordinary! I have never seen the like."

Lydia and Georgiana had taken inspiration from Shakespeare's *As You Like It*. Lydia was Rosalind but also Rosalind-as-Ganymede; one half of her costume was a long-sleeved gown, sumptuous enough to belong to the daughter of a duke. The other half was the evening garb of a young man of no very great family. The dark blue brocade gown displayed a bronze silk underskirt; a dark blue wool jacket topped a blue waistcoat, tan breeches and a tall black boot. The cravat on one side transitioned seamlessly to a high lace collar on the other, and her hair was carefully styled to display a simple ponytail on one side and an elaborate profusion of curls on the other.

Georgiana's costume was also split, but in much less astonishing fashion. As Celia she wore a pink silk gown embellished with pearls and lace, and an elegant white glove; her other half, Celia-as-Aliena, wore plain pink muslin. Darcy could not understand how her necklace had been fashioned; one side was sparkling diamond with half of a dangling teardrop, while the other was a plain gold chain with half of a Greek cross.

"Lydia has outdone herself with that notion, has she not?" Mrs. Bennet said. "She has promised to dance with any young man who can guess her identity."

Ganymede offered his arm to Aliena, and Bennet appeared beside his wife. "Let us greet our hosts and see if we might discover some fresh air before the dancing begins," he said.

Darcy extended his arm to Elizabeth. "Speaking of dancing," he said low in her ear as they climbed the stairs, "I should like to dance the first and the supper sets with my blushing bride."

Elizabeth coloured again faintly but the ghost of a smile was on her lips as she looked at him sidelong through her lashes. "Only those two, husband? I should think the king would wish to hear his wife's tale uninterrupted."

"He would, very much indeed," he growled. "But even the king must observe the forms."

She was silent for a moment and Darcy held his breath. *Dammit man, you are too forward.* When she spoke, however, he could not contain a bark of delighted laughter.

"Then she must be careful to end the first set in the middle of her story, that he might be eager to dance with her again to learn the rest."

On the first floor Darcy used his height and broad frame to advantage, opening a path in the sea of people. He noted the appreciative eyes of many ladies on him and was pleased to see no recognition, even on the faces of women he knew. Elizabeth, however, drew the gaze of nearly every person they passed. She walked like a queen, head high, hand feather-light on his arm. Darcy fairly burst with pride, and he silently gave thanks to Georgiana and Lydia.

The costumes of the other guests were elaborate and exceedingly varied. Many had painted their faces and a few even dared masks. He saw kings and queens, gods and goddesses, characters from the tales of a half-dozen countries. As they approached the receiving line, Darcy recognized their hosts as Emperor Justinian and Empress Theodora. The Kingsleys revealed themselves to be Petruchio and Katherina from *The Taming of the Shrew*. Darcy met Elizabeth's laughing eyes, equally amused by the irony.

Next came Paolo and Miss Kingsley as Marc Antony and Cleopatra. Miss Kingsley greeted Darcy with the rote pleasantry of one who is unacquainted, but her gaze sharpened into frosty daggers as it fell on Elizabeth.

Paolo was at first confused. "Miss Elizabeth?" he said, mouth hanging open.

Elizabeth nodded and congratulated the couple.

Swiveling, Paolo closely examined Darcy's face. Recognition dawned after several seconds and he laughed loudly. "My friend, you have chosen your costume – and your partner – exceedingly well. I hope to steal your lady from you for the space of a dance this evening," he added, addressing the last to Elizabeth.

"I shall be very pleased to allow it," she replied.

Darcy steered her away from the receiving line; they made their way to where the rest of their party stood with Annabelle Cooper and the Alessi girls, who were exclaiming over Lydia and Georgiana.

Darcy could not contain his mirth at Miss Cooper's costume. "Pray tell," he said, "who is the other half of the famous couple which includes the Virgin Queen?"

Miss Cooper only shook her finger at him and said coyly, "Nay, sir, you shall not winkle it out of me. A lady never reveals her secrets."

As they waited for the first set to begin, Darcy and Bingley secured the hands of each of the other ladies. Darcy could not recall a time when he had looked forward with such pleasure to dancing, though his anticipation was somewhat soured by watching the stream of young men – most of them friends of Paolo – who begged Elizabeth for the favour of her hand.

Her dance card was soon full through the supper set, though she declined to promise any thereafter. "The Sultan does not wish me to over-exert myself," she breezily explained. Darcy was chuckling darkly at the crestfallen expression of a young Big Bad Wolf when Bingley nudged him.

"I say, Darcy, who is that man speaking to Lydia? I have seen at least four men in eagle's masks with her in the last fifteen minutes, but this one has returned."

Lydia stood with a young man in a white half-mask with a prominent yellow beak. He was tall and wore a tawny suit of clothes. Looking about, Darcy saw four more men in eagle masks, though theirs were brown. Something tugged at his memory. He placed it only when the white eagle adopted a fencing stance.

"Dario Alessi," he said. "He and his friends were talking about eagles and gryphons in the changing-room the day we dueled."

"That would explain the color of the suit," Elizabeth said. "There is otherwise no acceptable excuse for it."

"What is the significance of the gryphon, then?" Bingley asked.

"Something to do with a family crest, I believe," Darcy said. "I confess I paid them little attention."

Dario took Lydia by the hand and walked to the dance floor, where his brother and Miss Kingsley were set to lead the dancing. Bennet and his wife also glided toward the floor, eyes on their granddaughter.

Relieved, Darcy held out his hand to Elizabeth. "Shall we?"

She placed her bare hand in his; his skin tingled where it touched hers. Miss Kingsley called a quadrille and they took their places in the set, Elizabeth silently regarding him with amused curiosity.

"I believe I was promised a story," he said as he took her hand for the first form.

She smiled. "Then you shall have one. This is the story of a princess, the second of three daughters. You may wonder that it is not the youngest daughter of whom I speak – all such tales are of the youngest daughter, are they not? – but hers is a story for another day."

"Nay, the youngest is ever the most beautiful and the purest of heart," Darcy said. "I weary of such perfection. Tell me of her sister."

Elizabeth nodded. "The king had no sons, and so he plotted advantageous marriages for his daughters – for what man does not understand the value of daughters to a king? The eldest daughter was beautiful, the second clever, the third bold. The king consulted his chief advisor, and together they laid their plans.

"The eldest daughter they would offer as bride for the heir to the neighbouring kingdom. The boy was good-hearted and biddable, and through this daughter the king thought eventually to rule both kingdoms. The youngest daughter would be wed to the general of all the kingdom's armies, ensuring his loyalty to the crown."

The ladies performed their chain. Elizabeth moved with unconscious grace, braid swinging and skirt billowing; she picked up the story immediately when she again stood before him.

"The second daughter would marry the chief advisor, who fancied himself even cleverer than she. By this the king sought to keep her wit close and tame her high spirits, for of all his children she was the best suited to rule after him. If only she had been born a man!"

"This story should hardly have been worth the telling if she had," Darcy said.

"Then it is well that she was not, I suppose," Elizabeth said with a raised brow.

With a properly chastised expression, he nodded for her to continue.

"The king was a good man and a decent ruler. Like all men, however, he was blind to that which he did not wish to see, which was that his chief advisor was cruel and ruthless and hungry for power. The clever daughter saw the chief advisor's true nature and avoided him. When her father insisted she marry him, she refused. The king was angry, but the chief advisor reassured him. 'All she needs is time, my liege,' he said.

"But secretly he plotted to abduct the girl and marry her in a private ceremony with only the priest and his loyal servants as witnesses, before locking her in a high tower under heavy guard. He could not permit her to remain in the castle while he put in motion his plan to succeed the king."

Darcy's brows rose. *How greatly is this tale embellished? Is this Mr. Pringle a greater villain than Bingley knows?* Aloud, he asked, "How did she escape such a fate?"

Elizabeth's answering smile was sly. "He suffered from a failing common to men with a very high opinion of their own importance: he paid no attention whatever to those he believed to be beneath him unless it suited his purpose.

"The young housemaid who cleaned his chambers – scarcely more than a child, in truth – was silent as a mouse as she went about her work, but she listened to every word he said. When he told his valet of his plan to wed the clever princess, the maid was horrified. The princess had always been kind to her, you see, and saw that she was protected from a stableboy who would have stolen her virtue."

Darcy smiled. Elizabeth had greeted every servant by name in every home they had leased on their journey and left small gifts when their group departed. He could easily envision her as an avenging Fury, insisting on the dismissal of a stableboy who preyed on the housemaids.

"The maid told the clever princess, and the clever princess went to the wise woman. The wise woman was a powerful seer whose husband was the chief magician. Before the arrival of his chief advisor, the king had trusted these two more than any others; together they ensured that the kingdom prospered and that its people were well cared-for.

"Upon hearing the clever princess's story, the wise woman consulted the stars. Fearful of what she saw, she went straight to the king's chamber, begging admittance even before he had risen for the day. The princesses must undertake an arduous journey, she said, accompanied only by the magician and the wise woman, or terrible tragedy would befall the princesses and the kingdom would fall to ruin.

"For all his flaws the king loved his daughters, and so he agreed. He stood firm even when the chief advisor insisted on accompanying the princesses instead. 'You are required here,' said the king, 'so that I might rule with wisdom while my daughters complete their journey.'"

The music began to slow, signaling the end of the first set. Darcy bowed.

As Elizabeth rose from her curtsey she said, "And so it was that the three princesses left the kingdom of their birth for the first time, accompanied by the wise woman and the magician, to seek safety in the wide world."

Darcy escorted Elizabeth to Bingley; the men were to trade partners for the second set. *Seek no further,* he thought. *I shall keep you safe. I swear it.*

CHAPTER TWENTY-FIVE

IN WHICH ELIZABETH CONCLUDES HER TALE

Palazzo Sforza, Rio de San Vio, Venice, February 13ᵗʰ, 1817

My Dear Charlotte,

I shall begin with a warning: before you read this letter ensure that you are seated comfortably, with refreshment to hand, and that you shall be uninterrupted for some time. There is so much to relate!

First to set the scene: imagine a large, stately salmon-colored home, three storeys, standing shoulder-to-shoulder with its neighbors on the Grand Canal. It boasts tall, narrow windows topped by Byzantine arches and a small but elegant garden to one side. The house is lit from top to bottom, gondolas clogging the canal as guests wait to disembark at the dock. The ballroom is on the first floor (we Americans would call it the second) and its wide balcony overlooks the Grand Canal. The other public rooms are on the same floor, and all are filled with guests. The food and libations are plentiful and delicious, the music lively, and many guests are unrecognizable behind their costumes and painted faces.

Mr. Darcy is among those. In an exceedingly un-subtle declaration of their opinion, Lydia and Georgiana dressed him as King Shahryar to my Scheherazade. Our costumes even matched – his long-sleeved tunic was cream and gold, the sleeveless over-robe and billowing trousers were scarlet, and the slippers were gold. He carried a curved dagger with a jeweled hilt tucked into a wide sash belt and he wore gold rings on his fingers. With his hair covered by a turban, kohl on his brows and around his eyes, and the great black beard, I might have walked past him on the street and never known him at all! We made an extraordinary picture, I must say; I caught sight of our reflection and even I nearly swooned!

You are perhaps thinking of the masques we have attended in the past, but I must tell you that the Venetians are far more dedicated to disguise than we, and unabashed about many matters which are treated with delicacy in other societies. For all that we were assured that the ball should be sober by comparison with the usual Carnevale revels, the general discourse had progressed from boisterous to positively risqué by supper! I feared poor Georgiana would faint, she was so flushed (though whether from heat, exertion or mortification I could not tell).

Jane bore it well; Lydia, of course, was entirely in her element. Grandpa and Nanna watched Lydia like hawks, but even their close attentions could not compete with the handful of young men wearing eagle masks. The gryphon with the white eagle mask was Dario Alessi (a nod to Lydia's country of birth, perhaps? I did not realize it at the time, but now I think on it, it seems likely). The rest were his friends – the jackals, Mr. Darcy calls them, and I wholeheartedly concur! Each of them danced with Lydia during the evening, and they looked so similar that it was impossible to tell which was which.

Lydia danced the first with Dario, and then danced with him again just before the furlana. Nanna was so incensed at her foolishness that she hauled Lydia from the ballroom and spent the next fifteen minutes turning her ears blue. I know not what Lydia said to prevent Nanna from removing her from the house right then and there, but they returned to the ballroom just as the furlana was concluding.

I must put down my pen for the moment, as Jane is calling for me. I shall take it up again as soon as I may, for I have yet to relate any of my news! –E.

Palazzo Alessi, Campo San Samuele, Venice, February 11th, 1817

Paolo Alessi escorted Elizabeth from the floor to wild cheers and applause.

As the only non-Venetian dancers on the floor for the *furlana* she, Jane, Georgiana and Annabelle were subjected to many curious stares – and a few jeers – when the music began. The music had steadily increased in tempo, and couples began to step out of the circle as they became too fatigued to keep pace. Elizabeth's habit of walking and riding stood her in good stead, as did her natural talent for dance; by the end the music was dizzyingly fast, and only she and Paolo and Dario and Giulia remained.

The music concluded with a flourish and Paolo bowed low to her before presenting her to the crowd. *"Elisabetta, di America,"* he shouted, and she curtseyed deeply as the cheering began. It followed them as Paolo returned her to Mr. Darcy, who appeared to pull his eyes from her heaving breast with some difficulty. Jane pressed a drink into her hand – cool water, thank the heavens! – and she drained it.

"Capital!" said Charles, including the other ladies in his compliment. "When did all of you learn – the *forlana*, is it called?"

"*Furlana*," Lydia corrected, joining them with Nanna trailing her. "We learned it a week or so past, when you lot were off hacking at each other with swords."

Elizabeth caught Philippa Kingsley's expression. "It is great fun. What a pity you did not also learn, Miss Kingsley."

"A great pity, Miss Elizabeth. You were so… energetic. I know not how a lady of breeding could manage such a thing! My congratulations to you." Without waiting for a reply, she attached herself to her fiancé's arm and glided away.

Their entire party burst into laughter. If Miss Kingsley was aware that her insult failed to hit its mark, she gave no sign. Elizabeth downed another glass of water and fanned herself in earnest for several minutes as dancers found their partners for the supper set. Mr. Darcy stood beside her, joking with Charles. He even responded in kind to Annabelle's occasional good-natured sallies.

Elizabeth was struck by his ease. *In London, Annabelle would have been far beneath his notice. Now he jests with her as though they had been friends for years.* She recalled that she had particularly recommended Annabelle to his notice at Lady Whiting's party and glanced up at him thoughtfully.

He made the effort to know her for me, she realized. She felt a rush of warmth and glanced back down just as his gaze shifted to her.

Mr. Darcy held out his hand. As his fingers closed around hers, a tingling sensation shot up her arm and she shivered. *Does he feel this also?* He raised a brow in inquiry; she squeezed his hand, reassuring.

Miss Kingsley called a minuet. An unusual choice, but Elizabeth understood it once she saw the elegance of Miss Kingsley's promenade. In fairness, the attention should be on the prospective bride. Elizabeth did not begrudge her the opportunity to display; indeed, she was grateful for the slow pace of the dance.

It allowed her to rest and speak, and the king was clearly opening his mouth to remind her of his due when she began.

"The three princesses traveled first to the neighboring kingdom," she said.

Mr. Darcy closed his mouth with a smile.

"The wise woman had seen that the king's choice for his beautiful eldest daughter was a good one – or would be, given time. The prince was indeed exceedingly biddable, which nearly cost him his bride; but that tale, too, is for another day."

Mr. Darcy's expression was curious, but he said nothing.

Perhaps I shall tell that tale, she thought, *if ever Jane tells it to me in full and permits me to share it.*

She had given some consideration to this part of her story. Mr. Darcy had used the tale of King Shahryar to explain his change of heart; in the weeks since, he had taken pains to show her the sincerity of his feelings. He never spoke the words, but Jane and Annabelle were right: she did not doubt that he loved her.

I have been stingy with my own heart. He must know that I no longer despise him, but he cannot know how well I love him in return. She had not admitted it even to herself until this evening, when she saw them reflected together in the window-glass and was struck by the thought – *we belong together.*

It was her turn to reveal her heart. But first, she must say words that could not but wound him.

"The prince's cousin was a wealthy nobleman, young and handsome and all too aware of his own importance. He esteemed only the nobility of his own kingdom, but even toward them he was rarely kind. He was widely known as a proud man, often thoughtlessly cruel; and like most proud men, he did not see those beneath him.

"The clever princess observed all this. She endured the proud nobleman's casual insults and his cold disdain. She knew he despised her even when he treated her with kindness, and she wondered that the good-hearted prince and his cousin could be friends.

"Eventually the time came when it was no longer safe for the princesses to remain in the neighboring kingdom, and they departed for a far distant land."

Mr. Darcy's countenance was pained, eyes filled with remorse. When she spoke of his homeland as a place of danger, however, he paled as though she had struck him a mortal blow.

"Elizabeth… I would wish you to know—"

"Hush, my king." Elizabeth placed her palm briefly against his chest, silencing him. "You must hear the rest before you speak of this."

Mr. Darcy swallowed hard and covered her hand with his, nodding.

"Months later in that distant land, the princesses encountered the prince and the proud nobleman again. Both men humbled themselves, each seeking a boon that only one of the princesses could grant. The princesses were angry, for what lady wishes to be treated as beneath the notice of a man who professes to esteem her? Were it not for the wise woman's counsel, they would have turned the prince and the proud nobleman away."

"What did the wise woman say?" Mr. Darcy's voice was hoarse, nearly a whisper.

"She advised the princesses to reserve their judgment and allow the young men to prove themselves. The princesses agreed, for the wise woman's sight was long and her counsel always sound.

"The clever princess struggled to set aside her anger and wounded pride. The proud nobleman treated her with greater kindness, but she mistrusted it because she still saw disdain in how he treated others. Then came a night when the proud nobleman was shamed into laboring alongside those who, the day before, he would have walked past without seeing. It changed him – only a little at first, but then a great deal.

"After that, the proud nobleman was not so proud. He treated those around him with genuine kindness – even those who were beneath him. The clever princess was not so clever, either. She saw these things with her eyes but would not permit her heart to understand. She was afraid, you see."

Mr. Darcy's brow knitted in confusion. "Afraid? Of what?"

"Afraid to care for him. Afraid that all his cold disdain would return when he was once again in his own kingdom. What lady, after all, wishes to be despised by the man she loves?"

The last strains of the music faded; Elizabeth had not even noticed when they ceased moving.

Mr. Darcy's eyes were troubled but hopeful as he tucked her hand into his elbow. "Is this the end of the tale?"

"No." She finally looked away from him to find the ballroom largely empty. She hesitated, blushing, before she gathered the courage to speak again. "I suppose you must ask me to dance once more to hear the rest." She felt his gaze burning into her hair and she looked up to find his eyes searching hers.

"The next set. After supper."

She nodded, heart in her throat.

He smiled – a broad, glorious smile – and turned to lead her in to supper. With his gaze no longer on her she found herself able to breathe again.

They stepped into the dining-room and immediately she felt the pointed stares. Glancing around she found that every member of her family – and his! – was watching them. Lydia was fairly bouncing in her chair, clearly desperate to ask the question in everyone's eyes.

Do we have an understanding?

Elizabeth registered Mr. Darcy's joyful expression and his hand covering her own as it rested on his arm. She realized that if she denied it, nobody would believe her. *Even I would be hard-pressed. I did just suggest that he dance with me a third time.*

Nanna bustled over. "There you are, my dears. We ensured that you should have seats near us; come." She led them to the table at which most of her family sat. Lydia and Georgiana were seated with Giulia and Silvia Alessi and Annabelle Cooper.

Lydia mouthed, "Well?"

Elizabeth pretended not to see. Seated between Mr. Darcy and Nanna, across from Jane's knowing smile and Charles's giddy grin, Elizabeth was nearly silent for the whole of supper. Fortunately, the rest carried the conversation.

Finally, Charles could stand the suspense no longer. "Darcy, I must know what Elizabeth was saying to you the whole of that set. You spoke perhaps three words the entire time. It looked as though she was putting you through the wringer, but here you are grinning like a monkey!"

Mr. Darcy merely shrugged. "She is Scheherazade, Bingley. She was telling me a story."

"Perhaps you might tell me one, my boy," Grandpa said. His smile was easy, but his eyes were serious. "Shall we stretch our legs?"

Under the table Mr. Darcy briefly clasped her hand in his before standing to follow Grandpa from the room.

"Have no fear, Lizzy," Nanna said. "I have been telling your grandfather for some time now that both you and Mr. Darcy would come around, but he must satisfy himself."

Elizabeth looked at her grandmother fondly. "I hope one day to be as wise as you are, Nanna."

Nanna patted her cheek with a gentle smile. "You are well on your way, my love."

The after-supper set had already begun when the gentlemen returned. Instead of Mr. Darcy, however, Elizabeth was approached by her grandfather.

"May I have the honor?"

She looked at Mr. Darcy, surprised. He nodded, his expression serious but not forbidding.

Elizabeth and her grandfather joined the other dancers. She waited, curious to know what he would say; as always, he came directly to the point.

"Mr. Darcy tells me that, despite your evident affection for each other, you do not have a formal understanding."

Elizabeth nodded.

Grandpa fixed her with eyes that were firm but loving. "I have no doubt that he will propose, my dear, and soon. I suspect that you have given a great deal of thought to what it shall mean if you accept."

Elizabeth nodded again. "In truth, that consideration – living in England, that is – has been the primary obstacle."

Grandpa grimaced. "I shall not envy you the *ton*, Lizzy. Only you can know if you love the man enough to accept all that comes with him. But you should also know that he must love you enough to accept all that shall come with *you*."

"I do not understand."

"I have recently come to a decision, in consultation with your grandmother. Bennet-Janssen will expand into railroads. This shall be a third company, separate from the real estate and the shipping businesses, and I should like to name you as its chairwoman."

Elizabeth stopped dead, stunned.

"Come, my dear," her grandfather said, "you must keep moving."

She propelled herself forward, moving through the steps as though in a dream. "I do not understand, Grandpa."

"You are meant for more than merely to be a rich man's wife, my Lizzy. You need a challenge; something that engages your mind and your passions. And you must stand on equal footing with your husband. You could not be happy, independent as you are, entirely under the power of any person – even one you love."

Elizabeth blinked back tears, unable to speak.

"There shall be a great many visits with solicitors in your future, I fear. I shall not approve any marriage settlement that does not preserve your interest in Bennet-Janssen Railroads. And, of course, there is the matter of finalizing those arrangements."

The music ended and she impulsively hugged him. "Thank you, Grandpa," she whispered.

He kissed her head fondly. "You are my dearest girl, and you deserve every happiness. Speaking of which, I believe I see a young man waiting very impatiently for another opportunity to dance with you."

Mr. Darcy did not wait for them to reach the edge of the ballroom; in three long strides, he met them halfway and took Elizabeth's hand from her grandfather. The men nodded solemnly to each other.

Mr. Darcy looked at her, care and concern in his eyes. "You are well?"

"Yes, I am well." *Fitzwilliam,* she told herself. *His name is Fitzwilliam.* "Did Grandpa tell you…?"

"About the railroad? Yes." He smiled. "You shall be brilliant; I have no doubt. But first may I beg the favor of your hand, that we might finish your story?"

She nodded and he led her back to the floor where couples were forming a circle, each gentleman standing to the left of his lady. Elizabeth's eyes grew wide. *This is a waltz!* Guiltily she glanced over to her grandmother, who merely lifted an amused brow. Relieved, she returned her attention to Mr. Darcy.

He took her left hand in his own, his right hovering by the small of her back. "Know you how to waltz?"

"A little. Lydia taught me on the day we learned the *furlana.*" She bent her right arm behind her, and he took her hand.

"A story I should like to hear another time," he said, brow raised. The music began and they stepped together in a slow promenade. "Now, however, I desire to learn the fate of the clever princess."

"There is little enough to tell," she said.

She turned toward him as he lifted her left arm high with his own; his right hand came to rest just above her left hip, his arm stretched across her body. She mirrored the position and they smoothly rotated, his hand gently guiding her, following the couple before them around the circle.

He said nothing, merely looked at her expectantly.

"The nobleman was more courageous than she," she said. "He asked for her opinions and followed her advice. He shared his thoughts, even going so far as to tell her that by her rebuke and her example, she had improved his understanding.

"By slow degrees she began to see that his esteem and admiration for her were unyielding, and that his heart had truly changed. No more the proud nobleman, he recognized and honored the good in others and condemned the evil, no matter their station or nationality. He became generous and liberal-minded, and easier in company."

His eyes never leaving hers, Mr. Darcy – *Fitzwilliam! His name is Fitzwilliam* – set Elizabeth's left hand upon his right arm. Adjusting his stance so that he stood directly facing her, he lifted her right hand in his left and pulled her closer to him, his right hand sliding to rest at the small of her back. They had never stopped moving, so skilled a dancer was he.

She took a deep breath; she was dancing in his embrace! She must reveal herself, but it was several moments before she could speak again. His eyes were the pale gray of an overcast sky, looking unwaveringly into hers as he waited.

She gripped his hand tightly. "Once the clever princess allowed her heart to see how the nobleman had changed, she also saw that her esteem for him had grown to such a degree that the word now seemed paltry."

His breath caught, and his next words were a whisper. "She loved him?"

Elizabeth's heart was thundering. "She did." She smiled shyly. "And she began to believe that by his side, she might live safely in his kingdom after all."

His steps faltered; she had never before known him to be clumsy, but now he seemed wholly inattentive to the dance. Glancing around, he pulled her out of the circle of couples.

Her head swam with the sudden stillness and she closed her eyes. The arm around her waist tightened, pulling her against his body; his other hand cupped her cheek. She opened her eyes only to be captured by his. The rest of the world faded.

He spoke with quiet intensity. "Elizabeth – dearest, loveliest Elizabeth – I cannot express how greatly I admire and love you. Words are wholly inadequate to the task. But I shall endeavor to show you every day for the rest of my life, if you will only consent to marry me."

Tears pricked her eyes. "I will. I love you with all my heart, Fitzwilliam, and I will marry you."

His face broke into that broad, glorious smile again and his arm tightened once more, crushing her against his chest. She wrapped her arms around his waist, ignoring a feminine gasp nearby and smiling up at him as a sudden warmth suffused her body.

When she was able to speak again, her voice was breathy. "Just promise me that you will try, at least, to find the words from time to time. I do so like to hear them."

"I promise, Elizabeth." His smile became wry and slightly pained. "Indeed, I must, for I cannot very well kiss you here with half of Venice looking on."

CHAPTER TWENTY-SIX

IN WHICH DARCY'S MEMORY IS TESTED

Palazzo Sforza, Rio de San Vio, Venice, 13th February 1817

Richard,

To say that the two days past have been eventful is akin to saying that Windsor Castle is a large building. I shall attempt to describe the events in the order in which they occurred, and thus I begin with the most momentous: my Scheherazade (for she was, indeed, so garbed) has consented to be my wife. I am endlessly grateful to the long-dead author of that tale, for the king and his clever bride have been almost entirely responsible for our current understanding.

You will laugh, I know, to hear that I declared myself and was accepted in full view of a ballroom full of people – during a waltz, no less! Elizabeth is an exceptional woman and I am happier than I have ever been. (Our engagement shall be of some duration, I fear, owing to the complexity of the necessary contracts, but more on that anon. The remainder of the tale awaits.)

It was folly, in retrospect, to permit Georgiana and Lydia to attend the ball. Several of the men were appallingly ribald in their jokes – particularly after several glasses of wine – and many ladies were noticeably attempting to avoid being pawed at. Georgiana stopped dancing quite early after experiencing this for herself and was only persuaded to join a Venetian folk dance by one of the Alessi daughters. Fortunately her partner was properly attentive to propriety, so her final foray onto the floor was an enjoyable one.

Lydia, however, was quite shameless in her flirtation with Dario Alessi. She appeared to me unrepentant despite her grandmother's forceful remonstrance. Had we departed then the evening would likely have turned out very differently, but on reflection I am unconvinced that the primary events could have been entirely avoided.

There remain many tasks requiring my attention and this missive shall certainly be long; I shall add to it whenever I have an available half-hour. For now, adieu. –F.D.

Venice, 12th February 1817

It was only with the greatest effort that Darcy kept himself from kissing Elizabeth soundly, for all his gallant words, after watching that beguiling smile spread across her face. It was paired with an expression in her eyes that he had never seen, and it set his heart racing.

Oh, what would I not give for a moment of privacy! He mastered himself as the music concluded and settled for kissing her hand for an indecently long moment, reveling in her blush of pleasure.

It was only then that he became fully aware of the eyes on them – not only their own party but most of the Alessi family and other assorted guests. Paolo grinned and bowed to them as he departed the floor, Miss Kingsley on his arm.

"Congratulations, my dears," said Mrs. Bennet as soon as they had gained the safety of the group. "I am delighted for you both." She planted a kiss on Elizabeth's cheek and then Darcy's.

"I am sure you shall be very happy," said Bingley, shaking his hand while Jane embraced her sister.

Georgiana squealed, clearly unable to decide which of them to kiss first. As Elizabeth was still speaking quietly to Jane, she settled on Darcy. "Oh, brother! I am so happy! I have never seen you smile so, and to have such a sister is all I could have wished for!"

The congratulations continued for several more minutes, though Miss Cooper's was predictably the most amusing. "You certainly took your sweet time about it, Mr. Darcy, but I applaud you. Elizabeth shall have a delightfully scandalous story to tell in the drawing-rooms of London!"

Shortly thereafter, the time came to gather up their party and depart; look where they might, however, none of them could catch sight of Lydia.

"She was here not a half-hour ago," said Mrs. Bennet. "I observed her when she and Georgiana went for some punch just before the waltz."

"She was talking to those young men in the brown eagle masks," Georgiana said. "I confess my attention was quite diverted by the waltz. I walked back to gain a better view and I know not if she followed me."

Darcy scanned the room again. "They are absent as well. Dario's jackals are all missing, though he stands over there with his siblings."

At the opposite side of the room Dario disappeared with his sisters through a hidden door. Darcy suspected it led to the stairs and the family apartments above. Paolo remained, striding over to where his parents said good-night to departing guests.

Darcy looked to Bennet. "I shall recruit Paolo's assistance."

Bennet nodded. "The rest of us shall search the other rooms and meet again in this spot."

Darcy swiftly pulled Paolo aside and explained Lydia's absence. "Is there any way to search the family apartments or the servant's areas? I have no reason to suppose that she would remain in the public rooms."

Paolo offered his immediate assistance. Corralling a manservant, he directed the man to escort Darcy below. He himself went above to seek out his siblings.

Ten minutes later Darcy returned to the ballroom, nearly colliding with Paolo. "Any luck?"

"None," said his friend. "Dario has already departed for another party and we do not expect to see him again until the morning is well advanced. Neither Giulia nor Silvia has seen Miss Lydia since supper."

"She was not below."

He caught Bennet's gaze as he and Paolo crossed the room; the older man shook his head. They rejoined the group and shared the news that Lydia was no longer in the house.

"Perhaps she returned to our palazzo," Jane said.

"Unlikely," said Bennet, "but it appears that we shall learn nothing further tonight. Let us away and attempt to catch a few hours' rest. We shall begin again in the morning." He looked at Paolo. "Signor, please send us word when you have spoken to your brother. Unless I miss my guess, he is the most likely to know where she may be."

Elizabeth kept the worry from her countenance until the whole party had boarded the gondolas and were underway. Darcy was glad of it; with Elizabeth's example before her Georgiana remained calm, tears beginning only when they were near to their palazzo. Elizabeth immediately took Georgiana's hands, her words soothing and confident.

Once inside, Darcy realized that Elizabeth had not spoken to him since they were in the ballroom and that she would not meet his eye. He took her hand as they trudged up the stairs. When she tried to pull away he whispered, "Elizabeth, please come with me for a moment."

Gaining the first floor he stepped into the hall, pulling her with him. Bennet gave him a brief, hard look but continued up the stairs. He led her to the sitting-room window; dim moonlight drifted in, illuminating her features. Darcy placed a finger under her chin and tipped her face up, forcing her to meet his eyes. The fear there was expected but he also saw a second emotion; it took him a moment to recognize it as mortification.

He spoke softly, fearing she would bolt. "What is the matter, dearest?"

She bit her lip, tears springing to her eyes. He cupped her face in his hands and brushed them away with his thumbs, waiting silently for her answer.

She spoke haltingly. "I know not whether I most fear that Lydia has been taken or that she went willingly. If the former, I can only imagine her terror and pain. If the latter... it is selfish of me, I know," she said, eyes closing to avoid his gaze, "but I cannot believe that you would wish to connect yourself with such a family."

"Oh, Elizabeth." He gently kissed her eyelids, which flew open in surprise. He smiled. "You shall not be rid of me so easily, dearest. It may be months yet before we speak the words before the priest and all our friends; but hear me now. You are mine and I am yours. Your family is my family. I shall never abandon you, love."

She was shaking now, kohl-stained tears streaming down her face. He took out his handkerchief and wiped them gently away. Then, taking her face in his hands again, he kissed her tenderly. She threw her arms about his neck and he embraced her, lifting her feet off the floor. She felt weightless in his arms.

"I love you, Fitzwilliam," she whispered.

They remained that way until, at length, she pulled back to look at him and he set her on her feet.

She placed her palms on his cheeks, chuckling for a moment at the ridiculous beard he still wore. Her eyes met his and she smiled. "You are mine and I am yours," she said, low and fierce, and then she kissed him.

He was not so tender this time.

~ * ~

The sun was barely above the horizon when Darcy met Bennet and Bingley in the small parlor where they usually broke their fast. He was inexpressibly grateful for the cup of espresso that a servant placed before him. He had been so filled with conflicting emotions that it had taken some time to fall asleep, and his valet had awakened him only a few hours later.

He frowned as he sipped. The nagging sensation that he was forgetting something important had begun when he was finally abed, and it had only intensified since.

"This city is a warren," Bennet was saying. "If she is here and wishes to remain hidden, it shall not be difficult for her to do so."

Bingley's eyebrows rose. "You believe she left of her own accord?"

"I am not convinced of it, but neither am I convinced otherwise. She asked the servant to retrieve her cloak, so at the very least she was cooperative, if not entirely willing."

"The trouble with remaining in the city," Bingley said, "is the gossip. Everyone seems to know every detail of their neighbours' lives."

"True." Bennet nodded thoughtfully. "It shall be difficult enough to search the city. We shall need assistance if we are to search further afield."

Bingley brightened. "We already have a proper boat. We were to sail to Lido today to explore the island."

Lido.

Darcy sat bolt upright as the memory finally resolved itself in his mind. "Lido... and Mestre," he said.

The other men looked at him blankly. Swiftly he told them of the snippets of conversation he had overheard at the fencing club that day.

"We cannot know that they were speaking of Lydia," Bingley was saying, but Bennet frowned.

"Montague... *Romeo* Montague, perhaps? Who then is Juliet, if not Lydia?"

Darcy nodded. "I believe we must pay another visit to Signor Alessi."

"This very moment," said Bennet.

The Alessi servant made every effort to turn them away.

"Yes, I know precisely what the hour is," Bennet snapped. "You may summon your master now, or the Governor's men shall do it forthwith. In either event, I shall not be moved from this spot until I have seen him."

They were shown into the house, where they were soon met by Giacomo and Paolo Alessi. In a few sentences, Bennet explained their errand.

"I am sure that even my Dario could never do such a thing," Signor Alessi began, but Darcy shook his head.

Paolo placed his hand on his father's arm. "What is it, Darcy?"

Darcy told them of the conversation in the fencing club.

"How is this possible? I was there, and I heard none of this."

"They entered the changing-room after you and Bingley went through to the armory and you were already warming up by the time I was selecting my foil. You could not have heard."

Paolo directed a furious look at his father. "He has been spouting this *Romeo and Juliet* nonsense for weeks!" He looked at Darcy. "When did they meet, do you recall?"

"At your party for the new year."

Giacomo Alessi nodded sadly. "It began after that," he sighed. "Our family owns a small house on Lido. We use it only for the summer; it would be empty now."

"Do you also own a home in Mestre?" Bennet's voice was sharp.

"No, but it is a simple matter to hire a carriage there. Many roads depart from Mestre. They could be anywhere."

"We are approximately eight hours behind them. If we move swiftly, we may yet catch their scent."

"What of the jackals?" Darcy asked.

"The what?" Paolo looked confused.

"Dario's friends. The pack of jackals that surround him. They disappeared last night when Lydia did; as Dario was still here, we must assume they aided her departure."

Paolo barked a laugh. "An apt description. I have no doubt I can find them; convincing them to talk is another story."

"I know who can assist with that," Signor Alessi said. He stood. "Signor Bennet, we shall do everything in our power to find her. And if my son was involved, I will see to it that he takes full responsibility."

CHAPTER TWENTY-SEVEN

IN WHICH THE LIONESS BARES HER TEETH

February 13th (cont'd)

I cannot tell you, Charlotte, how greatly comforted I was that ~~Mr. Darcy~~ Fitzwilliam noted my distress and acted so swiftly to assuage it. In my mind I had been engaged and repudiated in the course of a single hour, and only awaited confirmation. Instead he treated me very tenderly, and his words were such that I now consider myself as married in all but name.

I came down in the morning to find only Charles about; Grandpa and Fitzwilliam had already departed for Palazzo Alessi to seek their aid. By the time they returned with Paolo and Signor Alessi the other ladies were at breakfast as well, so the news need only be shared once – Dario had not returned, but Fitzwilliam had chanced to hear snatches of a conversation that hinted at where Lydia had gone: Lido, and Mestre.

The Alessi family have a cottage on the nearby island of Lido. Mestre is on the mainland, and thence Lydia and Dario could easily flee to parts unknown. The gentlemen determined to search both locations; Paolo and Charles took a boat to Lido and the others departed for Mestre. Jane and I longed to join them but were persuaded to remain, in the event that new information arrived that required action.

Not a half-hour after they departed, we were called upon by Signora Alessi. She had with her two other ladies, Signora Rossi and Signora Giordano – the mothers of two of Dario's friends. It was by this time well after nine o'clock, and none of the ladies had yet seen their sons. Signora Alessi knew our troubles, and to her credit she made no fond excuses for Dario. She came only to inform us that she and her companions would run their sons to ground if need be to find Lydia.

I believe that there is no creature so fearsome as an Italian matriarch! In every town – from the smallest hamlet to the largest metropolis – the men bluster, but the women rule. Every tall, strapping young Hercules becomes meek as a lamb when being stared down by a woman half his size. Jane is too meek to adopt this strategy, I think, but Annabelle and I agree that we must devote ourselves to learning the trick of it! –E.

Palazzo Sforza, Rio de San Vio, Venice, February 12th, 1817

Elizabeth sat at the pianoforte with Georgiana; she had no patience for reading or sketching just now, but music kept her mind and hands busy. Georgiana, though, was struggling. They came to a difficult passage – one Georgiana had played dozens of times – and again she struck a wrong note. She slumped on the bench, covering her face with her hands as she burst into tears.

Elizabeth wrapped an arm about her shoulders, fishing a handkerchief from her pocket. She exchanged concerned looks with Nanna and Jane. Slowly the sobs quieted, and Georgiana took the square of linen that Elizabeth silently proffered.

"Will you not say what troubles you, dear heart?" asked Elizabeth.

"I feel… Lizzy, I am to blame. I was with her and I turned my back, and now she is gone!"

"Dearest Georgiana, you could not have known that she would be spirited away just at that moment."

"No, but… there is more. Oh, Lizzy, she swore me to secrecy, but I knew it was wrong! I should have told you."

Elizabeth felt a cold weight in the pit of her stomach. The room was silent, Nanna and Jane both staring fixedly at Georgiana. "What do you mean?"

Georgiana avoided her eyes. "She… she was in love with him. They wrote to each other every day."

"What? How? How could she keep such a thing secret?"

"He arranged a place for them to hide their letters."

Sudden realization struck Elizabeth. "She walked out every day, even in the rain."

Georgiana nodded. "She let me read his first letter. He confessed to being selfish and irresponsible, impulsive, even a libertine. He said your grandfather scared him witless but that she was so captivating, he wanted to become worthy of her."

"And she believed him?"

"Not at first. I did not believe him either, but then his friends began to tease him about being too boring to come out with them. After that, they truly stopped inviting him."

"I knew it could not be by chance that we kept meeting him."

"No, it was not. I never saw any other letters, but she told me something of them. He quoted *Romeo and Juliet*, but also philosophy and business. He talked about the responsibilities he shall have when he inherits, and how she might continue with her painting and paper-marbling after they marry."

Elizabeth looked at her sharply. "Did she speak of elopement?"

Georgiana shook her head vigorously. "No. She spoke of their marriage as something that must happen in the future. She said that she must first find a way to convince your grandfather that Dario is not the villain we all believe him to be."

"Not a villain! How is he not? Georgiana, either he convinced her to elope or he abducted her. In neither case has he acted honorably."

Georgiana's gaze returned to her lap. "No. You are right, Lizzy. I should have insisted she tell you what was happening or told you myself. I am so very sorry."

Elizabeth hugged her again, sighing. "You were trying to be her friend, I am certain. Friendship is never more difficult than when one is asked to keep a dangerous secret."

Georgiana excused herself. Elizabeth sat down heavily next to her grand-mother, looking at the others in dumb amazement.

"They have both been very foolish," Jane said at length. "All of them, I suppose. But this news gives me hope that we shall find her well and happy."

Nanna's expression spoke volumes but all she said was, "We must pray that you are right, Jane."

They all started when the bell rang a few minutes later. Signora Alessi was shown in, Signora Rossi with her. That lady was dragging a sandy-haired young man along by his ear. Elizabeth did not recognize every word Signora Rossi was spitting at her son in rapid Italian, but she understood enough to know that many were not appropriate for ladies. Jane's eyes were wider even than her own.

Good heavens. It is a wonder he has not burst into flames.

Signora Alessi curtseyed to Nanna. "Good morning, Signora. I believe we have information that may be of use."

Signora Rossi shook her son's head by the ear. *"Vincenzo, dì alla Signora Bennet quello che sai!"*

Elizabeth silently translated: *Tell Mrs. Bennet what you know.*

"Mamma, per favore—"

"No! Non posso essere tua madre! Non ho cresciuto mio figlio per rapire ragazze innocenti!"

I cannot be your mother; I did not raise my son to abduct innocent girls!

"Dario me ucciderà se dico qualcosa, Mamma!"

Elizabeth suspected that Vincenzo was unlikely to be available for Dario to kill, given his mother's fury. Signora Rossi took her son's jaw in a crushing grip, her other hand still firmly holding his ear, and pulled until his face was inches from hers. Her voice was suddenly very quiet. *"Dovresti temermi. Ti ucciderò adesso se non dici alla Signora Bennet dove troverà sua nipote!"*

Elizabeth was duly impressed. *You should fear me. I will kill you now if you do not tell Mrs. Bennet where she may find her granddaughter.*

Vincenzo Rossi deflated. His gaze fixed on the floor, he mumbled, *"Ha no-leggiato una carozza—"*

"Più forte! In inglese!" Signora Rossi jerked her son upright again, facing Nanna.

"Dario hired a carriage to wait for them this morning at a hotel. He followed us to Lido. They left at sunrise."

"Why did he not take her directly to Mestre last night?" Nanna asked.

"He said it would be suspicious if they arrived in the middle of the night."

"And where is he taking her?"

"Verona. He is going to marry her."

"That is a long way to take a girl to marry her," said Paolo Alessi. He and Charles entered and came around to face a suddenly rigid Vincenzo. His tone was conversational. "Why not marry her in Mestre? Or even Padua?"

"Romeo and Juliet."

Paolo rolled his eyes. "I shall strangle him when I find him." His gaze sharpened. "So. Vincenzo. At which hotel did they meet the carriage?" He crossed his arms at Vincenzo's cagey expression. "I shall strangle *you* if I do not find him. I do not jest, boy. If you lie to me, you shall not see another sunrise."

The young man paled. "Mamma!"

"Digli la verità." Her voice was implacable. *Tell him the truth.*

There was a pause. "The *Albergo al Giardino.*"

Paolo's brows lifted. "Not the posting inn at Mestre?"

"No. He thought you would look there."

"And where, exactly, is the *Albergo al Giardino?*"

"Fusina. They sailed there directly from Lido."

Paolo nodded. "She was at the cottage, Signora Bennet, but it is empty now. Her costume was on Giulia's bed." He bowed to his mother and Signora Rossi. "Thank you. *Grazie per vostro aiuto.*"

Charles clasped Jane's hand briefly, then nodded to Nanna. "We shall find them and return directly."

Then they were gone, the visitors close behind them.

~ * ~

It was nearly twelve hours before the gentlemen returned.

Elizabeth, having discovered a reliable atlas in the library, had calculated that they were unlikely to return before ten o'clock in any event; when the search party entered the sitting-room at ten-fifteen they found a fire still blazing in the hearth and a light supper waiting for them in the dining-room.

They also found four women wearing varying expressions of anger and disbelief, for Lydia's fury at being returned to Venice was clearly audible from the moment she entered the house.

"And I daresay you have all been most high-handed!" she said as Grandpa propelled her into the room. They were followed by Charles, who appeared set to catch her if she attempted to flee. Mr. Darcy and Paolo manhandled an angry Dario just behind, and Signor Alessi brought up the rear.

Nanna fixed her eyes on Lydia. "Be silent, girl!"

Lydia took in Nanna's expression. Her mouth closed into a sullen frown.

Nanna turned to Grandpa. "Where did you find them?"

"They were nearly to Padua when we overtook them on the road."

"They were alone?"

"But for the carriage-driver, yes."

Nanna regarded Lydia for a long moment. "She would make an excellent actress, I suppose."

"Nanna! I—"

"Silence, Lydia! You shall speak when you are spoken to and not a moment before." She looked at her husband again. "Have any of you eaten?"

Grandpa smiled. "Very little, but we may delay a while yet before we expire of famine."

Elizabeth smiled inwardly. Six men in the room and not one of them spoke a word without the say-so of the tiniest woman present.

"Jane, Miss Darcy, Mr. Bingley, please escort Lydia to her room and ensure she remains there."

Glaring, Lydia spun on her heel and stomped from the room, her temporary gaolers following.

Nanna turned her attention to Dario. She pointed to a chair. "Sit."

Dario sat, the men fanning out around him. Nanna stood directly before him, arms crossed. His angry, sullen expression shifted to unease as he sat beneath her silent, measuring stare. More than a minute passed before he finally dropped his eyes. Only then did Nanna speak.

"When did you tell Lydia of your plan?"

"I told her last night that my friends would aid her to depart the ball unseen, that we might be together without—" his glance flickered upward. "Without her family always looking on."

"She consented to her compromise, then."

"She was not compromised!"

Nanna raised a single eyebrow.

"I swear it! I never touched her."

"You were alone together for twelve hours at least. Are we to credit the word of a self-confessed libertine?"

"I plan to marry her, Signora Bennet. I love her. I vow to you that I have not touched her, nor shall I before we are wed."

"You believe we shall permit her to marry?"

"You must!"

"I cannot imagine why."

"Because... well, because... as you said, Signora, we were alone together."

"Ah, so she *is* compromised."

"No!"

Nanna only lifted a brow again; the silence stretched.

"We had to elope! Like Romeo and Juliet. She said Mr. Bennet would never permit us to marry, so it was the only way. But I swear to you I did not touch her."

"Did she chance to mention the consequence if she marries without her grandfather's consent?"

Dario squirmed. "She said only that she must write to her father to release her dowry."

Nanna's grim smile was a mirror of her husband's. "It seems this child requires education, my dear."

"I shall be happy to provide it, madam. Even a boy must comprehend his situation if he is to make sensible decisions."

"I should first like to provide him some perspective, if I may."

Grandpa bowed slightly.

Nanna favored Dario with a dismissive gaze. "We are thousands of miles from New York. If what you say is true and Lydia shall not bear a child, so much the better. She may return home and marry a young man who is not a selfish, profligate ratbag, with her acquaintance none the wiser."

Elizabeth nearly swallowed her tongue; she had never heard Nanna use such language! Dario puffed up in anger, but Nanna merely stared him down once more.

"Come, Elizabeth," she said, "I believe it is time we spoke to your sister."

Elizabeth followed her from the room. As they passed, Grandpa whispered something in Nanna's ear that Elizabeth did not catch. Nanna gave him a hard look; he shrugged minutely, his expression apologetic but resolute. She frowned, then nodded.

On the stair she said, "The reason I wished you to remain with me, Lizzy, is to ensure that a sister – whose advice Lydia may be more ready to hear – may weigh Lydia's assertions against the evidence of her own eyes. And before you ask, I shall tell you tomorrow what your grandfather said to me just now."

They stopped by the door to Lydia's room; Charles stood outside.

"Has she spoken?"

"No. I have heard only Jane's voice since the door was closed."

Nanna nodded. "Thank you for keeping watch. You may join the gentlemen; I hope shortly to have things well in hand here."

He left with a bow. Inside Lydia was seated before the fireplace, staring into the flames. Jane looked up and shook her head sadly.

Nanna sat next to Lydia, looking into the fire for some time before she spoke. "Mesmerizing, is it not? What is it, I wonder, that so attracts us to something so dangerous?"

"I know not." Lydia's voice was flat.

"I am certain you have no desire to hear anything I say just now. I know it always angers me to be denied my heart's dearest wish."

Lydia glanced at Nanna but said nothing.

"I shall say only this: until today I was certain that we were right to bring you with us. Your father took a great deal of convincing, you know. I saw what happened to that foolish Miss Harding – how she threw herself into a compromise with a heartless young man who treated her like rubbish – and I feared that with only your friends to guide you, the same fate awaited you. It seems I greatly overestimated my influence."

"I did not throw myself into a compromise, Nanna. He is going to marry me!"

"Miss Harding thought the same of her young man, my dear. But no man of sense will marry without money and if the young lady is already ruined, her options are few. After your experience with Mr. Wickham, I thought you understood this."

"I am not ruined! And he has money even if Papa insists on denying me my dowry!"

"At present I believe he has only his allowance. He has no independent fortune."

"He will inherit after Paolo marries that awful Miss Kingsley."

"Indeed?" Nanna's tone was mild, but her look was pointed. "Think you that Signor Alessi will name as his successor a boy with a firmly established history as a ne'er-do-well, who abducted – from his own home – the granddaughter of one of his guests?"

"He has changed! He tells me every day that he has changed because of me."

"I see. You must have seen evidence of this transformation, or you would not be so certain. With your own eyes, of course, not merely what he and his friends have told you."

Lydia was silent.

Nanna sighed. "You say that you are not compromised, despite ample opportunity, so perhaps he is truly reforming his behavior."

"He never laid a finger on me. I would not have permitted it had he tried before we were married."

"And you truly wish to marry this young man?"

"I do! I love him, and only him."

"Understand, Lydia, that all we have seen from him today is deceit and selfishness. To my eyes, he is as dangerous to you as the fire in that grate." Nanna took Lydia's hand and turned fully to face her, waiting until Lydia met her gaze. "If you wish to gain my support, you must convince me that you have considered marriage to him with clear eyes and a rational mind."

"How am I supposed to do that?"

"Write two lists. First, what you have observed that convinces you that he is a good and honorable man. Second, your plan for your married life – where shall you live? What shall be your income, your expenses? How shall you provide for your children?"

"Is that not for him to manage?"

"A wife is responsible for her household; she must know what she may safely afford."

"I cannot know such a thing if I know not what my income is!"

"If you convince us to permit you to marry, you may safely assume that you shall have your dowry and he shall have his allowance until he inherits."

Lydia smiled in triumph.

"If you elope, you may safely assume that you shall have nothing."

Lydia's smile faded.

Nanna patted her knee. "We shall leave you for now. You shall not leave this house unescorted again and there must be no more secret letters or sneaking about, do you understand? To have any hope of changing our minds, you must both be entirely aboveboard."

Lydia nodded. "I understand."

They left her alone with her thoughts. Elizabeth embraced Georgiana as the girl went to her bed, then followed the others to where they stood before Jane's door.

"You would truly allow her to marry him?" Jane was asking.

Nanna sighed. "She has ever been the child who did precisely what she was told not to do, Jane. She shall not be happy unless she feels that she has won a victory over us. I shall not be happy if she marries a reprobate. If it is possible for us both to be satisfied by a marriage to that boy then I shall not be the one to deny her, but I shall require a great deal of convincing."

Elizabeth stood in the hall after the others entered their rooms. She dearly wished for her bed, but she had hardly spoken to Mr. Darcy – *Fitzwilliam!* – today, and not at all since his return. She could still hear masculine voices below; he was certainly more exhausted than she, and she could perhaps bring him some comfort. Though if she was honest with herself, she desired to be comforted nearly as much.

She descended the stairs, her soft house-slippers making no noise as she crossed the hall to the dining-room. She briefly caught Fitzwilliam's eye as she passed the open door to the sitting-room; pausing to listen, she felt certain that the Alessi men would be returning to their own home soon. She poured herself a glass of wine and sat down to wait.

CHAPTER TWENTY-EIGHT

IN WHICH DARCY OBSERVES A MASTER

13ᵗʰ February (cont'd)

Paolo, Bingley and I remained on horseback for the return journey to Venice, and the pace was considerably less punishing. Even so, for two months now I have been rarely in the saddle and nine hours of nearly continuous riding is more than most men can tolerate. I am certainly feeling the effects of it; even you might have had difficulty entering a boat after so many hours on horseback, particularly with two unwilling companions.

I prefer my lot to Bennet's, however; it was he and Giacomo Alessi who rode in the carriage with Lydia and Dario. The journey from Padua to Venice is nearly five hours by coach, and I understand that Lydia made her displeasure known for much of that time. She objected not only to the rescue but to the restrictions which made their elopement "necessary" in the first place.

Such is the principal drawback, I suppose, of encouraging young women to be independent and strong-minded. Bennet is quite sanguine about it; he assures me that once young ladies get over the most trying age, those with well-educated minds are quite as capable as any man at a task which requires intellect. (Hence his decision to place Elizabeth at the helm of a newly founded company.)

As Lydia has not yet achieved that hoped-for state, he deliberately fueled her outrage past the point of concealment and got out of her all the details of their correspondence and her knowledge of Dario's plan, which was very little. Though, in truth, there was little to know; he had thought ahead only so far as the wedding night and she had not even comprehended that much.

You are no doubt recalling my initial opinion of Andrew Bennet – I have just done so, and it is mortifying beyond description. Now I confess that in him I see the man I hope to become. At seventy years of age he rode like the devil for

250

*nearly four hours and interrogated his granddaughter for another five. Then –
at nearly midnight – he remained sharp enough to negotiate an agreement that
may satisfy all parties, if Dario proves himself worthy. All without losing his
sense of humour or showing an ounce of fatigue.*

*It is no wonder that the American Bennets ascended from nothing to one of
New York's first families in two generations! I shall sit at his knee alongside
Elizabeth and Bingley for as long as I may; I encourage you to do the same if
opportunity arises. I need not tell you that such tutelage is rarely to be met with.*

*We return to England soon; I may yet see you before this letter reaches
you. I look forward with great anticipation to returning to home and family,
though I shall miss this strange country more than I ever believed possible.*

Darcy

Palazzo Sforza, Rio de San Vio, Venice, 12th February 1817

Darcy glanced at the clock. It was after eleven, and Bennet had been shut
up with Giacomo Alessi for nearly twenty minutes now. Paolo had been pacing
the length of the room since the older men departed it.

Dario lounged insouciantly in his chair. "Say your piece, Paolo."

Paolo stopped and glared at his brother.

"The old people have lectured me. Surely you wish to be like them? Come,
mother hen, cluck-cluck."

Paolo resumed pacing, his brother watching with amusement. He finally
stopped before the window and stared out for several minutes before sighing
deeply. "I am foolish to be angry at what you have done to yourself, Dario. You
care nothing for me. You care nothing for the family. You care only for your
own pleasure." He turned and looked at his brother with dead eyes. "You must
face this alone. I will not speak for you."

Dario smirked. "Mamma shall support me. She always does."

"Ha! You did not see her face this morning, standing here with Signora
Rossi. You have shamed her even more than you have shamed me or Papà. She
has spent years telling everyone that your 'heart is in the right place,' no matter
who you injured."

Dario's expression of confident amusement cracked ever so slightly.

"But you never kidnapped the daughter of a guest in her home before, did
you? She was forced this morning to admit to all of the other mothers that her

251

favorite son is as reprehensible as they have said. No, Dario. She will not easily forgive this."

"I did not kidnap her. And take care how you speak to me. I care about our *famiglia*!"

"You tried to force a sixteen-year-old bride on our *famiglia*! If she went willingly it only proves that she is as selfish and headstrong as you are."

Dario glowered but Paolo gave him no chance to speak.

"To satisfy your childish notions of romance you endangered my engagement and insulted one of the most powerful men in America, with whom Papà is close to finalizing a very valuable shipping agreement. You have shamed us before all Venice; if you had succeeded in this idiocy you would have ruined us."

Dario scoffed. "You are an old woman, Paolo. Our family would not be ruined by my marrying Lydia and neither would your marriage to that harpy."

"I cannot speak for the financial state of your family, but I must agree with your brother on the matter of his engagement," Darcy said.

Dario turned, his surprise evident.

"Sir Robert Kingsley is a baronet. The aristocracy shall have difficulty accepting a foreigner into their ranks as it is; a foreigner whose brother eloped? With an *American*? Unthinkable. Kingsley would like to see his daughter settled, but he shall not do so at the expense of his own good name."

Dario's expression was dubious. He looked questioningly at Bingley.

"If Kingsley has not announced the engagement in the London papers, he could break it without damaging his daughter's reputation," Bingley said, shrugging. "And he will, if the risk to his own is too great."

"There is also the matter of the money," Paolo said. "Kingsley will give our family a title, but he does not risk his reputation on a Venetian son-by-law out of the generosity of his heart. He does not know that Tomasso Giardino has cut our legs from under us. Without the agreement with Signor Bennet, we go under."

Dario's cocky veneer vanished, and he surged to his feet. "What? Why was I not told of this?"

"Why would we trust you? Giardino's son is your friend, and you keep no secrets when you are drunk and whoring. As I said: you favour your own pleasure over our family."

"If I had known such a thing I would not have stolen away with Lydia!"

"You would never have believed it. I am an old woman, remember? You are a kidnapper who does not think of how his decisions will harm others."

"I am not a kidnapper!"

"You are." Giacomo Alessi's voice was like ice. He re-entered the room, appearing to loom over his son for all that he was shorter. "Sit down, *ragazzo*. You took an underage girl – a guest of our house! – without her family's knowledge or consent. She cannot give consent, by our laws or hers. That makes you a kidnapper."

"Papà—"

"I suppose you thought we would welcome you back with open arms? Buy you a house, increase your allowance? You told her you would inherit after your brother marries. You think I would trust such a boy with the future of my family?"

"Papà! You would never—"

"Do not think to tell me what I will and will not do! This man has spent the past half-hour convincing me to allow you to redeem yourself. I would prefer to throw you onto the street and be done."

Dario's face drained of color and he sank into his chair. "You... would disown me?"

"What reason have I to acknowledge a son who thinks nothing of bringing such shame upon his family?"

"I am sorry, Papà. I did not think it would be so bad."

"You did not think! You never do. I told Signor Bennet that he might bring you his proposal because it is only due to him and Mr. Darcy that we are not entirely ruined."

"Proposal? I do not understand."

Bennet stepped forward, towering over the now-seated Dario. "You say that you love my granddaughter."

"Yes, as Romeo loves Juliet."

"Juliet was thirteen years of age; Romeo scarcely older. Childish infatuation is not love, boy. Not by a large measure."

Dario bristled, but had the sense to say nothing.

Darcy sensed movement in the periphery of his vision; Elizabeth walked silently past the open door to the sitting-room. She looked exhausted and troubled, but she flashed him a small smile as she made her way to the dining-room.

It is easy to mistake attraction for love when one is not familiar with either. He knew now what it was to love, but he had been as foolish as this boy when first he had lost his heart to Elizabeth.

Bennet's challenging gaze never wavered, resting entirely on Dario. "What will you do to prove yourself worthy of Lydia's hand?"

"Anything."

"Truly? What I demand is not a small sacrifice."

"Truly. She is worth everything." He looked at his brother, then his father. "My *famiglia* is worth everything."

"Then your next three years belong to me. You shall start at the very bottom in our Lisbon office, under the watchful eyes of my manager and his wife. And do not think Mr. Lewis will go easy on you. My father started from nothing. As did I, before I was permitted to have any control of what was to be my own company. Mr. and Mrs. Lewis shall provide me and your father with regular reports on your conduct, including your behaviour outside of company time. You shall be paid standard wages but receive no other financial support."

Dario looked at his father in alarm; Signor Alessi's expression was hard.

"Have no illusions: if you are a gambler or a spendthrift, I shall know it. If you are a libertine and a drunkard, I shall know it. I make no allowances for the habits of youth. If you prove yourself the selfish, profligate ratbag you now appear, you shall forfeit your position and my granddaughter. What your father does with you then is his affair."

"I shall wash my hands of him," said Signor Alessi.

"If, on the other hand, you work hard and conduct yourself as a gentleman, you may earn a position of greater responsibility."

"What of Lydia?"

"She returns to New York. You may write to her, as you shall be provisionally engaged. If either of you wishes to break the engagement you may do so without penalty, so long as you behave honourably. If at the close of three years your conduct has been satisfactory and you both wish to marry, you shall be permitted."

"May I see her?"

"Before we depart, yes. Under close supervision. Beyond that I make no promises."

"And if I decline?"

"Then your father may do as he wishes. My terms are not negotiable."

Dario swallowed hard.

"But if you attempt *any* sort of sneaking or underhanded behaviour with Lydia again, both my offers are withdrawn – my offer to you and my agreement with your family. Dishonesty merits no support from me or mine."

Dario looked apprehensively at his father. "Is this to be my only opportunity to make my way?"

"If you prove yourself in these three years, *and* your brother's marriage goes forward, I shall reconsider whether to name you my heir. I also make no promises."

Silence descended. Dario looked badly shaken, but in truth he had little choice. He pushed trembling hands through his hair and hauled in a great breath before standing to face Bennet squarely. "I shall work hard to be a better man than I have been. Thank you for your generosity, Signor Bennet. I accept."

Bennet shook his proffered hand. "We depart within the fortnight." Glancing down with a sardonic grin at the tawny suit Dario still wore he added, "I suggest you acquire a more moderate wardrobe."

CHAPTER TWENTY-NINE

IN WHICH DARCY SHOWS HIS BEST SIDE

Darcy House, London, April 17ᵗʰ, 1817

Dearest Mamma,

This is the last letter I shall write as Jane Bennet. How surreal that it has come at last! Tonight, my sisters and I spent an hour on my bed, eating cookies and drinking chocolate together for what may be the last time.

Lydia wished to know if Charles's sisters have forgiven him for marrying me. I suspect not, though they are kinder than I anticipated. I thought at first that they had warmed to me, but Charles let slip that he threatened to cut them entirely if they had not the willingness to treat me with the courtesy due a sister. It is comforting to know that we shall see them but rarely, after our visit to Scarborough two weeks hence!

I guessed that Lydia might beg to come with Charles and me on our wedding tour to the Lakes, but she spoke instead with great enthusiasm about seeing our cousin Tommy again at Pemberley. I am most curious to see Georgiana and Fitzwilliam's home, having heard so much about it. I wish you might be there as well! I know that Lizzy especially wishes to see you and Papa before she is married, but this letter shall never reach you in time!

Lizzy was quite philosophical this evening; she spoke of how changed we all are by our Grand Tour. I do not feel so very different, but my sisters disagreed. Lizzy insisted that I "no longer perversely trust the untrustworthy," and Lydia applauded me for demanding that Charles treat me with the respect I deserve. Perhaps they are right; I certainly entertain more uncharitable thoughts now than I had been used to!

Lizzy keeps her merry wit, but its edge is tempered. She no longer clings with such tenacity to her first impressions; having come to forgive Mr. Darcy she has learned to believe that a person may improve, given time and proper guidance. Grandpa's generosity in the matter of the railroad has relieved her fears of dependency. In all she is the Lizzy you know but matured with grace.

Lydia, I think, you shall not recognize. This recent escapade with Dario Alessi has sobered her; I believe he shared with her the consequences to them both (and to their families) had they wed. She was exceedingly subdued on the journey to London and though she has now regained much of her liveliness, she is more thoughtful. She has written Aunt Louisa and hopes to join in her work with the Orphan Asylum Society when we return home.

Tomorrow begins a new chapter of my life; I close the cover on the old with gratitude and fond remembrances. Thank you, dearest Mamma, for permitting us all to undertake this journey. I have missed you very much, of course, but I cannot imagine being happier than I am now! I am ever

Your loving daughter,

Jane

Pemberley, Derbyshire, May-June 1817

Seated atop her favorite chestnut mare, Elizabeth looked down upon the grounds of Pemberley in awe. Mist hung over the lake and dew-covered grass sparkled in the early morning light. *Of all this I shall be mistress. It is certainly a far cry from New York.*

Fitzwilliam, beside her on his black stallion, pointed to a faint track in the distance which was invisible from the house. "Do you see that path there, that goes around the far side of the lake? It is a lovely walk, particularly once it enters the trees. Perfect for a solitary ramble."

"I have not enjoyed a solitary ramble since Hertfordshire! Did I ever thank you properly for saving me that day? Your intervention with Mr. Collins was exceedingly well-timed."

He made a show of thinking hard. "Nay; there were some words, I recall, but nothing like proper thanks." The gaze he leveled at her was heated. "I am willing to accept your belated gratitude, however."

Elizabeth chuckled and nudged her mare to side-step until her thigh pressed against his. Reaching for his cravat, she pulled his head down to whisper in his ear. "I am eternally grateful, sir, that you saved me from the mortification of a compromise with Mr. Collins… by arranging one with yourself."

She kissed him swiftly on the cheek, laughing gaily as she kicked her mount into a gallop; he grabbed at her but found only empty air. Racing down the hill with hoofbeats close behind, she caught up with the phaeton containing Richard Fitzwilliam – no longer a colonel – and Anne de Bourgh.

"Are you teasing my cousin?" Richard demanded.

"He clearly communicated his desire for teasing, sir. What is a lady to do but comply with her lord's wishes?"

"That is precisely how I feel, Elizabeth," said Anne.

"We are beset on all sides, Darcy! How shall we prevail?"

Fitzwilliam pulled up beside her. "If we divide our forces, we may attack on two fronts."

"Excellent notion, cousin! CHARGE!"

Richard snapped the reins and the ponies burst into motion, jerking the phaeton along behind them. Anne shrieked, grabbing at her bonnet. Elizabeth and Fitzwilliam laughed.

"'Tis a shame you did not know Anne before her mother died," he said. "You cannot appreciate the transformation. I do not know that saucy woman with the spring in her step and healthy glow in her cheeks."

"She and Richard shall do very well together, I think."

"They shall. They have only to wait another two months before her mourning is complete; I anticipate an announcement that very day." He smiled. "Come, I should like to show you that solitary ramble."

In their two weeks at Pemberley they had quickly formed the habit of riding out together in the early morning, before most of the house was awake. Elizabeth craved the time alone, and with a house full of guests – and more set to arrive before their wedding – Fitzwilliam required the quiet and relative solitude. Richard and Anne were their chaperones today, and one could not desire a more unsuitable pair to guard her virtue from the advances of her fiancé.

The path was wide enough to admit a horse, even in the trees; they followed it for a quarter of a mile before coming upon a clearing, in which stood a snug cottage. The roof was of sturdy shingles and the walls were brightly whitewashed. There was shelter for the horses with clean hay and a stack of chopped wood by the back door.

Fitzwilliam stole frequent glances at her, fighting to suppress a grin. He produced a key and the front door opened to reveal a small but comfortable room with a table beneath the front window, two cozy chairs before the fire, a wide bed with a thick, soft coverlet and fluffy pillows, and a wardrobe. A doorway led to a tiny kitchen.

"This is delightful, Fitzwilliam! How long has it been here?"

"It was long abandoned when I was a boy. Richard and I played here. I asked him to see to its restoration while I was abroad."

Elizabeth lifted an eyebrow. "Indeed? Had you a particular use in mind?"

He stepped close and encircled her in his arms. "I hoped to bring my bride here, that we might enjoy a truly private retreat."

"You came to Italy with the hope of winning my hand? That is positively an age to spend wooing a woman, sir."

"There were, I confess, several moments of crippling doubt. But when the lady is extraordinary, so must be the effort required to win her."

"You have put your obstinacy to excellent use, then, Mr. Darcy."

He lowered his head. "You shall find me very determined indeed, madam."

He kissed her then, not gently, his hands roaming down her back. She squeaked when he cupped her backside in his large palm. His low chuckle as he planted kisses on her neck and the hard press of his body against hers sent butterflies from her belly to the secret place between her legs.

"Oh," she breathed.

He drew back his head and gazed at her, his pupils large and black. "I should like to beg a favor of you on our wedding day." He gave her a lazy smile. "Please wear Scheherazade's corset beneath your gown."

She could not mask her surprise; it was so very unlike what she had expected him to say. "Of course, if you wish it. But why?"

"I shall be very pleased to be the only one who knows it is there." His smile became wicked. "And I shall look eagerly forward to removing it."

Her mouth fell open. *This* from the stern Mr. Darcy, with his upright posture and disapproving countenance? *Was this devilish man always there?* It had taken her far longer than it ought, to understand that the rigid façade was a mask he wore… but *this!*

She recalled the marriage ceremony she had witnessed only a few weeks ago: "With my body I thee worship," Charles had said as he placed the ring on Jane's finger. Elizabeth had not given it any consideration at the time, but clearly that phrase had a very particular meaning. She bit her lip, feeling a flush rising from her chest to her cheeks. Fitzwilliam's gaze only grew more appreciative.

Emboldened, she raised up on tiptoe. "Then it shall be my very great pleasure to wear it."

His kiss this time was deep and lingering, the pulse in his neck thudding beneath her thumb. He released her lips slowly and with evident regret. "We should return to the house; Richard can make only so many excuses before our absence becomes too suspicious."

She pretended not to notice him watching as she straightened her riding habit in the looking-glass. As they mounted, he was watching her again. She chuckled. "I recall a time when you found me not at all worth looking at. What could have changed?"

"I cannot account for it, I confess. But we had not left Hertfordshire before I desired always to be near you."

"Whereas you avoided other young ladies as though they were plague-stricken. I see how it is. You wanted me precisely because I made no pretense of wanting you."

"Lack of pretension is by no means your only endearing quality."

"Excellent! You are to have charge of all my best qualities and exaggerate them as greatly as possible. I shall undertake to tease you as often as I may, and poke so many holes in your conceit that it must inevitably shrivel to nothing."

Fitzwilliam shook his head. "Obstinate, did you call me? You know the saying about the pot and kettle, of course."

Elizabeth merely smiled.

~ * ~

It chanced to be unseasonably warm on Elizabeth's birthday. The party enjoyed a picnic under the trees, not far from the house.

Nanna and Grandpa rested comfortably on the soft cushioned chairs which had been carried out for them, occasionally gesturing to one of the youngsters and murmuring in amusement. Lydia and Tommy played cribbage with his newest deck of cards: Greek gods and goddesses illustrated the faces, while Lydia's marbled paper covered the backs. Richard and Anne partnered against Jane and Charles in a game of battledore and shuttlecock in the nearby clearing; groans punctuated the sound of racquets striking cork whenever the shuttlecock fell to the earth.

The rest lounged in the shade, listening to Fitzwilliam read the story of Sinbad's fourth voyage. Annabelle had arrived but two days past; she sat with Kitty in rapt attention, gasping as Fitzwilliam revealed the gruesome fate that awaited Sinbad on the death of his wife – to be buried alive with her.

Lord and Lady Matlock regarded their nephew with undisguised wonder. His reading was uncommonly good – embellished with broad gestures, dramatic changes of timbre and volume, and pauses for added effect. Over the course of many days reading *Une Mille et Une Nuits* aloud in the carriage across France, Lydia and Georgiana had encouraged him to liven up his performance; Elizabeth had heard this tale, though he did it better justice now.

Elizabeth herself sat with legs folded, sketchbook on her lap as she drew the scene. She had chosen to capture one of Fitzwilliam's more exaggerated poses, his arms spread wide and face frozen in a grimace.

"He shall not thank you for that," Georgiana giggled. She sat beside Elizabeth, observing her work.

"He may admire the drawings of himself in lordly poses all he likes. I prefer to catch him in the act of being ridiculous."

Richard interrupted the narrative. "I say, Darcy, were you expecting more guests today?"

The rest of them followed his gaze to where a carriage emblazoned with the Darcy crest approached the house.

Fitzwilliam sprang to his feet, grinning. "Hoping, but not expecting. Come, Elizabeth, let us greet our guests."

They arrived at the front of the house just as the carriage door was opened. A short middle-aged man with dark hair, a slender face, and long-fingered hands emerged, turning to assist his wife.

"Mamma Bianchi! Papà!" Elizabeth hurried over and threw her arms around the woman. "Oh, Mamma! *Che deliziosa sorpresa!*"

Mamma Bianchi embraced her and kissed her cheeks soundly, beaming. *"Mia bella ragazza. Hai finalmente deciso di sposarlo, eh?"*

Fitzwilliam laughed and submitted to kisses and a fierce, tearful hug. "Yes," he said, translating for his other guests, "this lovely woman did indeed finally agree to marry me."

Mamma Bianchi kept hold of his cheeks. *"Mio generoso figlio! Grazie per averci invitato."*

"Naturally I invited you! Our wedding would not be complete without you," he said, repeating his words in Italian as Papà Bianchi hugged him tightly.

"Elisabetta! William!" Stella and Luca stood in the carriage, Matteo waiting to help them descend. Luca, as ever, reached out for Fitzwilliam.

Fitzwilliam lifted the boy into his arms, nodding indulgently as Luca – now three – told him the barely-understandable but extremely exciting tale of their journey.

Stella held out a wilted bunch of wildflowers to Elizabeth. *"Tu e William vi state davvero sposando?"*

"Yes, William and I are truly marrying," Elizabeth said, kissing the girl's forehead.

The children had made a few endearing attempts to pronounce Fitzwilliam's name after that first terrible night, and Jane had swiftly suggested they call him William. From that moment, he had been William to the entire Bianchi clan.

Stella bounced on her toes. *"William è mio fratello, quindi sarai mia sorella!"*

"Yes, Stella," Fitzwilliam said as he finished the introductions. "I am your brother, so Elizabeth shall be your sister."

Having collected hugs and kisses from all the new arrivals, Elizabeth caught sight of Fitzwilliam's relations. She burst out laughing.

"What is it, love?" he asked.

She nodded at them. "I believe the word is 'poleaxed.' 'Stupefied' is too weak a term for that expression."

Fitzwilliam and Charles laughed heartily as they took in the faces of Lord and Lady Matlock, Richard, and Anne.

"If you wondered what transformed Darcy from a surly prig into a human being," said Charles, "I give you the Bianchi family."

Mamma Bianchi took in the scene and patted Fitzwilliam's cheek with twinkling eyes. *"Ah, William, non ti hanno mai visto sorridere?"*

"She suspects that you have never seen him smile before," said Charles.

Lord Matlock grinned. "I have not made it past the hugging and kissing."

"I cannot believe that I am truly seeing you snuggle a small child, Darcy," said Richard.

Fitzwilliam shrugged. "There are certain… inevitabilities, I suppose, when one is adopted into an Italian family."

"And those are?" Anne asked with a curious grin.

"One shall be thoroughly fed, loved, and teased," Elizabeth said. "And one does not *ever* argue with one's mamma."

"My notions of proper English decorum stood no chance against her," Fitzwilliam said, dropping an affectionate kiss on Mamma Bianchi's cheek. "Come, let us return to our picnic and allow our guests to refresh themselves."

Georgiana grinned as they settled under the trees. "Our relations are not alone in their astonishment, brother. The society column in the *Times* was fascinating the day after Jane's wedding. Shall I tell you what it said?"

"Can I prevent you?"

"No," Richard and Anne said together.

Georgiana looked skyward, reciting from memory. "'The editor would be remiss in failing to mention the astonishing transformation in the highly respected, yet formerly very grave, F.D., following his return from a mere ten months on the Continent. We cannot know if the Italian air or the company of Miss E.B. played the greater part, but a more complete alteration in disposition has never been seen.'"

"Difficult to argue against Miss E.B.," said Richard.

Elizabeth shook her head. "Do not discount the Italian air. We are all of us altered, in truth."

~ * ~

Fitzwilliam and Grandpa had been cagey about the completion of the marriage settlement; two weeks later Elizabeth learned why, when her parents arrived at Pemberley shortly after breakfast. She was delighted to see them and overjoyed at their warm reception. By evening her very proper mother and remote, preoccupied father appeared content in the company of their new relations, though Elizabeth's insistence that the Bianchi clan were now part of the family required some explanation.

Three days later she was less overjoyed by the arrival of a small army of American and English solicitors. The first day of meetings was interminable and left Elizabeth feeling impotent and furious. She stalked through the rose garden trying to soothe her tattered nerves; coming upon her grandmother and grateful for a sympathetic ear, she poured out her frustrations.

"Why must they behave as though I am not in the room?"

"Most men are unaccustomed to respecting a woman's intellect," Nanna said. "I daresay that if you alter your behavior, they shall alter theirs."

"How so?"

"Ladies often speak to men in questions – the tone, if not the words. It avoids giving offense, but it invites the man to believe that the woman's knowledge is lacking and that her judgment cannot be trusted."

Elizabeth stared at her grandmother, replaying conversations in her mind. *She is right; nearly every woman I know finishes her statements with a rising inflection, unless she speaks to a servant or a child. Even me.*

"Speak in statements. Give directions, rather than make requests. Do not permit a man to interrupt you. And ask your grandfather and Fitzwilliam to credit you whenever they reiterate your points. You shall find that your next meetings are more successful."

Nanna's advice proved sound. Elizabeth was able to finish her thoughts and was careful to ask questions only when she truly required an answer. By the end of the second day the solicitors were far more deferential, save one who continued to speak over her. She summarily dismissed him; the others stared at her, astonished.

"I shall not employ a solicitor to represent my interests who cannot be bothered to learn what my interests are," she said. "Shall we proceed?"

By week's end the negotiations were complete, the contracts signed; Elizabeth was the chairwoman and primary shareholder of the Bennet-Janssen Railroad Company, with offices in New York and London. She shared the details with Annabelle as they took a turn around the garden that evening. Her friend delicately suggested that Elizabeth would require a secretary, given the substantial volume of work before her.

Elizabeth gave her a shrewd look. "Are you seeking a position, my dear Annabelle? Your uncle still hopes to find you a suitable husband, I am sure."

"Naturally, but I am now twenty-six and free to do as I like. I have no interest in giving up my independence for the life of a dutiful helpmeet and mother. I am unlikely to have your good fortune, Lizzy, and I should much rather do something useful."

"Then I shall be pleased to welcome you to my staff."

~ * ~

The weeks leading up to the wedding were some of the most joyous that Elizabeth could remember. Their relations discovered that the voluble affections of the Bianchi family were indeed a force against which no proud reserve could stand, and the house rang with laughter. The skills of the musicians among them were much in demand, and impromptu dances were often held of an evening; even the housekeeper Mrs. Reynolds, clearly delighted by Pemberley's lively new atmosphere, was persuaded to kick up her heels.

"You must," Fitzwilliam said. "I warn you, come Christmas your mistress shall insist upon all the servants dancing with the family, and she shall not be gainsaid."

Richard, who partnered Elizabeth, shook his head. "I never thought to see the day that my cousin danced of his own accord. The servants talk of nothing but the changes in him and Georgiana, you know. You are very near to walking on water."

"You give yourself too little credit. He could not have been so altered had you not first intervened."

"Perhaps, but Georgiana's improvement I must lay entirely at your feet. She no longer resembles the timid mouse of only a year past."

"She wanted only assistance discovering her courage. She shall do well; as shall dear Matteo! How good it is of Fitzwilliam to support him at university!"

"Yes. Darcy wanted assistance discovering his heart, and it seems he has found it."

CHAPTER THIRTY

IN WHICH DARCY AND ELIZABETH
REVEL IN THEIR DISGUISE

Derwent Court, Matlock, Derbyshire, 28th June 1817

My dear Anne,

I hope this finds you and Captain Wentworth well and happy on your return from the Indies. I delighted in your description of the islands and the people there, but I selfishly cannot wait to see you again!

Fitzwilliam and Elizabeth were married two days past at Pemberley. Lizzy was lovely, though I thought it very bold of her to wear a scarlet underskirt! The rest of her dress was cream, with an over-layer of gold silk charmeuse so delicate it was nearly transparent. The dress beautifully set off the ruby necklace Fitzwilliam gave her as a wedding-gift. Her ring is even ruby! My brother wore a gold waistcoat and a dark blue coat, though I thought I saw Lizzy tuck a scarlet handkerchief into his inside breast pocket. They both wore scarlet and gold at the Carnevale masque, which must explain why they are so attached to those colors.

The wedding celebration shall be talked of for years, I think! Fitzwilliam said that observing the planning of it was like watching fencers circle each other. Mrs. Bennet (Lizzy's mother), Aunt Eleanor, and Mamma Bianchi were all exceedingly fierce. Thank goodness for Nanna! (Lizzy's grandmother insisted; "Nanna" it shall be henceforth.) She and Lizzy had already managed the wedding dress and the trousseau, and she negotiated a peace between the other three ladies.

My aunt planned the daytime entertainments following the ceremony and the luncheon. Mrs. Bennet planned the supper and the evening's music along with Mamma Bianchi, who wished only that some of her family's traditional dishes were served and that the trescone was danced. Lizzy said, "I care only that I am married at the end of it," and left them to it.

Thus, instead of a mere wedding-breakfast, the guests enjoyed a full day of feasting and delight. The weather was glorious, so the entirety of the day's festivities was held outside and the dancing went on well into the night. This is typical of an Italian wedding, though many guests seemed astonished to be dancing on the lawn under torches and moonlight, as though we were all faeiries.

My brother acquitted himself very well with the trescone and even danced with his new sisters, his mothers, and Nanna, but otherwise I do not believe he quitted Lizzy's side all day. He finds such events excessively draining, and we have entertained nearly two dozen guests for weeks already.

Dearest Lizzy! She handled it all very cleverly. She did the lion's share of socializing for them both, when she was not stealing him away for a private moment. Whenever he appeared particularly fatigued, she would send him on an errand that prevented him from speaking to anybody for at least a quarter of an hour. She even persuaded Mamma Bianchi to allow Luca to nap in Fitzwilliam's arms, which purchased him a full hour of solace.

It is unfashionable in some circles, I know, to be so passionately in love with one's spouse; but now I have seen it – in Fitzwilliam and Lizzy, Jane and Charles, you and the Captain, even Grandpa and Nanna – I cannot conceive of settling for anything less.

The newlyweds said their farewells in the evening and disappeared from the house, gone off by themselves for a week at least. Richard and Mrs. Reynolds know where they have gone, but neither of them will drop so much as a hint.

The guests all departed yesterday. I am to spend some weeks with my aunt and uncle, the Bianchis return to Orvieto, and the Bennets shall depart for New York in a fortnight. After so many months together, they have become my family. I already miss them!

I hope to see you very soon and hear all about your travels. Until then I remain

Your devoted friend,

Georgiana

267

Pemberley Woods, Derbyshire, July 1st, 1817

The morning was already well advanced. Elizabeth remained abed, Fitz-william's long body curled around hers. Neither of them wore a stitch of clothing under the coverlet.

She stretched luxuriantly, then snuggled into him again. "We should give this cottage a name."

"If you like."

"What would you call it?"

"Am I to instantly conjure a name? What a demanding wife you are! In that case I suggest... Sultan's Retreat."

"Preposterous! Entirely too grand. The next thing I know, you shall be in-stalling that ridiculous pink chandelier above our heads."

His chuckle was soft in her ear. "I suppose this cottage is a bit snug for such a monstrous thing. Though if it gives you any comfort, the gold-dust chandelier you selected shall be installed in the ballroom next week, along with two smaller ones flanking it and several wall sconces."

She turned over, regarding him with a delighted grin. "Truly? Oh, that shall be perfect! Why did you not say before?"

He laughed. "I forgot, in truth. I ordered them before we left Venice; there have been several items to attend to in the intervening months."

"Perhaps we should decorate the ballroom in cream, gold, and scarlet."

"Precisely my thinking, but you have quite forgotten your original purpose. What name would you give this cottage?"

"Pemberley Woods?"

"Definitely not. A name so obvious would encourage others to hunt for it!" He nuzzled at her neck. "*Casa d'Amore*, perhaps?"

She giggled. "I could not say that before others without blushing!"

"You need not speak of it before anyone but me, love."

"Ridiculous man! How shall I tease you if I cannot speak of it before oth-ers?" She thought for another minute. "What of *La Villetta*?"

To his credit, he gave it due consideration. "I like it. If this cottage were transplanted to the Peaks and one wished to be unbearably pretentious, one could indeed call it a chalet. *La Villetta* it is."

"I hope we shall visit often. I like you so improper."

He kissed her soundly. "And I am delighted to find such a wanton in my bed. But I fear we shall not be able to visit as frequently as I should like."

"Ah, yes. We shall not see Pemberley so often as you once hoped, I imagine."

"Perhaps not." He idly stroked her hip. "But we must certainly visit your family and your offices in New York quite as often as we spend the Season in London."

"September and October in New York each year, perhaps? Autumn is extraordinary in that part of the country."

"Excellent. Then we may spend Christmas at Pemberley and avoid London until February."

Elizabeth's eyes strayed to the shelf of books above their heads. Fitzwilliam had installed it so that they might read in bed; his choices thus far were universally salacious. The devilish man truly had been inside him all the while, she had discovered, but so had the romantic.

The shadow-box of the Duomo in Orvieto was tucked between the books; he had given it to her in this room on the morning of her birthday. *"That was the night I began to be worthy of you,"* he had said. So enthusiastic was her thanks that they had nearly been late returning to the house.

"We should return to Orvieto in the spring," she said. "Perhaps not every year, but I should like to visit every other year at least."

"Certainly. We shall purchase a home there. Something large enough to suit ourselves and the children."

"Well, naturally we shall bring the children. I suppose you shall add a third storey with your own hands?"

He chuckled. "Naturally. Perhaps more, depending on the number of children."

"You shall not prevent me from traveling when I am increasing, I hope."

His face grew serious. "I should not wish to be aboard ship when you are near your confinement."

"Oh, on that we certainly agree. So we might spend some years in Orvieto and some at Pemberley, for the spring and summer?"

He nodded. "And when we are here, I should like to visit *La Villetta* as often as we may." He kissed her again, long and deep, kneading her breast with nimble fingers. She arched into him and he moved lower, suckling her gently.

She recalled their wedding night, when he had first done this after peeling the corset from her body. An excited giggle escaped her.

"Hmmm?"

"I had an idea. What say you to hosting an annual masque for Carnevale?"

He paused in his ministrations, raising on an elbow to look directly into her face. "You are serious? In London, I suppose, in February?"

"That is when Carnevale usually falls, my love."

He considered her a long moment. "May we limit the invitations to only married couples, or ladies and gentlemen who are of age, whose company we truly enjoy?"

"Certainly. It shall be the most exclusive party of the Season. Besides, I should not like to entertain a house full of strangers or – worse – impetuous young people." She smirked. "Carnevale celebrations do become somewhat wild, after all."

His wicked grin returned. "If we may begin by requiring costumes from literature, my Scheherazade, I shall be very happy to begin such a tradition."

"Of course, my king," she said, and pulled him back down to her.

FINE

(The End)

ACKNOWLEDGEMENTS

This book would not exist were it not for Finch, who set the example of putting pen to paper (or fingers to keyboard, as it were) and encouraged me to do the same. They speak truth, who say that our children shall lead the way.

Thank you to my beta readers Elizabeth Tures and Craig and Suzanne Sheumaker for your thoughtful and detailed feedback; the book is the better for it.

Thank you to my husband Bruce for your patience and support, not only for this book but also for tackling the logistics for the Italian vacation which inspired it.

Finally, endless thanks to Jane Austen — for her brilliance and wit and for creating such compelling characters — and to you, dear Reader, for following old friends to new places.

ABOUT THE AUTHOR

Alexa Douglas loves traveling and inventing new adventures for the characters of her favorite books. These passions collide in her first novel, *The Re-education of Mr. Darcy*. An inveterate bluestocking, her other interests include science, psychology, cross-stitch and crochet; just don't ask her to sing in public or do anything requiring athletic prowess. She lives in Oregon but has seriously considered retiring in Italy.

www.ingramcontent.com/pod-product-compliance
Lightning Source LLC
Chambersburg PA
CBHW052035240626
47153CB00006B/2097